Save Me
Me

LISA SCOTTOLINE

EBURY
PRESS

3 5 7 9 10 8 6 4 2

First published in the US in 2011 by St Martin's Press

Published in the UK in 2011 by Ebury Press, an imprint of Ebury Publishing
A Random House Group Company

The Random House Group Limited Reg. No. 954009

Addresses for companies within the Random House Group can be found at
www.randomhouse.co.uk

A CIP catalogue record for this book is available from the British Library

The Random House Group Limited supports The Forest Stewardship Council
(FSC®), the leading international forest certification organisation. Our books
carrying the FSC label are printed on FSC® certified paper. FSC is the only
forest certification scheme endorsed by the leading environmental organisations,
including Greenpeace. Our paper procurement policy can be found at
www.randomhouse.co.uk/environment

Printed and bound by CPI Group (UK) Ltd, Croydon, CR0 4YY

ISBN 9780091944926

To buy books by your favourite authors and register for offers visit
www.randomhouse.co.uk

In loving memory of my dear friend Joseph Drabyak,
who understood the pleasure, and the power, of books

You give something up for ev'rything you gain.

—Bob Dylan, "Silvio"

Always use the proper name for everything.
Fear of a name increases fear of the thing itself.

—Albus Dumbledore, *Harry Potter and the Philosopher's Stone*

Chapter One

Rose McKenna stood against the wall in the noisy cafeteria, having volunteered as lunch mom, which is like a security guard with eyeliner. Two hundred children were talking, thumb-wrestling, or getting ready for recess, because lunch period was almost over. Rose was keeping an eye on her daughter, Melly, who was at the same table as the meanest girl in third grade. If there was any trouble, Rose was going to morph into a mother lion, in clogs.

Melly sat alone at the end of the table, sorting her fruit treats into a disjointed rainbow. She kept her head down, and her wavy, dark blond hair fell into her face, covering the port-wine birthmark on her cheek, a large round blotch like blusher gone haywire. Its medical term was *nevus flammeus,* an angry tangle of blood vessels under the skin, but it was Melly's own personal bull's-eye. It had made her a target for bullies ever since pre-school, and she'd developed tricks to hide it, like keeping her face down, resting her cheek in her hand, or at naptime, lying on her left side, still as a chalk outline at a murder scene. None of the tricks worked forever.

The mean girl's name was Amanda Gigot, and she sat at the opposite end of the table, showing an iPod to her friends. Amanda was the prettiest girl in their class, with the requisite straight blond hair, bright blue eyes, and perfect smile, and she dressed like a teenager in a white jersey tank top, pink ruffled skirt, and gold designer sandals. Amanda wasn't what people pictured when they heard the term "bully," but wolves could dress in sheep's clothing or Juicy Couture. Amanda was smart and verbal enough to tease at will, which earned her a fear-induced popularity found in all schools and fascist dictatorships.

It was early October, but Amanda was already calling Melly names like Spot The Dog and barking whenever she came into the classroom, and Rose prayed it wouldn't get worse. They'd moved here over the summer to get away from the teasing in their old school, where it had gotten so bad that Melly developed stomachaches and eating problems. She'd had trouble sleeping and she'd wake up exhausted, inventing reasons not to go to school. She tested as gifted, but her grades hovered at C's because of her absences. Rose had higher hopes here, since Reesburgh Elementary was in a better school district, with an innovative, anti-bullying curriculum.

She couldn't have wished for a more beautiful school building, either. It was brand-new construction, just finished last August, and the cafeteria was state-of-the-art, with modern skylights, shiny tables with blue plastic seats, and cheery blue-and-white tile walls. Bulletin boards around the room were decorated for Halloween, with construction-paper pumpkins, papier-mâché spiders, and black cats, their tails stiff as exclamation points. A wall clock covered with fake cobwebs read 11:20, and most of the kids were stowing their lunchboxes in the plastic bins for each homeroom and leaving through the doors to the playground, on the left.

Rose checked Melly's table, and was dismayed. Amanda and her friends Emily and Danielle were finishing their sandwiches, but Melly's lunch remained untouched in her purple Harry Potter lunchbox. The gifted teacher, Kristen Canton, had emailed Rose that Melly sometimes didn't eat at lunch and waited out the period in the handicapped bathroom, so Rose had volunteered as lunch mom to see what was going on. She couldn't ignore it, but she didn't want to overreact, walking a familiar parental tightrope.

"Oh no, I spilled!" cried a little girl whose milk carton tipped over, splashing onto the floor.

"It's okay, honey." Rose went over, grabbed a paper napkin, and swabbed up the milk. "Put your tray away. Then you can go out."

Rose tossed out the soggy napkin, then heard a commotion behind her and turned around, stricken at the sight. Amanda was dabbing grape jelly onto her cheek, making a replica of Melly's birthmark. Everyone at the table was giggling, and kids on their way out pointed and laughed. Melly was running from the cafeteria, her long hair flying. She was heading toward the exit for the handicapped bathroom, on the right.

"Melly, wait!" Rose called out, but Melly was already past her, so she went back to the lunch table. "Amanda, what are you doing? That's not nice."

Amanda tilted her face down to hide her smile, but Emily and Danielle stopped laughing, their faces reddening.

"I didn't do anything." Emily's lower lip began to pucker, and Danielle shook her head, with its long, dark braid.

"Me, neither," she said. The other girls scattered, and the rest of the kids hustled out to recess.

"You girls laughed," Rose said, pained. "That's not right, and you should know that. You're making fun of her." She turned to Amanda, who was wiping off the jelly with a napkin. "Amanda, don't you understand how hurtful you're being? Can't you put yourself in Melly's shoes? She can't help the way she is, nobody can."

Amanda didn't reply, setting down the crumpled napkin.

"Look at that bulletin board. See what it says?" Rose pointed to the Building Blocks of Character poster, with its glittery letters that read CARING COMPASSION COMMUNITY, from Reesburgh's anti-bullying curriculum. "Teasing isn't caring or compassionate, and—"

"What's going on?" someone called out, and Rose looked up to see the other lunch mom hurrying over. She had on a denim dress and sandals, and wore her highlighted hair short. "Excuse me, we have to get these girls out to recess."

"Did you see what just happened?"

"No, I missed it."

"Well, Amanda was teasing and—"

Amanda interrupted, "Hi, Mrs. Douglas."

"Hi, Amanda." The lunch mom turned to Rose. "We have to get everybody outside, so the kitchen can get ready for B lunch." She gestured behind her, where the last students were leaving the cafeteria. "See? Time to go."

"I know, but Amanda was teasing my daughter, Melly, so I was talking to her about it."

"You're new, right? I'm Terry Douglas. Have you ever been lunch mom before?"

"No."

"So you don't know the procedures. The lunch moms aren't supposed to discipline the students."

"I'm not disciplining them. I'm just talking to them."

"Whatever, it's not going well." Terry nodded toward Emily, just as a tear rolled down the little girl's cheek.

"Oh, jeez, sorry." Rose didn't think she'd been stern, but she was tired and maybe she'd sounded cranky. She'd been up late with baby John, who had another ear infection, and she'd felt guilty taking him to a sitter's this morning so she could be lunch mom. He was only ten months old, and Rose was still getting the hang of mothering two children. Most of the time she felt torn in half, taking care of one child at the expense of the other, like the maternal equivalent of robbing Peter to pay Paul. "Terry, the thing is, this school has a strict zero-tolerance policy against bullying, and the kids need to learn it. All the kids. The kids who tease, as well as the allies, the kids who laugh and think it's funny."

"Nevertheless, when there's a disciplinary issue, the procedure is for the lunch mom to tell a teacher. Mrs. Snyder is out on the playground. These girls should go out to recess, and you should take it up with her."

"Can I just finish what I was saying to them? That's all this requires." Rose didn't want to make it bigger, for Melly's sake. She could already hear the kids calling her a tattletale.

"Then I'll go get her myself." Terry turned on her heel and walked away, and the cafeteria fell silent except for the clatter of trays and silverware in the kitchen.

Rose faced the table. "Amanda," she began, dialing back her tone, "you have to understand that teasing is bullying. Words can hurt as much as a punch."

"You're not allowed to yell at me! Mrs. Douglas said!"

Rose blinked, surprised. She'd be damned if she'd be intimidated by somebody in a Hannah Montana headband. "I'm not yelling at you," she said calmly.

"I'm going to recess!" Amanda jumped to her feet, startling Emily and Danielle.

Suddenly, something exploded in the kitchen. A searing white light flashed in the kitchen doorway. Rose turned toward the ear-splitting *boom*! The kitchen wall flew apart, spraying shards of tile, wood, and wallboard everywhere.

A shockwave knocked Rose off her feet. A fireball billowed into the cafeteria.

And everything went black and silent.

Chapter Two

Rose woke up lying on the floor against the wall. She opened her eyes. Overhead sprinklers poured water, like cold rain. Acrid black smoke clouded the air. She rolled over onto wet debris and broken glass. Her head pounded. Her ears rang.

what happened what is going on

She propped herself up to a sitting position, in the water. Her face hurt. She touched her cheek. Fresh blood covered her fingertips. Dust caked her polo shirt and khaki capris, getting drenched from the sprinklers. Her legs splayed out in front of her, with a bloody cut on her ankle. She shook her head to clear her brain. She couldn't hear anything but the ringing in her ears.

She looked through the water and smoke. An inferno raged in the kitchen. Fire blazed from its doors. Hot orange flames spread upward. A jagged hole gaped in the kitchen wall. Rebar twisted from it like black tentacles. Wood studs lay splintered and broken.

Rose couldn't process what she was seeing. The perfect suburban cafeteria was a war zone. Tiles hung from the ceiling. Shattered skylights rained glass shards. The air felt furnace-hot. A burning smell filled her nostrils. Bits of flaming material blew around like a nightmare blizzard.

The kids!

Rose looked wildly around through the smoke. Amanda sat stunned on the floor nearby, then got up stiffly. Her mouth formed a terrified circle. Tears ran down her face. A cut bled on her arm. Emily lay near the door, crying in a little heap on the floor, like dirty laundry. Only Danielle was in motion, fleeing toward the door.

Suddenly, Rose could hear everything. Amanda was screaming. Emily was sobbing. Alarm bells were ringing. Fire roaring, sprinklers whirring, water *whoosh*ing. Flames billowed from the kitchen. Whoever was in there would have been killed. She had to get the kids out before they were, too.

Oh my God. Melly.

Rose stumbled to her feet, unsteady. Her knees buckled. Her head thundered. The room whirled. She struggled to get back up. The handicapped bathroom was across from the kitchen, where the explosion had been. Fear gripped her heart. Melly could have been killed in the blast.

Please God no.

Rose raced through the other possibilities. Melly could be trapped in the bathroom. If she hadn't gotten out, no one would come to save her. No one knew she was in the bathroom. Even if she got out of the bathroom, she wouldn't know how to get out of the building.

Rose staggered to her feet, panicky. She didn't know what to do. The smoke was getting thicker, the air hotter. Flames licked from the kitchen doors into the cafeteria. A skylight popped, showering glass.

Amanda and Emily were slowly moving around. Screaming. Crying. Stunned. They needed help. They were right in front of her. They were just kids. They couldn't save themselves.

Melly was in the bathroom, far away. Out the opposite side of the cafeteria and down the hall, at the very end.

Rose's mind reeled. If she got Amanda and Emily out of the cafeteria to the playground, she wouldn't have time to go after Melly. If she went to save Melly, she'd have to leave Amanda and Emily, who were right in front of her. She couldn't do that, and she couldn't leave her own child to die.

It was the choice from hell, in hell.

Rose could save Melly, or she could save Amanda and Emily.

She had to choose.

Now.

Chapter Three

"Come on!" Rose grabbed Amanda by the arm. She didn't choose, she merely acted. Danielle was already running out of the cafeteria.

"Mommy!" Amanda screamed. Smoke blew everywhere. Fire licked across the ceiling, superheating the air. Tiles dropped in flames. Sprinklers whirred, making more smoke.

"We have to get out, after Danielle!" Rose kept one hand on Amanda and ran with her to Emily, lying on the floor by the exit, crying.

"Mommy!" Amanda screamed again, as Rose hoisted Emily up by her arm. Her leg was cut, but she wasn't seriously injured.

"Come on! We have to go!" Rose hurried Amanda and Emily toward the exit doors, which were propped open. The hallway beyond was smoky and packed with older kids, Danielle among them, hurrying toward the doors to the playground. A teacher with blond hair stood at the threshold to the playground, getting kids outside.

"Go to the playground!" Rose whipped Amanda and Emily into the hallway, where they were swept along with the others. "Follow Danielle! Run! I have to get Melly!"

Rose turned around and ran back into the fiery cafeteria, dodging flaming tiles. Heat seared her throat. Smoke stung her nose and eyes.

Water soaked her long hair and clothes. A ceiling stud crashed. Insulation flared.

She tore past the fireball in the kitchen, almost slipping on the wet floor. She ran through the cafeteria, bolted through the exit doors, and veered around the corner into the hallway. She skidded to a stop, stunned. Fire blocked her path.

No, no, no!

The hallway ceiling had collapsed. Debris burned on the floor. Smoke billowed black and thick. Sprinklers squirted sideways, uselessly. Aluminum ductwork hung at bizarre angles. The handicapped bathroom was on the other side. The flames blazed too high to jump and would get higher still. Ceiling tiles, insulation, and studs burned.

Rose spotted a piece of wood sticking out of the debris, grabbed the end, and yanked. It came free, trailing burning debris. She coughed and coughed. Tears flowed from her eyes. She swung the stud like a flaming baseball bat, knocking aside smoky insulation to make a path.

Sparks flew. Smoke filled her nose. She spit dry filth from her mouth. Stirring the debris fed the fire. It roared in response.

She redoubled her efforts, whacking to clear a path. She could barely see or breathe. Her throat felt tight, closing. Her eyes streamed with tears. The stud caught fire at the end. She kept whacking until she'd cleared a fiery path. If she waited any longer, she wouldn't be able to run through.

She dropped the stud, got a running start, and leapt over the fire. Flames licked at her clogs and ankles but she was too adrenalized to feel anything. She charged ahead, running through an oven. It lasted forever, but she got through, the fire behind her.

She raced through the smoke to the end of the hall. A conflagration raged to her left, the kitchen and the teachers' lounge ablaze.

She reached the handicapped bathroom. Smoke was being sucked under its door. Melly would suffocate.

"Melly!" Rose tried the lever, hot to the touch. The door was locked, so Melly had to be inside.

"Melly!" Rose shrieked, frantic. She yanked on the lever. It didn't open. Tears of fright poured down her cheeks. She coughed and coughed. Black smoke rolled along the floor, enveloping her.

Fire flared closer. She pulled on the lever with all her might. She felt hotter and hotter. She couldn't breathe, her lungs choked with smoke.

"Melly!" Rose screamed, at the top of her lungs.

There was no reply.

Chapter Four

"Help!" Rose screamed. Nobody was in the corridor. The alarm bells rang continuously. Sirens sounded far away. She was on her own.

She threw herself against the bathroom door. It didn't budge. She raked at the hinges to see if she could take the door off, but no. She told herself to stay in control. She couldn't surrender to panic. She coughed and coughed. Tears blurred her vision.

She knelt down to look at the lever. It had a hole underneath. It locked from the inside, by pushing a button. She could unlock it if she could stick something in the hole. She tried her finger. The hole was too small. She needed something thin enough to fit through.

She looked wildly around. Smoke billowed everywhere. The blaze in the teachers' lounge was spreading. She had to hurry. She got up, bolted to the library, and burst through the doors. Smoke filtered the air, less than in the hallway.

She ran to the librarian's desk and tore open a drawer. It held pens, pencils, rulers, orange Tic-Tacs. She grabbed a pair of scissors. The blades were too big. She threw them aside. She whirled around, then saw a coat rack holding a red cardigan and a few wire hangers.

She ran to the rack, snatched off one of the hangers, and twisted it out of shape on the run. She bolted out of the library, horrified at the sight in the hallway. The fire was spreading to the handicapped bathroom. Fingers of flames stretched from the teachers' lounge. Black smoke enclosed the door.

"Melly!" Rose shrieked, agonized. She ran to the bathroom and threw herself on her knees in front of the door. She couldn't see the hole for the smoke and her tears.

She wrenched the hanger out of shape, slicing her palm with the pointy end. She bent the wire and tried to shove the end into the hole. Her hand shook too much. She tried again and again, her face next to the lever. She finally rammed it through. She felt a *click*.

She yanked on the lever. The door opened wide. Heat surged behind her, the flames sucked forward by new oxygen. Smoke filled the bathroom.

"Melly!" Rose screamed, but Melly sat slumped beside the toilet in the clouds of smoke, her head to the side, unmoving. Her arms hung down. Her feet flopped apart.

Rose rushed to her side and scooped her up. She couldn't tell if Melly was breathing, but black soot covered her cheeks and ringed her nostrils and mouth. Her body was limp, her eyes closed. Rose knew CPR but had to get her out while she still could.

She gathered Melly up, staggered to her feet, and ran out of the smoky bathroom. She bolted to the library, burst through the doors, and tore through the stacks to the exit, which led her down one smoky hallway, then another. She'd never been in that part of the school. She followed the sound of teachers shouting. Melly remained silent, lifeless.

Rose barreled toward the noise and saw an EXIT sign over double doors. Twenty feet away, then ten. Then five. She exploded through the doors into a stairwell, where a teacher was evacuating older kids, hurrying down the concrete stairs toward the exit for the teachers' parking lot.

"It's my daughter!" Rose shouted on the run, and the teacher blanched.

"Let her through!" she called to the kids, who parted as Rose wedged her way out of the exit and into the sunshine.

"Help!" Rose screamed, and the school librarian and a teacher came running. Smoke clouded the parking lot, and beyond it thronged teachers, staff, and students, abuzz with shouting, crying, and head counts.

Rose raced to a patch of grass, laid Melly on the ground, and put an ear to her chest to listen for a heartbeat. She couldn't hear breathing because the alarms were too loud. She put her cheek to Melly's face to feel breathing, but no. She began CPR, tilting Melly's head back, opening her mouth, and breathing for her, ignoring the stench of smoke on her lips.

Suddenly, Melly started coughing. Soot puffed from her mouth, a horrifying sight.

"Honey!" Rose cried with joy, but Melly's eyelids fluttered and her eyes rolled backwards into her head. "Melly, wake up! Please!" She shook Melly to rouse her, to no avail.

"Here's the ambulance!" The school librarian touched Rose's arm. The teacher stood behind. "Let us help."

"Thanks!" Rose scooped Melly into her arms, and the librarian steadied her as they ran through the parked cars.

The crowd surged forward, craning their necks, but the teacher and custodians with walkie-talkies shooed them back. Parents and neighbors held up cell phones and BlackBerrys, snapping pictures and taking videos. The ambulance sped onto the long driveway, and people shouted to flag it down until it veered into the teachers' parking lot.

Rose and the librarian hustled to meet the ambulance, which zoomed to a stop. A paramedic in a black uniform jumped from the cab and raced toward Melly. The back doors flew open, and two other uniformed paramedics, a male and a female, hustled out with a stretcher and a portable oxygen tank.

"She's my daughter." Rose met a male paramedic at the curb. "She's breathing but she's not conscious."

"I got her." The male paramedic took Melly from Rose as the two others materialized at his side. He laid Melly on the cushioned stretcher while the others hurried to fit a translucent oxygen mask over her face and secure her with two orange straps. They all rushed the stretcher to the ambulance, sliding it inside.

Rose was about to climb in behind, but shouted to the librarian,

"Please get word to my husband, Leo Ingrassia. He's a lawyer, his office is in King of Prussia."

"Will do!"

Rose hoisted herself inside the ambulance, hurried to Melly's side, and picked up her hand. It felt limp and oddly cool to the touch, but she clung to it, making a human tether to keep Melly in this world.

Please God let her live.

Chapter Five

"I'm locking, Jim!" the female paramedic shouted to the driver, to be heard over the sirens and the radio crackling in the cab. She twisted a large handle under the steel corrugation on the ambulance doors. "Go, go, go!"

"Is my daughter going to be okay?" Rose shouted, lifting up her oxygen mask to speak. They'd made her wear one and sit belted to a cushioned jump seat, but she could still reach Melly's hand. She held on as the ambulance lurched off. "I did CPR, and she was awake. Why is she unconscious?"

"Please keep your mask on." The female paramedic hurried to Melly's side. "You can ask the ER doc all your questions."

The male paramedic scrambled to Rose, shouting, "Let me see that ankle."

"I'm fine," Rose yelled, under her mask. "Take care of her, please."

"We have to treat you, too. You've got burns on your ankle and hand." The male paramedic slipped on exam gloves, grabbed a square white bag that read ROEHAMPTON STERILE BURNS DRESSING, and squatted at Rose's feet. "I'll start here. This might be uncomfortable."

"Please, take care of my daughter instead."

"My partner has her, don't worry. We have to treat you. It's the law." The male paramedic zipped open the white bag, but Rose kept her eyes glued to Melly, who looked so pale under the oxygen mask. The female paramedic was attaching circular electrodes to her chest, leading to an EKG monitor that began spitting out a spiky graph, almost instantly.

Rose shouted to the female paramedic, "She was trapped in a bathroom full of smoke. That means she was deprived of oxygen. How do you know if there's brain damage?"

"I'm doing everything I can." The female paramedic grabbed a transparent saline bag, hung it on a hook, and reached for Melly's hand, glancing over at Rose. "Sorry, may I have her hand? I need to start an IV line."

"Sure." Rose let go of Melly's hand, trying not to tear up. She held onto her stretcher instead, watching the female paramedic tapping Melly's skin to find a vein, then sliding the IV needle in, with a speed born of skill and practice.

"I'm dressing your burn now." The male paramedic unrolled yellow dressing and wrapped it around her ankle, keeping his balance in the moving ambulance. "It doesn't look too bad."

"Do you think my daughter has brain damage?" Rose shouted at him, through her mask. "Is that why she's unconscious?"

"Don't worry, the docs will do everything they can. Reesburgh is a great trauma center. Our job is to get her ready, so they can hit the ground running."

Rose could see they needed to work, so she shut up and kept an eye on Melly while the male paramedic finished dressing the burns on her ankle. The female paramedic was wrapping a blood pressure cuff around Melly's arm, but Melly's eyes were still closed, and she didn't move or react. A layer of coarse soot blanketed her face, arms, and legs, obscuring the Gothic lettering on her Harry Potter T-shirt and the flowery pattern of her shorts. A deep gash bled through her hairline, blackening its dark blond strands. Her eyelids looked swollen, and tears made heartbreaking tracks in the filth on her cheeks.

"Here, Mom," the male paramedic said, offering her a Kleenex.

Rose hadn't known she was crying. She nodded thanks, swabbing at her eyes, and the Kleenex got damp and sooty. The female paramedic blocked Melly from view, and the male paramedic dressed the burn on Rose's hand. She looked around the back of the ambulance, noticing things that didn't matter:

The windows in the back doors were tiny. There were six round dome lights in the ceiling. The first-aid bag was orange, and the plastic defibrillator was yellow. A half-open cabinet held plush teddy bears, with the sales tags still on.

Rose felt a wave of sadness. She wouldn't have expected to find toys in an ambulance, but she should have. Children got hurt every day in this world. Now it was her child, and her world.

Her gaze fell on a chart posted above eye-level. It read, EMERGENCY MEDICAL SERVICES FOR CHILDREN, and she found the line for School Age, 6–12 Years. It read, Respiratory Rate, 18–30. Heart Rate, 70–120. Systolic Blood B/P, Over 80. She looked over at the monitors attached to Melly, displaying her vital signs in multi-colored digits, but she wasn't able to decipher them.

She looked at the other wall, but there was only another chart. PEDIATRIC ASSESSMENT, said the top, and underneath, GLASGOW COMA SCALE. She read the three criteria for a coma. Eye Opening, Best Verbal Response, and Best Motor Response. The chart assigned point values to each of the criteria, and she applied the criteria to Melly, like a nightmare laundry list. Melly's eyes remained closed. Zero points. She had no verbal response. Zero points. She had no motor response. Zero points. Melly had no points. Zero, zero, zero.

Rose felt a bolt of fright. New tears filled her eyes. She craned her neck but couldn't see Melly. The female paramedic was bent over her, lifting her eyelid and shining a light in her pupils.

Rose kept her fingertips on the stainless steel of Melly's stretcher. The male paramedic dressed the burn on her hand. The female paramedic shifted position, and Melly's hand popped into view. Blood and bruises covered her little palm, and Rose realized that Melly must have bloodied her hands, banging on the bathroom door. Trying to get out. Pounding with her fists. Waiting to be rescued. Calling for her mother.

Mommy!

Rose wanted to scream at herself. If she had run to the handicapped bathroom first, Melly would be fine now. It was a matter of time, of minutes and seconds. Of oxygen deprivation to the brain. Of points on the Glasgow Coma Scale. Why had she spent those minutes on Amanda, and not on her own daughter? Why had she chosen to save Amanda over Melly?

She held tight to Melly's stretcher. Any mother would have saved her own child. So what if Amanda was standing closer? What difference did that make? What was she thinking?

Rose wiped her eyes. She'd thought she hadn't chosen, but she had, and she'd chosen wrong. She loved Melly more than life. If Melly didn't come through this, she would never forgive herself. She could never justify it to herself or Leo. He was Melly's stepfather, but he loved her like his own. He'd been her only father since she was four, when her father died. A wave of guilt washed over Rose, and she felt as if she were drowning in it, going under.

The ambulance raced down Allen Road. The hospital was only twenty minutes away. She tried not to count the seconds. The male paramedic finished treating the cut on her cheek. Her chest felt tight. She wasn't even sure she was breathing. She could only pray.

"Here we are, good luck!" The male paramedic hurried to the door, the ambulance lurched to a stop, and everything else happened in a blur. The back doors of the ambulance opened into the blinding sun, and the paramedics hurried Melly's stretcher out of the back, with Rose right behind, with portable oxygen. The legs on the stretcher snapped down, and they were all running to the entrance of the emergency department, where the doors slid open and a crowd of medical personnel fluttered to them like angels, bearing Melly away.

Rose didn't let go of her until the very last minute.

Chapter Six

Rose slumped in a cushioned seat, alone in the empty waiting room. Smoke clung to her damp clothes and hair. Her throat felt dry, and her eyes smarted despite the drops they'd given her. Melly had been in one of the ER examination rooms for half an hour, and still no word. The doctors hadn't wanted to discuss Melly's condition until they'd examined her thoroughly, and Rose had been sent to the waiting room after the nurses had cleaned her up and given her a tetanus shot. She'd left her purse and cell phone in the car, so she'd used the hospital phone to call the sitter, who'd said she could stay with John until tonight, if needed.

Rose sighed, telling herself to stay calm. Framed prints of generic pastures covered the pastel blue walls, and the sun streamed through the windows, whiting out the screen of the muted TV. She didn't bother picking up the wrinkled copies of *People, Time,* or the other magazines on the coffee table. She watched idly as dust motes floated through a shaft of sunlight, rudderless. A pot of stale decaf sat in a coffeemaker on a side table.

Her gaze fell to her lap. Her right hand was freshly bandaged, and the left had residual soot etched into the back of her hand, black and thick as ground peppercorns. She flashed on Melly, covered with the same grime, and imagined her beating on the bathroom door, calling out, like Amanda.

Mommy!

Rose got up and crossed to the bathroom, walking gingerly because of the bandage on her ankle. She closed the door behind her, using her good hand to flick on the light. A mirror hung over the sink, and in her reflection, she looked like a cleaned-up coal miner. Soot underlined her crow's feet, the wrinkles under her eyes, and each nostril, like parentheses. A small cut on her left cheek glistened with Neosporin, and her forehead was as gray as a stormcloud. Her long, dark hair was a dirty mop, weighed down by dust, water, and filth.

She didn't want to miss the doctor, so she opened the bathroom door in case he came back. She twisted on the faucets, popped the bulb of antibacterial soap, and washed her face as best she could. She dried off with paper towels, checked the mirror again. She looked nothing like the model she'd once been, if only in catalogs. Her blue eyes, wide-set, large, and bloodshot, tilted down at the corners, and her nose, slim and straight, had turned red at its bony tip, from crying. Her mouth, wide with thinnish lips, was drawn into a frown. She remembered what her ex-husband Bernardo always used to say.

You look like somebody's mom.

She sighed at the memory, bittersweet. Bernardo Cadiz was a handsome photographer she'd met on a shoot, and he'd always wanted more for her career, a better agent, bigger bookings, an exclusive with Almay or Dove. Rose knew she wasn't pretty enough for the big leagues, though her Black Irish features and wholesome suburban look made her perfect for the Land's End and L.L. Bean catalogs, and she regularly dolled-up as Snow White to model adult Halloween costumes. She wasn't vain about her looks, because they were God-given; she viewed them as a way to earn a living. She'd never wanted a big career; what she really wanted was to *be* somebody's mom, and when they'd gotten married, Bernardo had promised he'd leave behind his partying ways and downtown friends. What had happened after Melly was born surprised no one but her.

"Rose?" a voice called out, and she turned to see her husband, Leo, looking around the waiting room for her. "Honey?"

"In here," Rose called back, her heart full at the sight of him. If Bernardo Cadiz had been all style, Leo Ingrassia was all substance, and he still looked like the Italian-American altar boy and second-string left tackle he'd been in high school. He was average height, stocky and powerfully built, and his face was honest and open, with rich brown eyes, round in shape, a coarse nose that was on the big side, and a full, generous mouth. His jet-black hair was thick, curly, and unruly, which suited him, because he was the least vain person she'd ever known.

"My God, honey! Look at you!" Leo's eyes went wide with alarm, and he threw open his arms, reaching for her. "Are you okay? How's Melly?"

"I don't know, it's awful." Rose buried herself in his embrace, laying her cheek against the stiff starch of his oxford shirt.

"I was on the way home when Julie called. Where is she? What happened?"

"She's with the doctors." Rose hid her face in his shoulder. "She wasn't conscious, and I'm worried about brain damage."

"But they said you rescued her."

"No, well, kind of." Rose faltered, tears springing to her eyes. She didn't know how he'd react if he knew she hadn't gone immediately to Melly. She pulled away. "Leo, listen—"

Suddenly someone cleared his throat, and they turned around. A doctor she didn't recognize entered the waiting room, his expression grave behind his steel-rimmed glasses. He had the lean look of a runner, and he was tall, African-American, and in his late fifties, the short hair at his temples shot through with silver.

"Hello," the doctor said. "Are you the parents of Melinda Cadiz, the little girl from the school fire?"

"Yes," Rose answered, reaching for Leo.

"I'm Dr. Holloeri." He extended his hand and broke into a smile. "Your daughter is resting comfortably, and she's looking good, so far."

"Thank God!" Rose's body flooded with relief. Tears filled her eyes but she blinked them away.

"Leo Ingrassia." He shook the doctor's hand. "Doc, what's the matter with her? Is there brain damage?"

"No," Dr. Holloeri answered. "However, she suffered significant smoke inhalation. It causes the throat to swell, restricting the airflow to the lungs, and this can be dangerous in a child. There can be swelling in the throat and trachea for up to forty-eight hours after exposure. We need to monitor her levels for the next day or so."

Rose wiped her wet eyes, and Leo put his arm around her.

Dr. Holloeri continued, "One concern would be if she were exposed to fumes from plastics or other toxic materials. That can cause problems as she gets older, but I won't go into the technicalities. Right now she looks good."

"Can we see her?" Rose asked, recovering.

"Not yet. She's asleep, and we gave her a sedative."

"A sedative, is that a good idea?" Leo asked, and Dr. Holloeri turned to him.

"Yes. The sedation is light, and her physical symptoms are uncomfortable."

"Can't we see her, anyway?" Rose asked, again. "Even if she's sleeping? It's for my sake, not hers."

"You'll do her more good to go home now, clean up, and come back." Dr. Holloeri glanced at the wall clock. "I figure, say, about two hours. By then, she'll be coming around, looking for you. After she wakes up, she'll want you for the duration, and I'm guessing you'll want that, too."

"I do."

"Good." Dr. Holloeri touched Rose on the shoulder, and his eyes softened behind his no-nonsense glasses. "You saved your daughter's life today. If she'd spent another five minutes in that smoke, we'd be having a much different conversation."

Leo looked over, with a surprised smile. "Babe, jeez. That's amazing."

"No, not really." Rose reddened, secretly ashamed. She felt like an imposter, knowing that she'd rolled the dice with her daughter's life. It was dumb luck that had saved Melly.

"Okay, take care." Dr. Holloeri smiled. "I ought to get back to work."

"Thanks so much." Rose gave him a hug.

"Yes, thanks." Leo shook his hand again. "We really appreciate all you've done for her."

"You're very welcome. Stay well, folks." Dr. Holloeri left the waiting room, and Rose and Leo followed, bade him another good-bye, and passed through the automatic doors at the ER exit.

Rose took Leo's arm as they stepped outside, and her nose and throat stung in the humid air, an Indian summer that just wouldn't quit. The sun burned over the pin oaks surrounding the entrance, their large, spiky leaves turned splashy red and rich rust. They shed brittle leaves on the walkway, where a small crowd stood, their heads swiveling to Rose and Leo. One of them was a TV anchorwoman in thick foundation and a bright red suit.

"Hello, Ms. McKenna!" the TV anchorwoman called out, flashing a camera-ready smile. She made a beeline for them, a microphone in her manicured hand, and she was followed by a producer-type and a photographer, who rested a bulky videocamera on his shoulder. "I'm Tanya Robertson, at Channel 9. I'm so honored to meet you. You're so brave!"

"Oh, no, please." Rose stiffened, aware that nurses, orderlies, and a uniformed security guard were watching, since Reesburgh didn't get many visits from TV celebrities.

"Okay if we film?" Tanya grinned, raising her microphone. Behind her, the cameraman pressed a button with his thumb, and the videocamera whirred to life.

"No, please, I'm a mess." Rose put up a hand.

"Come on, you look great. How's your daughter Melinda? Her nickname's Melly, right? Is she out of the woods?"

"She's much better, thanks." Rose looked around for an escape route, but the producer and cameraman blocked the path.

"We understand that you saved her life. Tell us how."

"No, thanks." Rose wanted to forget about today, not relive it for TV.

"Aw, my wife is too modest." Leo squeezed her tight. "In five more minutes, our daughter would have been dead."

"Really?" Tanya's mascaraed eyes flew open, and the cameraman filmed away, the black lens hood moving forward and back. "Ms. McKenna, what did you do to save your daughter?"

"Nothing, no. Please." Rose cringed.

"Tell us!"

"I did what any mother would do." Rose took Leo's arm. "Now, excuse us. We have to go."

"But you're a hero, a hero mom!" Tanya practically cheered. "Don't be so modest. Your hubby's right."

"Let's go, hubby." Rose walked past her, and Leo fell into step.

"Wait, wait!" Tanya hurried to follow them, keeping her microphone pointed at Rose, her crew at her heels. "Ms. McKenna, your story is the silver lining. There were three fatalities in the explosion, a teacher and two cafeteria workers."

Rose stopped in her tracks, horrified. Leo looked over, equally stricken, but he got them moving when the TV reporter started in again.

"Ms. McKenna, your story can lift so many hearts. How did you feel when you rescued your daughter?"

"Please, no questions," Rose answered, shaken. She was thinking how easily it could have been Melly who'd died today.

"No comment," Leo said, on the fly, and they left Tanya talking into the camera, saying:

"Some people think we report only bad news, but here's some good. Today at Reesburgh Elementary, a hero mom risked her life to save her daughter. That's our reluctant hero, leaving the hospital, and her name is . . ."

Rose walked down the pavement with Leo and spotted Melly's teacher, Jane Nuru, hustling from the parking lot toward them, waving.

"Rose, Leo!" Mrs. Nuru called out, and Rose waved back, touched that she'd come. Mrs. Nuru was usually in complete control, but her forehead was knit with anxiety, her graying topknot slipped off her head sideways, and her blousy blue pantsuit looked rumpled. She met them on the walkway with a brief hug. "Rose, you poor thing! How are you and Melly?"

"Melly will be fine, thanks. She'll have to stay a day or two, because of the smoke inhalation, but she's okay."

"Thank God!" Mrs. Nuru shook her head, jiggling her Halloween earrings, funky skeletons on a string. "I was so concerned about her, and so was Mr. Rodriguez. We tried to reach you, but there was no answer on your cell. What happened?"

"She was in the bathroom, but she's fine now." Rose didn't go into detail because Tanya and her TV crew were standing close enough to eavesdrop. "I'll explain another time."

"And are you okay?" Mrs. Nuru's eyes flashed a worried blue. "What's the cut on your face?"

"Fine, it's all nothing."

"Goodness!" Mrs. Nuru looked at Leo, her hand fluttering to her chest. "Leo, would you ever think? What a tragedy."

Leo shook his head. "It's terrible. Both of my girls went through hell, and three people are dead."

"It's just horrible. Horrible!" Mrs. Nuru pursed her lips, her pinkish lipstick almost gone. "Marylou Battle was the teacher; she's been subbing since her retirement. My sons had her, everybody loved her. She was in the teachers' lounge. The cafeteria workers were Serena Perez and Ellen Conze. They were killed instantly in the explosion."

"That's awful." Rose felt stricken. She didn't know them, but she felt for their families, heartbroken today.

"So, Rose, tell me." Mrs. Nuru cocked her head. "What happened to Amanda? When I left, they didn't know where she was."

Rose blinked. "What do you mean?"

"The last time anybody saw Amanda, she was with you."

Chapter Seven

"Amanda ran out to the playground, with the others," Rose answered, puzzled.

"No, she didn't. We hadn't found her, at least as of twenty minutes ago, when I left to come here." Mrs. Nuru's face fell into deep lines, draping her downturned mouth. "So far, she and Melly are the only two in our class not accounted for. I had my class list, I did the head count. It was thirteen girls, twelve boys, with Raheem absent, from strep." Mrs. Nuru turned to Leo again. "We drill on these emergency procedures. We do fire drills, lockdown drills, sheltering drills. We have a fire drill once a month, it's state law, but we've only had one in the new building, and everything's different when it's a real fire."

"Naturally." Leo nodded, but Mrs. Nuru didn't need encouragement to continue, so nervous that her words almost ran into each other.

"We can't account for Amanda yet. We haven't found her. Nobody knows anything about her. It scares me half to death. Mr. Rodriguez is beside himself. You say she went to the playground?"

"Amanda? Yes. She went to the playground with Emily. They ran out after Danielle."

"Really?" Mrs. Nuru's forehead furrowed again. "Emily and Danielle were with the others, but not Amanda."

"Did you ask Emily? She was with Amanda. She should know."

"We didn't get to speak with her. She and Danielle were taken to their family doctors. It's confusing, back at school. All the parents were caught unawares. Some moms have already picked up, and others gave verbal approval to send their children home with friends. Excuse me." Mrs. Nuru slid a phone from her pocket, hit a button, and started texting. "I'm telling Mr. Rodriguez you don't know where Amanda is."

"Maybe she went home with one of her brothers?" Rose was thinking aloud. "They're older, and Eileen works, doesn't she?" She had seen Amanda's mother, Eileen Gigot, on Parents' Night, but they hadn't met. By then, the bullying had started, and Rose had called Eileen to talk about it, but she hadn't gotten a return call. "Amanda has a slew of friends in class, too. She could have gone home with any one of them."

Leo looked over. "What caused the explosion, Mrs. Nuru?"

"Don't know yet. The bomb squad was there when I left, and there were fifteen firetrucks putting out the fire."

"Bomb squad?" Leo shook his head, incredulous. "We used to get bomb scares in Worhawk, but I didn't think Reesburgh—"

"Excuse me, wait, Leo." Mrs. Nuru turned to Rose, her phone in hand. "Tell me, did you actually *see* Amanda go to the playground?"

"No, not exactly." Rose lowered her voice so Tanya couldn't hear. "I brought her and Emily to the hallway, to go out with the other kids going toward the playground. A teacher was there, at the doorway to the playground."

"Who? Which teacher?"

"I don't know. I didn't know her."

"What did she look like? Short hair, long hair?"

"Blond. That's all I saw." Rose rubbed her forehead, suddenly tired. "I'd recognize her if I saw her."

"I don't understand." Mrs. Nuru's eyes narrowed. "Did you take Amanda and Emily to the playground, yourself?"

"No, I didn't. I brought them to the hallway."

"Did you have Melly with you?"

"No. She was in the handicapped bathroom. Amanda had been teasing her. I got Amanda and Emily to the hallway. Danielle had gone out already. Then I went back for Melly." Rose avoided Leo's eye. He'd be surprised to hear she'd left Melly for last, but she couldn't deal with that now.

"I see." Mrs. Nuru nodded. "You didn't take them out to the playground because you went back for Melly."

"Right," Rose answered, and for an odd second, she felt as if she'd said something wrong.

Leo reached for her hand. "Babe, isn't the door to the playground at the end of the hallway?"

"Yes."

"So all Amanda and Emily had to do was to go out with the other kids, right?"

"Yes, right."

Mrs. Nuru frowned. "Rose, Mrs. Snyder heard from Terry Douglas that you were keeping Amanda in the cafeteria, to discipline her. You know that lunch moms aren't supposed to discipline the students. That's for teachers only."

"Oh, come on." Leo scoffed, but Rose squeezed his arm.

"I didn't discipline her, I only spoke to her. I wanted to deal with the teasing on the spot. We talked about the building blocks of character, that's all."

"Perhaps, but now you understand the problem." Mrs. Nuru lifted a graying eyebrow. "If you hadn't detained her, she would've been on the playground when the explosion happened, like the others."

Rose blinked, surprised.

"Are you kidding?" Leo asked, bristling.

"Procedures are procedures, Mr. Ingrassia." Mrs. Nuru stiffened. "Lunch moms have to follow them. You know, before you came, we had paid cafeteria aides. But the aide budget got cut, and this is the kind of thing that happens, which they'll never understand in Harrisburg."

They were interrupted by the sound of sirens, and Rose, Leo, and Mrs. Nuru turned as a group. Traffic had parted on Allen Road to allow an ambulance to speed to the hospital entrance. People in the parking lot were pointing to the street, and a man on the walkway flicked his cigarette to the pavement.

Rose tried to catch Leo's eye, but he was looking at the ambulance, his mouth a grim line. She took his hand just as Tanya came up from behind, aiming her microphone.

"Ms. McKenna, excuse me, since you're still here, would you reconsider giving me a sit-down interview?"

"No."

"Not now, I'm talking tomorrow or the next day. We could do a feature on you, one-on-one, in your home."

"No."

Leo turned to the anchorwoman. "My wife answered you nicely, but I'm not as nice. Leave us alone."

"Okay, fine." Tanya pointed her microphone at Mrs. Nuru. "Excuse me, are you one of the other parents?"

"I'm not going to speak with any reporters."

"I just wanted to know if—"

"I said *no*."

"Fine, thanks." Tanya turned and walked away as the cell phone at her waistband started ringing. The ambulance zoomed down the driveway toward the emergency department, and everybody watched, including Rose, Leo, and Mrs. Nuru, who covered her ears because of the siren.

"Hey, folks," Tanya called out, snapping her phone closed. "You might like to know that another student was found in the school. The name hasn't been released yet, pending notification."

"*What?*" Mrs. Nuru took her hands from her ears.

"Boy or girl?" Leo asked, but Tanya was already hustling toward the curb as the ambulance sped toward the entrance, followed by a blue minivan with its flashers on.

Rose watched, numb. Her mouth had gone dry. She didn't blink. She wasn't sure she even breathed. She pretended she hadn't heard what Tanya had said. That she hadn't been lunch mom today. That she was home with John, cuddling him. Leo's hand closed around hers, his fingers warm and rough.

There was a commotion behind them, and the emergency room doors *whoosh*ed open. Rose, Leo, and Mrs. Nuru stepped aside as a trio of nurses in patterned scrubs hurried outside. The ambulance lurched to a stop, cutting its siren. Its back doors flew open, and a paramedic jumped out, whirled around, and reached for the stretcher behind him. A second paramedic leapt from the back, and they slid the stretcher into the sunlight.

Rose almost fainted at the sight.

Chapter Eight

Amanda lay on the stretcher, unconscious. Orange foam blocks stabilized her head, positioned on both sides of her neck, and blood clotted in her silky blond hair. Her forehead was a mass of bandages soaked with blood, bright red in the sunlight. Soot and blood spattered her face under the oxygen mask. Filth blanketed her shirt and skirt. Her arms and legs flopped askew. One glittery Candie's sandal was lying sideways at the foot of the stretcher.

No, no, no. Rose couldn't speak, stricken.

"Oh my God," Mrs. Nuru said, hushed, and Leo put his other arm around the teacher. The three of them huddled in shock as the nurses rushed the stretcher toward the emergency room, where the automatic doors opened, admitted them, and closed behind them.

"I wonder what happened," Leo said quietly.

"Let's go see." Mrs. Nuru turned to the entrance, with Rose and Leo following, when the passenger door of the blue minivan flew open, and a woman jumped out, shouting.

"You!" the woman screamed. She hit the ground running and charged to the walkway, her blond hair flying and her features so contorted with rage that it took a moment for Rose to recognize her. It was Amanda's mother, Eileen Gigot.

"What's going on?" Leo gasped, astonished, as Eileen rushed toward them, shrieking at Rose.

"*You!* What kind of *person* are you? What kind of *mother* are you?"

Rose edged backwards, reeling, and Leo blocked Eileen's path, putting up his hands.

"Please," he said, his tone calm. "You're upset, and I don't blame you, but there's no call to—"

"You abandoned *my little girl*!" Eileen shouted at Rose, ignoring Leo. "You didn't care if she lived or died! You took care of your daughter, not mine!"

"No, I didn't. I took Amanda to the hallway—"

"Liar! Terry told me the whole thing! You yelled at Amanda! You had it in for her from the beginning, calling me to complain! Well, are you happy now? They found her in the building! She got hit on the head with something! She could *die!*"

Rose's mouth dropped open. She felt sick to her stomach. Mrs. Nuru and everyone else on the walkway stared at the scene, appalled. Tanya held out her microphone, and the cameraman aimed his videocamera at Eileen, who was still shouting.

"You were only worried about your own daughter! You didn't care what happened to mine!"

"Please, that's enough." Leo raised his hands, but Eileen smacked them aside.

"Screw *you*! You're as disgusting as she is!"

"Eileen!" shouted another woman, running from the minivan. She reached Eileen, wrapped her arms around her, and tried to tug her away. "Forget them, they're not worth it. We need to go see Amanda. Come on."

"It's *your* fault!" Eileen shrieked, as she was hustled past Tanya and the cameraman. "Her blood's on your hands!"

"Let's get out of here." Leo hurried Rose toward the parking lot, and she fled the scene like a murderer.

Chapter Nine

Rose sat at the kitchen table, chin in hand, feeling horrible, while Leo ate Thai leftovers. He believed that food cured everything, having grown up in his family's restaurant, and she wished she had a similar panacea. She'd showered and changed into a blue cotton sweater and clean jeans, but she couldn't stop thinking about Amanda. She'd brushed her teeth, but the taste of smoke lingered on her tongue. She kept hearing Eileen Gigot, yelling in front of the hospital.

It's your fault!

She'd told Leo everything that had happened in the cafeteria, and if he'd been angry that she'd left Melly until last, he'd been too kind to say so. It felt strange to be at home without her and John, who was still at the sitter's because they were going back to the hospital. Rose missed his warm little presence, always around her, happily cuddled on her lap or bouncing along on her hip. She hadn't known she could love a child as much as she loved Melly until John had been born, but then she learned that when it came to the human heart, one size fits all.

Mommy!

Her gaze flitted around the kitchen, and though it was the reason she'd fallen in love with the house, it gave her no pleasure today. It was big enough to eat in and was ringed with white cabinets, except for bay windows filled with French lavender, their tall green shoots showing tiny purple flowers. Ordinarily they scented the air, but Rose couldn't smell anything but smoke. Mint-and-white tile made a muted backsplash, the appliances were stainless steel, and the table was rough pine. Underneath was their little spaniel, Princess Google, who rested her soft red-and-white head on Rose's loafer, having sniffed her ankle bandage with curiosity.

Her blood's on your hands!

"Don't take this on, babe." Leo steered his tablespoon into his rice like a shovel into fresh snow. His tie was off, and his shirtsleeves folded up. "You didn't do anything wrong. By the way, a reporter called while you were upstairs, so I took the phone off the hook. The hospital has our cells."

"Good." Rose tried to rally, sipping some water, but her throat stung. "I pray to God that Amanda is okay."

"You got her out, and it's not your fault that she ran back in."

"You think that's what happened?"

"It has to be, doesn't it?" Leo stopped his spoon in mid-air, dripping red curry sauce. "They found her somewhere on the first floor."

"That can't be what happened." Rose felt sick at the thought of Amanda lying there, fire raging around her. "If she tried to run back in, the blond teacher would've stopped her."

"Either the teacher was gone by then, or she didn't see her. Amanda's short for her age, isn't she?"

"Yes."

"So she got through, somehow. She could have come into the hallway on the opposite side, away from the teacher. With the hallway full of kids in between, it would be easy to miss her." Leo scooped more sauce onto his rice. "The teachers and staff on the playground missed her, too. You heard Nuru, it was confusing. They had only one fire drill in the new school, so I don't blame them. But I don't blame *you* either, that's for damn sure."

Rose tried to imagine the scene on the playground. It would've been like the teachers' parking lot, only worse. Smoke, tears, shouting. "Mrs. Nuru said she was out there, with the class list."

"Yep. Nuru missed her, too. That's why she's pissing on you."

"That's not nice."

"But it's true." Leo scoffed. "I was surprised at her. Giving you grief about procedures. I mean, really."

"Maybe Amanda ran out of the cafeteria, then ran back in, before she went outside. Maybe the blond teacher didn't see her."

"Anything's possible. All I know is, it's not your fault."

"My God." Rose ran shaky fingers through her wet hair. She could still feel the grit, near her scalp. "Nobody can blame me for going back for Melly, can they?"

"Of course not, that's ass backwards." A flicker of disapproval crossed Leo's face, and Rose sensed they should clear the air.

"Are you mad that I got the other kids out first?"

"Look." Leo shifted forward, his forearms on the table. "I understand why you did. They were in front of you. You couldn't turn your back on them."

"Right." Rose felt relieved.

"It was luck of the draw, who was closer. Bottom line, I'm glad Melly's okay. We dodged a bullet. You wouldn't normally put another kid ahead of your own."

"No." Rose flushed. It sounded awful, put that way.

"Plus it was an emergency. You had to react on the spot. Explosion. Fire. Ka-*boom!*" Leo glanced away, then his gaze shifted back to her and he set down his fork. "But I'm curious about one thing."

"What?" Rose wasn't sure she wanted to know.

"Imagine this hypothetical. Let's say that you're supposed to take somebody's kid home, in your car. But you only have one car seat. Two kids, but one car seat." Leo wiggled two fingers. "Which kid gets the car seat? Your kid or hers?"

"You want me to say that my kid gets the car seat."

"Uh, hello, yes." Leo laughed uncomfortably.

"What would you do?"

"I'd give it to my kid, no question."

"I might not. Maybe. I'd feel guilty about it if I did."

"Why?" Leo asked, incredulous.

"Because if there were an accident on the way home, and something happened to the other child, I'd feel responsible for her. And I'd feel horrible if my kid got hurt, too."

"And we always treat other people's things better than our own, right?"

"Right."

Leo shook it off. "On that we agree to disagree, and anyway, that's not this case. You took care of the other kids, you went back for Melly, and in the end, you saved all of them. You were multi-tasker extraordinaire."

"Not at all." Rose shook her head. "What about Amanda?"

"You got her to safety. But next time, give Melly the car seat." Leo smiled, but Rose couldn't.

"Here's what's killing me. If I had delivered Amanda all the way to the playground, she'd be fine now."

"But then you wouldn't have had the time to go back for Melly. That's five minutes more, like the doctor said." Leo gulped some ice water. "Also, the way you told me, there's more variables, like the fire in the hallway could have been too high for you to get through. It was no-win, and somehow you managed to win."

"Not with Amanda hurt." Rose flashed on Amanda, on the stretcher. The fresh blood on her bandages. "You saw her."

"But what caused Amanda to get hurt? Who's at fault? How about the blond teacher who didn't see her run back in? How about the other lunch mom? What's her name again?"

"Terry. How's it her fault?"

"How many lunch moms are there?"

"Two."

"Okay, two. Two lunch moms for two hundred kids isn't much." Leo nodded. "And I would imagine that the lunch moms are supposed to stay in the cafeteria until lunch is over, right?"

"Yes, until all the kids are out, then we go home."

"So Terry didn't follow procedure. If she'd stayed in the cafeteria instead of leaving to tell on you, she could have taken Amanda and the other girls to the playground while you went to rescue Melly." Leo eyed her, trying to see if his message was hitting home. "All of these causes are only 'but for' causes. By which I mean, *but for* Amanda's running back into the building, she wouldn't have been hurt. *But for* Terry's leaving her post, Amanda wouldn't have been hurt. *But for* you talking to the kids about bullying, Amanda wouldn't have been hurt. *But for* the bomb or whatever blew up, Amanda wouldn't have been hurt. You get the idea? If you say yes, I'll stop."

Rose smiled. "Yes."

"No single 'but for' cause, including you, caused what happened."

"Then what did?"

"All of the above. The perfect storm of a terrible situation. No one thing. Everything went wrong, and that's why Amanda and Melly are in the hospital and three people are dead." Leo reached across the table and touched her hand. "For you to take the blame on yourself, to the exclusion of everything else, makes no sense."

"Eileen thinks I didn't even try."

"Eileen doesn't know the facts and she wants someone to blame. She doesn't know us, either." Leo cocked his head. "Please, who do you think Eileen would rescue? Melly or Amanda?"

Rose didn't reply. "That poor kid."

"Which poor kid? Melly or Amanda? Don't get mixed up."

"Amanda is the poor kid. Melly is fine, Amanda isn't."

"Point taken." Leo paused, his eyes softening. "Listen, I know it's terrible, but you have to be realistic. Amanda might not make it."

Rose suppressed the emotion that welled up. "I'd hate to be responsible for that."

"Then don't. You're not. We just went through the analysis."

Mommy!

"Please stop beating yourself up, Ro." Leo pushed out his chair and got up heavily from the table. "You're supposed to save your own child. That's why we each get a mother. My mother would've saved me, no question. My mother would've walked on bodies to save me, and you're an even better mother than she was."

Rose managed a smile. Leo was a great man, and she was lucky to have him, especially when the chips were down.

"Come on, sweetie." Leo picked up his silverware, let it clatter onto the plate, and lifted his dish. "The baby's at the sitter, but the clock is running. Let's go to the hospital."

Chapter Ten

Rose looked out the window of Leo's sporty Audi, dismayed as they pulled into the hospital parking lot. They'd picked up her car at school and dropped it back off at home, since Leo didn't want her driving herself to the hospital. It turned out he'd been right, but for a different reason. The main entrance was crowded with people, security guards and reporters with videocameras. Klieglights on metallic stalks sprouted above everyone, like steel sunflowers.

"We got company," Leo said, cutting the ignition. The air conditioning hissed into silence.

"Do you think that Amanda—" Rose started to say, but the sentence trailed off.

"No. I checked online before we left the house."

"I wonder how she is."

"We'll see. First, we gotta get through the media. Here's some free legal advice." Leo patted her leg. "Stay with me. Say nothing. Keep moving. Don't put your head down, it makes you look guilty."

"I feel guilty."

"You shouldn't. Please, remember, we're going to visit our daughter. It's not about Amanda, it's about Melly, who almost died today."

Rose flashed on the smoke in the bathroom. "You're right."

"As usual." Leo flashed her a grim smile, and they got out of the car. The air was barely cooling, though the sun had dropped behind the trees. The streetlights along Allen Road were beginning to glow, as was the red neon CVS sign, the McDonald's, the Olive Garden, and the Target. Rose drove the main drag so often she felt as if she'd lived here five years, but she hadn't been to the hospital until today.

Leo took her arm and walked with her toward the entrance. Heads started to turn as they approached, then klieglights and video-cameras. She held her chin up and kept pace with him, moving forward even when Tanya and her TV crew came running toward them, followed by other reporters and photographers.

"Hello, Ms. McKenna!" Tanya called out, on the run. "A few questions, please. What happened with Amanda in the cafeteria this morning? This is your chance to set the record straight."

"No comment." Rose masked her worry. She hadn't realized there was a record.

"Ms. McKenna, talk to me and get your story out. My offer's still good on that one-on-one. Tell me what happened, from your point of view. Can't we set that up?"

"She said no comment, thanks." Leo put up his hand, keeping them both walking ahead, but Tanya fell into step with them.

"Ms. McKenna, if you don't tell your side of the story, it leaves everyone to speculate. Eileen Gigot alleges that you chose to rescue your child to the detriment of three other children, including Amanda. Is that true?"

Oh no. Rose kept her chin up, even as other reporters joined the flock, yelling more questions.

"Ms. McKenna, did you complain to anyone about Amanda, calling her a bully?" "Ms. McKenna, did you place Amanda Gigot in a time-out?" "Ms. McKenna, over here!" "Rose, has Amanda ever struck your child?" "Ms. McKenna, did you move here because you claim your daughter was bullied?" "Any comment, Ms. McKenna? How about you, Mr. Ingrassia?"

Leo ignored the reporters, holding Rose close as they threaded their way through the crowd. She recognized parents from Melly's class, and they craned their necks, their expressions collectively solemn. She lowered her head as Leo steered her up the walkway, followed by reporters, shouted questions, and videocameras. They reached the entrance, where a few women stood together.

"Rose McKenna?" one woman called out. She had short black hair and wore a blue dress with a laminated Homestead ID on a yellow lanyard around her neck, as if she'd come from work.

"Yes." Rose approached, tentatively.

"I'm Wanda Jeresen. My daughter Courtney is in Nuru's class, too, and Amanda is my goddaughter. I want to know how you justify what you did." Wanda's dark eyes flashed under light makeup, and her tone was angry, but controlled. "Terry and Eileen told me you ran to the bathroom to get Melly instead of helping her and Emily."

"No, that's not true," Rose answered, and the crowd of parents and reporters closed in around them.

"Excuse me." Leo put up a flat hand, turning to Wanda. "If you want to talk, we're happy to do that, but not here."

"Why not?" Wanda shot back. "I'd want an answer, here and now. We all do. I called you at home, but you didn't answer."

Leo raised both hands. "Hold on now—"

"Why am I talking to you anyway?" Wanda turned back to Rose. "Can't you speak for yourself? You have to hide behind your husband? Don't you think you owe me, or anybody, an explanation? We're mothers, so talk to me, mother-to-mother."

"Okay, well, that's not the way it happened—"

"Then how did it happen?" Wanda's dark eyes glittered. "Danielle had to run out of the fire, all by herself. I called and talked to Barbara, her mother. She didn't even see you. You went to get your daughter and ignored her and Emily."

"No, wait, listen." Rose put up a hand. "I fell unconscious, and when I woke up, Danielle was running. Ask Emily, I took her and Amanda to the door."

"Nice try, but I called Jerusha, too. Emily's mother. We've been friends since the girls were in first grade. All Emily remembers is that you went to get Melly. She even remembers you saying that's what you were doing. You told her that, didn't you?"

"Yes, but—"

"No buts about it! And thank God that Danielle ran. If she hadn't run, she'd be upstairs now, like Amanda. Or dead!"

"Wanda, hold on!" another woman shouted, making her way through the crowd. She had glasses and long dark hair, and wore a striped top with jeans and flats. "Rose, I'm Cathy Tillman, Sarah's mother, from class. Tell me, since when is it okay to *desert* a child?"

"I didn't desert her. I helped her. The first thing I did was take Amanda and Emily to the hallway leading to the playground."

"What about Danielle?" Wanda demanded, hands on hips.

"Danielle had already gone. She was in the hallway with the others. I told Amanda and Emily to follow Danielle—"

"Follow *Danielle,* that's *it*?" Cathy interrupted, her light eyes round with astonishment behind her glasses. "You don't put an eight-year-old in charge of another eight-year-old. They're just kids, and it was an emergency. You should have taken them out to the playground yourself. Danielle wasn't the lunch mom, you were. That's your responsibility."

"Right," Wanda joined in. "I heard what happened. You punished Emily and Danielle for something they didn't do, and so what if Amanda was joking around with your daughter? Kids are kids. You have to let them fight their own battles."

Cathy leaned closer. "Let's talk turkey. You're just jealous of Amanda because she's popular and Melly isn't. Harry Potter this, Harry Potter that. Melly's a freak!"

"She is not!" Rose's temper flared. "She reads, that's all!"

"Oh, please!" Cathy's hand shot out, waving Rose off, but it startled her and she stepped backwards, bumping into a tall cylindrical ashtray, then losing her balance and falling to the hard concrete with the ashtray spilling sand, cigarette butts, and gum wrappers.

"That's it!" Leo bellowed, pulling a stunned Rose to her feet.

Cathy burst into nervous laughter. Wanda's mouth dropped open. The reporters surged forward, the photographers held their cameras overhead, and the crowd reacted with gasps, chatter, and a hoot or two.

"Let's go!" Leo hurried Rose through the glass doors into the hospital. The lobby was like a refuge, quiet and cool, filled with potted plants and soothing framed landscapes. A few older people sat in sectional furniture, one holding Get Well balloons weighted with a small sandbag. Leo touched Rose's arm. "My God. Are you okay, honey?"

"Yes." She brushed cigarette ashes from her jeans. "And Melly's not a freak."

"I know." Leo smoothed down his suit jacket. "Sorry about that. I should've seen that coming."

"It was an accident."

"Right. Yes, but they still laughed about it."

Shaken, Rose tried to recover. "You told me not to talk to them, but I thought they deserved an answer."

"They didn't want an answer. They wanted to vent." Leo put an arm around her. "Damn, I should have anticipated this. Hubby let you down."

"Hubby never lets me down."

Leo gave her a quick kiss. "You good to go?"

"Yes."

"Okay, then we need an information desk." Leo looked around.

"There." Rose pointed, and they went to the information desk, where they gave their name and asked for Melly's room.

"She's in 306," answered the receptionist, who was an older woman with a button that read VOLUNTEER. "She's one of the little girls from the school, isn't she?"

"Yes, she's our daughter." Rose leaned over the counter. "Where is the other little girl, Amanda Gigot?"

"Let me see." The receptionist hit a few keys. "Yes. She's in 406. That's Intensive Care."

Rose felt her stomach tense.

Leo leaned on the desk. "What floor did you say is Intensive Care? The fourth?"

"Yes, but you can't visit. Only immediate family is permitted."

"I understand, thanks." Leo took Rose's arm, and they left for the elevators.

"Do you want to visit Amanda?" Rose asked, incredulous.

"No, I want to avoid the fourth floor."

Chapter Eleven

Rose stood at Melly's bedside, suppressing a surge of emotion. It was one thing to know that Melly was in a hospital, and another to see her lying there, asleep. She took up only half of the bed, and her feet made little mounds in the white coverlet, midway. Her hospital gown was too big, and its scoop neck exposed her collarbones. Her eyes were closed, and even though she was only sleeping, she could so easily have been gone, forever. Rose watched her chest move up and down, to make sure she was breathing. There wasn't a mother in the world who hadn't done the same thing, more than once.

Mommy!

Melly's head lay tilted to the right, displaying her birthmark in a way that would have mortified her, if she'd been awake. It was as red as fresh blood, covering her left cheek at its upper edge, roughly roundish in shape, about the size of a small plum. A greenish oxygen tube lay across it under her nostrils, and her index finger was covered by a plastic cap that connected her to a boxy monitor, flashing her vital signs in multi-colored digits.

"She looks good," Leo whispered, a wet shine in his eyes.

"Thank God she's alive."

"Let me get you a seat." Leo picked up a wooden chair and moved it close to the bed, near the thick plastic guardrail. Behind them, a TV mounted on the wall played on mute. "Here, sit."

"Wanna share? I'll move over."

"No, you."

"Thanks." Rose sat down, resting her hand on the bedrail. As happy as she was that Melly was alive, she couldn't forget that a different scene would be playing out a floor above them, in Intensive Care. She tried to shoo away thoughts of Amanda, but the images were too fresh in her mind.

"Oh no. We left your overnight bag in the car."

"It's okay." Rose flashed again on Amanda, on the stretcher. The bandages on her forehead had been blood-soaked, and Eileen had said she'd gotten hit on her head with something, so she might even need brain surgery.

"You'll have to brush your teeth with your finger, like I did in the old days, when I used to stay at your apartment. That was before the guest toothbrush. Remember the guest toothbrush?"

"Yes." Rose thought of the soot on Amanda's face. She'd been in the school a lot longer than Melly, but probably not in as enclosed a space. She could have brain damage, not only from whatever fell on her head, but from the oxygen deprivation.

"You can sleep in your clothes, too. Do you want me to ask for a cot, or do you want to sleep in the same bed with her? Babe?" Leo took her hand. "You with us?"

"Yes, sure."

"Take a look at your daughter. Now. Do it."

Rose looked at Melly. "She's sweet, huh?"

"She's a great kid. My bonus kid."

Rose smiled. Leo always said that, and she loved hearing it.

"Remember when we met, on the train? I went to the food car, starved and beat, and there you were, this stunning young mother with her brainy little girl, who recommended I try the hot dogs. We bonded over our shared love of sodium nitrate."

Rose smiled. It was true. They'd all met on the Acela between New York and Philadelphia. She wouldn't have talked to Leo if it hadn't been for Melly. She didn't think he was her type. She'd been into bad boys, and Leo was not only a good boy, but an altar boy.

"You did the right thing today. You saved her life. Don't listen to those crazies out front, or anybody else. We love Melly and we're blessed to have her. Looking at her, being here now, would you change anything you did?"

"No." Rose heard the truth in his words, but she still felt torn. "I keep thinking of Amanda and Eileen, just one floor up. How can I not?"

"I'll tell you." Leo let go of her hand. "Because it could get worse, honey, and you need to keep your head on straight."

"What do you mean?"

"Let's not talk about it now." Leo shook it off. "Like I said outside, this isn't the time or the place."

Rose didn't like his expression. The shine had left his eyes. "No, what do you mean?"

"We could get sued, babe. Eileen could come after us. Best case scenario, Amanda is fine, but she'll have monster medical bills. Eileen's a single mom. How will she pay?"

"She wouldn't win if she sued, would she?"

"She could. When you volunteer at school, you're exposed to liability."

"You are? I am?"

"Look, I'm a humble general practitioner, but I don't see why you wouldn't be. You took on the responsibility for her kid, and she got hurt, end of story." Leo jerked a thumb to the hospital window. "And those women out front, the *moms,* will be the first witnesses testifying against you."

Rose felt her chest tighten. She sensed he was right, but it felt wrong to worry about being sued when Eileen was worrying about her child dying.

"Eileen could sue the school, too, for letting her run back into the building, and don't even think about what happens when they find out whatever blew up. Plus the family of the cafeteria workers could sue, and so could the teacher's." Leo spoke in his professional voice, albeit softly. "This could be a holy mess for the next few years, while the litigation goes on and on. Win or lose, we'd get hit for the legal fees, because I couldn't represent us. It could cost us everything we have. We could lose the house."

Rose's mouth went dry. The thought of losing the house shook her. Leo made a good living, but she had stopped working. They didn't have much in savings apart from the kids' college funds, and they had loan payments on two cars and a hefty new mortgage.

There was rustling from the bed, and they both looked over. Melly shifted under the covers, moving her head back and forth, and they lapsed into silence, waiting for the moment to pass.

"Uh-oh," Leo said, nudging Rose. "Look at the TV, babe."

She turned around to the TV, then did a double-take. The screen showed her own face, then a shot of the firetrucks and burning elementary school. "Oh my God," she said, appalled.

"I know."

Rose felt her heart sink. The TV screen changed to Tanya, talking into a microphone. The closed captioning read, A LOCAL MOM IS A HERO TODAY, then the film was of Rose again, at the hospital after they'd gotten the news that Melly was fine. The captioning said, I DID WHAT ANY MOTHER WOULD DO.

"Mom?" said a voice from the bed, and Rose turned.

"Melly!"

Leo got up and hit the POWER button on the TV, willing the screen into blackness.

Chapter Twelve

Rose lay in darkness, cuddling with Melly in her hospital bed, by now accustomed to the smoky smell in her hair. Leo had left at the end of visiting hours, gotten John from the sitter, and taken him home. Melly had been quiet during the evening, drowsy as a result of the drugs.

"You sleepy, honey?" Rose asked, and Melly looked over, resting her head on Rose's left arm.

"A little. Are you going to sleep here?"

"I sure am. Want more water, or Jell-O?"

"No."

"How's your head?"

"Okay.

"Mom?" Melly's voice sounded raspy, from the irritation. "When I was in the bathroom, the floor felt like an earthquake."

Rose thought back. "Yes, it did."

"Why?"

"Because of the explosion in the kitchen." Rose and Leo had explained to Melly generally what had happened, but she wasn't ready to hear about the deaths yet, or Amanda.

"Was it a bomb? It sounded like a bomb."

"They don't know for sure. Whatever it was, the fire is already out, and they'll make it safe to go back."

"Is it from a terrorist?"

"I doubt that very much." Rose cursed modern times. When she was little, the only bombs she saw were in cartoons, round black bowling balls with wiggly cotton strings.

"It was a *big* noise."

"Sure was. Did it scare you?"

"Yes. I didn't come out of the bathroom."

"I know. Is that why?"

"No. Remember Fire Safety Week?"

"Not really." Rose remembered nothing, and Melly remembered everything.

"At our old school, we went to the firehouse on Fire Safety Week. You came, and we climbed on top of the firetruck, and they gave me a green sticker for my bedroom window and for Googie. It says, Save Our Dog."

"Okay."

"They said, don't open the door if it's hot. The bathroom door was hot, so I didn't open it, then I couldn't breathe. I hit the door and hollered so people would know I was inside, but nobody came to get me."

Rose felt a pang. "Well, it's all right now."

"How did I get out?"

"I got you out."

"Is that how you hurt your hand?"

"No," Rose lied. She'd burned it when she'd picked up the burning stud. "It got burned in the cafeteria, but it's nothing."

"Remember when Quirrell gets burned by Harry's scar? He gets burned on his hands, too."

"This wasn't that bad." Rose flashed on the mothers making fun of Melly's love of Harry Potter, then put it out of her mind. She and Melly had read the Potter books aloud before bedtime, and it was easy to see why Melly identified with a kid with a scar on his face.

"I'm sorry I ran to the bathroom, Mom."

Rose felt a twinge. Sometimes she thought motherhood was full of twinges. "It's okay, I understand why you'd be upset. Does Amanda tease you like that a lot?"

Melly fell silent.

"Huh, Mel? Does she?"

Melly didn't answer. She wasn't a whiner. She hadn't complained about any of the teasing at their old school because she thought if they did anything about it, it would get worse, and she'd been right.

"Mel, I won't do anything, I promise. I just want to know." Rose looked over, but she could barely make out Melly's profile in the dark. "What does Amanda do?"

"Yesterday we were finger-painting with Ms. Canton."

"Okay," Rose said, keeping her tone drama-free. Melly, Amanda, and two other children in Mrs. Nuru's class were in the gifted program, spending an hour in the afternoons with Kristen Canton, twice a week.

"I was painting a picture of Dumbledore, and Amanda put poster paint on with her finger and painted on her cheek, like with the jelly. Ms. Canton told her it's not funny or caring, and how we're a community. I *love* Ms. Canton."

"Me, too," Rose said, hearing Melly's voice warm.

"Her favorite Harry Potter is *The Sorcerer's Stone,* and she has a cat named Hedwig and a Hermione wand. She says it looks just like it came from Ollivander's. It doesn't light up, but it sounds cool."

"I bet." Rose felt lucky that Melly had found a fellow Harry Potter fanatic in the gifted teacher. "Maybe we should get some sleep, honey."

"I'm not tired."

"Okay, we'll just rest." Rose held her closer, feeling her body grow heavier. In the next few minutes, Melly fell quiet, her breathing grew regular, and she fell asleep.

Rose lay awake in the dark, and found herself wishing that Melly had never had the birthmark. It wasn't the first time she'd fantasized about how their life would be different, without. The birthmark had come to define Melly and their family, and they all revolved around the red circle as if it were the sun itself, setting them all in mad, dizzying orbit.

Rose let her thoughts run free, knowing it was forbidden, like a family dog running through an electric fence. It was the birthmark that had started the sequence of awful events today, whether Leo would say that was a *but for* cause or not. Funny, Rose hadn't even seen the birthmark when Melly was first put on her chest, as a newborn. In her first instant as a mother, Rose felt suffused with such wonder and happiness that she saw only a beautiful baby. The nurses all cooed happily, but Bernardo had asked the doctor, in disgust:

What the hell is that red thing on her face?

His awful words had a hang time in the cold delivery room, chilling Rose to the marrow. The doctor had replied that it was a *nevus* even before he'd announced that the baby was a girl, and the nurses had receded, their tones newly subdued and their smiles stiffening at Bernardo's reaction. Rose had gotten what she'd always wanted, a baby girl looking at the world with eyes the hue of heaven itself.

I love you, Rose had told the baby then, and when she saw the stain on her cheek, she'd added silently, *I love all of you.*

Rose's parents were both gone by the time Melly was born, but her in-laws had flown in to see the baby, bringing their *She'll grow out of it, don't worry.* But the baby didn't grow out of it, and Bernardo obsessed more and more on the birthmark, as if it marked him. He was a photographer, but rarely took pictures of Melly, and then only from her right side. Toddlers would stare at baby Melly in her stroller, and he would pull down the Perego's top, hiding her in their walks through the West Village. Children would ask questions, and Bernardo would ignore them, leaving Rose to answer with the medical facts, much as Melly would later, fielding questions like the most patient of family doctors.

The teasing had started in pre-school, and Rose had watched as Melly's grin disintegrated, bit by bit. She became withdrawn and quiet, wanting to stay home and avoid strangers, begging to quit Mommy & Me and Gymboree. Meanwhile, Bernardo scheduled her with Manhattan's best dermatologists, who judged the birthmark too big for surgery, then he dragged them all over the city for more opinions and different treatments, shooting the birthmark with pulse-dye lasers, treating it with bipolar radio-frequencies, and even covering it with custom-made foundation, to no avail.

It was a thicker *nevus* than most, and all the time, Rose had hated the message they were sending Melly. Their marriage cracked under it and other strains, mainly Bernardo's partying, and they divorced when Melly was three years old. Bernardo was killed the very next year, crashing his Porsche, and around that time, Rose and Melly met Leo on the train. They'd fallen in love and married the next year, and she'd left the city to move to southeastern Pennsylvania, near where Leo had grown up in Worhawk. On her own, she felt free to help Melly accept herself, even after her fifth Halloween, when she wouldn't take off her Dora the Explorer mask.

Mommy, I hate being me.

Rose stared at the ceiling, then closed her eyes, and her thoughts returned to the room above. She wondered if Eileen was holding Amanda right now, or if that wasn't permissible in Intensive Care. She tried to put it out of her mind, but gave up. She eased Melly off her chest, rolled quietly out of bed, and left the room. The hallway was empty at this hour, and there was only one nurse behind the desk. Rose crossed the polished hall, and the nurse looked up.

"Oh my God, I know you!" The nurse's eyes sparkled. She was young and tanned, with short, sunbleached hair and a line of gold studs in one ear. "You're the mom who saved her daughter, aren't you?"

"Well, yes." Rose felt her face warm.

"I have a baby at home, and I give you so much credit. How'd you do it?"

"It's a long story, but I'm wondering if you could help me." Rose leaned on the desk. "There's another little girl who was caught in the fire. Her name's Amanda Gigot, and I was wondering how she's doing. Last I heard, she was in Intensive Care with a head injury. Can you find out how she is?"

"Hold on." The nurse turned to a computer keyboard and pressed a few keys. "She's still in Intensive Care."

"Is there any way I could get some details on how she's doing, or maybe you can?"

"We're not supposed to divulge that information."

"Please?" Rose put her hands together in mock prayer.

"Let me see." The nurse shifted her gaze down the hallway, then picked up a desk phone and hit a few buttons, turning slightly away.

"Suz, what up? Can you give me some info on the girl up there from the school? Name's Gigot?"

Rose waited while the nurse nodded on the phone, listening for a few minutes, saying only "uh-huh" from time to time. When the nurse hung up, her expression was unreadable.

"Well?" Rose asked, breathless.

"I'm sorry, I can't really say."

"Please?" Rose begged, but the nurse shook her head.

"Sorry," she answered, looking away.

Chapter Thirteen

It was morning, and Rose had watched the light in the hospital room change from darkness to dawn, as the outlines of the TV, wooden chairs, and night table acquired definition in increments. She had barely slept, worrying about Amanda, and said more than one prayer for her.

Well, are you happy now?

Outside the closed door, there were sounds of people talking, metal carts rattling, and an unidentified beeping, something mechanical. She caught a whiff of breakfast being served, an eggy smell rather than the proverbial coffee aroma, and either way, she wasn't hungry.

We could lose the house.

Melly was still asleep, so Rose leaned over carefully, slid a hand into her jeans pocket, and pulled out her BlackBerry, checking the time. 8:26 A.M. She wished she could call Leo, but the cell phones supposedly interfered with the medical equipment. Last night, she'd texted him, and the red stars on her phone meant that she had new texts, emails, and calls. She pressed the button to see if he'd texted back.

Babe, Hope Amanda pulls through. Call me. Love you.

Rose thumbed the rollerball to check her email and skimmed the list of senders. They were parents of kids in Melly's class, who must've gotten her email address from the class list. She opened the first email:

You have a helluva lot of nerve acting like you're a hero when you were happy with letting those kids die. All you did was save your own hide and child

Rose swallowed, closed the email, and opened the next.

I will never understand how some people can be so blind to the needs of others. God will judge what you did

She closed the email, and didn't want to read the next one, but the sender's name caught her eye. **Barbara Westerman.** Danielle's last name was Westerman, so Rose clicked Open:

I am outraged that you would care so little about my daughter's safety. She was terrified and had to run out of the building all by herself. She could have died or been gravely injured, like Amanda! We don't need selfish people like you in Reesburgh, and you should go back to

Rose closed the email, shaken. She clicked over to her phone calls. The log showed new calls from Unknown Numbers, and she didn't call her voicemail to listen to the messages. She had a sense of what they'd say.

Melly was shifting in bed, her eyelids fluttering and her oxygen tube slipping, so Rose readjusted the oxygen, forwarded the last three emails to Leo, turned off the BlackBerry, and slid it back into her jeans pocket. She turned to Melly and brushed a stray hair from her forehead, just as the door to the room opened and a young orderly stuck his head inside.

"Anybody hungry?" he asked, with a smile.

"Sure, come on in, thanks." Rose motioned to him, then returned her attention to Melly. It was the first chance she'd had to get a look at Melly in the daylight, and she eyed her with more care than usual, like Dr. Mom:

Her eyes, large and blue, still looked bloodshot, and her skin, which was on the fair side, seemed reddish, whether from the antiseptic used to clean it or from the smoke's irritation. Her nose was small and turned slightly up, but showed redness around the nostrils, which was to be expected, and her lips, also thin like Rose's, looked dry and parched. Bernardo had always said that Melly looked exactly like Rose, except in a dark blond Bernardo wig, and Dr. Mom decided she looked fine.

"Hi, Mom." Melly raised her arms and hugged Rose around the neck. "I love you."

"I love you, too, Mel. I hope you got some good sleep. You conked out." Rose eased Melly back onto the bed. "Do you feel like waking up and eating a little breakfast? Or do you wanna rest?"

"I want to wake up." Melly rubbed her eyes. "Can we go home?"

"Not yet, not until the doctor says."

"Breakfast!" The orderly placed the tray on the night table, then blinked when he spotted her birthmark. He pointed at the scrambled eggs under their steamed-up cover of thick amber plastic. "Eat up. Help you grow up big and strong."

"Thank you," Melly said, raspy, getting into a sitting position as he left the room, closing the door behind him. She lifted the lid, releasing the smell of institutional eggs. "Is this all for me?"

"Yes."

"My throat hurts. Do I have to go to school today?"

"No, it's Saturday. You'll feel better soon. Drink this." Rose opened the water bottle, poured some in the flexible cup, and helped her sip some.

Melly swallowed, grimacing.

"It'll be okay soon."

"Do you have my *Beedle the Bard* book?"

"No. Sorry." Rose had forgotten to ask Leo to get it in the car. There was another knock on the door, and she looked over. "Come in."

The door opened, and Kristen Canton, the gifted teacher, popped her head inside the room. "Hello!" she called out, with a grin.

"Kristen!" Rose got up to greet her, calling her by her first name because she was only twenty-five, and preferred it. "How nice of you to come."

"I'm so sorry I didn't get here yesterday." Kristen gave her a warm hug, then whispered in her ear, "I've been upstairs."

"Oh." Rose released Kristen, and close-up, she could see that the pretty young teacher was a wreck. A normally bouncy redhead with warm brown eyes, a small, straight nose, a sprinkling of adorable freckles and an omnipresent grin, Kristen wore a forced smile today, and her eyes looked puffy under fresh makeup.

"Ms. Canton!" Melly shouted.

"Hey, girlfriend!" Kristen crossed to the bed. Her hair had been gathered into a messy ponytail, and her usually hip shirt-and-jeans combo had been replaced by a gray hoodie, which she had on with black yoga pants and flats. "How you doin'?"

"Good!"

"Great. I'm so happy to see you're all right. I'd hug you but I'm a little sick."

"There was a fire in the school, Ms. Canton. My mom found me."

"What a great mom!" Kristen winked at Rose, then turned back to Melly. "Guess what? I have a get-well present for you."

"What is it?"

"Check it out." Kristen slipped a hand into her shoulder bag, pulled out a longish box with flowery gift wrap, and presented it with a flourish. "Ta-da!"

"Yay!" Melly tore off the gift wrap, which covered a forest green box. She flipped open the lid, and inside was a green velveteen channel that held a magic wand, of fake wood. "Mom, look! It's a Hermione wand!"

"Honey, what do you say?" Rose smiled, touched.

"Thank you, Ms. Canton!" Melly took out the wand and started waving it around, letting the box and wrap fall to the bed. "*Alohomora!* I opened a lock, just like Hermione."

"Good for you."

"Thank you so much. I have Harry's wand but not Hermione's. Now I can put out fires."

Kristen grinned. "Like in *Deathly Hallows*."

Rose didn't remember. "There's a fire in *Deathly Hallows*? Remind me, Mel."

"Hermione puts out the fire in Mundungus's eyebrows after Harry sets him on fire by accident. Water squirts out the top of the wand." Melly waved the wand around, almost hitting her metal IV pole. "I don't know the incantation, though."

"Me, neither," Kristen said, frowning.

Rose smiled. "You haven't memorized every spell in Harry Potter?"

"I'll put out the fire in the school!" Melly looked over, then her face fell. "Did the school burn down, Ms. Canton?"

"No," Kristen answered, growing serious. "The school is fine. Only the section with the cafeteria was damaged, and we're going to fix it, as good as new."

"Was it from a bomb?"

"No, there were no bombs."

Rose looked over. "Kristen, do they know what caused the explosion?"

"They think it was some kind of gas leak and faulty electrical wiring. Mrs. Nuru says they rushed construction to open on time, and the snag list didn't get done." Kristen checked her watch and turned back to Melly. "Oops, sorry, it's late and I've got to go, sweetie. See you at school." Kristen gave Melly another hug. "Good-bye."

"Bye, Ms. Canton." Melly released her, waving the wand, and Kristen shot Rose a meaningful look.

"Rose, will you walk me out?"

"Sure." Rose turned to Melly. She knew it had to be about Amanda and she wanted to know what was going on upstairs. "Honey, I'll be right back. Ms. Canton and I will be outside the door. Call if you need me."

"Okay, Mom. Thanks for my wand, Ms. Canton!"

Chapter Fourteen

Rose led Kristen to a window well near Melly's room, but away from the nurses' station. Sunshine poured through the glass, bathing the young teacher in light as she leaned against the ledge and heaved a heavy sigh. Now that they were alone, she dropped her perky mask, and the naked sadness in her eyes made her look like a little girl.

"They don't prepare you for this, in school," Kristen said, exhaling. She shook her head, and her long, dark red ponytail slipped from side to side. "They don't tell you that something horrible could happen to kids. I've been the gifted teacher for two years, and until now, my biggest worry was my math skills. I'm like, how can I help these kids with broken fractions, when I don't understand them myself?"

Rose patted her back, sympathetic. "I know, this is tough."

"I'm happy that Melly's okay. It did me good to see her."

"Thanks so much for the gift."

"No worries. I love that kid. She's awesome."

"She loves you, too. She looks forward to school, because of you." Rose couldn't wait to ask. "Kristen, how is Amanda? I'm so worried about her. She was in a coma, last I heard."

"She's worse," Kristen answered softly. Her pretty features contorted with pain, and she heaved a sudden sob, her hands moving to cover her face. "They just gave her last rites."

Oh my God. Rose sagged next to her on the window ledge, feeling as if she'd been punched in the gut.

"The family is all up there," Kristen said, between sobs. "The two brothers, their priest, the grandparents. They're a mess, a total mess."

Rose hung her head. Air conditioning blew onto her face, through a grate on top of the window well.

"I'm sorry, I just feel so lost, she's just a little kid." Kristen's shoulders shuddered. "It's so awful to see her that way."

Rose ached for Eileen and the family, and her regrets rushed back at her. She should have saved Amanda when she had the chance. It wouldn't have taken that long to get her out of the building. Both girls could be fine now, alive and well.

"I'm so sorry." Kristen's sobs began to subside, and she fumbled in her purse, found a soggy tissue, and dabbed underneath her eyes. "Things like this aren't supposed to happen."

"No, they're not," Rose said, but she knew better. Things like this happened all the time. Ambulances stocked teddy bears for a reason.

"I was so excited to get the job, running the gifted program." Kristen sniffled. "Reesburgh is such a great district, and they were like, make it your own, go with it, develop your own curriculum and enrichment programs. It was the job everybody wanted. Now I'm sorry I got it."

"Don't say that." Rose put an arm around the young teacher's shoulder. "You do such a great job. Melly loves the gifted program and all the things you do, like when you bring in a speaker, that guy with the falcons or that poet. And Senator Martin and the Phillie Phanatic? The kids adore you, you relate so well to them."

"That's the problem, you know." Kristen blew her nose noisily, causing her face to flush under her fair, freckled skin. "Mrs. Nuru says I'm too close to the students, that I lack professional distance. She says that I . . . I don't know, oh, forget it."

"What?"

"She thinks that I'm too close to Melly and that's why she got so upset when Amanda teased her at lunch, or when we meet, in gifted. She says Melly's too sensitive, and I shouldn't encourage it."

Rose stiffened. "That's blaming the victim. What Amanda did was downright cruel, and you weren't even there."

"I agree, but not everybody does." Kristen blew her nose, with finality. "They're all talking about it. Everybody has an opinion, because of what happened."

"What happened? You mean that I got Melly out, and not Amanda?"

"Forget it, I shouldn't have mentioned it." Kristen rolled her eyes. "God, I'm such a motor mouth."

"Kristen, no matter what you heard, I want you to know that I thought I got Amanda out of the building. I took her and Emily to the hallway door before I even went to get Melly, and I thought she'd keep going—"

"Wait, stop." Kristen raised her hands. "I'm not accusing you of anything, and I know you. I know you wouldn't just leave Amanda in a burning school. If you tried to get Amanda and the others out, then went back for Melly, no one can blame you. I don't blame you. You couldn't leave *Melly*." Kristen blinked. "That's crazy! You were in a terrible position. You did your best."

Rose felt a warm rush of gratitude. "They think I chose Melly over Amanda, but I didn't."

"Don't let them get to you. No one has the facts, and I heard Emily's traumatized. Eileen's losing Amanda, and it's so horrible that she's totally crazy. Everybody's crazy! Her, Mrs. Nuru, Mr. Rodriguez, all of them. You don't know the half of it. My mother would say, we're 'undone.' I'm 'undone,' and so are you." Kristen looked up, her tired eyes glistening. "Have you told Melly about Amanda and the others?"

"Not yet, no." Rose didn't want to fast-forward to that conversation. "I'd like to get her home first, and get her feet under her."

"Good. I'll be glad to come over when you tell her. Call me, whenever. You have my cell number. I think it's on my email to you."

"Thanks," Rose said, grateful. "I'll talk to Leo, to see what he thinks."

"We'll have grief counselors at school, and the guidance counselor. Mrs. Nuru's been through this, and she says the counselors really help. She's lost three students in her time. One to leukemia, one to bone cancer, and another died in a car crash with a drunk driver."

Rose reeled. Leukemia. Cancer. Car crash. Now, Amanda. It made a blotchy red birthmark seem like nothing. She felt tears rising, then willed them away. At least her child was alive. "How the hell do you outlive your child?" Rose asked, half to herself.

Mommy!

"Don't ask me, I have both my parents, and my only kid is a cat." Kristen looked down the hall, distracted, and Rose turned to see Mr. Rodriguez striding toward them. He'd been a teacher for thirty years before he became principal, and he was in his fifties, if less than fit. Six feet tall with a blocky build, he came off like everybody's favorite uncle in a navy polo shirt that showed a paunch hanging over gray suit pants.

"Rose." Mr. Rodriguez smiled when he reached her, but his brown eyes showed the strain. He ran a hand through short, dark hair. "I'm sorry about what happened, and I'm sorry it took me this long to come see you. How is Melly? I hear she's on the mend."

"Yes, thanks. We're hoping she goes home tomorrow."

"Wonderful." Mr. Rodriguez's brow relaxed, his relief genuine. "Where's Leo?"

"Home with John, the baby."

"Of course. Great guy. I'm so happy you were there for Melly. Your acts were positively heroic."

Rose flushed. "I only wish I could have saved Amanda, too. I did take her and Emily to the hall leading to the playground."

"I'm sure." Mr. Rodriguez frowned deeply, his dark eyebrows joining like gathering nimbus clouds. "I was just upstairs. You should know that Amanda's been given last rites."

"Kristen told me. I'm so sorry."

"It's just tragic." Mr. Rodriguez sighed. "Fortunately, Eileen's got a lot of support, and her family will get her through whatever she has to face, whenever the time comes."

"I can't imagine losing a child."

"Nor can I. My daughters are my life. I've had challenges in my career, but never like this. Eileen will have to go on, for her boys."

Mr. Rodriguez nodded, as if trying to cheer himself up. "You'll find that there are real advantages to being a member of such a small community. We support each other in Reesburgh. Most of the people here have watched the Gigots grow up, and you'll see how tight we are, when we reopen on Monday."

"Back to school, so soon?" Rose asked, surprised.

"Routine is really the best thing for the students, and school becomes a constant in times of stress. We'll eat in the classrooms during the clean-up and put up plywood fencing so they don't see the cafeteria. We'll start with half a day on Monday and dismiss at noon." Mr. Rodriguez stuck his hands in his pockets, jingling his change. "We're asking the parents to drive the kids in, and we'll have a special assembly in the morning for Marylou, Serena, and Ellen."

"When are the funerals?" Rose felt a step behind, playing catch-up.

"They'll hold the wake on Sunday night, at Fiore's, with private burials on Monday. We'll have grief counselors in the auditorium for the next two weeks. The healing can begin, right away."

"It seems soon, doesn't it?"

"Feel free to keep Melly home if you wish, we'll count it as excused, but if she's well enough, I'd send her. We need her to assimilate into the school community, and I'll look out for her, and so will the staff." Mr. Rodriguez turned to Kristen. "You have a special relationship with Melly, don't you?"

"Yes, I'll take care of her."

Mr. Rodriguez turned back to Rose. "Please, don't think I'm callous. Under state law, we have to hold class a certain number of days, come hell or high water. We can't afford to lose the days now, in case we get as much snow as we did last winter."

"But it was such a big fire." Rose flashed on the horrific scene in the cafeteria.

"Perhaps it seems that way to you, but in fact, it was fairly confined. The only damage was to the cafeteria, teachers' lounge, and hallway, and those will all be closed."

"What about water damage? The sprinklers went off."

"The sprinkler system is zoned. The sprinklers went off only where there was fire." Mr. Rodriguez straightened, his manner turning official. "I spent all afternoon yesterday with the county Fire Marshals, the Fire Chief, the state police, and the district supervisors. We even hosted the FBI. Quite the command center, for a tragedy of this scope."

"My condolences, too."

"Thank you." Mr. Rodriguez pursed his thin lips. "The Fire Marshals have already certified the rest of the building as structurally sound, and we hope to rebuild the cafeteria by the end of February."

"This time they better get the wiring right."

"Excuse me?" Mr. Rodriguez frowned. "What makes you say that, Rose?"

Rose blinked. "I heard there was faulty wiring, maybe something left off the snag list."

"Where'd you hear that?"

Rose hesitated, sorry she'd mentioned anything, but Kristen answered, "I told her."

Mr. Rodriguez turned to the teacher, his eyes hardening. "Kristen, this is a difficult situation, with three fatalities, and there shouldn't be any idle speculation about its causes, especially from my own staff. The cause of the explosion and fire haven't been determined as yet."

Rose interjected, "I asked her. She wasn't speculating."

"Just the same." Mr. Rodriguez's gaze bored into Kristen, then shifted back to Rose, his brow relaxing just a little. "We've all been instructed by legal counsel not to discuss the particulars of this tragedy with anyone. You can imagine, with three families grieving and two children in the hospital, even Melly, that we need to keep an even keel, going forward." Mr. Rodriguez squared his shoulders. "Rose, I have my work cut out for me, this weekend. I'd like to say hello to Melly, if that's okay with you, and then we'll go. Kristen, you'll leave with me, please."

"Sure." Kristen nodded, nervously, and Rose couldn't process it all fast enough. Everybody lawyering up. Amanda, dying upstairs. School, opening after the weekend. It was a lot to wrap her mind around, and it would be even harder for Melly.

"Right, let's go see Melly," Rose said, summoning her composure and leading them to the door, but when they opened it, Melly was sound asleep.

Mr. Rodriguez looked over, a twinkle in his eye. "Usually this happens *after* I speak," he said, with a tight smile.

Chapter Fifteen

"Sure you're not thirsty?" Rose asked Melly, sitting at the edge of her hospital bed, when they were alone. She felt devastated that Amanda had been given last rites, but she masked it for Melly, who was waking up, having napped only briefly.

"No."

"No water?"

"I drank some." Melly touched the oxygen tube under her nostrils with her fingernail, polished pink, now chipping. "Did Ms. Canton go home?"

"Yes. She told me to say good-bye. Mr. Rodriguez came to meet you, but you were asleep, so I didn't wake you."

"Maybe because she's sick. That's why she wasn't in school." Melly let go of the oxygen tube. "Do you have my DS?"

"No. It's in the bag I left in Leo's car, with the book. Sorry. I don't have my laptop either."

"It's okay. I miss my friends on Club Penguin. We always talk on Saturday morning."

"I know." Rose limited Melly's time on Club Penguin, a safe chat site for children, though for a kid self-conscious about her looks, the site was a godsend.

"Can we watch TV? Cartoons are on."

"No, let's not." Rose didn't want to take a chance that any newsbreak or screen crawl could update the school fire, especially the fatalities.

"So what can we do?"

"I can run down to the gift shop and see if they have any magazines, and we can read together."

Melly brightened. "Do they have *Teen People*? It's my friend's favorite magazine."

"Which friend?"

"A girl on Club Penguin. She likes all those magazines. She likes Harry Potter, too, but she only read *Chamber of Secrets*."

"Okay, I'll go get the magazine." Rose rolled the night table out of the way and stood up, just as the door opened. It was Leo, and he had John asleep on his shoulder, in his yellow onesie and a white receiving blanket. Oddly, Leo looked dressed for work, in the white oxford shirt, tan Dockers, and penny loafers of the American lawyer on a Saturday.

"Hey, boys! Let me see my Johnnie Angel." Rose got up and took the sleeping baby, who filled her arms. John was big for his age, making a nice warm bundle, and he resettled his head on her shoulder. She was happy to see him, even if it wasn't the greatest idea to bring a sick baby to a hospital. She stroked John's tiny back in the soft blanket, cuddling him, and given what was happening with Amanda, she felt vaguely more comforted than comforting.

"Hey, girls!" Leo dropped the diaper bag on the chair by the door and went over to Melly. "How's my melba toast?"

"Leo!" Melly knelt in bed and threw open her arms, and Leo gathered her up in a bear hug, ending with his trademark grunt.

"I'm so happy to see you, kiddo."

"Leo, I have oxygen."

"Great." Leo laughed. "I love oxygen."

Rose watched them, counting herself lucky that Melly loved her stepfather so much, whether she called him Daddy or not. Her family was finally complete, even if it wasn't exactly the way she'd planned it, and she felt a deep stab of guilt over her own happiness, when she knew that upstairs the scene would be one of profound grief. She went over and impulsively kissed Leo on the cheek, catching a whiff of his spicy aftershave, also unusual for a Saturday. "Why do you smell so nice?"

"Because I'm a sexy beast?" Leo smiled crookedly, but Rose saw a flicker of regret behind his eyes.

"You're not going in, are you?"

"I have to, babe." Leo's brown eyes met hers, his emotions now plain. "I'm going to trial, in *Granger Securities*. I'm so sorry, honey, but it can't be helped. We were number ten in the trial pool, but everything settled and we're up on Monday. I got the call an hour ago, from the law clerk."

"On a Saturday, they call?"

"Yep. It happens. Judges can't afford down time in their dockets."

"But what about John? They won't let him stay here tonight, and if they find out he's sick, they'll throw me out."

"I couldn't get a sitter." Leo shook his head. "Babe, believe me, if I could avoid this, I would, but I can't. My hands are tied. You know how big this case is."

"I know." Rose did, it was true. He'd been talking about *Granger Securities* for three years. "But what about Jamie, couldn't she sit?"

"No, she's busy. I even called the backup sitter, and she has exams. I told her she can study at our house, but she said no. Plus I asked the neighbor, Mrs. Burton. She's going out, and I don't know anybody else. I'm out of options."

"What about the sitter from the old neighborhood. Sandy?"

"No answer." Leo shrugged. "I'd take him with me to the office, but I have witnesses flying in from Denver, and it's all hands on deck. I have to work all weekend, and next week will be sheer hell."

"Oh, jeez." Rose was getting that Peter and Paul feeling again, torn between the two children. She didn't want to go home with John and leave Melly alone in the hospital. "On the bright side, he's cooler. Is his fever gone?"

"Yes, but I packed the Tylenol and amoxicillin, just in case. Also I fed the dog and left the dog door open."

"Leo, Leo!" Melly called from the bed. "Ms. Canton gave me a Hermione wand!"

"Lemme see."

"I forget the incantation to make water come out, though. Oh, wait. *Aguamenti!*" Melly grabbed the wand and waved it around, and Leo ducked.

"Cool. Let me try. I don't speak Harry Potter." He took the wand and waved it in the air. "Bibbity, bobbity, boo! What's the spell for a babysitter?"

Melly frowned. "Leo, Mom says I can't watch *iCarly.*"

"She said that? She's such a meanie." Leo turned to Rose, waving the wand. "Let's make her change her mind. Presto!"

"No TV." Rose flared her eyes meaningfully, but Leo scoffed.

"Come on, she won't see anything bad on Nickleodeon."

"What's anything bad?" Melly asked, and Leo caught himself, cringing.

"Nothing."

"Step outside with me, will you, Merlin?" Rose went to the door with John, then turned to Melly. "Honey, stay in bed. We're going into the hall a minute, to talk."

"Later, tater!" Leo kissed Melly and gave her back the wand, and Rose led him outside to the window well, dreading the task at hand. Her heart felt so heavy, and she leaned against the ledge, with the air conditioning cold on her back.

"Leo, there's terrible news about Amanda. They gave her last rites. She may already be—" Rose still couldn't finish the sentence, and from the expression on Leo's face, she didn't have to. His forehead collapsed into folds, and he winced.

"Aw, no." He wrapped his arms around her and John, holding them close and rubbing her back. "That's terrible, so terrible. That poor kid."

"I know. I just feel so awful for her, and for Eileen. I wish we could do something."

"We can't."

"You sure?"

"Of course." Leo released her, squinting against the sunlight. "There's nothing we can do."

"Just to tell them we're thinking of them."

"You'd make yourself feel better, but not them. You're the last person they want to hear from right now."

Rose felt stung, if only because it was true.

"Plus anything you say can look like an admission of guilt, later." Leo frowned. "Let it go. Can you let it go?"

Rose had been here before. She could never let anything go. She didn't even know what letting go meant.

"Listen." Leo rubbed her arms, and John stirred, but stayed asleep. "I got a bunch of calls from reporters today, and there are messages at work, too. We have to be smart about this. I realize that this trial comes at the worst time, but it's out of my control."

"Can't you get an extension from the judge? You have a child in the hospital."

"Melly's coming home tomorrow, right?"

"Yes, around noon."

"Then no." Leo gave her a quick kiss on the cheek. "Look, I have to leave. Tonight, take John and go home."

"I don't have a car."

"Yes, you do. I parked yours out front."

"Thanks. How did you do that?"

"By cab. Listen, Melly will be fine tonight. I put her new book in the diaper bag, plus the DS. You can call her every hour. I'll call if I can, too."

"Leo, no." Rose felt so confused. Her head thundered. "I can't go home and leave her alone. She just went through a major trauma."

"Then go home until one of the sitters frees up, and maybe you can come back."

"I don't want to leave her alone. She could have died. Amanda is dying. This is real, and it matters." Rose felt herself get worked up. She flashed on the teddy bears in the ambulance. "These kids are real, not packages you can drop off. They live and they die."

Leo blinked. "I know that."

"Melly's always accommodating John. It's never the other way around."

Leo frowned in confusion. "That's because he's the baby."

"Or is it because he's *your* baby?"

"What?" Leo's lips parted. "Are you crazy?"

Mommy!

Rose blinked. Maybe she was. She felt it, a little. She was responsible for a child's death. She couldn't take anything back. She couldn't replay anything. It was too late to make a different decision. Time wasn't her friend, it had never been. It didn't care about children, life, or death. It just ticked ahead, moving on, ever forward, always later.

"Ro, it's not a choice between Melly and John, or between Melly and Amanda. You're all over the place. Hang on to yourself." Leo touched her arm, and John shifted, his nose bubbling. "I love both kids the same, you know that. Right now, the only family that matters is ours. Not theirs, ours. You, me, Melly, and John. Even Googie. That's the family that means everything to me."

"Is that why you're going to work?"

"*What?*"

"You heard me." Rose knew she was wrong, even as the words escaped her lips. She was digging herself a hole and she didn't know why, but she couldn't stop herself, either.

Leo's eyes widened, a bewildered brown, the hue of earth itself. He shut his mouth, pursing his lips, and she could see he didn't want to say anything he would regret. Without another word, he turned on his heel and strode back to the hospital room, where she knew he would put on a happy face and give Melly a good-bye kiss.

Rose remained frozen in the sunlight, and when Leo emerged from Melly's room, she didn't apologize or try to stop him.

She let him walk down the hall.

Away.

Chapter Sixteen

Rose began walking and rocking John, who was fussy and unhappy. He'd slept most of the afternoon, but his second dose of Tylenol was wearing off and he must've been hungry. She replaced his pacifier and sang him "Oh Susanna," her go-to song, but it wasn't working. She didn't know what had happened to Amanda, and she felt cut off from the world, tense, and out of sorts.

John wailed, and Melly looked up from her *Beedle the Bard* book. "Mom, what does he want?"

"I don't know. His ear must hurt."

"Why don't we tell the doctor?"

"They're all busy, and he's not their patient."

"Why not?"

"That's not how it works.

" 'Oh, don't you cry for me.' " Rose sang and swayed, but John kept crying. She walked him to the window, but he wouldn't be distracted by mere trees and a setting sun. She had to quiet him before the nurses got wise to their pajama party. She paced back to the bed. "Melly?"

"Yes?" She looked up from the book, pressing her oxygen tube dutifully into place.

"I'm going to go downstairs and get us some more food. I'll be right back, okay?"

"Okay."

"If you need anything, you can always ask the nurse." Rose picked up her purse and slung it over her shoulder, then grabbed the remote control and tucked it under John. She wiped his nose with her sleeve, then slipped out of the room. An older nurse and a young intern looked up from behind their counter, and Rose flashed them a smile. "We're going down for some food, and my daughter Melly will be alone. Can you keep an eye on her?"

"Sure," the nurse answered. "Take the stairs, it's quicker. The cafeteria is to the right, at the bottom, first floor."

"Thanks."

John cried, and the intern winced at the sound. "No lung trouble on him, eh?"

Rose faked a laugh and wished parenthood on him, then headed down the hall toward the stairs. Visitors and orderlies turned as she passed, and when she went through the stairwell door, John quieted abruptly, at the change in scenery. He sighed a baby sigh, his chest heaving, and he looked around in wobbly wonderment. The tip of his nose was red, his cheeks pink and chubby, and his curly brown hair damp where he had sweated. His brown eyes shone with tears, but were round and lively, like Leo's.

Is it because he's your baby?

"There you go, honey bun." She rubbed his back between his tiny shoulder blades, and his sleeper felt warm and nubby under her palm. "It's all right, honey. Everything's all right."

John smiled at her, and Rose felt her heart fill with love. She gave him a kiss, then climbed down the stairs, cradling him close to her chest. She adored John, and she adored Leo, and she felt terrible about what she'd said about him favoring the baby. It was a terrible thing to say, and it wasn't even true. She must have been crazy.

Mommy!

She stopped on the stairwell, slid her BlackBerry from her pocket, and thumbed her way to the phone function. She didn't think she'd screw up any cardiac monitors if she called from here, but there was only one bar left on the screen. She thumbed her way to the text function, texted I'M SORRY LOVE U, and hit SEND. But the text didn't transmit, either because of the low battery or poor reception.

She hit the first floor, opened the door, and entered the bright, glistening lobby. It was an uncrowded, sleepy Saturday night, and for that she was grateful. She passed a sign for the cafeteria and followed it past bronze plaques that listed major donors and corporate sponsors, knowing she was getting closer to the cafeteria by the comforting aromas of grilled cheese and tomato soup. She kept going, and the hallway wound around to an institutional cafeteria signed THE GROTTO, where papier-mâché salamis and ersatz wheels of provolone hung above a stainless steel lineup of trays and silverware. She grabbed a red plastic tray and got in line behind a man and a woman, sliding the tray along with one hand and holding John with the other, giving him a kiss on the cheek.

"Let's see what they have, huh? Hot dog, grilled cheese, mac and cheese." Rose talked to John all the time, like the narrator of their everyday life. She didn't know why she did it, but she'd done it with Melly, and she knew he understood the gist. Science didn't give babies enough credit, and every mother knew it.

"Johnnie, look at all this good stuff." Rose eyed the hot sandwiches wrapped in aluminum foil and picked two grilled-cheese sandwiches for them, hoping to find something easier on the throat for Melly. John started pumping his fists happily, which he did when he was hungry, and it caught the attention of a female cafeteria worker, whose nametag read DORIS.

"What a cute little guy!" Doris walked over with a tray of wrapped hamburgers, flat and silvery as flying saucers. "Is he a good baby?"

"The best. Easy as pie." Rose thought of the cafeteria workers killed in the explosion, then shooed it away. She plucked a French fry from the bag and offered one to John, who closed his little fingers around it and throttled it before it got to his mouth, where he stuffed it in, sideways. "Yummy, huh?"

"He loves my cooking." Doris smiled.

"He sure does." Rose went down the line, looking for pizza. The man in front of her skipped ahead to the coffee station, and she closed up behind an older woman with a short, steel-gray ponytail, who was squinting at the vats of soup, the deep lines in her face illuminated by the under-counter lights.

"Excuse me, can you read that, dear?" the older woman asked, frowning at Rose. "I forgot my reading glasses. Does that say 'vegetable'?"

"Yes, it's vegetarian vegetable."

"Thank you." The woman smiled, her hooded eyes lighting up when she saw John. "Goodness, a baby! How I miss those days! She's adorable."

"Thanks." Rose didn't bother to correct her, and Doris tried to get the older woman's attention.

"Ma'am, did you want some soup?"

"Yes, please, just one. Vegetable. Small."

"And you want the burgers, too. All eight?"

"Yes, I've got to feed a lot of people."

"Good for you," Rose said, trying to leave. The heat lamps shone blood-red onto pizza slices in cardboard triangles, and next to that were glass shelves of cherry Jell-O and chocolate pudding, which she slid onto her tray for Melly.

"They sent me down for the food. I'm the one who pays, naturally. I'm always the one who pays." The older woman chuckled, and Rose took three bottles of water from a well of chipped ice.

"That's nice of you," she said, to be polite.

"My grand-niece is in a bad way," the older woman said to Doris, who was putting the hamburgers in a large paper bag. "She got hurt real bad, in that fire at the school."

Rose froze. The woman had to be talking about Amanda. It was a coincidence, but not that strange. Reesburgh Memorial was a small hospital in a small town. It meant that Amanda was still alive. Her heart leapt, and she wanted to hear more. She handed John another French fry to keep him quiet, eavesdropping.

"Sorry for your trouble." Doris pitched ketchup packets into the bag. "I saw that fire on the news. They broke in right in the middle of my stories."

Rose kept her head down. She wanted information, but she didn't want to be recognized.

The older woman was saying, "The doctors thought she was going to pass this morning, but she proved 'em all wrong. It's a rollercoaster, up and down, down and up, day and night."

"I'm so sorry." Doris frowned. "I'll say a prayer."

"Thank you. We drove across the state from Pittsburgh, when we heard. They won't let us in to see her, for more than fifteen minutes every hour."

"Rules are rules." Doris handed the bag to the cashier, then turned to Rose. "Would you like to go first, miss? You have the baby, and this lady has a large dinner order."

"Yes, thanks, I should hurry." Rose went ahead to the cashier, keeping her head down, but she could still overhear the conversation.

"I believe in the power of prayer," the older woman was saying. "I pray every day. Ever since my husband passed, it brings me peace and tranquility. You ask me, the rest of my family could use some good old-fashioned religion. My nephew, he's a lawyer, and he's just plain angry all the time. He's up there now, ranting and raving. Hard to believe he was raised a Christian."

"I hear that." Doris put a floppy packet of napkins in the bag.

"He wants to sue the school and everybody in sight. He says, 'Heads will roll!' "

Oh no. Rose got her wallet from her purse, but the cashier was taking forever, pecking the register keys. Another cafeteria worker, a tattooed teenager, came over and helped the older woman. Rose kept her head down, and the cashier stuffed the food in a bag, firing lids for the Jell-O and pudding, while the machine came up with a total.

"That'll be $18.36," the cashier said finally.

"Keep the change." Rose left a twenty, grabbed the food bag, and hurried from the cafeteria. She hit the hallway, her thoughts racing. She wanted to call Leo and tell him that he'd been right. People were lawyering up. Amanda's family, the school district, and God knows who else.

She took her phone from her pocket, juggling John, purse, remote control, and food bag. She glanced at the screen but it was still a single bar, so she headed for the hospital entrance, figuring she'd get better reception outside. But when she looked up through the glass doors, she stopped in her tracks.

Reporters mobbed the walkway, drinking sodas and smoking, their videocameras and microphones at rest. She turned on her heel and hustled back to the stairs.

Chapter Seventeen

Rose lay next to Melly on her bed, with John snoring on her chest, induced to slumber with Tylenol and carbs. The TV played softly on the Nickelodeon channel, and the saturated colors of the cartoons flickered around the darkening room. She checked her watch. 8:15 P.M. Her phone battery had gone dead, and she hadn't heard from Leo on the hospital phone. She'd called him and left a message, then she'd called every sitter she could think of, with no luck. She could hide out in the room for only so long after visiting hours.

Rose turned to Melly, watching TV. "Mel? We have a problem, and I need your help."

"What?" Melly looked over, her long hair messy on the pillow and her eyes tired.

"I can't stay much longer with John, and Leo can't take him, so I might have to go home for tonight."

Melly frowned. "Do I go, too?"

"No, you stay here. Later tonight, if I can get a sitter, I can come back, but if I can't, I'll be back in the morning. You'll have to be alone tonight, like a big girl, but I think you'll be fine. I'm not worried about it." Rose always said she wasn't worried when she was, which was professional parenting.

"I would be here, all by myself?"

"You won't be alone. There are nurses and doctors right outside the door. They sit there all night, at their desk. We can go meet them, right now."

"I don't want to."

"Okay, well, before I go, I'll make sure they'll check on you. That's their job, to check on the patients."

"Why can't I go home with you?"

"You can tomorrow, but not tonight. They want to keep an eye on you, to make sure your oxygen level is okay."

"But I was good, Mom. I kept it on." Melly fingered the oxygen tube, wounded.

"Yes, you were, but they need it on all night, one more night."

"Why do you have to leave?" Melly boosted herself up on the pillow.

"They don't let babies stay, and I can't get a babysitter. You heard me on the phone. I have a problem, and you could really help, if you'd just stay here by yourself." Rose went into bribe mode. "You can watch TV as late as you want, but only *Nick at Nite*."

"Really?" Melly perked up as the door opened, and the nurse entered, with a smile.

"Hello, ladies," she said, cheery. She was a young brunette, heavyset, with a broad smile. Her pink scrubs were covered with a puppy print, and taped to her stethoscope was a laminated photo of a white poodle. "I'm Rosie, the night nurse."

"Ha!" Melly laughed, sitting up. "Same name as you, Mom."

"Right." Rose edged out of bed, holding the sleeping baby. "My name's Rose, too. And we both love dogs, right?"

"Guilty as charged. I have a poodle named Bobo."

Melly perked up. "We have a Cavalier King Charles spaniel. Her name is Princess Google Cadiz McKenna Ingrassia."

The nurse laughed. "That's a long name."

"We have a lot of names in our family. We just call her Googie because she has googly eyes."

"Cute!" The nurse lifted the blood pressure cuff from a wire basket in the wall. "Melly, I'm going to take your blood pressure. You know how this works?"

"Yes. It hurts."

"Not the way I do it." The nurse picked up Melly's arm, and her gaze shifted to Rose. "I'm sorry, but you can't stay here at night, with the baby."

"I know, I'm leaving." Rose smiled, to send the right signal to Melly. "I was telling Melly that you'll be right outside the door, and she shouldn't be worried about a thing. I'm going to let her stay up and watch *Nick at Nite*."

The nurse nodded, wrapping the cuff with care. "That's right, Melly. We're going to have fun. I like your nail polish. I love pink."

"Me, too."

"Know what?" The nurse strapped the cuff closed with Velcro. "I have some nail polish at my desk, and we can do each other's nails, later on."

"Yay!" Melly grinned, scrambling to her knees. "I know how to do it, all by myself."

"Really?" The nurse pumped up the cuff. "We'll have a good time, you and me."

"Do you like pudding?"

"I love pudding! See my hips?" The nurse chuckled, eyeing her watch. "I like it all gooey and yummy and chocolaty." She released the cuff. "All done. You're doing great, cutie patootie."

Melly smiled, surprised. "Hey, that didn't hurt. How did you do that?"

"That's my secret."

Melly turned to Rose, bright-eyed. "Mom, you can go now."

"Okay, good idea." Rose cuddled John to her chest, gave Melly a quick kiss on the cheek, hoisted her purse and diaper bag to her shoulder, then noticed the remote control on the chair. She picked it up and wedged it into the diaper bag, just to be on the safe side.

"There was a fire at my school," Melly told the nurse.

"I know, I heard."

"My mom got me out."

"She's amazing. You know why?"

"Why?"

"Her name is Rose." The nurse winked, then turned to Rose. "Bye now, other Rose!"

"Bye, and thanks!" Rose went to the door. "Sweetie, I'll call you on the phone in about an hour."

"Okay, Mom!"

"Have fun! Love you!" Rose hurried down the hall and took the stairs, trying not to jostle John. She got her car keys from her purse, held John close, put her head down, and barreled through the doors.

Heads started to turn as soon as she hit the pavement, and the crowd surged toward her. Klieglights burst into brightness, cameramen hoisted videocameras, and microphones were brandished. Leading the crowd was Tanya Robertson, and she thrust her microphone at Rose.

"Ms. McKenna, how's Melly? Is she still being discharged tomorrow? Can't we get that one-on-one interview? Just say the word!"

"No comment." Rose looked around for her car, but the klieglights blinded her, and the commotion woke John, who burst into tears.

Tanya persisted, joined by the other reporters. "Any comment on the condition of Amanda Gigot, Ms. McKenna?" "Did you administer CPR to any child besides yours?"

Rose spotted her blue Explorer in the lot and picked up a jog, holding the crying baby to her chest.

"Is it true that you have complained to school officials about the behavior of Amanda Gigot toward your daughter?" "Has the Gigot family or their lawyer contacted you?"

Rose chirped the door unlocked, buckled John into his car seat, jumped behind the wheel, and hit the gas, leaving their questions behind.

Chapter Eighteen

It was dark by the time Rose got home and pulled into the driveway. Her neighbor across the street was putting out his trash, and she waved to him. He didn't wave back, though he had to have seen her. She cut the engine, got out of the car, went around the backseat, and lifted John, still asleep, from his car seat. Stale Cheerios fell to the driveway as she hoisted him to her shoulder, grabbed the diaper bag, and closed the door. She walked the sidewalk to the house, grateful for the darkness, the starless night like a cloak, hiding her from view.

She went up the sidewalk, then the flagstone path to the house, a four-bedroom colonial of solid gray stone, with a half circle of white roof sheltering the entrance. It seemed impossible that they could lose the house, but everything that had happened since Friday seemed impossible. She found her house key and let herself in, waking Princess Google, the world's worst watchdog.

She set her bags on the couch and went straight upstairs with John, walking evenly so she wouldn't wake him. She switched on the hall light, changed him, and put him down. He stayed asleep, his arms open, his fists balled, and his legs flopped apart like a frog's. She tiptoed from the room and was going downstairs to try to find a sitter when the phone started ringing. She ran to the wall phone in the kitchen, and the caller ID read REESBURGH MEMORIAL.

Rose picked up instantly, alarmed. "Yes?"

"Mom?" It was Melly.

"Honey! I was going to call you soon. How are you doing?"

"They put a little girl in my room."

"Oh well." Rose should have thought of that, as a possibility. "That happens, sometimes."

"That's what Leo says. He called to say hi."

"That was nice."

"The mom is sleeping over with her. She's on the other side of the curtain."

Rose heard noise in the background. "What's that sound?"

"She has the TV on, really loud. I can't even hear *Nick at Nite.* I don't know where the nurse went and we didn't do our nails."

Rose hated that Melly was there alone. "I guess she got busy. Do you see the button—"

"Mom, it said on their TV that Amanda was in the hospital. I heard it. They said her name, Amanda Gigot. Is Amanda in the hospital?"

Oh no. "Yes, she is."

"*This* hospital?"

"Yes."

"Is she sick?"

"Yes. She has what you had, from the smoke." Rose didn't want to lie, but she couldn't tell the whole truth, not with Melly by herself. "She needs more oxygen, and they're keeping an eye on her."

"I don't want her to come in my room, Mom."

"She won't."

"She better not." Melly sounded anxious. "I'm already sharing it with a little kid. I shouldn't have to share it with Amanda, too. Mom, can I come home?"

"Not yet."

"But I don't want to stay here, all by myself."

Rose felt a guilty pang. "I'm going to call some babysitters and see if I can get someone to stay with John, so I can come back to the hospital. Okay?"

"Please come soon, Mom."

"I'll try. In the meantime, can you rest a little?"

"No, the TV is so loud. If you were here, you would say, 'turn that down!'" Melly did a fair impression of Rose as fishwife.

"Let me see if I can do something about that TV, then get a sitter." Rose checked her oven clock. 9:25 P.M. "I'll call you as soon as I can. I love you."

"Love you, too."

"Hang in there. Bye." Rose hung up, then hit redial to get the main switchboard at the hospital. The operator picked up, and she asked, "Can you transfer me to the nurses' station on the third floor?"

"Certainly," the operator answered. There was a click, and the phone rang and rang. Nobody picked up, so Rose hung up and re-dialed.

"I'm the one calling the third floor," Rose said, when the operator answered. "My daughter is in the hospital, and I want to speak with the nurse outside her room. Her name is Rosie, and the TV in—"

"Hold the line."

"No, wait!" Rose heard the same clicks and the same ringing. She waited ten rings and hung up. She took her phone from her pocket and plugged it into the charger near the toaster. The phone came to life, the red star telling her there was a message, so she pressed to the phone function. The last call was from Leo's cell, and she pressed voicemail, for his message:

"Babe, I got your text, and I'm sorry, too. I'm up to my ass in alligators here, so don't wait up. Hope you found a sitter and give the kids my love. You, too."

Rose pressed END, happy to hear his voice, then pressed her way to her address book, thumbed to her B-list babysitters, and got busy. Almost half an hour later, she hadn't been able to beg, borrow, or steal a sitter. She checked the clock, and it was almost ten o'clock. She felt terrible, but she had to call Melly with the bad news. "Honey?" she said, when Melly picked up.

"Mom! When are you coming?"

"I'm so sorry, sweetie, but I can't. I tried, but I can't get a sitter. I'll keep trying, and if I get lucky, I can—"

"Mom, please? I don't like it here."

"Did the nurse come back?" Rose could hear the TV, blaring in the background.

"She did but she had to go. Mom, please. Please come."

"Did you tell her about the TV?"

"No, I felt funny."

"Mel, see the button on the side of the bed? It's a white plastic thing and it's attached to a white cord. Can you press it?"

"Yes. I'm pressing it, but the nurse isn't coming."

"Keep pressing it, and she will."

"She's not, Mom." Melly started to cry, softly.

"Honey, don't cry, everything's all right. Don't be upset. When the nurse comes, put her on the phone. I'll tell her to tell the lady to lower the TV." Rose heard Melly sniffling, then some noise and talking, and it sounded like the nurse was in the room. "Melly, put the nurse on. Melly? Hello?"

"Yes," replied a cool voice, clearly not nurse Rosie.

"Hi, this is Rose. Who is this?"

"It's Annabelle. Are you the mother?"

"Yes, please, help her. She was in that school fire yesterday, and the woman in her room is blaring the TV. The news is upsetting her."

"Relax. I have it under control. Hang on, please." The nurse sounded calm, and in the next minute the background noise stopped and the TV silenced, but Melly was still crying softly, which broke Rose's heart.

"Hello, Annabelle?" she said. "Are you there?"

"Pardon?"

"Can you just comfort my daughter? She's a good kid, she's just scared, and she's been through a lot in the past few—"

"I'm sorry, but we have to hang up. There are no calls permitted this late."

"No, wait. Don't hang up. I want to talk to my daughter."

"There's an automatic cut-off for phone calls after ten. I'll take good care of her."

Rose felt her temper flare. "Let me say good night to her, for God's sake."

"Please, hold on."

"Melly? Melly?" Rose said, but the line went dead. She tried to call back, but there was no answer. She tried the switchboard and asked again for the nurses' station, but the phone rang and rang, all over again. She hung up, noticing the red light was blinking on her phone, which meant incoming email.

She pressed the button to see the list of senders, but they were all messages sent from Facebook. She scanned the names in the messages: Kim Barnett, Jane Llewellyn, Annelyn Baxter, moms from the class and school committees. When she'd moved to Reesburgh, she'd friended everyone in the class. She clicked the first name, and the email came on the screen:

Kim Barnett has sent you a message on Facebook. "I KNOW THE GIGOT FAMILY AND THEY ARE HEARTBROKEN! HOW DO YOU LIVE WITH YOURSELF?"

Rose set down the BlackBerry. Reesburgh was a small town, and the Internet made it even smaller. She didn't need to read any more.

She got the gist.

Chapter Nineteen

Rose stood at the kitchen counter, drinking Diet Coke and waiting for the TV news. She didn't relish seeing the story of the school fire, but she wanted to know what Melly might have seen or heard. She scratched the sleeping dog with her foot while the turbocharged theme of Philly News started. A handsome anchorman came on the screen, with a photo of the burning elementary school behind him, above a banner, FATAL SCHOOL FIRE.

"Good evening, Tim Dodson here. In our top story, life in Reesburgh is getting back to the new normal, after a cafeteria fire in an elementary school that left three dead, a beloved teacher and two female cafeteria workers. Tanya Robertson is on the scene at Reesburgh Memorial Hospital, where young Amanda Gigot remains in Intensive Care, fighting for her young life . . ."

The screen changed to Tanya, holding a bubble microphone to her lipsticked lips, standing in a pool of manufactured light. "Tonight, the two students injured in Friday's school fire remain in this hospital. They're little girls from the same third-grade class, but that's where the similarity ends. The lucky one, Melinda Cadiz, age eight, will be going home tomorrow after being treated for smoke inhalation. Melinda, called Melly, was rescued from the flames by her mother, our reluctant hero Rose McKenna. We were the first to show you that viewer video yesterday, of Rose running out of the smoky school, with her daughter in her arms."

Rose shuddered, but wasn't completely surprised. So many people had phones and BlackBerrys. She'd carried a flip camera around since the day John was born.

Tanya's expression darkened, and a school photo of Amanda popped onto the screen. "Not so lucky is Amanda Gigot, also age eight, who remains in a coma, after a head injury and significant smoke inhalation. Amanda's the only daughter after two sons, and the Gigot family is headed by hard-working single mom Eileen Gigot, whose husband was killed in a forklift accident seven years ago. The entire extended Gigot clan is now by Amanda's side, hoping and praying for her recovery."

Tanya changed her tone, to investigative mode. "Authorities say that the school is set to reopen on Monday, but a spokesman for the Gigot family tells me they're considering legal action against the school, the school district, and the school's general contractor for negligence. The Gigot family has already filed for an emergency injunction, trying to stop the school from demolishing the damaged cafeteria until the cause of the fire can be independently determined. They've also called for the county District Attorney to investigate the matter for possible criminal charges."

Rose shook her head. So the Gigots really were going to sue, and she hadn't known about the injunction. She thought back to her talk with Mr. Rodriguez. No wonder he'd been angry at Kristen for talking about the cause of the fire. Things were about to go from bad to worse, and she hoped that didn't include suing her and Leo.

"We'll keep you posted on developments in this heartbreaking story, and I'll have my exclusive interview tomorrow, my one-on-one exclusive with Eileen Gigot. Back to you, Tim."

Rose took a final slug of soda. The story was getting bigger, spreading like the fire itself, and she didn't know how long it would burn. She switched off the TV, troubled. Her gaze fell on her black laptop, which she kept on the kitchen table, off to the side. She pulled up a stool, sat down, and hit a key. A screensaver came on of Leo, Melly, John, and her, grinning in a cottony mass of matching sweatshirts on the beach. She went online, plugged in the website of the TV station, and its website popped onto the screen. PHILADELPHIA'S BIGGEST NEWS, read the top of the page, and underneath were headlines, among them, SCHOOL FIRE IGNITES CONTROVERSY, above the banner, Share, Print Email, Buzz up, Twitter, Facebook.

She skimmed the story, which said nothing that hadn't been reported on TV, but at the bottom was a bright red banner, SEND US YOUR VIEWER VIDEOS! There were a bunch of thumbnails: scenes of the burning school, frozen in time, with the title on top. The Most Watched was *Hero Mom.* Rose clicked *Hero Mom* and watched. The video showed kids and teachers milling around the teachers' parking lot, with the sound of head counts and other snippets caught on audio—"it's only in the cafeteria," "the fourth grade got out first," "because it's a new school, so they didn't have the drill down yet."

Suddenly the camera turned, jittery, to the building, where students streamed from the double doors by the library, and Rose recognized the older kids she had seen in the stairwell. Their flow stopped abruptly, and she saw herself running out of the building, her expression stricken, with Melly limp in her arms, her legs swinging. "Help!" she heard herself scream, on the video. Her cry was barely picked up by the audio, but Princess Google woke up, blinking and cocking her head.

Rose watched herself run and lay Melly down on the grass, then the view was obstructed by heads and feet as the crowds surged forward, until there was the ambulance siren and the tape ended. The video left her heart pounding. The sights, the sounds, the very picture took her back to the fire. She sat there a moment, staring at the titles of the other clips: *Hero Mom Carries Daughter to Ambulance. Mom Gives CPR to Daughter. Cafeteria Fire.* She moved the cursor over *Cafeteria Fire,* and hit PLAY, and the first frame of the video wasn't a sunny parking lot, but a nightmare.

Rose swallowed hard at the sight. The view was from the playground, and the screen showed the front of the school, with the cafeteria front and center. Smoke billowed from the playground exit and from holes in the cafeteria walls and roof, where windows and skylights used to be. The air grew increasingly gray and hazy, and frantic children popped from the fog, being shepherded by teachers, janitors, and staff. The audio picked up a cacophony of screams, shouts, tears, yelling, and people shouting "oh my God," "look at that," "this way, this way," and "help!"

Rose watched, galvanized, and suddenly she saw a terrified Danielle running out of the smoke, and after her, Emily, running in tears. Teachers surged forward to meet them, and the older students kept coming out of the smoke, hustled out in lines, until the video ended.

Rose remained motionless at the laptop, her hand still on the mouse. She wished she could play it again and have it end with Amanda fleeing the building, her blond hair flying behind her, her tanned legs churning, her arms open as she ran into the waiting embrace of Mrs. Nuru.

Mommy!

Rose didn't move for the longest time. Princess Google fell back asleep on the floor, and the kitchen went completely silent. A light rain began to fall outside, and the leaves of the trees rustled with the drops, making the softest of sounds, an undercurrent of hush.

Tears came to Rose's eyes. She'd been holding them back for so long, but this time, she let them flow.

Chapter Twenty

Rose woke up, hearing her name called softly, then feeling a gentle touch on her back and a soft kiss on her cheek. She had fallen asleep in front of the laptop, on her folded arms. She lifted her head, blinking. "Leo?" she said, muzzy from sleep.

"Hi, honey." Leo knelt beside her, so that they were eye level, and he put his arm around her. "I was worried about my best girl, so I snuck out."

"Aw." Rose let herself be hugged, their heads touching. Princess Google pressed between them, pawing for attention with moppet feet, her tail flopping back and forth. "That's so sweet of you."

"I can sleep here if you want to go back to the hospital. I'll work from home tomorrow morning, then come by the hospital at noon and pick up you and Melly. Sound like a plan?" Leo kissed her again, and Rose felt the delicious scratchiness of a late-day beard.

"Yes, thanks. I'm sorry I was a jerk."

"I'm sorry you were, too." Leo smiled, and Rose smiled back.

"I don't like when we fight."

"Me, neither." Leo kissed her again, more deeply. His mouth was warm, soft, and familiar. A best friend, and a best lover.

"I love you."

"I love you, too, which brings up an option I didn't mention. We forget the kids and go upstairs and make love like people who have orange crates for furniture and read the liner notes on CDs."

Rose smiled, then felt it disappear. "Amanda's doing better, but still in a coma. Melly heard about her on TV."

"Oh no." Leo frowned, and Princess Google jumped up on his leg again. He scratched behind the ear, burying his knuckles in her fluffy coat. "You'd better get to the hospital. Unless you want me to."

"Thanks, but I will." Rose stretched, feeling stiff. "The Gigots have a lawyer in the family, and they're suing to stop the school from opening and cleaning up the site. Think they'll sue us, too?"

"Here we go." Leo stood up, then steadied her to her feet, his lips pursed. He looked tired, his tie gone and his shirt unbuttoned, showing the collar of his undershirt. "The state and the school district have deeper pockets than we do, but as I said, I'd name us, too."

"So what can we do? What does it mean, exactly? Can we really lose the house? Do they just take it, and sell it?" Rose couldn't wrap her mind around it. "What about the mortgage? Do we owe the bank then, too?"

"Relax." Leo held up a hand. "I have to look at the insurance policy and see if we're covered. I refuse to worry about it now. It's late, and we're both beat."

"Would you represent us?"

"Not now. Please." Leo held up his hand, his expression tense. "I can't deal. One thing at a time."

"I'm sorry."

"It's okay. I said for better or worse, and I meant it."

"Then I'm a lucky woman." Rose hugged him tight, and Leo held her close for a second.

"Is this sex?" he asked.

Rose laughed.

Leo gave her a final squeeze, with his trademark grunt, like a punctuation mark. "Want some coffee before you go?"

"Good idea."

"I'll get it." Leo made a beeline for the coffeemaker. He was a coffee fetishist, always on a quest for the perfect cup, trying out French Presses, Cuisinart brewers, and now a single-cup Keurig. He slid a mug under the spout and hit the blue button, and Rose leaned against the counter.

"How's trial prep going?"

"Not bad. I have a ton to do, but I'm on it."

"Melly gets discharged at noon. Can you really be there?"

"Yes, I planned on it. I don't want you running that gauntlet of press alone."

"Thanks." Rose knew it wouldn't be easy for him. His office was an hour's drive away. "Also, I know you can't swing it, but the wakes are tomorrow night for Marylou, Serena, and Ellen."

"You're not going, are you?" Leo turned, frowning. Behind him, coffee poured into the mug in a stream, releasing a rich aroma.

"Yes, I have to. I lined up a sitter."

"You shouldn't, babe."

"What will it look like if I don't?" Rose gestured at her computer. "You should see the email I'm getting. They think I'm heartless."

"All the more reason you shouldn't go. If we're getting sued, we have to clam up and lay low."

"But the whole town will be there. Everyone loved the teacher. You heard Mrs. Nuru."

"My point exactly."

"We'll look disrespectful."

"So send flowers, lots of flowers." Leo handed her the coffee mug, and Rose set it down, letting it cool.

"I don't know."

"Well, I do. Don't go. Please. As a favor to me."

"Come on. Don't be that way."

"What way?" A wounded look crossed Leo's tired eyes. "You don't know what can happen, or what they'll do, what you'll do."

"What would I do? I won't do anything wrong."

"You could say the wrong thing." Leo started to take a sip of coffee, then stopped. "Like how guilty you feel, or how sad that you couldn't get them both out of the school. All the things you say to me."

Rose blinked. "I might say that, but only to you or a friend."

"Like who?"

"I don't know. I guess Kristen, maybe. She'll be there."

"The gifted teacher? Who works for the district that's about to be sued, who would testify against you or lose her job?" Leo's eyed flared. "Babe, we don't have any friends. Nobody knows us, and what they know, they don't like."

"We can't just accept that. It could be our chance to show them that we're not what they think."

"No way." Leo's tone flattened. "It ain't gonna happen."

"It *has* to, Leo. You can go to the office every day, but this is my world. I have to make it work, for my sake and for the kids."

"Not now, not tomorrow night. Stay home, will you? Haven't you done enough?"

Ouch. Rose stood, stunned.

"Oh, jeez." Leo rubbed his forehead, irritably. "I didn't mean that. I'm sorry, really."

Rose turned away, hurt, and headed for the living room. "I'm going to the hospital. See you tomorrow."

Chapter Twenty-one

Rose walked down the quiet hall of the hospital, empty at this hour. There had been no press out front, and a janitor in baggy blue scrubs was shining the floor with a large rotating polisher. The nurses' station held only the goateed intern, who was on the computer and barely nodded at Rose when she approached the counter.

"I'm Melly's mother, back to stay the night."

"No problem." The intern glanced up from the computer, and Rose could see tiny playing cards reflected in his glasses.

"I understand there's another child in the room."

"Not anymore. A new bed opened up, and her parents wanted a private."

"Great." Rose looked around. "Is Rosie here, the nurse?"

"Saw her a while ago, but not sure where she is now."

"Okay, thanks. See you." Rose crossed the hall to Melly's room and opened the door. It was still and dark, except for the vital-signs monitor, pulsing red, blue, and green digits.

"Mom?" Melly asked softly, and Rose felt a rush of tenderness, shedding her purse on the chair and coming over to the bed.

"How'd you know it was me?"

"You're my mom."

Rose smiled. "How you doin', night owl?"

"You came back."

"Leo's with John. Why aren't you asleep?"

"I'm not tired."

"Well, I am." Rose lowered the guardrail, kicked her loafers off, and eased onto the bed. "Roll over, Beethoven."

"They said on the TV that cafeteria ladies died in the fire."

I hate TV. "That's true, sweetie, and a teacher died, too. Marylou Battle."

"I don't know her."

"I didn't think so."

"Did they burn up?"

Rose shuddered. Another truth she couldn't tell, another necessary lie. "No, the smoke got them."

"The smoke almost got me, too."

"But it didn't, in the end."

Melly fell silent, her breathing shallow. The oxygen tube was in place under her nose, and she'd been taken off the IV. "Did they go to heaven with Daddy?"

"I'm sure they did, Mel," Rose answered. Bernardo had died when Melly was four, and she brought him up often, though he hadn't bothered to see her much, after the divorce.

"If Amanda dies, will she go to heaven?"

"Yes." Rose swallowed hard, caught unawares. "Absolutely."

"I think so, too," Melly said, after a moment.

Chapter Twenty-two

"You look cute!" Rose was trying to make the best of things. She hadn't gotten a change of clothes for Melly, so she'd had to buy her a pink Hello Kitty sweatsuit and flip-flops in the hospital gift shop.

"Nobody in third grade wears Hello Kitty." Melly sulked at the end of the bed. She'd taken a shower and shampooed her hair, so the smell of smoke was almost completely gone. "It's for babies."

"You can take it off when we get home."

"What if kids from my class see, like Amanda? She's in the same hospital, you said."

"She won't see." Rose hadn't heard anything about Amanda, and she was hoping no news was good news. She hadn't slept well and couldn't wait go home, having signed the hospital's discharge forms and gotten a flurry of papers with instructions for aftercare.

"I wish I had my Harry shirt. The nurse said they had to throw it away, but I wish they didn't."

"We'll see if we can get you a new one."

"They don't make that one anymore, Mom. It was from the first movie."

"We'll look on eBay." Rose wondered if the Harry Potter shirts were such a good idea, anymore. "Now, listen, if there are reporters outside, don't say anything to them. They'll know your name and they'll call it out, but don't answer."

"Okay." Melly looked over as the door opened, and Leo came in, dressed for work and holding John, awake and gurgling, in a blue onesie. "Leo, did you bring my clothes?"

"No." Leo looked from her to Rose. "Was I supposed to?"

"No, hi." Rose was sorry they'd fought, but she still felt distant. John smiled and reached for her with wet, outstretched fingers, and she took him and gave him a kiss without meeting Leo's eye. "How's he doing?"

"All better. No fever. Slept like a baby. Ha!"

"Hugs, Leo!" Melly called out, and Leo scooped her up and gave her a big kiss on the cheek.

"Wow, I like your cat shirt. Very fashionable."

"Yuck." Melly wrinkled her nose. "I wish I had my Harry shirt."

"Aww, this is nice for a change. It's pink, like cotton candy. You know I love cotton candy." Leo buried his face in her neck and blew raspberries, sending Melly into gales of giggles. The sound made John laugh, and he reached for Melly, his chubby hand outstretched and flapping happily.

"Let's go home." Rose picked up her purse and went to the door. "Is there a lot of press outside?"

"Some." Leo carried Melly out of the room and down the hall to the elevator, where he set her down. "Want to press the button, tater? Go for it. When we get inside, hit L."

Melly pressed the DOWN button, then led them into the elevator cab when the doors slid open. They piled inside, and she hit the lobby button. "*Descendo!*"

"You okay, babe?" Leo asked lightly, after the doors closed, but Rose busied herself with John's pacifier.

"Fine. You?"

"Good. By the way, I brought your phone. It was on the counter." Leo slid her BlackBerry from the pocket of his khakis and handed it to her.

"Thanks." Rose accepted it with a pat smile.

"You going out tonight, still?"

"Yes." Rose knew it was code for the wake, but they never fought in front of Melly, who undoubtedly knew whenever they were fighting. The kid wasn't gifted for nothing.

"Too bad," Leo said, pleasantly. "I wish you wouldn't. You might want to rethink it."

"I don't think so."

"I'll walk you to the car." Leo pursed his lips as they reached the ground floor. "Ready, everybody?"

"Ready!" Melly said, and Leo took her hand. When the doors slid open, they filed out into the carpeted lobby, which was quiet except for a few people sitting on the sectional furniture. Outside the glass entrance was a throng of reporters and cameras.

"Melly, just walk and keep going, no matter what." Rose hoisted John higher, and Leo picked up Melly on the fly.

"Let's go. Melly, where's your wand?"

"In the diaper bag."

"Too bad. Can you make those reporters disappear, anyway?"

"Let's put on our invisibility cloak!"

"Now you're talking." Leo smiled.

"It's on! Go, Leo!" Melly looped one hand around his neck and pointed forward with the other, and they moved as a pack out the entrance and into the sunlight. The reporters flocked to them with cameras, microphones, and questions.

"Any comment, Rose?" "How are you feeling, Melly? Are you friends with Amanda?" "Melly, you going to school tomorrow? What was it like when your mom came to save you?" "Melly, were you afraid in the cafeteria?"

Tanya Robertson caught up with Rose, running alongside, bubble microphone outstretched. "Ms. McKenna, please, I've done an interview with Eileen. You'll want to respond to what she's saying. This is your last chance."

"No comment." Rose kept moving, hugging John close.

"Back off!" Leo said, and Melly buried her face in his neck.

Rose hurried ahead, chirped the doors unlocked, and hustled John into his car seat while Leo took Melly to the other side, buckled her in, and closed the door behind her, as the press swarmed the car, firing questions.

"Mr. Ingrassia, what do you have to say about the injunction the Gigots have filed?" "Did you join in the injunction? Will you be suing the district as well?" "Is Melly going back to school tomorrow?"

Rose jumped inside the car and shoved the key in the ignition. Her phone started ringing, but she ignored it. Reporters edged away as she backed up, and she hit the gas and drove toward the exit, leaving them behind, relieved. She stopped at the first traffic light, slid the phone from her purse, and checked the display. The call was from her best friend, Annie Assarian, so she pressed REDIAL. "Hey!"

"Girl, I've been calling you and leaving messages. What's going on? There's all kinds of nastiness on your Facebook wall. Is Melly okay?"

"Fine." Rose kept her tone light because Melly was listening. "Can I call you back? I'm driving."

"I'm in Philly this week and next on a movie shoot, and we just finished for the day. You wanna have drinks?"

"I can't go out."

"How about I come over? I have my car."

"I'd love that, if it's not too much trouble."

"I'll be there as soon as I can."

"Great." Rose brightened. "See you then." She hung up and set the phone in the cupholder as the traffic light changed to green. "Guess what?"

"Aunt Nemo's coming? Yay!"

Rose smiled. "How did you know? Did you hear?"

"You always smile when you talk to her."

"I bet I do." Rose felt better. She didn't get to see Annie that much anymore, and she fed the car some gas, wondering if there was any food in the fridge.

"Mom, think I'll ever get a friend like Aunt Nemo?"

"I know you will, honey," Rose answered, though her throat caught.

Chapter Twenty-three

Rose made pizza bagels for the kids, then put John down for a nap and installed Melly in the family room with Princess Google and a Harry Potter DVD. Sunshine poured through the lavender in the bay window, and while the two women cleaned up the kitchen, Rose told Annie the whole story.

"You didn't do anything wrong, Ro." Annie shook her head, a stiff cap of onyx curls. Her eyes were large and a rich brown, with a faint almond shape that hinted at her biracial parentage. Her warm skin tone freed her from makeup, though she was one of the most-sought-after makeup artists in New York.

"Still, I feel terrible." Rose rinsed a dish and loaded it into the open dishwasher. "I wish I had gotten them both out."

"You did, essentially. Amanda ran back in, and you couldn't have known that."

"I should have."

"You're not superhuman. You're just a model."

Rose smiled. She had stopped thinking of herself as a model, ages ago.

"I'd have done the exact same thing, if it were Joey or Armen." Annie had two boys with her husband Simon, a sculptor and art history professor at NYU.

"You would?"

"Totally." Annie twisted the plastic bag of bagels closed and put it back in the freezer. "Meanwhile, these were good, for frozen."

"I know, they're fine, right?"

"Totally." Annie yanked up the skinny strap of her purple boho sundress, which showed off tattooed arms encircled with fire-breathing red dragons, Chinese symbols, and an orange koi that had reminded a younger Melly of the cartoon Nemo, so a nickname was born for her godmother.

"Remember when we had to have Murray's? They were the cool bagels." Rose rinsed tomato sauce from a tablespoon. "We'd stand in line every Sunday morning with all the investment bankers?"

"I still do that." Annie smiled.

"Well, I still do this." Rose dropped the spoon into the silverware holder in the dishwasher, keeping it with the other spoons.

"Oh no!" Annie burst into laughter. "Set that spoon free. Let it hang with the knives and forks."

"I'm telling you, sort the silverware before you wash it, then it saves time when you put it away."

"It saves *no* time," Annie shot back. It was an historic disagreement, from their years sharing a one-bedroom in the East Village, which was so small that they stored their boots in the oven.

"Melly agrees with me. She thinks Aunt Nemo's crazy."

"Aunt Nemo *is* crazy, but that's not why."

"But for real, tell me the truth. You would have done the same thing?"

"Yes."

"You don't think I'm a horrible person?"

"I *know* you're not. You're the sweetest person I know."

Rose smiled. "Should I keep fishing for compliments?"

"Go right ahead. I love you, and you know it." Annie's smile vanished. "And I *hate* how Melly gets bullied. If Amanda hadn't been teasing her, they both would have been outside on the playground when the fire started. Ever think of that?"

"I did, but Leo would say that's only a *but for* cause."

"Whatever. All I know is that Melly could have died of smoke inhalation because of that brat."

Rose winced. "Don't say that."

"I know it seems mean, but what about you guys? You moved once already because of the bullying. You can't move again. You're running out of planet." Annie picked up the sponge and wiped the kitchen table. "When I read what they were saying about you on Facebook, it made me nuts."

"Was it bad? I'm afraid to look."

"You should remove all those posts. Those people are insane."

"They're just upset about Amanda."

"Please. Did you read them? Those women are jealous of you, just because of the way you look." Annie finished wiping the table and rinsed out the sponge. "You're going through hell, but nobody ever feels sorry for the pretty one."

"That's not what's going on, and I'm only 'catalog material,' remember?" Rose was quoting her old modeling agent.

"What an idiot he was! You were better than the other girls. Not only were you gorgeous, you were the only one who was nice to everybody, even the makeup gypsies."

Rose didn't reply. She liked the past to stay past. She needed it to.

"You know, if Melly hadn't come along, you'd be making a fortune. Even Bernardo said so. It was the only thing he was right about."

"Nah, they all use actresses now. I got out just in time, and luckily, Melly did come along. Anyway, let's talk about here and now. What if we get sued? We could lose the house. Now that scares me."

"Oh, man. That would scare me, too." Annie frowned under her dark curls. "You can't get sued for saving your own kid, can you?"

"Leo seems to think you can, but it's not his field." Rose screwed the cap on the jar of tomato sauce and returned it to the fridge. "He doesn't want me to go to the wakes, but I really feel like I should pay my respects, and it's tonight. It's too bad that the one night you're in town, I ditch you. Sorry."

"Oh, you're not ditching me. I haven't seen you in, like, six months. I'm going with you."

Rose felt touched. "You are?"

"Sure. You shouldn't go alone, and I have nothing else to do."

"But you don't even know these people."

"Neither do you." Annie smiled, crookedly. "Besides, I go to lots of parties where I don't know anybody."

"It's a wake, not a party, and don't you have to get back to Philly?"

"I'll follow you there in my car, then leave. Lend me a sweater, to cover my tats."

Rose smiled. "Now, *that's* a best friend."

Chapter Twenty-four

Rose braked in the traffic for the funeral home, which anchored Old Town, the historic district of Reesburgh, bisected by Allen Road. The late-day sun tarnished the quaint brick homes, with their Victorian porches, and next to them was a stop-time corner grocery, a mom-and-pop drugstore, and a funky independent bookstore called READsburgh.

Rose circled the block looking for a parking space, with Annie following in her car, and they ended up finding them about ten blocks away from Fiore's. She parked and slipped on sunglasses, having worn her hair tucked under a raffia hat. "Quite a crowd, huh?" she said, getting out of the car.

"Yes." Annie sniffed the air. "Hey, do you smell that? Is that French fries?"

"It's potato chips from the Homestead factory. You smell it stronger here in Old Town, because it's closer to the plant, downwind."

"How many carbs in one breath?"

"Don't ask." Rose fell into step with her on the sidewalk. The humidity was still high, making her black linen dress uncomfortable. They passed a series of graceful brick homes with restored façades and generous wrap-around porches, surrounded by tall, ancient trees in resplendent autumn leaf.

"Where are we?" Annie's neat head swiveled left and right. "Mayberry?"

Rose smiled. "This is called Bosses Row, where the Allen brothers lived when they started Homestead. The company used to be family-owned, but it's not anymore."

"No surprise. Families aren't even family-owned anymore. Look at these houses. They're beautiful."

"They're over a hundred and fifty years old."

"Yes, massa. Remind me to take potato chips back to the boys. I'll say they're from Tara."

"You have this place all wrong." Rose shook her head, walking along, her black flats slapping against the pavement. "It's not homogeneous at all. It's a company town. Most people who live here work at the Homestead plant, and there's plenty of professionals, too. That's what I like, it's a cross-section of people. Normal people."

"Snore."

Rose laughed. "You're a snob."

"I'm a New Yorker." Annie tugged at her black cardigan. "And I'm so hating on this sweater. You wear this?"

"Sure. It's useful."

"It's so boxy, it makes me feel like a nun. Are you dead below the waist, too?"

"Uh-oh." Rose spotted a group of reporters on the pavement ahead of them, with cameras and klieglights. "On the left, ahead, is the press. When we get in the line, stay to the right."

"Gotcha." They reached the end of the receiving line, which flowed down Fiore's flagstone walkway and onto the sidewalk. There had to be a few hundred people here, somber and teary-eyed. Rose hadn't realized how many people these deaths had affected, but she should have. A single life, and death, could touch so many people, and a teacher was forever.

"Sorry, it could take an hour to get inside."

"I don't mind. I'm used to waiting on line." Annie shrugged. "The air is adding years to my life."

Rose felt a wave of sadness for Marylou, Serena, and Ellen. She flashed on the billowing smoke, the raging fire, and Amanda.

Mommy!

"Are you okay?" Annie pulled her closer, by the elbow. "You look so sad. You didn't know any of them, did you?"

"No." Rose understood what she was feeling, but there was too much to say, and she'd never said any of it to anybody, not even Annie. "I keep thinking of Amanda."

"I understand."

Rose noticed a few of the teachers leaving the funeral home, making their way down the driveway to the sidewalk, a downhearted group that included Mrs. Nuru, dabbing her eyes with a Kleenex. "That's Melly's teacher," Rose said, leaning over to Annie. "I should go say hi."

"Go. I'll hold our place."

"Thanks. Be right back." Rose crossed to Mrs. Nuru, who stopped and smiled stiffly at Rose, her hooded eyes glistening.

"Hello, Rose. How's Melly?"

"Home, thanks. I'm so sorry, and Leo sends his condolences, too."

"Thank you."

"Is Kristen here?"

"She came and left. The school staff all came early, at the invitation of the families." Mrs. Nuru pursed her lips. "I heard from Mr. Rodriguez that she told you what I said about the faulty wiring. That was imprudent of me, and of her. I trust you'll keep it confidential."

"Of course."

"Kristen is young, and she has lots of growing up to do. She needs to learn judgment."

"Do you really think so?" Rose asked, defensively. "I think she's such a great teacher."

"Experience tells, in my opinion." Mrs. Nuru sniffed, glancing at the other teachers. "I should go, they're waiting. Will Melly be in school tomorrow?"

"I'm not sure I'll send her." Rose remembered that Mrs. Nuru thought Melly was too sensitive, so she didn't elaborate. "I haven't decided yet."

"If she's well enough, I'd send her. If you decide not to, give her my best."

"Will do, thanks. Bye now." Rose turned and went back to the line, trying not to notice that people started whispering among themselves when they spotted her.

"Everything okay?" Annie asked, when Rose got back to the line.

"I guess. She's upset. They all are." Rose was troubled by what Mrs. Nuru had said about Kristen, and now heads were turning and people were talking about them. "Um, look around."

"I know, I noticed before you did. And here comes the press."

Rose turned to see Tanya Robertson approaching from the left. Her crew followed, switching on klieglights, and the cameraman started filming, his camera perched on his shoulder.

"Ms. McKenna, please." Tanya thrust her microphone forward. "Can't we chat for a moment?"

"No comment." Rose put up a hand, though she knew it would make her look bad on TV. "Please, show some respect."

"We're on public property, and if we could speak one-on-one, as I did with Eileen, this would go much easier. Did you see my interview with her? Do you have a response to her allegations about you?"

"I said, no comment." Rose didn't look over. She didn't know Eileen had made allegations against her. The women in front of her edged away, and other people in the line kept turning around, whispering, and staring at them.

Tanya held her microphone out. "Eileen alleges that you intentionally left Amanda because you think she teases your child, and you've even called her about that. Do you have animosity for Amanda?"

"Stop it!" Annie interrupted, stepping over. "Are you *insane*? If you knew this woman, you'd never say anything like that!"

"Annie, no, it's okay." Rose put a hand on her arm, but Annie wasn't listening.

"This is harassment. I'm calling the cops. Where are the cops?" Annie looked around, then tried to flag down a funeral home employee in a gray suit, who was directing traffic. "Sir? Sir!"

"Annie, that's okay, no." Rose wanted to defuse the situation. Everyone was watching, and a short woman in a black pantsuit got out of line and stalked toward them, her forehead creased with anger.

"How can you show your face here?" the woman shouted, and people reacted with shock, chatter, and nervous laughter.

Rose edged away from the woman. The situation was getting out of hand, and she hadn't counted on the press being there. "Annie, we should get—"

"Aren't you ashamed?" The woman kept charging toward her, then pointed down the street. "Get out of here. You don't belong here."

"What?" Annie shouted at the woman, in disbelief. "What's the matter with you? She didn't do anything wrong, and she has every right to be here. What is this, Salem?"

Tanya held the microphone out, recording audio. The cameraman zoomed in, the large black lens telescoping forward and back.

The woman was yelling, "She abandoned a *child* in the fire, to burn alive!"

"You're wrong!" Annie yelled back. "She tried to get the girl out, but she must have run back in!"

"How dare you blame that child? She's a child! A little girl!"

"Ladies, please!" The funeral home employee came over, waving his hands. He was bald and on the slight side. "This is inappropriate at such a time. Please."

"Sorry, we're leaving." Rose took Annie's arm, but she pulled it away and pointed at the woman.

"This woman is insane!" Then Annie pointed at Tanya. "And *this* woman is harassing us to sell commercial time on TV, so a grateful nation can have enough toothpaste, beer, and deodorant!"

"Let's go." Rose hustled Annie away, but Tanya and her crew followed on their heels.

"Ms. McKenna, what do you say to the court's denial of the emergency injunction? Do you think the school is reopening prematurely? Do you expect to be sued by the Gigots? Are you suing the school? Will you attend the candlelight vigil Monday night?"

Rose and Annie broke into a jog toward their cars.

Chapter Twenty-five

Rose parked in Allen's Dam, the public park outside of Old Town, its tall trees ablaze in rich reds, oranges, and golds, a conflagration of hues that only reminded her of the fire that had brought so much destruction and death.

Annie climbed into the car and sat in the passenger seat, having followed her in her car. "What a disaster!"

"I feel like such a screw-up." Rose took off her sunglasses and tossed them onto the console. "I shouldn't have gone."

"Of course you should have. You're a member of the community. The problem was, where were the cops? In the city, we would've had a swarm."

"There are no cops. Only state police."

"What?" Annie looked over, incredulous. "Of course there are cops."

"No." Rose shook her head. "Not every town in America has its own police force. I didn't know that either, but it's true. Most of the rural townships don't have a police force, or they share. The area's too sparsely populated, and when the economy tanked, they cut the funds for it."

"For police?"

"Yes."

"How about fire?"

"We have a fire department, and if there's a crime, we're supposed to call the state police. The realtor said they'd come, but it could take a while. She didn't even know anybody who'd called them, except for hunting out of season."

Annie shook her neat head. "I wouldn't feel safe without cops."

"I do, now. There's no crime here. Most people don't even lock their front doors. It's paradise. At least it was, until recently."

"Whatever, I'm sorry I lost it at that woman." Annie frowned, and the corners of her mouth tugged downward, as if by strings. "I hope I didn't make it worse for you. It'll pass, it has to."

"It's okay." Rose rubbed her forehead, thinking. Leo had a small cabin near Lake Harmony, which Melly loved, and their neighbors at the lake, Mo and Gabriella Vaughn, were like her honorary grandparents. "Maybe we should take a break, up to the cabin. Leo's busy anyway, and we could all use a little R&R while it's still hot, and Melly loves the Vaughns. What do you think?"

"No."

"Why not?"

"I know you love the Vaughns, but it'll all be here when you get back. You can't run from this, Ro."

"I'm not running," Rose said, stung.

"I think you are."

"What am I supposed to do? How can I send her to school on Monday? They'll take it out on her."

"I think you should send her. Tell you why." Annie cocked her head, her expression thoughtful. "This whole thing, with the fire, the deaths, and Melly and Amanda, it's all of a piece. Getting through it is going to be a recovery process. All grief is, and all trauma. That recovery process is starting at school tomorrow, with the memorial service."

Rose set her ego aside, listening. Annie was honest, if blunt.

"If Melly's not a part of that, she's more on the outs than ever. She'll be a step behind everybody else, and that sucks. Like when you start the day late, you know that feeling? You never quite catch up. You spend the day unsettled, off-balance, left behind. True?"

"Yes."

"You say she has a relationship with this Kristen. She'll look out for her."

Rose mulled it over. "Mrs. Nuru thinks I should send her, but she's mad at Kristen and thinks she favors Melly. It's gotten political, all of a sudden."

"Great." Annie curled her upper lip. "I like the one who likes Melly. I'm Team Kristen."

"Me, too." Rose smiled. "I wish I could ask her about all of this. She said she'd look out for Melly, but that was before they came down on her. I'm not sending Melly, unless Kristen keeps an eye out for her."

"So call and ask her."

"I have her number somewhere at home." Then Rose realized something. "You know what? Kristen's apartment is two blocks from here. I dropped cupcakes off there once."

"So why don't you just go over? If she likes Melly that much, she won't mind. You have the sitter until nine, you might as well use her." Annie checked her watch. "I should go, too. Forget the chips for the boys. Mom's tired."

"Okay, it's a plan." Rose leaned over and gave her a hug. "You're the best. Thanks so much for coming."

"I'll be in Philly all week. Call me if you need me. Give everybody kisses for me, would you?"

"Yes. Same to Simon and the boys. Love you."

"You, too." Annie opened the door and climbed out of the car, her eyes glittering with mischief. "By the way, I'm keeping this sweater. I'll give it to the homeless lady on my corner."

"No!" Rose smiled. "Gimme back my sweater."

Annie laughed. "Why, you going to a funeral?"

Rose blinked, caught up short, thinking instantly of Amanda.

Annie's smile faded. "Oops, sorry. I just stuck my foot in my mouth, didn't I?"

"Nah, and keep the sweater." Rose tried to rally. "Then maybe I won't need it, right?"

"Right!" Annie said, closing the door.

Chapter Twenty-six

Rose walked up the brick walkway to Kristen's house, a boxy duplex on a street of older rowhouses. A man in a white undershirt and jeans was washing a red Ford pickup in the driveway, and he shut off the hose when he saw Rose.

"Whoops, didn't mean to spray you," he said with a grin. "Hi."

"Hello, I'm here to see Kristen. I'm a parent of one of the kids in her class."

"Jacob Horton. I live on the first floor. Just a heads-up, Kristen came home, upset. She was over at Fiore's."

"Thanks, bye." Rose went to the set of exterior steps, climbed to the second floor, reached the wooden landing, and knocked on the screen door. "Kristen!" She waited but there was no answer, so she knocked again. "Kristen?"

The door opened, and Kristen stood in the doorway, dressed in a black cotton dress, wiping tears from her eyes. "Rose?"

"Can I come in, for a minute?"

"Okay." Kristen sniffled and stepped aside, and Rose entered and gave her a big hug.

"I know it's a hard time for you and the other teachers."

"It's so awful, everything's so awful." Kristen hugged her back, then released her, wiping her eyes. "The wakes were so sad, and Mrs.

Nuru and Mr. Rodriguez are so angry, and there were even reporters there, asking me a zillion questions, like how Melly and Amanda got along."

"I know. I was there." Rose looked around, her eyes adjusting to the light in the small living room. A black suitcase rested on a red-checked couch, and T-shirts and shorts sat stacked in a pile on top of a painted bookshelf, ready to be packed. "Are you going somewhere?"

"I'm sorry, I'm leaving. I can't take it anymore. I quit."

"*What?*" Rose asked, aghast. "When? *Why?*"

"It's all too much. I messed up here, I talk too much, and I can't work here, watching everything I say, walking on eggshells." Kristen's eyes welled up again, her freckled skin mottled with emotion. "Mr. Rodriguez said I have bad judgment and loose lips sink ships. I give up. I'm not cut out to be a teacher, at least not here, not anymore. I'm going."

"Wait, slow down." Rose thought of Melly. "I was just saying this will pass, it has to."

"No, it won't, and it doesn't have to."

"Yes, it will, Kristen. You're young and you don't realize. Time changes things. Things you don't think you'll survive, you do. I know, I've lived it."

"Sorry, I've made my decision. I'm leaving. I'm sorry." Kristen turned on her heel, picked up two T-shirts, and tossed them into the suitcase, startling a white cat that bounded out of the room, his tail high.

"But what about Melly? And what about the other kids in the program? They just went through a trauma, and Amanda's still in the hospital. They need you, now more than ever. Melly needs you."

"I'm just the gifted teacher, and not that experienced, as Mrs. Nuru keeps reminding me."

"But the kids love you. Melly loves you."

"I have your number, I'll call her." Kristen placed a quilted toiletries case into the suitcase. "I'll stay in touch with her."

"It's not the same."

"Don't you think I know that? Don't you think I feel guilty enough?" Kristen picked up some socks and wedged them into the case. "I have to live my own life."

"Kristen, please stay. *Please.*"

"Don't you see, if I stay, I make it worse for her?" Kristen turned, stricken. "They think I favor her, and now they'll be looking for it in everything I do. It's best for her if I go."

"That's *not* what's best for her. I know what's best for her."

"Look, I'm sorry, I really am, but this is messing up my life, too."

"Then why don't you slow down, see how you feel in two weeks?"

"No. I emailed Mr. Rodriguez my resignation. I said to tell people I had a family emergency. It's a done deal."

"You're really leaving *now*?" Rose asked, incredulous.

"Yes. I'm going to my parents', and I'd appreciate it if you'd keep it confidential. I don't want any of these crazy parents emailing me or posting any more crap on my Facebook wall. No more reporters, either." Kristen's pretty features softened, and she became her old sweet self. "I really am sorry, so sorry, for everything, but I have to go now. Please, go. I'll call Melly in a day or two."

"Do you swear? You'll break her heart if you don't. You owe her that much. She's a person, with feelings."

"I said I will, and I will." Kristen crossed to the door, and opened it wide, and Rose went to the threshold, bewildered.

"You're not who I thought you were."

"None of us is," Kristen said, unsmiling.

Chapter Twenty-seven

Rose steered down Allen Road, the window open, her elbow resting on the door, and a breeze blowing through her hair. She'd called Leo to tell him about Kristen, but he hadn't answered, and she'd left a message. Kristen was leaving Melly without her only ally, and Rose wasn't sure what to do. She didn't know whether to send Melly to school or how to tell Melly that Kristen was leaving, and in the end, either way, it would be a terrible blow.

Rose stopped at a red light, and the traffic had lessened, once she was on the outskirts of town. The sky was darkening, and she scanned the neat houses with their glowing lights, a typical Sunday night in the suburbs. Parents and kids would be hunkering down around kitchen tables, doing math and French homework, or building volcanoes with baking-soda lava or teepees ribbed with Popsicle sticks. Not all the Sunday night scenes would be so idyllic, and Rose knew that, too. That, she had lived, too.

She hit the gas, and the homes disappeared among the commercial outskirts and the chain stores like the CVS, Giant, Costco, Walmart, and Target. Beyond them, she could see the distant outline of the school, with its long, low roofline and large wings on either side. The wings held the classrooms, and the entrance and administrative offices were nearer the left wing, on the north side. The cafeteria was also near the left, but it was built on the front of the school like an addition, with no second floor because of the skylights. Rose stopped at a traffic light, and from this distance, she could pretend that nothing had ever happened. No fire, no women in coffins, no daughters in hospitals, no angry parents, and no young teacher quitting a promising career, leaving Melly on her own.

Rose fed the car gas when the light changed, braking as she approached the school. As she got closer, she could see that the street in front was marked off by orange cones and sawhorses. Pickups and construction vehicles sat parked along the curb, ending in a rusty dumpster. The few cars around her slowed down, rubbernecking, and she found herself pulling over in front of the school, parking behind a dusty pickup with a bumper sticker, UNION CARPENTERS HAVE BETTER WOOD. She cut the ignition, and the breeze through the window smelled like burned things.

She scanned the school and understood what Mr. Rodriguez had meant. Most of the building looked the same, its brand-new brick façade and classroom wings perfect, and only the cafeteria had been damaged, like a black eye on a pageant queen. The cafeteria windows were empty holes, dark smudges marred the windowsills and brick, and a blue plastic tarp covered the roof.

Rose thought of the people who had died inside, and the long lines at Fiore's, and to her mind, public property had become hallowed ground. It seemed impossible that there would be recess tomorrow, with kids throwing basketballs, jumping rope, and playing kickball. She could almost feel the flames licking at her ankles, all over again. She flashed on Melly, slumped in the bathroom. Emily, crying, and Danielle, running terrified. Her thoughts ended where they always did, with Amanda.

Mommy!

She got out of the car, closed the door behind her, and walked through the playground toward the cafeteria, which had been cordoned off in different sections with yellow caution tape, sawhorses, and a temporary fence of orange netting. She stood behind the sawhorse, eyeing the scene.

Klieglights lit up the façade of the cafeteria, making supersized shadows of the workmen as they went back and forth from the cafeteria to the dumpster with wheelbarrows, tarps, and trash bags of charred debris. Some of the workmen were building a plywood wall, probably the one that Mr. Rodriguez had mentioned, and a workman in a T-shirt and Carhartt overalls smiled as he walked to the pickup in front of her car. He was carrying a heavy-duty laptop, and he stowed it inside, slammed the door, and came over to her, with a confident stride.

"Can I help you?" he asked, in a friendly way. In the reflected light, Rose could see that he had an easy grin, a longish nose, and dark eyes under a white plastic hardhat with a Phillies sticker. "Name's Kurt Rehgard." He stuck out a large hand, and Rose shook it, feeling her fingers crunch.

"Rose. I'm just looking around."

"Been a lot of that today."

"I bet." Rose eyed the bustling scene. "You guys are working late."

"All night. The bigwigs want this school up and running, time is of the essence, and we don't mind, I'll tell you that. We're all loving the OT, especially in this economy." Kurt gestured to the work crews behind him. "My crew is all from Phoenixville, the electrical contractor's from Pottstown, and the GC's from Norristown. The district wanted all new on site, on account of the lawsuits they expect."

"There's more than one lawsuit?" Rose felt her chest tighten.

"Hell, yeah. Everybody's pointing fingers and who's responsible for what, who caused this, who did that."

"I heard it was a gas leak and faulty wiring."

"I'm not supposed to say, on pain of death." The carpenter drew a dirty finger across his throat. "You a reporter?"

"No way." Rose smiled. "Just a mother. You were saying, about the lawsuits?"

"Startin' in already. The first electrical contractor says it was the GC's fault, and the first GC says it was the gas company's fault, and the HVAC guys are in trouble because the ductwork was too close for code, and somebody said the fire used it to spread so fast." Kurt shook his head. "All the fire marshals, building inspectors came around, even the FBI, because of the fatalities. Then the lawyers and the so-called experts they hired, all taking pictures. It's a damn circus."

Rose's head was spinning. It sounded like the lawsuits that Leo talked about at dinner, and she hoped they wouldn't be caught in the middle, becoming the lawsuit that people talked about at dinner.

"You say your child goes here?"

"Yes. My daughter's in third grade, and school's open tomorrow, which seems kind of strange to me."

"Not at all. It's not unsafe or anything. The kids can't go in the cafeteria, and there'll be fire and water damage crews in the hallways, but your kid will be safe in the rest of the building. Don't worry." Kurt cocked his head. "I thought you were a lawyer, that's why I came over. That, and to see if you were married."

"Thanks, but I am married. To a lawyer."

"No!" Kurt pretended he'd been shot, staggering backwards comically. "Dump his lame ass!"

Rose laughed.

"Hey, if you like, I'll show you inside. You'll see, it's safe. You want a quick tour?"

"I'd love to," Rose answered, intrigued. "Is that kosher?"

"The bigwigs are gone, and my guys don't care. Act like a lawyer."

"I can do that." Rose ducked under the tape.

Chapter Twenty-eight

Rose followed Kurt beyond the cordon, past a paint-spattered boom-box blasting vintage Aerosmith. Heads turned as they stepped into the klieglights and tramped across the playground, churned to muddy spots by the wheelbarrows and foot traffic. She smiled in a professional way, though she knew they weren't fooling anybody. Workmen looked up and nodded hello before they returned to their tasks. Their faces were streaked with sweat, and they seemed not to recognize her, either because they weren't local or they'd been working nonstop, with no time for TV news.

Rose asked, "I guess you rebuild the cafeteria after you throw all this stuff out, huh?"

"Basically, yes. I'm with Bethany Run Construction, and we'll do the demo, then the framing and construction. Here, follow me." Kurt led her to the threshold of the playground exit, where the blackened double doors had been propped open with cinderblocks. Calcium-white light flooded the area, illuminating the hallway. Soot blanketed the walls, and the glass ceiling fixtures had been shattered.

"My God," Rose said half to herself.

"The hall is messy, but structurally sound. There's nothing unsafe about it, see? Got certified right off. It'll be good to go as soon as we clean up the water." Kurt walked ahead, gesturing at a series of noisy black machines. Hoses sprouted from each one, affixed to corrugated black mats that were duct-taped to the grimy floor. "Bet you're wondering what these puppies are."

Rose was drawn to the cafeteria, which was a hellish sight. The tables, chairs, and decorated bulletin boards had been removed, leaving a black shell of a room. Smoke had blackened the walls, obscuring the cheery blue-and-white tiles, and the ceiling was gone, exposing steel joists, aluminum ductwork, and electrical wiring.

"I'll explain, hold on. It's so damn noisy, I can't stand it." Kurt stepped to the first machine and pressed a red POWER button. The machine shuddered into silence, though the others thrummed loudly. "See, these are Injectidry machines. They're on day and night. The water sprinklers went off here, and the machines suck the moisture out of the subfloor, so it doesn't warp."

"Got it," Rose said, but she couldn't tear her eyes from the cafeteria. The floor tiles were cracked, and charred rubble lay in piles where it had been swept; broken ceiling tiles, split wooden beams, and filthy debris. The skylights were gone, and the blue tarp covering square holes they left behind made an azure glow, like a tropical sky.

"Those machines over there, they're different." Kurt pointed down the hall to a series of tall gray machines, also boxlike and attached to a generator. "They're dehumidifiers on steroids. Not the kind you have in your basement when the sump pump goes out, if you get me. They make sure no toxic mold gets a chance to form, in case you were worried about that for your kid. Did you say you have a boy or a girl?"

"A girl." Rose took a step toward the cafeteria, where the front wall of the kitchen had been demolished. She could see through to the industrial ovens and stainless steel shelving in the kitchen, which lay twisted and in pieces, like the residuum of a twenty-car collision. She could imagine how the blast had killed poor Serena and Ellen.

"I have a niece that I've taken to Disney World, my sister's kid. Her dad's in Iraq, so I'm spending a lot of time with her. I taught her to throw, and she goes to the Phils games with me, too." Kurt gestured at the hallway. "See, it's all sound. I'd send my own niece here. You got nothing to worry about."

"Great." Rose took another step down the hall, and from the new perspective could see that the explosion had blown away the wall between the kitchen and the teachers' lounge, which was only partially blackened, but full of broken cabinetry and a yellow Formica counter that had been cracked into pieces, like a nightmare puzzle.

"We'll have this fixed up good as new. Better." Kurt leaned over, lowering his voice. "You ask me, they opened too soon. You can't rush a job, especially the electrical. It always bites you in the ass."

"I bet." Rose came out of her reverie. "It's sad to see where somebody died."

"Nobody suffered, if that helps you. The explosion was in the gas line in the back wall of the kitchen, a three-quarter inch pipe that feeds the oven in the kitchen and the teachers' lounge. It took out everything instantly."

"How terrible," Rose said, heavily. "A gas leak? Why didn't they smell it?"

"It was in the wall, and maybe they did, for all we know. Tell you something about the smell of gas, you get desensitized. You smell it in the beginning, then you stop noticing it." Kurt seemed to catch himself. "That's not the official cause, they didn't say that yet, and you didn't hear it from me."

"Hear what?"

Kurt laughed. "Let's go." He motioned, leading Rose back down the hall, out the exit door, and into the blinding klieglights. She put up her hands, shielding her eyes, and he held her elbow. "Watch out for that pile of junk."

"Oops!" Rose looked down at a heap of blackened debris on a tarp, a heartbreaking sight. Twisted pieces of rebar and busted dry wall mixed with a *Toy Story* lunchbox, a crushed juicebox, and a broken Sony PS2. She flashed on Amanda, showing her new iPod to the girls at the table. Suddenly, it struck her why Amanda had run back into the school. The blond teacher could have missed her running back in, like Leo had said, because she'd been on the other side of the students being evacuated to the playground.

"An iPod," Rose blurted out, and Kurt looked over.

"Excuse me?"

"Nothing," Rose answered, saddened. Amanda lay in a coma tonight, because of a shiny new toy. And because of her.

"Here, take my card." Kurt dug in his pocket, extracted a wrinkled business card, and handed it to her. "Call me if you need a deck, or if you dump that husband of yours."

"Thanks." Rose smiled.

"Feel better, now that you've seen the school?"

"Yes," Rose lied, and when she turned away, she dropped the smile.

Chapter Twenty-nine

"Hi, sweetie." Rose entered Melly's bedroom, where she was reading in bed, with Princess Google. The butterfly lamp on the night table cast a warm glow over her yellow comforter, whitewashed bureau, and matching desk, but the rest of the room was a Harry Potter shrine. A black Hogwarts banner hung above the headboard, and the bookshelf contained the thick books, figurines, a Sorting Hat, and new Hermione wand. The lower shelves held B-list books, which was everything not Harry.

"Hi, Mom." Melly peered over the top of *Beedle the Bard*. Her hair had been brushed out and lay wavy on the pillow.

"How was your night?" Rose sat down on the edge of her bed and gave her a kiss. "What did you and Julie do?"

"We watched *Up*."

"Sounds good." Rose had told the babysitter, DVDs only. "Did you like it?"

"Yes." Melly placed her laminated bookmark carefully in the page, making sure the blue tassel showed, and closed the book.

"Good. Hi, Googs." Rose scratched Princess Google, and the spaniel raised her small, flat head and tucked into a ball of red-and-white patches.

"Googie's so cute."

"She is. Did she eat any underwear?"

Melly smiled. "No, she was good, Mom. I let her out in the back-yard. Two times."

"How was John?"

"He pooped, and his face got all red."

"Great. Just so he didn't eat any underwear."

Melly giggled. "You're silly."

"Thanks."

"Was the funeral sad?"

"Yes. It's hard when people pass."

"Like Daddy." Melly frowned, showing a tiny buckle in her smooth forehead.

"Right." Rose felt a surge of love and worry, eyeing Melly, who looked so happy and comfy in Leo's Phillies T-shirt. "We have to make a decision about whether you should go to school tomorrow."

"Is it open?"

"Yes. The cafeteria isn't open, but the classrooms are. I was just there to see it."

"I know, I can smell." Melly scrunched up her nose. "You smell like fire."

"Gross." Rose hadn't realized. "Anyway, it's a half-day tomorrow. They're going to have an assembly in the morning, about the people who died, then go back to class, then you'll come home."

"Okay, I can go."

"Do you feel well enough?"

"Yes." Melly shrugged. "I'm not sick. The doctor said."

"I know, but if you feel tired or you just want to rest another day, you can stay home." Rose was stacking the deck, but she couldn't help herself. She was worried about the reception that Melly would get tomorrow. "How's your throat?"

"Okay. I can go. I'll go."

"Well, then let me say this. You know that Amanda was caught in the fire, and you should know that there are some people who blame me about that."

"Why?"

Rose kept it simple. "They say I saved you instead of her."

"I'm your kid."

Rose smiled. "I know, but really, I got Amanda to the door of the cafeteria, and when I went to get you, she ran back into the cafeteria. I think, after her iPod."

Melly blinked, and it seemed not to register that she'd been left for second. "I heard her talking about that iPod. It was her big brother's. He got it for his birthday."

"Anyway, the other kids might say things to you, about that. Try to ignore them, and don't answer, okay? Like the reporters, in a way."

"I'll tell Ms. Canton. She'll tell them not to."

Rose felt her heart sink. "Mel, listen, I have some news for you about Ms. Canton. She had an emergency with her family, and she had to leave school and go home."

"When is she coming back?"

"She's not. She had to move home, to be with her family."

"Why?" Melly frowned, confused.

"I don't know more than I told you. Somebody in her family is sick, and she has to take care of them. She went home for good."

"Forever?" Melly's eyebrows flew upward, and Rose nodded, not hiding her disappointment.

"Yes. I know you like her, and you know she likes you, so much. But she can't help it, she has—"

"She *has* to come back." Melly raised her voice, anxious. "She's the best teacher I ever had."

"She won't be able to come back, but I hope she can call us, to talk and say hi to you, if she's not too busy."

"But I like her. I *want* her to be my teacher." Melly's lower lip buckled, and Rose gave her a big hug.

"I know, sweetie. I'm hoping they'll get a new teacher you'll like as much as her. You know, you don't have to go tomorrow if you don't want to."

"I want to, I just want her to be there." Melly's blue eyes glistened the way only a child's can, showing all the hurt, unguarded and guileless. "Why didn't they tell us this before?"

"Nobody knew. Things like this happen, in life. Unexpected things, and people have to take care of their families." Rose shifted on the bed, waking Princess Google, who moved her head to Melly's leg and gazed up at her with round, melty brown eyes. "Look. Googie knows you're upset."

"I know. It's okay, Googs." Melly stroked the dog's head, her fingernails bright with pink polish, probably from the babysitter. "Don't be sad, Googie Girl. Everything will be okay. Everything will turn out okay."

Rose fell silent, listening and watching, and it struck her that Melly was comforting herself.

"Don't worry, Googie. Don't worry." Melly kept petting the dog, who closed her eyes.

"I think you're making her feel better."

"I tell her all the time, don't worry. But she still does."

"It's hard not to, sometimes."

"She knows that." Melly ran her hand down the spaniel's coat to her feathery tail. "See, Mom, how this part is all white? Like a wiggly line down her back? That's like a river, all along on her back, and the red parts are down the side."

"I see." Rose smiled, and Melly walked her fingers up to the spaniel's fluffy neck, then scratched her ears.

"She likes it when I scratch here. She has mats in back of her ears, and I try to get the mats out. She doesn't like the mats. She likes to look her best, so I help her." Melly touched the russet patch on the spaniel's head. "This is from the Countess's thumb, in England."

Rose had taught Melly that, one of the breed's characteristics. "Remember what it's called?"

"Her 'Blenheim spot,' because the Countess of Marlborough used to rest her thumb there, waiting for her husband to come home from the Battle of Blenheim."

"Good for you."

"The Countess lived in Blenheim Palace, in England. Harry Potter is from England, too."

"Right." Rose smiled.

"That's what I like about Googie. We both have a spot."

Rose blinked. Funny, she'd never made the connection. They'd gotten a Cavalier because she'd had one as a child and they were great with kids.

"I tell her not to be sad about her spot. The Countess gave it to her, and that's just the way she is." Melly shrugged, stroking the little spaniel. "I tell her, the spot is part of her. Just like Harry Potter. She has other spots, too." She pointed to the small spots on the dog's leg. "I told her she shouldn't worry about any of her spots."

"What does she say?"

"She says she doesn't. Other people do." Melly kept petting the dog, whose eyes stayed closed, fringed with red eyelashes. "When I see her, I don't see the spots, I just see her. And she's beautiful."

Rose felt her throat catch. "I feel the same way. She's the most beautiful dog I ever saw."

Melly looked up. "Am I beautiful, Mom?"

"You sure are."

"As beautiful as you? You were a model, in magazines."

"Yes, and you know what I learned from all that?"

"What?"

"That beauty doesn't really have anything to do with what we look like. It's who we are inside, and what we do, in life. Googie's beautiful because she has a beautiful little spirit inside her, and so do you."

"And so do *you,* Mom." Melly smiled sweetly, and Rose smiled back.

"Thanks, honeybun."

"I can go to school tomorrow."

"Okay, good idea," Rose said, hoping it sounded like the truth.

Chapter Thirty

Rose tucked Melly in, checked on John, changed into jeans and a T-shirt, then went downstairs. She padded into the kitchen and hit a button on her laptop, and while it woke up, placed a decaf pod in the coffeemaker, got a mug from the cabinet, and hit BREW. Hot coffee spurted into the mug, and she thought of Leo. He hadn't called her back yet, and she knew he must be busy, so she texted him.

Love you. Canton quit. Call anytime.

She grabbed the mug of coffee, took it to the laptop, and sat down. She logged onto Facebook and looked at the first three messages on her wall. She didn't know the people who had posted, but she recognized the names from class, and the messages were familiar:

I think you are a terrible person . . .
You should leave and go back . . .
I saw you at Fiore's and you must be crazy if you think . . .

Rose didn't read any further. She logged onto Account Settings, then Deactivate Account, and clicked Yes, ending her Facebook account. She sipped her coffee, strong and bitter, then logged into her email account and read the list of senders. She didn't know any of them, and their email wasn't friendly:

You are so fake . . .
I will not let my son . . .
If I am unlucky enough to see you at school . . .

Rose was about to delete them but spotted an email from **Principal Lucas Rodriguez** to the **Reesburgh School Community**, and she opened it:

We all mourn the loss of Marylou Battle, Serena Perez, and Ellen Conze, and we will have an assembly in the gym to honor them, on Monday morning (students only). We'll also hold a meeting for parents (parents only) in the auditorium, at 9:00 a.m., and administrators and dignitaries will be there to answer any questions you may have. Please drive your child to school and try to calm any emotional reactions. It's time to put the past behind us and move on. . . .

Rose read between the lines. Mr. Rodriguez wanted peace at school tomorrow, and so did she. She went into her email account and navigated around until she figured out how to deactivate it, then did. It left her with one thing to do. She logged onto the website for the TV station, which burst into the screen with PHILADELPHIA'S BIGGEST NEWS at the top. She skipped the SCHOOL FIRE EXPLODES IN CONTROVERSY and scrolled down until she found Tanya's one-on-one interview with Eileen Gigot. She wanted to know what was going on to prepare Melly, if she had to. She plugged in the earphones she used when John was sleeping, and clicked the play arrow on the video.

"I'm Tanya Robertson," the anchorwoman said. She was sitting across from Eileen at a dining room table, in front of family photographs and a breakfront. "Tonight, I'm with Eileen Gigot, the mother of young Amanda, who remains in Intensive Care, as a result of being trapped in the school fire at Reesburgh Elementary." Tanya turned to

Eileen. "Thanks for agreeing to meet with me. I know this is a diffi-cult time for you, and I will keep this short. First, how is Amanda?"

"She's still in a coma, and we're praying for her." Eileen looked exhausted, and smiled wanly. She wore little makeup, and her short blond hair was pulled into a ponytail. She looked like an adult ver-sion of her daughter, except for the dark circles under her bloodshot blue eyes and the despair that formed deep wrinkles at the corners of her mouth.

"I understand that you're a single mother, a widow, and in addi-tion to Amanda, you have two sons at home, Jason, thirteen, and Joe, ten. Can you tell our viewers how they're coping with this terrible accident involving their sister?"

"The boys always help, because I work. I'm a secretary in an ac-countant's office, in Reesburgh. They pull their own weight and then some. Amanda's the youngest, and they act like she's a mascot, or their pet."

Rose felt her gut clench. Eileen had been going through hell. And now this, with Amanda.

Tanya continued, "Now, you've made certain allegations regard-ing alleged negligence by the school district, the general contractor, and the subcontractors."

"Yes, but I can't elaborate on that. My lawyer has said we shouldn't discuss it, and we'll do our talking in court." Eileen stiffened. "We're not going to let this happen to another family, is all I'll say."

"Of course." Tanya shifted closer. "When we were talking earlier, you told me that you're upset with the way the school handled evacu-ating the children to safety. Can you elaborate on that?"

"Again, I can't go into detail, on my lawyer's advice. But I don't think they had enough safety procedures in place. They only held one fire drill." Eileen held up an index finger. "Also, when the fire started, the school left it to certain volunteers to get the children out. Those volunteers did not follow correct procedures. That's why Amanda was trapped in the fire."

Rose gasped.

"What do you mean?" Tanya asked.

"Again, all I can say is that these volunteers are other mothers, and I have been advised not to name names. But one of these mothers made sure her child was brought to safety, and Amanda and the others were left on their own." Eileen faltered, pursing her lips. "I just wish I had been there, like the moms who don't work. I keep thinking, if I had, Amanda would be healthy and happy today."

"I understand." Tanya leaned over. "You also told me that this mother called you and complained that Amanda was bullying her child."

"Yes, she did call me to complain." Eileen scowled, deeply. "But Amanda is *not* a bully. She'd never tease or raise a hand to another child, ever. She's just a little girl, a wonderful child, and everybody knows it. If she occasionally acts up, all kids do, especially one who's lost her daddy. Kids work this stuff out, and moms who interfere are the worst."

Rose's mouth dropped open.

Tanya said, "But to return to your point, do you think this mother intentionally left Amanda behind?"

"I'm not allowed to say more. I have turned this matter over to the District Attorney and asked him to press criminal charges."

Rose felt her heart stop. She remembered Mr. Rodriguez talking about criminal charges against the school district. But could there be criminal charges against her, too?

Tanya asked, "Are you saying that you have filed a criminal complaint against this volunteer, for intentionally failing to help Amanda?"

"The District Attorney said—" Eileen caught herself, then stopped talking. "Well, I was instructed not to speak about it. I won't, any further."

"Thank you, Mrs. Gigot." Tanya turned to the camera with a satisfied smile. "Back to you, Tim."

Rose yanked out the earphone, jumped up, and got her phone.

Chapter Thirty-one

"Leo?" Rose said, anxious, when he finally picked up.

"Babe, I was going to call you, but I'm crazy busy. Got people with me in the conference room. Hold on a sec." Leo covered the phone. "Folks, gimme five minutes. Be right back. Mark, hold the fort."

Rose waited while there were some voices, then the sound of a door closing, and she used the time to take a deep breath.

"Okay, I'm back," Leo said, himself again. "So Canton quit?"

"Yes. She couldn't take the pressure."

"What's wrong, babe? You sound weird. Did something happen at the wake?" Leo's voice carried no judgment, and Rose loved him for it.

"Yes, but that's not the problem. Did you see the TV news tonight?"

"Are you kidding? I don't have time to pee."

"Eileen implied that she asked the D.A. to bring criminal charges against me. What does she mean? What did I do that's criminal?"

"Really." Leo paused. "I expected a civil lawsuit, but criminal charges?"

"What is she talking about? Should we call the D.A. and ask?"

"No, that's the worst thing to do. Wait, hold on again." Leo paused, then his voice sounded muffled. "They're in the file on my credenza, with the eagle statue."

Rose waited, panicky. It was bad enough to lose the house. It was impossible to go to jail. It seemed inconceivable, but then again, so did school fires and a little girl in a coma.

"Honey, did she say the District Attorney? Are you sure?"

"Yes, the D.A. That's criminal, right? That's different from civil, right?"

"Yes, sure. Criminal charges are criminal, with criminal penalties. A negligence suit would be civil, that's money damages only. Wait, wait." Leo covered the phone again, his tone newly tense. "The *back* credenza, under the eagle. Next to the softball trophy."

"Does this mean they won't try to charge me with something or they will?"

"Please, hold on." Leo sighed heavily. "A credenza is a file drawer. Is this a hard one? How's Melly?"

"She's sad about Kristen."

"Babe, tell you what. The trial looks like it'll take two weeks, and we're all staying in Philly, at the Omni near the courthouse. But we need to get ahead of this criminal thing, if they're talking about charges against you. Let me get a hold of somebody who can answer your questions. Dean will know a criminal lawyer. I'll let you know."

"Okay, thanks."

"Hang in, and I'll get back to you. Love you."

"Love you, too," Rose said, relieved, but Leo had already hung up.

Chapter Thirty-two

Pewter clouds hid the morning sun, and Rose carried John on her hip and held Melly's hand as they wound their way through the school parking lot, which was full to bursting. It hadn't been designed for every parent to drive, and she'd had to park on the grass because they were running late, to boot, having had one of those hectic mornings.

She'd had to dress up, in a blue cotton shirtdress, because Leo had gotten her a meeting with two lawyers, and she'd changed the bandages on her hand and her ankle. Melly had tried on three different outfits, implicitly anxious about her return to school, and she'd decided on a flowery T-shirt and pink cotton shorts. Rose hadn't rushed her, secretly relieved that Harry Potter had stayed home.

She shifted John higher onto her hip, and he was back to being his sweet self, bouncing happily along, kicking his chubby legs and sucking his light-blue pacifier. He'd slept well, and looked natty in a blue-striped polo and denim pants, which fit him like Mom jeans. She was taking him to the lawyers' office with her, because she took him along whenever possible. She hadn't had children to leave them home with a sitter.

She kept walking, pleased to see that the press stood off school property, behind a cordon, and that Tanya and her TV crew were nowhere in evidence. The last of the parents and children were heading to the entrance, where Mr. Rodriguez stood on a receiving line with the vice principal, guidance counselor, gym teacher, computer teacher, and the librarian who'd helped the day of the fire. The air still smelled faintly, though Rose wondered if she was the only one who noticed. She found herself thinking of the charred Sony PS2, then Amanda. She'd checked online and there'd been no more news about her condition, and Rose had avoided all the news stories about her, including HERO MOM?.

"Mom, come on." Melly tugged her hand. "We're going to be late."

"How you doing, sweetie? You okay?"

"Fine." Melly faced forward, and the slight breeze blew her hair from her cheek, revealing her birthmark. Reflexively, she patted it back down.

"Don't worry. Everything's going to be okay."

"I'm not worried."

"They'll have an assembly in the gym, then you'll go to class for a little while and come home before lunch. I'll come get you, and maybe we'll do something fun. Wanna eat out?"

"Okay."

"Mrs. Nuru wanted you to come in today." Rose felt Melly's fingers tighten on her hand. "She likes you a lot, you know."

"Maybe Ms. Canton will be there, like a surprise."

Rose felt a twinge. "No, she won't, Mel. But she'll call you."

"When?"

"Soon, I hope. When she can." Rose fell in behind a first-grade boy and his mother, and he glanced behind him to see who was there. When he realized he didn't know them, he turned away, then back again, an obvious double-take at Melly's birthmark. "Mel, don't let it bother you if people bug you today. It could happen, with the fire and all."

"Will Amanda be there?"

"No, she's still in the hospital."

"What about Emily and Danielle?"

"Yes, I assume. You can just steer clear of them, if you want. Are you worried about them bothering you?"

"No. I'll use my *Protego* charm. It makes a shield against them. Or sometimes I just tell myself they're just Slytherins. Amanda is like Draco Malfoy, and Emily and Danielle are Crabbe and Goyle."

Rose was about to reply, but Mr. Rodriguez was coming toward them in a jacket and tie, his suit pants flapping. "Melly, here's Mr. Rodriguez."

"Hello, Rose! Hi, Melly!" Mr. Rodriguez made a beeline for them, and Rose met him, shaking his hand.

"Good to see you again."

"You, too." Mr. Rodriguez bent down to talk to Melly. "I'm glad to see you on your feet, and I'm glad you came to school today."

"I'm not sick, and I have to go to school. Is Ms. Canton coming?"

"No, she had to go home," Mr. Rodriguez answered, without missing a beat. He tousled her hair, which Rose knew she hated, because it exposed her birthmark. "Mrs. Nuru's inside waiting for you, and she's proud you came, too." He held out his hand, palm up. "Wanna walk with me?"

"Can my mom come?"

"She's going to her own assembly, with the parents." Mr. Rodriguez's hand remained extended, like an unanswered question.

"Melly, go with Mr. Rodriguez, and I'll see you later, okay? Love you." Rose let go of Melly's hand and bunny-dipped to give her a clumsy kiss, which she returned with an awkward hug, wrapping her arms around Rose and the wiggling baby.

"Bye, Mom. Bye, John."

"Bye, sweetie. We love you."

Rose lingered, watching Melly trundle along, her pink-and-purple Harry Potter backpack bumping up and down. The vice principal, the guidance counselor, the librarian, and the gym teacher all came forward to meet her, greeting her with open arms and broad smiles. Rose felt a rush of gratitude for their kindness, praying that Melly would be okay. Sometimes, it was the most a mother could do.

Mommy!

Ten minutes later, Rose had joined the parents waiting in the hallway to go into the auditorium. Windows filled the corridor with light, reminding her of the skylights in the cafeteria, before they'd exploded into shards, but she told herself to get a grip. John made an adorable armful, smiling up at her and reaching up to play the got-your-nose game. She caught his outstretched hand and gave it a kiss, glad of something to do.

The line of parents shifted forward, and Rose shifted, too, wiggling her index finger with John's finger curled around it. He giggled behind his pacifier, and she would have talked to him, doing her life narration routine, but she didn't want to draw attention to herself. She didn't know the parents ahead of her in line; two were men in casual dress with the yellow ID lanyards of Homestead employees, and the other was a woman in a pantsuit, paging through her email with a skilled thumb.

They reached the doors to the auditorium, which were propped open, and Rose could hear the harsh noise of a microphone being bumped around and someone saying, "testing, one, two, three." The men went inside, then the woman with the BlackBerry, and Rose with John. The auditorium was packed to bursting, with standing room only, and the air conditioning struggled to cool so many bodies. Rose found a place in the crowd under the balcony, happy to be less conspicuous. She dreaded seeing Danielle's mother, or Emily's, and wanted to avoid any confrontations.

The stage curtain was closed, with its blue-and-white pattern in school colors, and the gym teacher was at the podium adjusting the microphone while Mr. Rodriguez ushered a group of public officials into brown folding chairs. The audience talked, finished cell phone calls, or wrote last-minute texts and emails, the artificial light from their various hand-helds illuminating their faces from below.

Mr. Rodriguez took the podium, tapping the microphone and making a *bonk* sound. "Good morning, everyone," he began, and though Rose couldn't see his expression at a distance, his voice sounded heavy with the gravity of the occasion. "Thank you all for coming. I know these last few days have been very difficult for all of you, as they have for all of us in the school community. We have a lot to get to, so let's get started, because I know many of you have questions and we want to address as many as we can in this next hour."

"Damn!" said a well-dressed woman, standing near to Rose. She was typing on her iPhone, her head down. "I'll never get used to this thing. My daughter wants a dress for her American Girl doll, but I can't work this touch screen, to order one."

Rose didn't say anything. She didn't want to risk being recognized, and she never talked while someone else was speaking. It was a pet peeve of hers, and she was always surprised at how rude people could be, even adults. She kept her eyes forward.

Up on the stage, Mr. Rodriguez was saying, "However, we cannot begin our program until we honor these three precious lives we have lost, each of whom was special to our community in her own way. I'm speaking, of course, of Marylou Battle, Ellen Conze, and Serena Perez. To lead us in a moment of silence, let me introduce a man who needs no introduction, the Mayor of Reesburgh, Leonard Krakowski. Mayor Krakowski?" Mr. Rodriguez stepped aside, gesturing at Mayor Krakowski, a short, bald man in a dark suit and tie, who seemed to scoot to the podium.

"I miss my buttons." The woman with the iPhone kept talking, still fussing with the keypad. "But I love this gadget, otherwise. I'm a real gadget hound. You have an iPhone?"

"No," Rose answered, to shut the woman up.

Mayor Krakowski bent the microphone down to his height, then cleared his throat. "Good morning, ladies and gentlemen. Like all of you, I am positively grief-stricken over the loss of these wonderful women, and over the weekend, I took the time to mourn them and reflect on the meaning of their lives, and of all of our lives. Ironically, it's a tragedy like this when a town like Reesburgh can be at its best, because we all come together, as a family."

"Do you have a daughter or son?" The woman kept tapping her iPhone, but her voice made heads turn in the back row.

"A daughter," Rose whispered, getting nervous.

Mayor Krakowski continued, "Let us pause for a moment of silence this morning, to honor these fine women and reflect upon all they meant to all of us, and to our community as a whole." He bent his head, as did most of the crowd. There was the sound of a sniffle or two, though the woman with the iPhone kept fussing with the touch screen. Rose looked down, cuddling John so he'd stay quiet, but there was rustling in the back row as more people turned around and glanced in their direction. She hoped they were looking at the woman next to her.

"Is your daughter into American Girl, too?" the woman asked, turning to her.

"Shh," Rose whispered, but the woman's eyes widened slightly.

"Oh, my! You're the one who left Amanda."

Rose snapped her face front, mortified. Her cheeks flushed, her mouth went dry. She didn't know what to do. She didn't know whether to stay or leave. More heads turned in the back row, and Rose knew it was about her.

Mayor Krakowski raised his head, finishing the moment of silence. "Thank you, and allow me to introduce another person who needs no introduction, Senator Paul Martin. Senator Martin?" He stood aside as Senator Martin rose, tall and slim in a dark suit, with tortoiseshell glasses. His thick, graying hair caught the auditorium lights as he took the podium, raised the microphone, and said, "Good morning, Mayor Krakowski, Mr. Rodriguez, members of the school board, parents, and friends."

Rose kept her eyes to the stage, pretending not to notice that the woman with the iPhone had turned away and was murmuring something to the woman beside her, who had been digging in her purse. The woman with the purse looked over and both of them edged away. More heads were turning around in the audience, as word spread to the back rows. They were all looking at her, talking about her.

Senator Martin continued, "I feel honored to address all of you this morning, on the loss of an amazing teacher, Marylou Battle, and two very dedicated cafeteria workers, Ellen Conze and Serena Perez. I see the expressions of loss and grief on your faces today, and I know that all of you will pull together and stay strong for your families, and particularly your children. Reesburgh is small, but strong, proud, and the very definition of community, and having been at Homestead like many of you, I know that you will persevere through this tragedy."

Rose ignored the commotion to her right, where the women were talking to someone else, their heads together, their whispers behind manicured fingers. She held John closer, hugging him protectively, as people in the seats twisted around to get a look at her. People standing in the back were shifting away from her, leaving her alone. She felt surrounded by shuffling, rustling, and murmuring, but nobody said anything to her.

Rose swallowed hard. She realized that there weren't going to be any more yelling matches, like at Fiore's or the hospital. People would ignore and avoid her until she became invisible, someone they talked about, but not to. And she understood, for the first time, how Melly felt.

Every day of her life.

Chapter Thirty-three

Rose was let into a small conference room, dominated by a floor-to-ceiling panel of windows and a round walnut table covered with papers, briefs, and a laptop. The two lawyers rose instantly, their backlit silhouettes markedly different; the man on the left was reedy and tall, and the one on the right was stocky and short. Until Rose's eyes adjusted to the light behind them, she couldn't see their features at all, and it added to her feeling of surrealism, that she found herself meeting with two faceless lawyers, one of whom represented criminals.

"Thanks for seeing me on such short notice," she said, hoisting John higher on her hip, and the tall lawyer strode around the table toward her, extending a hand with long fingers. His polished smile came into focus first, then his light eyes behind hip rimless glasses, and a lean face framed by thick, reddish hair cut in expensive layers.

"Oliver Charriere." His handshake was strong and brief, and he looked more styled than dressed, in a superbly tailored Italian suit with discreet pinstripes. "Great to meet you."

"I'm Tom Lake," said the other, who had a big folksy grin and the handshake of a weightlifter. His hair was short and bristle cut, his eyes brown behind aviator frames, and his tan suit strained at the seams. His neck was so big that the collar of his blue shirt cut into his jugular. "At this point, we usually say we're Mutt and Jeff, but I can see you're too young to get the joke."

"Not at all, but thanks." Rose smiled.

"Coffee?" Oliver asked, gesturing.

Tom smiled. "He takes your drink order, and I make the doughnuts. I've been baking all morning."

Rose chuckled. "Coffee would be great, thanks."

"Cream and sugar, correct?"

"Yes. How did you know?"

"My Spidey sense." Oliver crossed to the credenza, which held a tall coffee container and a flat box of doughnuts. He picked up a styrofoam cup and raised it to the coffee dispenser, pressing down the button on the lid. "Women like cream and sugar. Very few women drink black coffee, and I can tell who they are with my eyes closed. You're too lovely to be one of them."

Tom snorted. "Believe it or not, Oliver's inherent sexism helps when he picks a jury."

"If not a wife," Oliver added, and they laughed.

"Allow me." Tom rolled a maroon Aeron chair from under the table for her. "Please, sit down. You okay with the baby?"

"Yes, thanks." Rose took a seat, resettling John, who smiled up at her, then sucked his pacifier with such vigor that it moved up and down. "Thanks for letting me bring him."

"Not at all, we allow pets." Oliver strolled over with the coffee, and Tom shot him a comically dirty look.

"Please, show respect. That's Leo Ingrassia's son."

"Right." Rose felt herself relax. "And he bites."

"So do I." Oliver set the coffee on the conference table in front of Rose, then leaned over slightly, unfastened a button on his jacket, and sat down opposite her.

Tom took a seat next to him, sitting down heavily. "And so begins our lesson on the difference between criminal lawyers like my partner, and civil lawyers like me. He's an obnoxious peacock, and I'm straight."

Rose laughed.

Oliver shook his head, then glanced at Tom. "Same old jokes, over and over. You're fired."

"You can't fire me, I quit, and we're here for her." Tom pointed an index finger at Rose. "So you're married to Leo, the lucky bastard, and he knows Dean. I was in JAG with Dean's brother. It's lawyers all the way down. Let's get started." Tom looked over at Oliver with a crooked grin. "Should I clear the deck, first?"

"Oh, please. Not again."

"Yes, again. Clean up time!" Tom stuck out his arm, placed it against the clutter of stapled briefs, newspaper clippings, and Xeroxed legal cases, then swept it off the edge of the table and onto the maroon rug.

Rose burst into laughter, and Oliver rolled his eyes behind his cool glasses.

"Rose, please, don't encourage him. Now, you probably already know this, as a lawyer's wife, but let me explain one thing at the outset. You need to see both of us this morning, a criminal lawyer and a civil lawyer, because criminal charges may be filed against you, by the D.A., and you may also be sued in civil court, for damages. They're two different things. Understood?"

"Yes."

"Here's how we'll run this meeting this morning. Criminal law is more important than civil because locks and keys are involved. That means I'll talk first, while Tom tries not to pick his nose. Still with me?"

"Yes." Rose kept her smile, even though she didn't like the joke about the lock and keys.

"We're both familiar with your case. We've seen the TV and online video, but tell us what happened at school last Friday. Omit nothing."

"Well, I was lunch mom," Rose began, and told them the whole story, from the jelly circle to the debris she'd seen at the school last night. Oliver took notes on the laptop, and Tom wrote on a fresh yellow legal pad, pressing so hard that he embossed the paper with his handwriting. When she finished, she braced herself, managing a smile. "Okay, what's the verdict, gentlemen?"

Oliver leaned back in his chair. "First, don't look so worried. You're in excellent hands with us. We're smarter than we look. At least I am."

"Good." Rose shifted John onto her lap, and he leaned backwards, lying in the crook of her arm and gazing up at her, in his sweet way.

"Let me lay out the criminal side for you. Under Pennsylvania law, specifically 18 Pa.C.S.A. Section 301(b)(2), criminal liability can be imposed for an act, or for the failure to perform an act, when one is imposed by law." Oliver spoke with authority and confidence. "In other words, you're not criminally liable for an omission, unless your duty to act is imposed by law. Understood?"

"Yes."

"There are circumstances in which adults do have a duty to a child imposed on them, and one such time is when there is a 'status relationship' to the child." Oliver made quote marks in the air. "Parents, for example, have that duty to their children, merely by virtue of their status. Make sense?"

"Yes." Rose glanced at John, and he was dozing off, sucking away.

"Now, the duty isn't only for parents. It can apply to anyone in control and supervision of a child, like a babysitter, a day-care worker, or a boyfriend or girlfriend who lives with the child. In Pennsylvania, that was established in the *Kellam* case."

Rose nodded.

"If someone can be said to have assumed a status relationship to the child, that forms a basis for criminal liability, in this and most other jurisdictions."

"Like being lunch mom?"

"Yes, exactly, and many other volunteer situations in schools, volunteers in the library, computer lab, music room, also coaches and chaperones on field trips."

"Really?"

"Yes."

"Jeez." Rose considered the implications, with dismay. "You mean if anybody in one of those situations screws up, they can be charged with a crime?"

"Let's not speculate that broadly. To be precise, all of those situations are fraught with liability, not only civil but criminal."

Rose had had no idea. She smoothed John's hair into place, but had the feeling she was comforting herself again.

"To digress, every summer, I'm asked to speak to baseball coaches. The first hour they have a doctor tell the coaches—all parents, like you—about medical care in case of emergency. Then, the second hour, I advise them to forget everything they just heard. I tell them that the only thing they should do in an emergency is call 911. That's it. Period."

"Why?"

"Because they could incur civil and criminal liability, otherwise."

Rose thought it was awful that they'd come to this point, as a civilization. It was hardly civilized. "Does criminal liability mean go to jail?"

"Not always, but usually."

"Am I going to jail?" Rose asked, her heart in her throat, but Oliver held up a hand.

"Wait. Stop. Don't get ahead of us, please. When you became a lunch mom, you arguably assumed such a status relationship to the children."

"'Arguably'? What does that mean?"

"It means that if I were to represent you, we'd argue you didn't, but it's a tough argument to win, and criminal liability arises under *Kellam* when you have prevented others from rendering aid."

"But I didn't do that."

"Yes, you did. You just told us you kept the girls in the cafeteria after dismissal to recess." Oliver's gaze was direct, yet without judgment, behind his tiny glasses. "They couldn't go outside where there were teachers and others to help them. Then the other lunch mom, Terry, left."

"That was her decision." Rose shook her head. "I didn't want her to go."

"True, but that's not legally significant. At the point at which she leaves to tell Mrs. Snyder, you detained the children and put them in a position where they couldn't be helped by others. Then, the D.A. will say, you failed to adequately help them, under *Kellam*. And it doesn't help that there's a suggestion your actions were motivated by dislike for Amanda, since she teases Melly."

Rose felt her stomach twist. "Can you contact Emily and her parents, or Danielle and hers, and try to get the facts? They can say I took them to the door."

"We'll try but they won't talk to us, I'm sure. If they're thinking of suing you or the school, they won't be permitted to talk to us."

Rose nodded. She should have known. It was a nightmare, replayed. They'd never get the truth now. Justice would be kept at bay by the lawyers.

"In addition, under *Kellam,* their testimony can hurt you. The kids will say you had them in time-out, yelling at them. One of them cried, right?"

"Yes," Rose admitted, miserable.

"*Kellam* is a bad case for you, though the facts are very different. Mr. Kellam was a child abuser."

"How long did he go to jail for?"

"Ninety to 240."

"Days?"

"Months."

Rose gasped. "That's twenty years!"

Tom pursed his lips, and Oliver held up his hand, again. "Look, there's nothing saying you'll be charged."

"How do we know if I'll be charged?" Rose felt panicky. "Who decides?"

"The D.A."

"So can we ask him what he's going to do?"

"No. Better to wait and see—"

"But this is my life, and the uncertainty is awful!"

"The uncertainty is better than provoking him. Keep your eye on the ball. We want this to blow over. The D.A. will be hard pressed to charge a pretty mommy with a crime, unless public pressure is too great not to do so. Lucky for us, it's not an election year."

Rose wasn't feeling so lucky. "If they charge me, do they arrest me?"

"We'd ask for bail, and we'd get it. You're not a flight risk."

Rose's mind reeled. Bail. Arrest. Flight risk.

"Also there's a separate statute, for criminal endangerment of a child, that we need to worry about." Oliver turned to the laptop and hit a few keys. "The criminal endangerment statute provides that a parent or guardian or 'other person supervising the welfare of a child'"—Oliver made quote marks again—"may be criminally liable for endangering the welfare of the child. And the Pennsylvania Supreme Court, in the *Gerstner* case, has interpreted the term to include babysitters and others who have 'permanent or temporary custody of the child.'" Oliver turned back to her, his gaze steady. "Much of this jurisprudence evolved under child abuse law, which is clearly not this case, but the law is the law."

"So how does that apply to me? As you said, I'm no child abuser."

"Of course not." Oliver leaned over. "But again, not legally significant. You were in supervision, it was exclusive, and you didn't take the kids all the way to the playground. I don't blame you, but that's not the point."

Rose couldn't believe her ears.

"Assume the facts that they have are true, namely, that you chose your child over the others, abandoning Amanda and the other two. That's straight-up endangerment."

"But that's not what happened."

"I know, but that's a matter of proof. They'll have to prove their set of facts, and even though we don't technically have the burden, we'll have to prove ours. Now, is there surveillance videotape in the cafeteria or elsewhere in the school?"

Rose hadn't thought of that. "I don't know, I doubt it. They videotape on the buses. Melly doesn't take the bus."

"Understood." Oliver nodded. "The D.A. will need more information to charge you, and they'll try to get it, in the days to come. If one of the assistant D.A.s calls you or drops by, say nothing and call me. In the meantime, say nothing to anybody about this case. Don't talk about it at all. Understand?"

"Yes."

"If it starts to look like they'll charge you, we'll have an opportunity to tell them the way it really happened. I don't think a jury that has all the relevant facts would convict you beyond a reasonable doubt."

"Are you sure?"

"No, but I've been doing this for twenty-six years and I'm not bad at it. It helps that Amanda is still alive. The D.A. will be far less likely to charge you if she lives. If she doesn't, you could be looking at third degree murder."

Rose felt vaguely sick. It was a double-whammy. Amanda dying, and her being arrested.

"Keep calm and carry on. That's my motto, which I stole from British royalty." Oliver permitted himself a crooked smile. "Third degree murder is like gross negligence. It's killing done with legal malice, but without the specific intent to kill." He turned to the laptop again and hit a few more keys. "Malice is defined as 'principal acts in gross deviation from the standard of reasonable care, failing to perceive that such actions might create a substantial or unjustifiable risk of death or serious bodily injury.' That's *Yanoff.*"

"This is a nightmare."

"No, this is a situation that we can deal with, and we will. For the present, some things are up in the air." Oliver smiled. "Now, it's time to turn the floor over to my genius partner, who will tell you the relevant civil law and also a brilliant legal strategy we came up with."

Rose turned to Tom, who was at the credenza, pouring water into another styrofoam cup. She'd been so focused, she hadn't noticed that he'd left the conference table.

"Hold on." Tom returned to the table and placed the cup of water in front of her. "Have some."

"Thanks."

"Ready?" Tom asked, his tone sympathetic as he sat down in his chair.

"Sure," Rose lied. "I'm all ears."

Chapter Thirty-four

Rose took a sip of water while Tom glanced down at his handwritten notes, flipped through the pages, then looked up.

"Rose, let me ask you a few questions, for starters."

"Okay."

"When you were lunch mom, were you given any instruction in any emergency or fire procedures at the school?"

"No."

"Were you asked to take part in a fire drill at the school?"

"No."

Tom made a note. "Have you ever seen a fire drill at the school?"

"No. It's a brand-new school. We just moved here, in June."

Tom made another note. "Ever been in a school fire drill elsewhere, as an adult?"

"No."

"New topic. You said there are lunch-mom procedures." Tom looked up, his expression businesslike and his elbows resting on the table. His fingers throttled his Bic pen. "How were these procedures communicated to you?"

"One of the other moms told me."

"Who?"

"Uh, Robin Lynn Katz."

"She's another parent, isn't she? She's not employed by the school or the school district?"

"No. Yes. She's a mom." Rose was getting confused. She tried to adjust to the cadence of his speech, so different from Oliver's.

"How did Robin Lynn Katz find out about the procedures, if you know?"

"I don't know."

"Are the lunch-mom procedures written anywhere?"

"Not that I know of."

"In any event, you were never given written instructions about them, correct?"

"Correct. No."

"Were you given any instructions by anyone at the school with respect to emergencies or fire safety procedures?" Tom gestured at Oliver, who remained silent, listening. "Like Oliver was saying, with the baseball coaches."

"No."

"New topic." Tom checked his notes. "Let's talk about the blond teacher at the door to the playground. You sure she was a teacher and not a mom?"

"Yes."

"Why?"

"I don't know. She appeared to be getting them outside, in some official way. She acted like a teacher."

"Good enough." Tom made a note. "When you ran back into the cafeteria, was she still there?"

"As far as I know, yes."

"Did you see her? In other words, you didn't see her go out, did you?"

"No."

Tom made another note. "Now. Reesburgh is a new building, finished in August, correct?"

"Yes."

"And you told us what Kristen Canton told you, about the gas leak and the faulty wiring. The carpenter, Kurt Rehgard, told you the same thing. Were they the only people who told you about that?"

Rose thought a minute. "Kristen told me that the teacher, Jane Nuru, said something about them rushing the job and not doing the snag list."

"Right. You mentioned that. Sorry. My error." Tom made a note. "Okay, shifting gears again, tell me how you get in and out of the school, particularly through the playground door."

Rose didn't understand. "You walk?"

"No." Tom shook his head. "I'm being unclear. In my son's middle school, only the main entrance to the school is unlocked, and it leads to the office and only to the office. All visitors check in."

"Right. Reesburgh works the same way."

"You need a keycard to get in the other doors?"

"Same as Reesburgh." Rose thought a minute. "One time I went into the side entrance and it was locked. The teachers have the keycards. They wear them around their necks."

"Good." Tom made another note. "In my son's school, the doors lock automatically when they close. Also the fact, in Reesburgh?"

"Yes."

"So think back to that morning. Tell me about the kids in the hallway, running out to the playground. Are they moving in a continuous stream?"

"Mostly."

"But not always?"

"No, I think. I don't know." Rose could imagine how scary it would be to get cross-examined by Tom, and felt glad he was on her side.

"Does each kid open the door himself, on the way out?"

"I'm not sure."

"See it now." Tom held up his hand, almost like a hypnotist. "Close your eyes. Focus on the kids. What do you see?"

Rose obeyed. She saw smoke. Fire. The kids, a moving stream of heads.

"Do you see the door closing in anybody's face? Do you see them hitting the bar in the middle to open it?"

Suddenly Rose knew the answer, and she opened her eyes. "No. The door was open the whole time, propped open."

Tom broke into a grin.

Oliver looked over with a sly smile. "Bingo."

Rose didn't understand. "Does that matter?"

"Patience, grasshopper." Tom cocked his head. "Why was it propped open, if you know? Is that typical? Have you seen that before?"

"Yes, I have seen that, when I pick Melly up." Rose shifted, and in her arms, John stirred but stayed asleep. "It's been hot this month, and they keep it propped open, to make it cooler in the hallway."

Tom frowned. "But what about the air conditioning?"

"The hallways aren't air-conditioned. Only the classrooms."

"Yes!" Tom turned to Oliver and raised his hand for a high five. "Hit me, bro!"

Oliver recoiled, smiling. "Quiet. You'll wake up the puppy, and I don't high-five. Also, *never* call me *bro*."

Tom grinned at Rose. "Boy, am I feeling better!"

"Why?"

"Here's why." Tom set his notepad aside. "First, the basics. There's no duty to rescue in civil law. In other words, you had no duty to rescue Amanda. But under common tort law, in Pennsylvania and mostly everywhere else, once you undertake to rescue someone, you have to do so with reasonable care. The only exception is for doctors under the Good Samaritan statutes, but they don't apply to you."

"Okay."

"So the question for the jury would be, what is reasonable care in these circumstances? The jury will have to ask themselves, what would *I* do?" Tom put a finger to his head, mock-thinking. "Would I take Amanda and the others out to the playground all the way, and risk losing my own child in the fire? Or would I do what Rose did, strike an on-the-spot compromise that tries to save all of them? Or would I ignore Amanda and the others altogether and go save my kid?"

Rose's mouth went dry. She picked up her water and sipped some.

"I've listened to your account, and we have an obvious proof problem between what you say you did and what everybody else says you did. We'll have to overcome that, but the best way to get you off the hook is to put someone else on it."

"Who?"

"The school, and the state. We can either wait for Amanda and her parents to sue you and the school, or we can take a more aggressive position and file suit against the school."

"What? No." Rose recoiled. "I like the school."

Tom raised a hand. "Keep an open mind."

"I would never want to sue the school."

"Why not?"

Oliver clucked, shaking his head. "She's cream and sugar. Black coffee would sue, no question."

Tom ignored him, leaning over. "You're injured. Your kid was injured. She almost died. You'll have expenses you haven't gotten the bills for yet."

"Yes, but—"

"Hear me out, please. Leave aside the faulty wiring for a minute, because we don't have all the facts on causation, and right now I want to focus on you. You need to change the way you see yourself." Tom pointed at her. "Let me paint you a picture. You're thrown into the school as lunch mom, with no instruction on fire safety, either written or oral, and you could have died. So could your daughter."

"I don't want to sue anybody, least of all the—"

"The teacher at the door doesn't notice that a kid is running back inside, which is clear negligence, and the exit door is left propped open, which is a patently unsafe procedure, because a kid could run back inside undetected, and she did, and that's why she was grievously injured."

Rose listened, trying to keep up with him. "But how did anything the school did cause harm to me, or Melly?"

"You weren't told the procedures in case of fire emergency, which put you in jeopardy. You could've been killed."

"Okay, but what about Melly? How did the school do anything to her?"

"It has no fire procedures in place to convey to volunteers, to save kids in a fire emergency. Also, the school could have three or four lunch moms, not just two. That would have helped, right? Or maybe one of the lunch moms should stand in the hallway to the bathroom, to see what's going on." Tom shook his head. "Rose, you should sue the school for the same reason that the Gigots might sue the school. You stand on the same footing. Melly equals Amanda, legally speaking."

"But Melly is fine, and Amanda might die."

"That makes no difference, again, legally. That's a damages question, and goes to extent of recovery."

"What does that mean?"

"Money." Tom spread his hands, palms up. "Look, we don't have all the facts on causation yet, for sure. Our firm investigator is a former detective and fraud investigator, and he's very experienced. He'll get started fleshing out all the details, obtaining the fire and state police reports, and he'll do his own investigation. When we find out who's really at fault—the school, the general contractor, or the electrical contractor, the inspector, whoever—we'll develop and refine our theory."

"Still." Rose shook her head. "I don't want to sue the school. You don't know what it's like. They'll crucify my daughter. I sat in an assembly like I was radioactive. We just moved, and we can't move again."

"Okay. Relax. Fine." Tom pursed his lips. "You're in charge. You make the decisions, we only make the recommendations."

"Good."

"But if you get sued, this is the best argument you have, and I think you might prevail with it, even if Amanda dies. You weren't at fault, you were a victim, the same as Amanda and the others. All of you were victims of a school system that saves money by throwing unpaid and untrained moms and dads, normal people like you, into a situation they're ill-equipped and ill-prepared to handle." Tom leaned forward again, his gaze intense. "You cannot do more with less, not now and not ever. Bet on it. This economy is in trouble, and the more our state government tries to cut corners in school budgets, the more *children will die.*"

Rose blinked. Tom fell silent as the words sank in, and the only sound in the conference room was John sucking on his pacifier, in a baby dream.

Oliver clapped softly. "Best jury speech ever. I love the send-a-message closing."

Tom looked over, then grinned. "I got myself all worked up, right? But I can feel it. It's a winner."

Oliver turned to Rose, with a smile. "Now you see why he's my partner. He seeks and destroys."

"But I still don't want to sue," Rose said, shaken. "I have to make a life for us in Reesburgh. They're already against us. I had to disable my email and they posted about me on Facebook."

"I see that all the time now, in my cases." Oliver nodded, knowingly. "The mob doesn't need burning torches and clubs anymore. It's trial by Facebook. That's why you have to be realistic. Your duck-and-cover posture isn't the best. If we don't file suit against the school, then at least you know you have a defense, and it could work. Understood?"

"Yes."

"I do recommend, however, that we get the word out in the press. We can leak it or go with a press release, or both. We have to start to shift public opinion in your direction. You have a side of the story, and you need it out there."

"Why?"

"If you're charged, the first thing I'd do is ask for a change of venue, and I won't win. There's enough press to make you look bad, but not enough to make you look bad enough."

Rose felt bewildered. "I wouldn't know how to leak something or send a press release. I thought you told me not to say anything."

"You don't, we do. We have people, sources. We write the release and put it out there. You say nothing." Oliver seemed to think aloud. "You need an official statement, especially in a place like Reesburgh. It's a small town, and views become self-reinforcing. We have to reverse the tide."

Tom's lips made an unhappy line. "Rose, if you were my wife, I'd give you the same advice. You need to get ahead of this situation, public relations–wise, whether it's civil, criminal, or both, and whether you file a lawsuit or defend one. You're getting killed in the press, and that taints the jury pool against you, civil and criminal."

Rose hadn't even thought of that. There was a lot to process, it was overwhelming.

"Look, Rose." Tom's expression softened. "You need to act, but you have a day or two. Think it over. Talk to Leo. If you want to get a second opinion, feel free to do that, too. Get back to us as soon as you can."

Oliver rose slowly, buttoning his jacket. "You're in a terrible bind. You don't want to sue the school, but if you did, it would help your criminal case, too. It would make a statement that you're not at fault. It could even deter the D.A. from charging you. The best defense is a good offense, to cite a cliché."

Tom got to his feet. "This comes down to one thing. Them or you."

Rose cuddled John and stood up. "Well, thanks so much, gentlemen. I do appreciate the time, and the advice."

"Last word. Think about what you hold dear." Tom gestured at John. "That little guy. Your daughter. Leo. Your home. That's what you need to protect. Not the school."

Rose heard the truth in his words, though it tore at her heart. She was remembering how kind Mr. Rodriguez and the staff had been to Melly this morning.

"Never hesitate to shoot." Tom eyed Rose, hard. "It's self-defense."

Chapter Thirty-five

Rose hit the gas, keeping her eyes on the road, relieved she could find an excuse to avoid Melly's gaze. The notion of being sued was bad enough, but she couldn't begin to think about going to jail. Meeting with the lawyers had left her shaken, but letting it show would defeat the purpose of their lunch outing, so she put on a happy face. "Mel, how was your morning?"

"Fine."

Rose braked for a yellow light, turning red. She'd picked Melly up at school without incident, and the other parents ignored them as they went to their car. The press stayed behind the cordon, and even though they snapped photos of the car as they drove past, nobody followed them. "What did you do in school?"

"More *Flat Stanley*."

"Was it fun?"

"Ms. Canton wasn't there. She's not coming back."

"I'm sorry."

"She had to take care of her mom. She's sick."

"I see. Did Mrs. Nuru say when they're getting a new gifted teacher?" Rose glanced over, and Melly kept her head to the window, which was open.

"No."

"Did you spend much time with Mrs. Nuru?"

"No. Sammy and Seth got in a fight. They always do."

"What happened at assembly?"

"Nothing. It was sad."

"Mine was, too." Rose thought back to the parents' assembly. Aside from feeling like she had leprosy, it was an hour of boilerplate assurances that the school would return to business as usual, which was the best thing for the children. "We had a moment of silence. Did you?"

"Yes."

"What else did they say? Anything?"

"That we shouldn't be scared and there's no more fire, and we'll get a new cafeteria and still have the Halloween parade." Melly looked over. "I want to be Hermione again, okay?"

"Sure."

"Now I have the Hermione wand, it makes it better."

"Perfect," Rose said, though she was beginning to feel otherwise. As great as Harry Potter was, she was worrying that it was just another thing to set Melly apart.

"They said we should make get-well cards for Amanda, so we did. Mine was really good."

"That was nice. I'm proud of you." Rose smiled, meaning it. It couldn't have been easy to make a card for your bully. "So, where should we eat?"

"I don't know."

"What do you feel like? I didn't have time to make any sandwiches this morning." Rose eyed the McDonald's, Saladworks, and the other fast-food joints. This section of Allen Road was one strip mall after another, all with tan stucco façades and fake-English names like Reesburgh Mews, Reesburgh Commons, and Reesburgh Roundabout. Traffic was busy, with school dismissed early and the noontime rush. "Want a Happy Meal? Or chicken? Want a hamburger?"

"Ms. Canton doesn't eat hamburgers. She eats veggie burgers. We ate together. It was really good."

"When was that?" Rose hadn't heard anything about Kristen and Melly eating together. The traffic light changed, and she hit the gas.

"She showed me how to make a veggie burger."

"Really, when?"

"At lunch. She gets a veggie burger out of the freezer, puts it the microwave, then she puts a Stackers pickle on top, and ketchup." Melly made a motion with her hand. "Stackers pickles are flat. She said we can buy them at the Giant, and the veggie burgers, too. She showed me the box, and it says Amy's Burgers, but I said they were Kristenburgers, and she laughed."

Rose still didn't understand. "Why were you eating with her?"

"She saw me going to the handicapped bathroom and she said I could." Melly turned, her eyes hopeful. "Can we get Stackers pickles at the store? And Kristenburgers?"

"Sure." Rose wanted to know what had happened, though. If it was what had prompted Kristen's email to her, about lunchtime, she didn't know the details. "Why were you going to the bathroom? Was there a problem? I'm not going to do anything. I just want to know."

"Ms. Canton said I needed a break. She calls it 'me time.' She says she eats alone on Friday, like me. She doesn't mind, because that's her 'me time.'"

Rose knew the weekly schedule, but that wasn't the point. On Friday, the teachers ate in the classrooms, because they made folders that got sent home with the kids, containing work from the week prior. Kristen, as a gifted teacher, wasn't responsible for making any folders, but that still didn't explain why she was eating with Melly. "So why were you eating with her? What happened?"

"She says I needed 'me time' from Amanda and Emily."

"Were they teasing you?" Rose tried to put it together, like a puzzle.

"They were saying that Harry Potter is for boys, and I said, he's not. They only saw the movies, so they don't know. He saves Hermione from the bathroom. Remember, Mom? Like you saved me. I knew you'd come."

Rose felt a twinge. "I love you, Mel."

"I love you, too." Melly twisted to the backseat and waved to John, who was asleep. "I love *you*, John!" she whispered, then turned back to Rose, cheered. "He's cute, isn't he?"

"He's very cute." Rose brightened. "I have an idea. How about we get some lunch, go over to the park, and have a picnic?"

"It's not a sunny day."

"You don't need the sun for a picnic. It won't rain."

"Okay." Melly nodded. "Then can we get the Kristenburgers?"

"Yes."

"Yay!" Melly cheered, and Rose steered the car into the turn lane.

Two hours later they'd had a picnic at Allen's Dam, found the reddest fallen leaf, and gone to the grocery store. Rose wanted to make one last stop before home, in one of the strip malls. She pulled into the lot, cut the ignition, and turned to Melly. "I thought we'd get some books."

"Goodie!" Melly turned to John, who was babbling away in the backseat. "Johnnie, books!"

"Careful, it's a parking lot. You have to hold my hand." Rose grabbed her car keys and purse, and Melly was already in motion, climbing out of the car and closing the door. Rose went around to the backseat, unclipped John from his car seat, found his pacifier, and lifted him into her arms. "Hey, buddy, how're you?"

"Bababsbsbsb," he answered, and Rose kissed his cheek as Melly came around and took her other hand.

"Mom, can I lock the car?"

"Sure." Rose handed her the car keys.

"*Colloportus!*" Melly pointed the key fob at the car.

"Good job." Rose knew the basic Harry Potter incantations, since it was Melly's second language. She dropped the keys into her purse and took Melly's hand. "I want to get a book for me, and you can pick some out, too."

"There's a new one about Quidditch. My friend on Club Penguin told me. She's Harryfan373 and I'm HarryP2009. She loves it!"

"Mel, do any of the kids in your class like Harry Potter? I would think there'd be a few."

"William does."

"Nice. Did you talk to him about it?"

"No. I only know because he has a Gryffindor beanie, too. It's maroon like mine."

"So maybe we can make a playdate with him."

"Mom." Melly rolled her eyes. "He likes the video games, not the books."

Rose walked her toward the store. "A woman at assembly told me her daughter loves the American Girl books. She said they're good."

"They're not." Melly kicked a stone, sending it skidding across the rough surface of the asphalt.

"Have you ever read one?"

"No."

"Do kids in your class read them?"

"All the girls do. They have the dolls, too."

"Really?" They reached the bookstore, and Rose opened the heavy door. "So how's it work? You read the book and you get the doll that's in the book?"

Melly let go of her hand, skipping ahead. A woman standing at the octagon display of hardcovers looked up from behind her reading glasses, her gaze lingering a fraction too long on Melly's face. Oblivious, Melly was already heading toward the Harry Potter books, in Fantasy. A cardboard Dumbledore presided over the section, his magic wand in hand. Behind him was a Hogwarts flag, its shield covered with fake spiderwebs.

"Mel, come check this out," Rose called out, and Melly turned, her eyes bright and alert. She came alive in bookstores.

"Check what out?"

"This way." Rose gestured at the children's books section, a pastel-hued kingdom of pink mushrooms, cartoon parrots, and a papier-mâché cottage. "They probably have American Girl books, and we can pick some books for John."

"I don't want American Girl, Mom."

"What about John? He needs books, too." Rose smiled in an encouraging way, then walked toward the children's department. "Follow me. Let's do this, then go over to Harry Potter."

"Okay." Melly skipped ahead.

"Do you see the American Girl?"

"Over here." Melly stood at a yellow shelf, her knees bent so they bowed backwards. It was her characteristic stance; she was double-jointed, one of the reasons she didn't do well at sports.

"Find anything that looks good?"

"Nah."

"Lemme see." Rose came over and slid an American Girl paperback from the shelves. On the cover was a dark-haired girl in an old-fashioned straw hat. "*Rebecca and the Movies.*"

"She looks dumb."

"Okay." Rose shrugged, which was reverse psychology, the hallmark of professional parenting. "Maybe there's a better one."

"Here." Melly slid one off the shelf and eyed the cover, which showed a girl with straight blond hair and a big smile, touching a butterfly.

"*Lanie's Real Adventures.*" Rose thought it looked fine. "Wanna give it a try?"

"Amanda likes Lanie. She has a Lanie doll, too."

Oops. "Amanda looks like Lanie, doesn't she?"

"Yes." Melly put the book back on the shelf, wedging it between the others with care. "Get it, Mom? You like the books that look like you. You get the doll that looks like you. You go on the website and make the doll that looks like you. Like Build-A-Bear, only with dolls."

"Oh." Rose wanted to kick herself, realizing the problem. None of the American Girls had a birthmark. She spotted one hugging a cute tricolored dog and picked it from the shelf, trying to recover. "Look at this one, about Nicki. She likes dogs, and we like dogs."

"Bbsbssbsb." John pumped his arm, and Rose put on a smile.

"He likes it. Let's get it."

An hour later, Rose pulled into the driveway at home, with sleeping kids, groceries, and a shopping bag of books. The clouds had darkened, and it looked like rain, so they were just in time. She cut the ignition and was about to wake Melly when she noticed a strange car parked in front of the house. It was a navy blue Crown Victoria, and in the next minute, two men in suits were getting out of the front seat and walking toward her car. They didn't look like reporters or door-to-door salesmen, if there was such a thing anymore. She stayed in the driver's seat and slid the key back in the ignition.

"Excuse me, Ms. McKenna?" one of the men called out, reaching into his pocket as he approached. He was young-looking, his sandy hair stiff with product, and he had on a dark suit and an edgy patterned tie. He held up a slim black billfold that flopped open to reveal a heavy, gold-toned badge.

Rose felt her heart stop.

"I'm Rick Artiss, with the District Attorney's Office, Reesburgh County. Can I speak with you a minute?"

Chapter Thirty-six

Rose's mouth went dry. Melly slept in the passenger seat, and John snored in the back, but for a split-second, she forgot they were there, that they even existed, and she was transported back to another time. Everything came rushing back, conflating the days of her life, collapsing the past into the present, making them one and the same, as impossible to separate, one from the other, as waves in an ocean.

"Mrs. McKenna?" The young assistant district attorney was frowning, and so was the other man with him, older and taller, in horn-rims, a dark suit, and a preppy striped tie. Behind them, one of her neighbors, Sue Keller, was walking down the sidewalk with her dog, an old gray poodle.

Rose blinked, recovering. It wasn't the lawyers or the neighbor that snapped her out of her reverie, but the poodle. His name was Boris, and he'd growled at Princess Google last week, scaring her and Melly. The incident anchored Rose in time, and she came zooming back into the present, shaken and seared, as if she'd traveled through the atmosphere of Earth itself.

"Whoa, don't be afraid." The young assistant district attorney closed the billfold and slipped it into his back pocket. "We're just lawyers. We just want to talk with you for a minute or two."

Rose signaled to him with a jittery index finger, mouthing *hold on a sec.* She thought of Oliver and Tom, who'd told her not to talk to the prosecutors, but she didn't want to look guiltier than she did already. She slid the key from the ignition, trying to get in control.

"Mom?" Melly started to stir, and Rose leaned over.

"Melly, go back to sleep. Everything's all right."

"Okay," Melly said, drowsy, and Rose reached for the door handle, got out of the car, and closed it behind her.

"Sorry, we didn't mean to startle you." The young assistant district attorney backed up, deferring to his older colleague, who stepped forward with a confident air. Deep crow's feet creased his eyes behind his bifocals, and a bald spot left him with a sparse fringe of grayish-brown bangs.

"Sorry, young Rick comes on like a carjacker," he said, extending a hand. "I'm Howard Kermisez, also an assistant district attorney with the county. Call me Howard."

"Rose McKenna." She shook his hand, managing a smile. Sue Keller eyed the scene as she walked by, with Boris sniffing the breeze.

"We didn't mean to scare you. We thought you saw us. Sorry about that." Howard leaned over, peering into the car. "And that must be Melly."

"Yes." Rose edged reflexively in front of the window, blocking his view.

"Welcome to Reesburgh. It's great to see new folks moving in, especially babies. This is a great town, in a great state." Howard smiled in a pleasant, if impersonal, way. "How are you and your husband enjoying it? He's from Worhawk, I understand."

"We love it, thanks. But excuse me, I have to get the kids inside." Rose gestured behind her, as if that explained it all. She couldn't go to jail because she had to make dinner, then there were fractions to practice, and another Flat Stanley to be pasted into the scrapbook, from a cell phone picture taken at the picnic. Melly had already thought of the caption: Flat Stanley Meets a New Newt.

"Of course, you're busy now, I can see that. I have three sons. They're older, but you know what my wife says? Little kids, little problems, big kids, big problems." He smiled coolly, again. "So we won't take long. We just have a few questions. You were volunteering at the elementary school last Friday, when the fire broke out, weren't you?"

"No, wait, listen. I've been told not to speak with you. My lawyers are Oliver Charriere and Tom Lake." Rose almost blanked on Tom's last name, she felt so panicky. "You should call them if you have any questions for me. I have their card. Hold on."

"I'm not sure we need to get formal about this."

"I'd prefer it that way." Rose opened the car door, grabbed her purse, extracted the card, and handed it to Howard. "Now, excuse me, but I should really get the kids some dinner."

"Sure, okay." Howard's smile flattened. "I know Oliver well. I'll give him a call, then get back to you."

"Great," Rose said lightly, as if it were a date, not an arrest. She opened the car door, and Melly was sitting upright in the seat, awake.

"Mom, who are those guys?"

"Just lawyers." Rose reached in, unbuckled Melly's harness, and let it retract. She wanted to get the kids inside and call Oliver, right away. "Let's go, honey. Got your backpack? Get your backpack."

"Like Leo?" Melly stretched slowly.

"Not as much fun as Leo." Rose glanced over her shoulder, and the Assistant District Attorneys were getting back into their car. Sue Keller and Boris were on their way back, for the return trip. "Hurry up, let's go."

"Are you okay, Mom?"

"I'm fine, I just have to go to the bathroom. Let's go, okay?" Rose hurried to the backseat, opened the car door, and unbuckled John's car seat.

"Mom, don't forget the bag from the bookstore."

"I'll get it later." Rose slipped the seat belt over John's head and lifted him up to her shoulder, where he flopped, staying asleep.

"But I want my books."

"Then can you get the bag?" Rose checked over her shoulder. The sedan was still parked in front of the house. They hadn't even started the engine.

"It's heavy." Melly had her backpack and was struggling with the bag of books.

"If you can't do it, leave it. I'll come back for it." Rose glanced behind her, worried. Still, the sedan hadn't moved. She felt her heart start to pound. Prosecutors, lawyers, charges. She had been here before. "Mel, please, hurry up."

"Mom, you don't have the Kristenburgers."

"I'll come back for the groceries."

"Can we still have them for dinner tonight? You said."

"We will, just hurry. I have to go to the bathroom, please." Rose hurried down the sidewalk, reaching the sedan. The prosecutors were inside talking, and she slowed her pace so she didn't look like a fleeing felon. "Mel, do you need help?"

"No. I can do it myself."

"Okay, hurry." Rose could see that Howard Whatever was pressing a number into his cell phone, and she wondered if he was already calling Oliver. Meanwhile, Sue Keller was catching up to them, with Boris yanking her forward. The cranky dog was getting close, so Rose hurried back to Melly. "Let me help, sweetie."

"I was doing it, Mom. I can do it."

"I know." Rose bunny-dipped with John and picked up the plastic bag of books. "I don't want Boris near you. Remember last time?"

Melly turned. "Oh, right. Norbert the dragon. Tried to bite me and Googie."

"Yes. Come on." Rose herded Melly up the sidewalk and past the sedan, where Howard was talking on his cell. The younger prosecutor sat in the driver's seat, watching her. She turned with Melly onto their front walk and went up the flagstone path.

"Mom, we didn't lock the car."

"I will later. When I come back out."

"*Colloportus,*" Melly said, anyway.

They reached the front step, where Rose set down the bag of books and handed Melly her purse. "Can you get the keys and open the door? I can't with my hand."

"*Alohomora!*"

"No unlocking spells, please. Use the key with the red thing on it."

"I know, I see you do it, all the time." Melly dug in the purse, found her keys, slid the key in the lock and twisted it, then pushed open the door. "Did it!"

"Good for you. Close the door. I'll be right back." Rose left Melly in the living room with the new books, went upstairs and put John down, then hurried into her bathroom with her purse. She got out her phone, and Oliver's number was still in the text function. She highlighted it and pressed CALL. "Hello?" she said, as soon as a woman picked up. "I'd like to speak to either Oliver or Tom. I'm a new client. Rose McKenna. I was there today."

"I'm sorry. Tom is in court, and Oliver is on the phone. May he return—"

"Is he on the phone with an Assistant District Attorney from Reesburgh?"

"I'm sorry, I'm not permitted to give out that information, but I can ask him to return your call."

"Thanks." Rose left her name and cell number, then hung up and dialed Leo's cell. It rang and rang, then the voicemail came on. She told herself to calm down when the beep sounded, and she left a message: "Leo, I met with the lawyers, and two assistant D.A.s were here at the house. Give me a call when you can. Love you."

Rose pressed END, then sank to the edge of the bathtub, her thoughts bounding back in time, a wild animal set free. She knew these woods. She had brought it on herself. She had it coming, truly. Her heart raced, she broke a sweat, and her gaze flitted around the picture-perfect bathroom, finding the his-and-hers pedestal sinks and the cornflower-blue accents in the shower curtain, which matched the hue of the thick bathtowels.

She had picked everything out for the new house, and seeing it all now, she knew she didn't deserve any of it; neither the pretty Italian floor tiles, nor the overpriced shampoos on the rim of the tub. She'd wanted to start over, to have one last starting-over in a lifetime of starting-overs, of endless moving from apartment to apartment, and from base to base. The only difference in each place was the color of the bathtowels.

Rose blinked. Her mother lay on the bathroom floor in her robe, passed out again. She'd need to be awakened, picked up, washed off, sobered up. Long, dark hair hid her once lovely face. The bathtowels in that apartment were yellow. Then pink, then white. The bathtowels were the only thing that changed in the apartments where her mother lay on the floor, until one day, she couldn't be awakened, at all.

Mommy!

"Mom?"

It was Melly, at the door. The door knob was twisting.

"Yes, honey?" Rose asked, coming out of her reverie.

"Why is the door locked?"

"Here I come." Rose got up and caught sight of her reflection, but didn't recognize herself. Her eyes, dark and blue, looked haunted.

"*Alohomora.*" Melly giggled, on the other side of the door.

Chapter Thirty-seven

Rose was cleaning up the dinner dishes when her phone rang, and she dried her hand hastily, reached for the cell phone, and tucked it into the crook of her neck. "Hello, yes?"

"Rose. It's Oliver. I heard you got a visit today."

"Yes. Did they call you? What did they say?" Rose peeked around the corner and double-checked that Melly was out of earshot in the family room, sitting at the computer desk and printing the Flat Stanley picture. John was in his high chair in the kitchen, mashing his rotini, his hand a small starfish. His palm made a *bum, bum, bum* sound when he banged the tray.

"They want a meeting tomorrow. Our offices, at ten in the morning. Can you make it?"

"My God, so soon?" Rose felt stricken. "What's going on?"

"Remain calm and carry on, remember?"

"Does this mean they're thinking of charging me?"

"It means they're investigating the facts."

Rose's gut tensed. "But why so soon?"

"The sooner, the better for us. We want to meet with them while Amanda's still alive."

Rose shuddered. "Why?"

"As we discussed, now there's less public pressure to charge you, and less pressure from the Gigot family. At present, the worst-case scenario is still a hypothetical. Understand?"

"Yes, but why are they moving so quickly?"

"Lots of reasons. They could be following up when your memory is fresh, or trying to show how responsive they are and how hard they work. Or they want to have their ducks in a row, in case Amanda dies."

"Do you have to talk that way?"

"What way?" Oliver paused, his voice warmer. "Sorry. I really am a nice man. You recall."

Rose didn't smile. She eyed John, banging the tray. *Bum!*

"Rose, be of good cheer. I'd like them to hear your side of the story before they get entrenched. If we put on a strong enough case, I hope we can back them down."

"We have to put on a case?"

"Not in a strict sense. I'll explain when I see you. Can you come in around nine, so I can prepare you before the meeting?"

"Yes. Sure." Rose thought a minute. "What if I can't get a sitter that quick? What do we do?"

"Melly's in school, correct?"

"Yes."

"Don't get a sitter. I want Howard and his lackey to see what the jury will see. Bring the baby."

"You talk like he's a prop."

"Well said. He's a prop."

"Oliver, he's my son," Rose said, upset. It was getting worse and worse.

"Did you speak with Leo yet?"

"No."

"By way of housekeeping, am I correct in assuming that you'd like us to represent you, on both the criminal and the civil side?"

"Yes."

"Excellent. We're delighted, and I know I speak for Tom. If you tell me your email address, I'll email you an engagement letter and when you get a second, send us a check for the retainer, which is five thousand dollars."

"Okay." Then Rose remembered. "Wait. I disabled my email."

"Get a new account, and we'll keep it private. What do you want to do about the press release, or me talking to one of my sources? May I go forward?"

"I'm not sure. Let me think and talk to Leo."

"Sure. Let me know. See you. Take care."

"Thanks." Rose pressed END, then L to speed-dial Leo, and waited while it rang, then went to voicemail. She composed herself before leaving another message: "I'm meeting with the D.A. tomorrow morning. Please call."

She pressed END, and her gaze fell on John, happily sucking his fingers. She couldn't imagine what would happen to him or Melly, if she had to go to jail. Leo would have to hire a full-time caretaker, and even if John could adapt, Melly would be devastated. She'd already lost her father, now she'd lose her mother. And there'd be no backstop for her at school, now that Kristen was gone.

Rose felt a wave of sadness so profound that she had to lean on the counter until it passed. It killed her that her children, and Leo, would have to pay for what she'd done, and even so, she sensed that she was entering eye-for-an-eye territory, the ultimate payback. She pressed the emotion away, trying to stay anchored in the present. There were dishes to rinse, counters to spray-clean, and a baby to bathe; the tasks of home life, the very stuff of being a mother. She had always taken satisfaction in the tasks, because she knew that each one mattered; it was the little things that made a house a home, and moms did all the little things.

Rose went to John, pulled out his tray, picked him up, and hugged him close, breathing in his damp baby smells and feeling his reassuring weight. He looped his fleshy arm around her neck, and she rocked him, told him she loved him, and nuzzled his warm neck with her nose, trying not to think about how much longer she'd have him, or he'd have her.

"Let's go say hi to your sister," she whispered into his ear, swallowing her emotion. She carried him into the family room, where Melly looked up from the computer printer, her blue eyes expectant.

"Mom, was that Ms. Canton on the phone?"

"No, sorry."

"When is she going to call?"

"I'm not sure, but soon, I hope."

"She said she would."

"She will," Rose said, uncertain.

After the kids were in bed, she went back down to the kitchen, cleaned up, and sat down in front of the laptop, logging onto the web and checking philly.com for news of Amanda. The earlier stories hadn't changed, which meant that she was still alive.

Thank you, God.

Rain fell outside the window, and the sky had grown dark, a backdrop like a final curtain, of dark velvet. She could see the peaked roof of the house next door, which had in-ground floodlights that shone upward at its brick façade, lighting the place like a stage set. The tall trees in the sideyard were shedding leaves, but night and rain had obliterated their colors, so they looked black and shiny.

She wondered which leaf would fall next, playing a waiting game with herself, which felt uncomfortably familiar. She'd been waiting to see what would happen to Amanda. Waiting to see if she'd be charged with a crime or sued. Waiting for decades, since it had happened.

It had been a night just like this, and the rain was a slow, steady downfall. Her downfall. Rose could call up the memory of that night, without thinking. In fact, it took thinking *not* to call it up. She could see it now as if it were in front of her. It had happened around this time of year, too, but at the end of October. Halloween night, the leaves fallen, dead on the street.

Rose blinked, and the memory vanished. The kitchen was dim, the halogens under the counter working their suburban magic. The only sound was the patter of the raindrops on the roof and the thrumming of the dishwasher, which shifted gears. The blue digits glowed on the door, counting down until the end of the cycle. She watched the number change, 36, 35, 34, finally permitting herself to have the thought she'd been suppressing, almost constantly since the fire.

I need a drink.

She got up, went to the side cabinet, and reached into the wine rack, sliding out the first bottle she touched, then closing the door. The label read LOUIS JADOT, which would do just fine. She went into the drawer for the corkscrew, peeled the metal wrapping off, and did the honors with difficulty because of her bandaged hand. She poured herself a glass of merlot, and still standing at the counter, drained the glass like she used to, in the bad old days. It tasted more bitter than she remembered, but it could have been her state of mind.

"Don't tell anyone," she said, when Princess Google looked up.

She grabbed the bottle by the neck and set it on the table, then took the glass over to the laptop and sat down. She poured another glass, drank it, and her gaze fell on the laptop through the glass, an alcoholic wash of the newspaper's front page. HERO MOM? read the sidebar, and underneath that, *New Viewer Videos*!

She set down the glass, palmed the mouse, and muted the volume on the laptop. She clicked on the link for the videos, and it brought her to a list in bright blue, each one titled: School Fire, Cafeteria Fire in Local School, First Responders Arrive, Ambulance Leaves with Amanda Gigot, and so on, the list reading like a chronological description of her nightmare. Luckily, she was starting not to feel anything.

She poured another glass, drank it, and clicked one of the links, of the kids running from the school and onto the playground. She watched them come, numbing to their stricken faces, racing into the camera. The video ended, and the arrow froze, and she clicked and watched it again and again, until she felt absolutely nothing. She clicked on another video, titled Copter Shots, and watched the roof of the cafeteria smolder, then flare into flames. She slid the bar back and forth, forward and back, moving time backward and forward, so the past became the present, then they traded places and the present came before the past, her life a palindrome.

Rose came out of her reverie, realizing the cell phone had been ringing. The screen read LEO, so she reached for it and answered, "Hello?"

"Babe, is that you? You sound funny."

"I was sleeping. I went to bed early."

"Sorry. You wanna go back to sleep? How are you with this D.A. meeting?"

"Fine, but I need to go back to sleep."

"Sure, okay. Oliver's a great lawyer, so don't worry. Just listen to what he tells you when you meet with the D.A. Don't let them rattle you. If you wake up, call me, no matter how late. Love you."

"Love you, too." Rose hung up, set the phone down, and reached for the bottle.

Chapter Thirty-eight

Rose sipped her coffee, but it couldn't cure her cotton mouth from last night. They were in a larger conference room than yesterday, containing a long walnut table that held only a stack of fresh legal pads. The windows showed off a view of the woods behind the corporate center, with picturesque autumn foliage, a sharply blue sky, and a cool sun.

Rose stayed seated with John in her lap, while Oliver introduced himself to the two prosecutors. She had on a navy dress with a matching sweater, light makeup, and her hair in a half-ponytail, and John was in a white polo shirt and his Mom jeans, sucking his pacifier and clutching his Fisher-Price car keys. Long ago, she had posed almost the same way, for the Hanna Andersson catalog.

"Gentlemen, be my guest." Oliver gestured at the walnut credenza against the wall, which held two canisters of coffee, fresh bagels, and cream cheese, the delicious smells scenting the air. "Get yourself some coffee, and we have the best bagels of any law firm in the county."

"Thanks, but no," Howard said, evidently for both of them. He rolled out a chair for Rick, then unbuttoned his khaki jacket before he sat down, with a warm grin for Rose. "Hello again. Now that I can see the baby, he's cute, and the resemblance is remarkable."

"Thanks." Rose flashed a professional smile, wary. During their meeting prior, Oliver had warned her that Howard would use the friendly approach to get her to talk, and he'd told her to clam up, which should be easy, because she was terrified.

"Let's begin, shall we?" Oliver pulled up his chair and sat next to Rose. Their backs were to the window, forcing the prosecutors to squint against the brightness. Oliver had told her that the seating plan was intentional, but she hadn't reminded him that yesterday, she'd been the one squinting.

Oliver cleared his throat. "I suggest that we proceed as follows. Rose will tell you what happened at school, then you may ask questions, for clarification purposes. Understood?"

"Fine."

"Let's be clear. Rose is here today because she wants the truth to come out, and it hasn't, as yet. Between us, she's considering whether she will file a civil action against the school and the school district, for damages arising from their negligence."

Rose said nothing. Oliver hadn't told her he would say that, but she let her smile mask her dismay.

"I see." Howard lifted an eyebrow. His eyes were brown behind his hornrims, and there was a small scab under the softness under his chin, as if he'd cut himself shaving.

Oliver nodded. "Frankly, I have advised her to file suit, as has my partner Tom, but she and her husband have yet to decide. Her daughter Melly, as you may know, almost perished in the fire, and as you can see, she herself was burned on her hand and ankle." He gestured in Rose's direction, and John banged his plastic keys on the table. "In addition, Howard, let me ask you if the Commonwealth intends to file criminal negligence charges against the school and the school district in connection with the fire?"

"We're undecided, at this point." Howard's smile faded, and beside him, Rick looked down, as if the conference table needed examining.

"I would hope so." Oliver leaned back in the chair. "Who makes that decision, anyway? The District Attorney himself? And you make a recommendation to him, go or no?"

"Something like that." Howard looked annoyed.

"You've got 'em dead to rights, don't you? Even I've heard rumors there was faulty wiring and a gas leak. What did the Fire Marshal determine as the cause?"

"We haven't yet released that information."

"Of course, whatever, I'll play along." Oliver shrugged it off. "Obviously, the general contractor and all of the subcontractors—electrical, HVAC, and the like—were under the school and the district's exclusive control and supervision. I assume that the district chose them, and were I in your chair, I would examine the bidding method by which they were selected with a close eye." Oliver sniffed as if he'd caught a whiff of something stinky. "I know that state and local politics often play an unfortunate role in the awarding of major construction projects, and that should be investigated, too. If the district awarded the job to the low-ball contractor, they'd get haphazard construction, which resulted in foreseeable loss of life. That's criminal negligence."

Rose was surprised at how strong Oliver was coming on, and it was ratcheting up the tension in the room. Across the table, she could see Howard stiffen.

"Not to mention the elementary school's failure to have adequate safety procedures, which your discovery will reveal, if it hasn't already." Oliver gestured again at Rose. "My client is happy to speak with you now, however. We hope it will help you build a case against the people responsible for the deaths of three innocent citizens—and a little girl, if Amanda Gigot doesn't recover, God forbid. I assume you've been in contact with the Gigot family, and I would hope that your office isn't succumbing to their pressure to scapegoat Rose and her family."

"No, nothing of the sort." Howard frowned.

"Then I'm at a loss to understand why you visited my client at her home, yesterday. I would think she's the last person you would want to speak with, a mother who's as much a victim as the Gigot family. I trust you understand, whether we file suit or not, that's our position."

"I do." Howard shifted forward. "Now, if we could get on with—"

"Finally, of course, Rose is in no way waiving any of the constitutional rights that she may seek to assert later, such as self-incrimination, which we expect will not be necessary. Understood?"

"Yes."

"And, one questioner only. That's you." Oliver pointed at Howard. "If at any point, Rose wishes to break, we will. If she feels uncomfortable, we stop. If she wants to end, we do. Understood?"

"Yes," Howard answered, and Oliver turned to Rose, with a confident smile.

"Rose, why don't you begin?"

"Okay." Rose hoisted John higher on her lap and launched into the story. She told it in brief strokes, the way she had to Oliver and Tom, and Howard listened quietly, his expression sympathetic. When she got to the part where Melly was taken away in the ambulance, Oliver leaned over, raising his hand like a school crossing guard.

"And the rest is history," he said, to Howard. "So you see, no matter what the press or the Gigots may be saying, it's not as if Rose chose to rescue Melly over Amanda and Emily. On the contrary, she chose Amanda and Emily *over* Melly. There's simply no basis for any criminal charges against her."

Howard's gaze shifted from Oliver to Rose, then back again.

Rose held her breath. It was hard to believe she was sitting here, in front of a man who determined her and her family's fate. He wielded all the power and resources of the Commonwealth of Pennsylvania. He could send her to prison for twenty years.

Oliver kept talking. "I cannot imagine a jury in the world who would find anything blameworthy in her conduct, because she *is* a hero. The fact that Amanda was eventually injured is the fault of the construction deficiencies, the school's non-existent fire safety procedures, and the negligent supervision of the blond teacher in the hallway, who permitted her to run back in after an iPod."

Rose remained still. John banged the keys on the table, but everyone ignored him.

Howard looked deep in thought, eyeing Rose. "Just to clarify, where was the other lunch mom, Terry Douglas, when you asked Amanda and the other students to stay behind?"

Rose swallowed, hard. "She was—"

"Stop." Oliver raised his hand again. "I object to the phraseology 'stay behind,' and Rose has been clear about that. I won't have you go over and over it."

"I was clarifying."

"It's clear enough."

"Not to us." Howard shook his head. "The Commonwealth's concern is that Rose assumed and insisted upon exclusive control of the three children, including Amanda."

Rose felt her gut clench.

"We dispute that," Oliver shot back, coolly. "As soon as Rose regained consciousness, she delivered Amanda and Emily to the hallway and the supervision of the teacher there. She excluded no one, at any time. There was no one helping any child, except Rose." Oliver checked his watch. "We've been here an hour. That's an hour you should have spent interviewing the contractor, subcontractors, school district officials, and a teacher who let a child run into a burning building." Oliver rose, suddenly. "This meeting is over. Good-bye, and thank you for coming."

Howard looked up, pursing his lips. "Grandstanding doesn't help your client, Oliver."

"Oh, please." Oliver didn't bat an eye. "I'm not grandstanding, I'm merely standing. If you persist, I'm going to have to wonder why you're so intent on *not* investigating the school district and state officials who made the decision to hire whomever they hired. Please tell me it's not because they pay your and your boss's salaries, because the jury won't like that, not one bit."

"What?" Howard's eyes flared an angry brown, and he got to his feet, as did Rick. "What are you suggesting? That I'm in somebody's pocket?"

"I didn't say that, did I?" Oliver strode around the table, went to the door, and opened it calmly. "No more free discovery. Know that if you come after her, I'm coming after *you.*"

Chapter Thirty-nine

Oliver eased into Howard's vacated chair across from Rose, exhaling with a smile. "So, now we can talk. How are you?"

"Worried sick." Rose sipped her coffee, which was cold. "Tell me how you think it went. Will he charge me?"

"That, I don't know." Oliver buckled his lower lip. "But you did well. Your account was brief and to the point."

"Thanks."

"This isn't in our control, and you have to understand that. We shot our wad, we bloodied his nose." Oliver paused. "I'm mixing my metaphors."

"It's okay."

"You heard the question he asked. That's our problem. The *Kellam* case, as I told you."

"Tell me if you think he'll charge me. Take a shot."

"We have to wait and see, about Amanda, and so forth, as I told you."

Rose gave up. "Why did you say all that, about me filing suit?"

"To back him down, to show him he's at risk if he moves against you." Oliver's smile vanished. "This is war, Rose. Make no mistake. Tom is right about that."

Rose didn't know what to say. She felt worried sick.

"This is no time to hesitate. You don't want to be sitting in cell-block C, thinking, 'I wish my lawyer had been more aggressive, I wish he'd fought harder for me.'"

Rose didn't want to admit it, but he was right. "So, do you think there's some payoffs going on, with the school district?"

"Of course not. I just said that to scare him. To let him know I'll go after him and his boss if I have to. I don't want him going after you instead of the district. I won't let that happen."

"Thanks," Rose said, meaning it.

"I do think we have to put our story out now. Let me proceed with a press release, please. I'll tell it from your point of view, and at the end, I can suggest that you're thinking about suing, not that you actually are going to."

"Why can't you put out my side of the story, without talking about me suing anybody?"

"It's not as newsworthy, and the first question they'll ask me is, is she suing? If I say no, you'll look weak." Oliver shook his head. "I'd rather say nothing than say that. Then at least they'll think you're contemplating suit."

"Then don't say anything. To the outside world, saying I'm thinking about suing is the same as saying I *am* suing. These are distinctions that only lawyers make, Oliver."

"Please, at least talk to Leo. See what he says."

"Okay, fine."

"You'll see a change for the better, as soon as we do. In the short run, it will get more intense, but we want to win, in the end. Keep the long run in mind."

"I will." Rose was about to get up, and John had fallen asleep, now that the meeting was over. She slid the plastic keys from his hand as his grip loosened. "Such a good baby."

"He earned his keep today, our little Exhibit A."

"His name is John."

"Exhibit J, then."

Rose didn't smile as she dropped the plastic keys into her purse, then raised John to her shoulder and stood up. "Thanks for everything today."

"You're welcome." Oliver stood up, too. "You know, I get it, seeing you with Exhibit J."

"Get what?"

"Why people want offspring. I never did, but all my wives did."

"Children are all that matters, Oliver." Rose met his eye and spoke to him from the heart. "This baby needs me, and so does Melly. They love their dad, but I'm their world. You have to keep me free, for them. Not for me, for them."

Oliver dropped his cynical expression, seeming to get real. "Listen. I'll try my best, but I can't guarantee anything."

"I know," Rose said, aching. She picked up her purse and left. There was something she wanted to do, and she had no time to waste.

Chapter Forty

Rose steered into the school parking lot, her face hidden behind sunglasses, but Tanya Robertson and the other press at the cordon recognized her car. They snapped photos and shouted questions she couldn't hear, with the car windows up and Disney lullabies on the CD player. John listened contentedly in his car seat, shaking his plastic keys, a toy worth its weight in gold.

She hit the gas, cruised as far from the press as she could go, and parked. The lot was almost empty because it was too early for dismissal, but she was a mom on a mission. She twisted off the ignition, grabbed her purse, got out, and slid John and his toy keys from the car seat. She gave him a big kiss on his fleshy cheek, and his tiny arm went around her neck.

"Bbsbb," he gurgled, with a wet grin that revealed a white flash of tooth nugget on his lower gum.

"A new tooth!" Rose hadn't noticed, with all the horrible stuff going on. She walked toward the school, reached the concrete ramp, and went inside through the door signed, ALL VISITORS MUST CHECK IN. It was the only door open to the public, and she thought of Tom. She couldn't imagine filing suit against the school, shook it off, and entered the office. The room was large, with a sunny panel of windows, soft blue walls, and matching patterned carpeting. An oak-like counter divided the office lengthwise, and the front part served as a waiting room, containing four blue-cloth chairs, an end table, and a wire rack with tri-fold brochures for the PTO.

"Hi, Jill." Rose slid her sunglasses onto her head and walked to the counter. The main secretary's desk was on the other side, a petite, friendly woman named Jill Piero.

"Hello, Rose." Jill looked up from her keyboard with a smile that hardened like ice. "How's Melly?"

"Fine, thanks." Rose wasn't completely surprised by the cold shoulder. "I was wondering if you could help me. Melly was really close to Kristen Canton, and she's so sad that Kristen's gone."

"Yes, it's too bad." Jill pursed her lips.

"Kristen said she'd call us to say hi to Melly, but so far she hasn't. Do you have a number where I can call her?"

"I don't know if we have it, but even if we did, I wouldn't be permitted to give that out."

"But Kristen was close to Melly, and she wouldn't mind."

"Sorry, no can do." Jill glanced behind her at the other secretaries, but they were both on the phone at their desks.

"Then can you call Kristen and ask her to give us a call? I'll give you my cell number."

"If we have a number for her, I will. I don't even know if we do."

"Can you check?" Rose thought a minute. "Or if you have a home address for her parents, I'd take that too. Then I could send her a note or maybe Melly could send her a card."

"Hold on." Jill turned and went behind the wall, which connected to the hallway to Mr. Rodriguez's office.

Rose could hear talking, but couldn't make out what anyone was saying. She waited a minute, but sensed where this was heading and decided to get proactive. She went to the right, down the hallway, about to find Mr. Rodriguez and ask him herself when she spotted the teachers' mailboxes, to her left. Neat oak slots lined the wall, and each one was open, many with mail.

Rose scanned the nameplates, in alphabetical order, and reached the C's. Kristen Canton. Her mailbox was lower than eye-level, and there was a thin packet of mail inside. The school must have been accumulating mail, to forward it when they had enough. She slid it out quickly and read the forwarding address, printed in ballpoint pen next to the crossed-out school address. **765 Roberts Lane Boonsboro MD.** She committed it to memory, went back to the counter, and waited for Jill, who returned after a few minutes.

"Sorry, we don't have her cell and we can't give out her parents' home address."

"Thanks for trying, bye." Rose left the office, flipped down her sunglasses, walked from the building, and slid out her phone, adding the Cantons' address to her list of contacts, so she wouldn't forget it. She started to go back to her car with John, but it was too nice a day to sit in a car, until dismissal. On impulse, she walked to the back of the building and through the teacher's parking lot, shaking off some unhappy flashbacks.

Here's the ambulance!

She went around the back of the building and ended up on the far side of the school. The township parking lot lay to her left, and the school buses sat parked against the cyclone fence like a row of yellowed teeth. She passed the grassy stretch of athletic fields, with their soccer goals outlined, and approached the cafeteria from the other side.

She was downwind, where the breeze carried the stench of burned plastic, and the sight filled her with renewed sadness. A new plywood wall concealed the cafeteria, which had been state-of-the-art, and she walked along on grass blackened and filthy with mud and charred debris. Workmen flowed in and out of the site through an opening in the plywood, pushing wheelbarrows of charred debris, or carrying building materials. One of the workmen, in a white Bethany Run T-shirt and Carhartt pants, was her carpenter friend from the night before, Kurt Rehgard.

Kurt looked over, recognizing her, with a slow grin. "Hey, Mrs. Lawyer," he called out, coming over as his buddies exchanged glances, behind him. "How's your daughter?"

"Back to school."

"I didn't hear from you, so I figured you're not getting that divorce." Kurt grinned. "And I know who you are, even with those big shades on. I saw your picture online. The article wasn't very nice."

"I didn't mean to keep it from you." Rose reddened, and Kurt met her gaze directly, his eyes flinty under his hardhat.

"Yes, you did."

"Okay, maybe I did." Rose felt unmasked. "I guess they know who I am, too. Your buddies."

"Those clowns?" Kurt gestured behind him. "No way. If they go online, it's for porn. I went to one year of community college, and they think I'm Einstein."

Rose couldn't smile. "I didn't leave that little girl behind. I thought I got her out, but she ran back in."

"I didn't think you'd just leave her there. I can tell. I'm a good judge of character. Also, you keep coming back here, looking so sad, like you're visiting a grave. It said online that that little girl's family wants to sue you. Are they for real?"

"Evidently."

"That's crap." Kurt frowned. "It's not your fault. I told you the wiring was bad, and the gas leaked, too. The general contractor was Campanile. Those are the guys who need to get their ass sued."

Rose made a mental note of the name. "Are they a good contractor?"

"Yes. Campanile is top-drawer, but mistakes happen, even with the best outfits. The electrical contractor messed up, and the building inspector shoulda caught the mistakes. He certified it, so he messed up, too."

"But the inspector would've certified it before the school opened, right?"

"Yes."

"So why did it blow up now, in October? School's been open for a month."

"You ever put a penny in a fuse box? A lotta guys, they do a jury-rigged job, down-and-dirty, to get it done when the client wants in. They tell themselves they'll come back later and do it right, but they don't. Or they forget. Or they get canned. If that's what happened, that's on Campanile, or the building inspector. Not you."

"What a mess." Rose shook her head, thinking down the line. "This is going to be the lawsuit from hell, and that's if they don't bring criminal charges."

"Against you? That's ridiculous. Tell you what." Kurt checked behind him again. "Let me do some asking around, and I'll see what I can find out about how it happened. Off the record."

"Really? Thanks."

"No sweat. When I read that article, I thought of my niece, the one I told you about. Kids are precious, and we gotta take care of 'em, and sometimes, like with Iraq and all, we gotta take care of each other's. You really stepped up for those kids."

"Thanks," Rose said, touched.

"S'all right. Gimme your phone number, for official use only." Kurt slid out his cell phone, Rose did the same, and they added each other's numbers to their contacts.

"Aren't we so modern?" Rose asked, and Kurt grinned.

"Hell, to me, that was phone sex."

Chapter Forty-one

Rose walked around the back of the school, shifted John to her hip, checked her phone for the address of Kristen's parents, then dialed information. She got their home phone and let the call connect, stopping in front of an empty parking space.

"You have reached the Canton residence," said the voicemail, and Rose waited for the beep, disappointed.

"Hello, I'm Rose McKenna, trying to reach Kristen. She taught my daughter at Reesburgh Elementary, and she was going to call us. We hope to hear from her. Please call when you get a sec, thanks." She left her home and cell number, pressed END, and dropped the phone back into her purse.

She checked the time on the phone, and it was 2:25—ten minutes until dismissal. The buses were lined up and idling at the long driveway, and SUVs and minivans were pulling into the parking lot. A group of walkers, who lived close to the school, were assembling at the entrance ramp, standing with babies in their arms or in strollers. They were talking, still abuzz from the morning, but none of them noticed Rose. Suddenly, she spotted a boxy white newsvan stop at the entrance to the parking lot, open the sliding door, and disgorge Tanya and her cameraman behind the cordon.

Rose stalled, hugging John, uncertain. She didn't want Tanya to get an early bead on her, so she stayed where she was, apart. The school's front doors opened, and fifth graders emerged, carrying heavy backpacks looped over one shoulder or banging against their legs. More kids started flowing out, headed for the buses or for parents who had walked or driven.

Rose eyed the kids for Melly's class, but they weren't out yet. She took a few steps forward, but one of the moms spotted her as she approached, then the others noticed, and she caught their collective frowns. One of them was Janine Rayburn, whose son was in Melly's class, and when Rose smiled at her, she turned away.

The kids in Mrs. Nuru's class started to leave the building, then Melly appeared. Her head hung lower than usual, though her back was characteristically straight, with the padded loops of her backpack placed on both shoulders; it was a habit of hers that touched Rose, because it told so much. Melly had to be perfect, controlling what she could because there was so much she couldn't.

"Melly!" Rose waved her free arm, and Melly hurried down the ramp, as the other moms followed her with their eyes, talking behind their hands.

"Hi, Mom, hi Johnnie!" Melly hugged her and John, but when she pulled back, Rose noticed a long reddish bruise on her arm.

"What's this?"

"Oh." Melly put a hand over the bruise. "Just a bump."

"How did you get it?" Rose asked, surprised. Melly wasn't the kind of kid who got a lot of bumps.

"I'm fine, Mom." Melly stood on tiptoe to kiss John, her blue eyes shining. "Hi, baby boy. Love you." John made a pass at her with his fingers, outstretched, and Melly giggled. "He almost got me that time!"

"What happened to your arm?"

"Did Ms. Canton call?"

"Not yet." Rose didn't tell her she'd called Kristen's parents, because she didn't want to get her hopes up. "Answer me, about your arm."

"I got in a fight, that's all."

"A *fight*? How did that happen?"

"I pushed Josh and he pushed me and I fell down."

"You pushed him first?" Rose felt incredulous. It was unprecedented. "Why?"

"Let's go home, Mom."

"Why did you push Josh?" Rose took Melly's hand, and they walked through the noisy parking lot. Kids shouted, minivan doors rolled shut, and hatchbacks came down. Engines started, and buses lurched off with hydraulic squeaks, spewing exhaust. Rose squeezed Melly's hand to provoke her answer. "Mel?"

"Josh said you let Amanda burn up like a French fry. So I pushed him and he pushed me back and I fell down."

"Oh no." Rose felt a stab of guilt. "Mel, you don't have to defend me. I don't care what people say about me."

"Okay."

"I'm sorry it happened."

"It's not your fault. You didn't do it."

"What did Mrs. Nuru say?"

"She didn't see."

"Did you tell her?"

"No." Melly shook her head. "Can we not talk about it anymore?"

"Okay." Rose squeezed her hand, and they reached the car. "Let's go home and get lunch."

"Can we have Kristenburgers?"

"You got it." Rose shifted John to the back of her hip, found her keys in her purse, and chirped the car unlocked.

"I wanted to unlock it, Mom."

"Sorry, honey. I forgot. Give me your stuff." Rose opened the front door for Melly, then took her backpack and lunchbox so she could climb in unencumbered. Melly clambered into the passenger seat, and Rose went to the back, opened the door, tossed the stuff onto the floor, and lowered John into his car seat, buckling him in. An SUV pulled into the space next to her, not leaving her much room to maneuver.

"Ms. McKenna, excuse me," said a woman's voice in the SUV behind her, and Rose turned around. The passenger slid down the window to reveal Tanya Robertson, squinting so hard in the sunlight that her false eyelashes stuck together.

"What are you doing here? You're not allowed on school property."

"It's about my 'More on Moms' feature. It's very popular, and I've already interviewed Eileen—"

"Get off of school property before I call somebody." Rose looked around for a teacher, but no one was close enough to see. "I told you, I'm not giving you any interviews."

"I'm not asking for one, about Amanda, anyway. I'm trying to help you."

"The hell you are." Rose turned away and went to the front door, but Tanya stuck her hand outside the window, with her business card.

"Call me. We need to talk about Thomas Pelal."

Rose stopped, stunned.

"Ms. McKenna? Do yourself a favor. Take my card. If I don't hear from you by five o'clock today, I'm going with my story."

Rose willed herself into action, got inside the car, closed the door, and twisted the ignition key with a shaking hand. She was being called to account, to atone. To explain, when there was no explanation. She had waited for it to catch up with her for years, and now, finally, it had.

"Mom?"

"What?" Rose hit the gas, aimed to the exit behind the other cars, and reached into her purse for her phone. "What, honey?"

"Do you think we should have Muenster cheese on the Kristenburgers or Swiss?"

"I don't know." Rose thumbed her rollerball in a panic.

"Mrs. Canton likes Muenster, and so do I. A kid in my class calls it monster. Monster cheese. I think that's so funny and cute."

"Me, too." Rose swung the car out of the school parking lot onto Allen Road, trying to find Oliver's office number in her phone. Her heart thundered in her chest. All hell was about to break loose.

"Mom, remember, you said the car is a no-phone zone."

"This is important, honey." Rose fed the car gas, thumbing to the phone function. Traffic flowed steadily, and she kept pace. Everybody but Reesburgh Elementary parents avoided Allen Road when school was dismissed. Her thoughts raced ahead. She wished she could reach Leo, but he'd be in court and wouldn't pick up. She could have texted him, but it wasn't the kind of message you left by text.

"You said, no phones, it's a rule. You told me to yell at you if you did it, like being on a diet."

"Well, this is an exception." Rose fed the car gas. The rollerball was stuck for some reason, and she couldn't get it to move to the phone function. Sunlight flooded through the car window, obliterating the small screen.

"Why is it an exception?"

"It's okay, just this once. It's a school zone, so don't worry." Rose finally got to the phone function and scrolled down to the call before last.

"So why does that matter, that it's a school zone?"

"People drive more slowly in a school zone." Rose rolled the rollerball to highlight the phone number, but it got sticky again.

"Mom, watch out!"

Rose slammed on the brake before they almost crashed into a minivan in front of them, its left turn signal blinking. They shuddered to a stop, the ABS stuttering and the tires screeching. The sudden movement tossed them all forward, then back into their seats.

"We almost hit that car!" Melly cried, her eyes agog, and in the backseat, John burst into tears.

Rose exhaled, coming to her senses. She set the phone down on the console and looked over. Melly looked bewildered, her frown deeper than any child's should ever be. Rose prayed she'd never see that look on her daughter's face again, but now she wasn't so sure. "Mel, I'm so sorry. Are you okay?"

"Yes." Melly nodded, still wide-eyed. "Are you?"

"Yes." Rose smiled, touched. She loved Melly so much it hurt. She could have cried out loud at what was going to come, for all of them. She checked John in the rearview, and he was crying full-blast, his tiny features clustered and his pacifier gone. "Aww, Johnnie, I'm sorry, I love you."

"What's the matter, Mom?"

"Nothing." Rose knew that Melly would find out, soon enough.

The minivan in front of them took its left turn, oblivious to the near disaster, and Rose hit the gas. She'd wait to call Oliver until Melly was out of earshot, but she knew there wasn't anything anybody could do. Some crashes could be averted, and some couldn't. This one was head-on, barreling faster than an express train.

Hurtling toward everyone she loved the most.

Chapter Forty-two

Rose closed her bedroom door, having put John down for a nap and left Melly downstairs, reading her new book. The ride home had given her a chance to think, and she had even more questions than before. What interest did Tanya have in Thomas Pelal? Would she even report on it, and could Rose sue her if she did, maybe to stop her? Or should Rose try and call her to talk her out of it?

If I don't hear from you by five o'clock today.

Rose checked the clock on the night table; it was 3:13. She sank onto the bed, pressed CALL, and waited for the call to connect to Oliver.

"Charriere and Lake," the receptionist answered, and Rose identified herself.

"Is Oliver or Tom there?"

"They're both in court, Ms. McKenna. May I take a message?"

"Can we interrupt them, either one? Can we reach them? It's an emergency."

"Are you calling from the police station? Are you under arrest?"

"No. It's almost as bad as that, though."

"Are you in physical danger?"

"No, not at all, sorry." Rose hated being so mysterious, but she didn't want to talk with anyone but a lawyer. "Do they call in? Can you leave them a message, asking them to call me as soon as possible?"

"Yes, certainly. They both just did call in, but if they call again, I'll make sure they get back to you, top priority."

"Thanks, bye." Rose hung up, tense, then pressed L for Leo, and waited for the call to connect. Leo's voicemail came on, and she left him a message. "Something's come up, and it's really important that you call me ASAP. I love you."

Rose thumbed her way to the text function and left him a text message, saying the same thing, then pressed SEND. She hated to think of how hurt he'd be, and what impact it would have on their marriage. The phone rang in her hand, and she jumped. The screen showed Oliver's office number, and she pressed answer. "Yes, hello?"

"Ms. McKenna?" It was the receptionist. "Sorry, I can't reach them or the paralegal. They're both in court, on separate trials. I'll keep trying."

"When's the next break?"

"As I said before, they just called, and I know they're both putting on witnesses this afternoon. I'll keep trying, as I say."

"Okay, thanks. Bye." Rose pressed END, sitting at the edge of the bed, feeling pressure building. She couldn't prevent what was going to happen, and it clarified her greatest fear. It didn't matter what the world thought of her. What really mattered was her family. She'd made mistakes in her life, and the worst part was that everybody she loved was about to pay for the biggest one. How they'd feel, how they'd be impacted. She had to tell Leo before he heard about it on TV.

Haven't you done enough?

Rose sighed, looking around the sunny, peaceful bedroom that they'd worked on together. She'd unpacked the moving boxes while Leo had painted the walls, a soft powder-blue that they'd joked would induce falling asleep, if not making love. They'd agreed on the matching blue rug, and refinished as a team an Irish pine dresser from a Lambertville antiques store. Above it hung a matching mirror and a panel of scribbles that a younger Melly had drawn for their wedding, which Leo had framed; crayoned circles in red, blue, and yellow that represented the three of them, a new family.

If I don't hear from you . . .

Rose tried to hold at bay the sensation that everything in the bedroom was about to explode, flying into smithereens like a picture-perfect cafeteria. Her phone rang again, and she looked down at the screen. LEO, it read. She didn't know how to tell him, but she would find a way.

She pressed ANSWER.

Chapter Forty-three

Rose spent the afternoon dreading the TV news, but going through the motions, making Kristenburgers again, cleaning her countertops, helping Melly take a picture of Flat Stanley with fallen leaves in the backyard, changing and feeding John, and fussing at Melly about being on Club Penguin too long. Leo had said he'd be home around eight o'clock, and she'd prepared him as best as she could without telling him over the phone. It was a conversation they could have only in person.

"Mel?" Rose called into the family room, checking the clock. It was 4:45. She wiped John's face, and he squeezed his eyes closed whenever the paper towel touched his cheek, which made her laugh, on any other day. She realized she wasn't narrating their life either, but that was no surprise. "Mel, I want you to go up and take a bath."

"Now?"

"Yes." Rose didn't want Melly anywhere near the TV at five o'clock. She held John tighter on her hip, opened the base cabinet, and tossed the paper towel in the trash, then left the kitchen, already formulating a plan for the next few days. "And I want to talk to you about something else."

"Okay, I'm signing off." Melly hit a key on the computer keyboard, and Rose went over and stroked her head. There was a window next to the desk, and sunlight poured through the window sheers, bringing out the gold in her long hair and casting a fuzzy square of light on the patterned Karastan, where Princess Google was lying flat, her feathery white legs stretched out like Superdog.

"Let's get you in the bath, and I'll tell you what I'm thinking."

"Okay." Melly rose from the computer, and Princess Google woke up, stretching her front legs, then trotting behind as they headed upstairs with John, who was making bubbles with his spit. "Mom, look, he's doing motorboat again. He loves it."

"He sure does." Rose followed Melly up the stairs, keeping her moving with a gentle hand. "He's talented."

"He's a baby wizard."

"Mel, you know what I was thinking?" They reached the landing, and Rose guided her upstairs, down the hall, and into the bathroom. "I was thinking that maybe we could take a break, like a few days, up to the lake."

"When?"

"Maybe even tomorrow."

Melly looked up, her eyes a surprised blue. "I have school."

"I know, but it's just for a few days." Rose sat down on the edge of the bathtub and held John closer as she leaned over and twisted on the faucet, then ran her fingers through the water to check the temperature. Princess Google settled onto the bathmat, curling like a cinnamon bun. "Wouldn't that be fun? We could take Flat Stanley to the creek and take pictures of him with the minnows. That would be cool."

"Would I miss school?"

"Yes, but just for a few days."

"Who would go?"

"Me, you, and the motorboat." Rose smiled in a way she hoped was reassuring. "Leo has to work. He's on trial. He'll be home tonight, but that's it for the week."

"Would Googie go, too?"

"Of course, the Googs. We can't live without her."

"Why do you want to go to the lake?"

Rose wasn't about to lie to her, at least not much. "There's just so much stuff going on, with what happened with Amanda. I think if we went away for a few days, things would cool down and then we could come back, next week."

Melly stood a little forlornly, her arms at her sides. The only sound was the water rushing into the tub. "Is it my fault? Because I pushed Josh?"

"No, not at all." Rose wished she could say, it's not your fault, it's mine. "It's okay to take a break, even if it's during school, like 'me time.' We could get you an excused absence. You were in the hospital, just two days ago."

Melly blinked. "Did Amanda die?"

"No."

"Do you think she will?"

"I don't know." Rose looked at Melly, eye-level, because she was sitting on the bathtub. "I pray she won't, and I didn't leave her in the fire, no matter what Josh said."

"I know, Mom." Melly wrapped her arms around Rose's neck, mashing John, but he didn't protest. "I love you."

"I love you, too, sweetie." Rose swallowed hard, then released Melly and stood up. "Let's go, okay?"

"Okay." Melly brightened. "Are Gabriella and Mo gonna be there?"

"They sure will, and we'll get to see them again. And we've never been up this time of year, so I bet all the leaves are pretty. There might even be foxes."

"And owls!"

"And raccoons."

"Yay!" Melly kicked off her sneakers, and Rose tested the bath water again.

"Good, then get yourself cleaned up. Call me when you're finished." Rose kissed her on the cheek, left the bathroom, and went downstairs with John, checking her watch. Five minutes to go. She went to the TV in the family room, dug the remote from between the couch cushions, and pressed POWER, then lowered the volume. The TV was large, forty-two inches built into a cherrywood entertainment center, and everything on the screen looked gigantic. A commercial was ending, and the massive face of a handsome male reporter appeared, his smile a canoe.

Rose sat down cross-legged on the rug, cuddled John on her lap, and offered him her index finger, which he brought to his mouth and gnawed on, teething. The TV screen segued from the male anchor to a huge picture of Tanya Robertson, her head larger-than-life and her lipsticked mouth big as a swimming pool. Behind her was a banner in pink that read MORE ON MOMS. Rose felt her heartbeat thunder.

"I'm Tanya Robertson, and I continue my 'More on Moms' report, which tonight examines the role of the parents who volunteer in our schools. You've heard the expression, 'Who guards the guards?' Well, we're wondering, 'Who guards the volunteers?' Many schools rely on parent volunteers, sometimes even in emergencies, as shown in the recent fire at Reesburgh Elementary. The life of Amanda Gigot still hangs by a thread at Reesburgh Hospital, where she remains in Intensive Care."

Rose's mouth went dry as the screen behind Tanya changed to footage of the fire at school, with children running from the building.

Tanya's expression turned to photogenic concern, writ large. "We're asking, how much do you *really* know about the volunteers who serve as lunch moms, softball coaches, library aides, or chaperones on field trips? How much do you *really* know about the moms who take care of your child in a life-threatening emergency, like at Reesburgh?"

Rose watched appalled as the film of the school fire was replaced by her own Facebook photo, from before she'd closed her account.

Tanya continued, "If you watched my first installment of 'More on Moms,' you saw my expanded interview of Eileen Gigot, but today we focus on Rose McKenna, one of the lunch moms the day the fire broke out at Reesburgh Elementary. At first, Ms. McKenna seemed like a hero because she saved her child Melly from the fire. Then little Amanda Gigot was found injured in the same fire. The Gigot family alleges that Ms. McKenna was negligent in her failure to rescue Amanda, and the District Attorney is investigating the matter."

Rose swallowed hard, aghast. The screen morphed to her at eighteen years old, in her mug shot. She was a mess, her dark hair disheveled and her eyes puffy from crying. Her expression was unfocused, her head tilted slightly. She looked drunk in the photo, but she was stone cold sober. She'd just had the worst moment of her life.

"We've discovered that Rose McKenna was arrested when she was eighteen years old and charged with suspicion of driving under the influence, after a fatal auto accident involving a six-year-old boy, Thomas Pelal. The accident occurred outside of Wilmington, North Carolina, and police determined that the little boy ran in front of her car and was killed. Though Ms. McKenna was arrested, the charges were later dropped. Ms. McKenna has declined any comment."

Rose gasped. It was true, but it wasn't the whole story, and the fact that she hadn't commented made it worse, as if she were hiding something.

Tanya said, "Here's what we're asking, at 'More on Moms.' Don't you have a right to know that information about Rose McKenna, if she were volunteering in your child's school? Would you want her taking care of your child? Shouldn't we do background checks on moms who volunteer? How about drug and alcohol testing? Some schools background-check paid aides, but why should we restrict it to paid personnel? Shouldn't anyone who cares for *your* child be proven safe, in addition to being drug- and alcohol-free?"

Rose felt tears in her eyes, watching her photo fade on the screen, replaced by a black question mark. The whole thing was worse than she had imagined. Or maybe it was just seeing the face of that sweet little boy broadcast before her eyes, in high-definition. She didn't need the photo to remember Thomas Pelal. What she had done haunted her, and she thought of him every day.

Tanya paused. "Don't you have a right to know *more* about the parents who take care of your children at school, on the ball field, or at the field trip to the pumpkin patch? What do *you* think? Weigh in at our website. This series has produced a record amount of email and tweets, so give us your opinion. I'm Tanya Robertson, looking out for *you*."

Rose clicked POWER, silencing the TV, but she could still hear the scream of little Thomas Pelal, just before she hit the brakes. It would echo in her brain, and her heart, forever.

Mommy!

Chapter Forty-four

Rose was packing in Melly's room when she heard the front door close, downstairs. Melly was reading in bed, with Princess Google curled up on the pillow beside her. Leo was home, and she steeled herself, glancing at the clock on the night table. It was 7:30, so he'd booked it from the city.

"Leo!" Melly called out, looking up from *Beedle the Bard*. "Leo! We're up here!"

"Shh." Rose folded Melly's pants in two and set them inside the open bag. "Don't wake John."

"Sorry." Melly placed her bookmark into her book, set it aside, and climbed out of bed. She looked small and skinny in the oversized T-shirt, and took off for the stairway. "Be right back."

"Okay, but make it fast." Rose wanted Melly asleep by the time she and Leo started talking, and she hid her worry. She'd been hiding her worry all afternoon. Or maybe since Thomas Pelal.

"Leo, here I am!" Melly whispered, standing at the top of the stairs. Below was the sound of Leo's heavy tread on the hardwood floor of the entrance hall as he walked to the coat closet, took off his suit jacket, and closed the door, then came to the stairs.

"Tater! How's my girl?"

"We're packing."

"Packing?" Leo climbed the stair, chuckling. "Where are you going?"

"The lake house, to see Mo and Gabriella. And raccoons!"

Rose cringed. She hadn't told Leo about the trip yet. She turned as Leo reached the landing and scooped Melly into his arms. Hurt flickered across his face, but it vanished when he let Melly go, replacing it with the suburban blank that parents reserve for their children whenever there's trouble.

"How you doing, tater tot?"

"Good! Did you win your case?"

"Not yet. I came home to say hi to my girls." Leo took Melly's hand, then spotted the bruise on her arm, frowning. "What happened?"

"I don't want to talk about it anymore."

"Okay." Leo came upstairs, and his gaze went to the open suitcase. He avoided Rose's eye, impassive. "Going to the lake house?"

"Yes, I'll explain later." She gave him a quick kiss on the cheek, which smelled of faded aftershave. "Sorry I didn't mention it to you."

"No matter." Leo went to Melly, helping her back into bed, next to the drowsy little spaniel. He picked up the comforter, tucked her in, and sat down next to her. "Mel, didn't you finish your book yet?"

"Almost." Melly showed him her bookmark. "I have ten more pages."

"What? Slacker, get on it. You've had that thing for a whole day."

Melly giggled. "Mom wants me to read American Girl."

"Why should you read American Girl? You *are* an American Girl!"

"I know. I don't want to."

"Then don't. Read whatever you want. It's a free country. I'm a lawyer and I know. Tell Mom, your lawyer said you have First Amendment rights."

"I will!" Melly's eyes lit up when she looked at Leo, and Rose could see how much she loved him. They had actually succeeded in creating a family, despite divorce and death, and Rose couldn't bear to think they could lose it all. She dreaded the conversation to come, but it was time.

"Bedtime, Melly," she said, managing a smile.

"Kiss, Leo." Melly held out her arms, and Leo gave her a hug and a grunt, then got up, brushing down his pants.

"Get some sleep, you. I'll try to come home tomorrow night to see you, but I don't know if I can."

"We won't be here."

"Oh right. Sorry. Then here's another kiss to hold you over. Have fun at the lake. Bye now." Leo gave her another big hug.

"Leo, say good-bye to Googie, too."

"Bye, Googie."

"Kiss her!" Melly giggled, playing their game, because Leo would never kiss the dog.

"No way, I don't kiss dogs, only girls." Leo stroked the spaniel, who barely opened her eyes. "See ya, Googie."

Rose went to Melly's beside, gave her a quick kiss, and patted Googie. "Good night, sweetie. Sleep tight."

"Mom, did Ms. Canton call when I was in the bath?"

"No."

"Can we call her again?"

"I will, tomorrow."

"If she calls tonight, will you wake me up?"

Rose brushed Melly's hair from her forehead. "I doubt she'll do that, but if she does, I'll wake you up. Say your prayers."

"I will. I'll say one for Amanda."

"Me, too. Pleasant dreams."

Chapter Forty-five

Rose followed Leo downstairs, and they both went automatically to the kitchen. She lingered behind the table, while he walked ahead and opened the refrigerator. She didn't know how to start the conversation, suddenly uncomfortable with her own husband, in her own kitchen. The setting sun came through the window, making spiky shadows of the lavender shoots, like a bed of needles.

"You hungry?" she asked.

"No." Leo grabbed a Yuengling beer by the neck, turned around, and pulled out a chair, sitting down heavily. "I had a sandwich when I stopped for gas. Sit, please." He gestured.

"I'm sorry about the lake thing." Rose sank into her chair, behind the watery Diet Coke she'd had before she went upstairs. Her mouth was dry, and she took a sip, then forced herself to look at him directly. He held her gaze for a second, and she could see the hurt, plain in his eyes. "I decided on the spur of the moment."

"Right." Leo's mouth went tight, and he made much of opening the beer bottle, as if he hadn't done it with ease, a hundred times before. "You're not leaving me, are you?"

"No." Rose laughed, a release of nervous tension. "No, of course not."

"Good." Leo leaned back in the chair, regarding her in a remote way. "I got a call from Martin when I was on the way home. His wife saw it on the news and called him. Also Joan called me and told me."

Rose reddened. Joan was his secretary, and Martin was an old friend from Worhawk. "I'm so sorry."

"Joan said we're getting more than a few calls, from clients."

"Oh, no. I'm sorry, really. What will you say to them? Are you worried—"

"I'll deal with them, but what gets me is what's between us. It would have been nice to hear it from you when we met. Or when we got engaged. Or when we got married."

Rose felt vaguely sick. Leo's tone was controlled, and he was too kind to yell, which made it worse. Outside, the peaked tops of the trees bent in the wind, and the sky was turning a lurid pink, an unearthly hue.

"I can think of lots of times, going back, when you could have told me, but you didn't. Even this thing with Amanda, it would have been a good time to mention it."

"I know. I'm so sorry."

"It explained a lot to me, like why you were taking it all so hard, so personally. It explains why you've been feeling so guilty. So why don't you tell me now, the whole story?"

Rose swallowed hard. "Okay, well, to keep it simple—"

"Don't keep it simple. It's not simple, and I have time."

Rose nodded. "It happened on Halloween, and I was eighteen years old. I'd just had a fight with my mom."

"What did you fight about?"

"It was Halloween night, sorry, I said that already, and I was having some friends over, from my job. It was during my year off, after high school, when I was living with her and working, modeling to save money for college. She'd said she'd stopped drinking, and I actually believed her, God knows why. She'd seemed fine for almost a year, doing AA again, so I figured it was okay to have friends over." Rose paused, trying to remember, and trying not to remember, both at once. "We all had costumes, I was Cleopatra, and we were giving candy to the kids who came to the door, trick-or-treating. My mother said hi to us, everything was fine, then she went upstairs."

"Okay."

"Later, she came falling down the stairs, drunk, and, randomly, topless." Rose felt mortified, even at the memory. "She came down the stairs with no bra or anything, only in her panties and high heels, my high heels, oddly, and she hit on one of my guy friends. She actually tried to sit in his lap, with her breasts in his face, and it was, well, you get the idea." Rose shook it off. It wasn't anywhere near the worst part of the story. "Anyway, the party broke up, and I ran out crying. I got into the car, and drove to my old high school. I was in her car, I didn't have a car. I sat in the parking lot, which was empty. I stopped crying, I calmed down, then I left for home. I was upset, but not too upset to drive, and I hadn't been drinking."

"I know that. You don't have to tell me that. You never drink."

"Right." Rose never drank, except for the backsliding the other night in the kitchen. She'd spent her college years partying harder than she should have, then stopped after she'd graduated and started working, full-time. She'd wanted to be a mother, and not *her* mother. Her mother's drinking had driven her father away, when she was only ten. Rose hardly remembered him, and he never came around again, though he always sent checks, to support them.

"So what happened?"

"I was driving home, and most of the little kids were done trick-or-treating. It was like nine o'clock. Only the older kids were left, the hoboes and the basketball players, too cool to dress up. But still, I was going slow, the roads were slick from the rain." Rose could see the scene, in front of her. "Wet leaves were everywhere, so I was careful. She would never want anything to happen to her car, not a scratch. I could see everything. I was paying attention. I didn't even have the radio on. I was driving fine, I was—"

"Okay, you were being careful."

"Right, I was." Rose could see it happening all over again, in her mind, and she could tell him the story in real time, like a horrifying play-by-play. "Something flew out in front of me, a white blur. I heard a noise. I stopped right away, but the car skidded on the wet leaves, and I heard a scream. A child, a scream. It was him." Rose held back tears that came to her eyes. "Thomas Pelal."

"The little boy."

"He was six."

"Where were his parents?"

Rose could hear a change in Leo's voice, and he sounded almost professional. Already he was thinking like a lawyer, constructing a legal argument for her, finding a way to absolve her of responsibility. It had been his first instinct, even as angry as he was at her, and Rose felt so much love for him at that moment that she couldn't meet his eye.

"Babe?"

"His parents were up the street, talking to a neighbor. He was with his sister."

"How old was she?"

"Fourteen. She had gone up on their porch. It happened right in front of their house. He'd dropped a jawbreaker, one of those big ones they used to have." Rose formed a ball with her fingers, for some reason. Maybe because she'd seen the jawbreaker later, when the ambulance and the police came, with their sirens and lights. The jawbreaker made a yellow dot among the wet leaves, like a discarded sun. "It rolled into the street. He was going after it. I didn't see it roll, it was too small. He'd gotten it that night, in his Halloween bag."

"So then what happened?"

"I heard this sound. *Thud.*" Rose knew she wasn't telling the story in order, but it didn't matter. It would end the same way. "And I realized I'd hit a child because he screamed, 'Mommy!'"

Mommy!

"I jumped out of the car and ran around the front, and he was lying there, crumpled, on his side, turned away. He had on his costume, a white pillowcase with holes cut out for the neck and arms." Rose blinked, but the sight, and her tears, wouldn't clear. "God knows why I thought this, but I remember thinking, it was such a sweet, old-fashioned costume. I mean, here I am, in this Cleopatra outfit, all eye-makeup and turquoise polyester, bought at the store. And here he is in his little white pillowcase, a real pillowcase. He'd must've made it himself. He was a ghost."

Leo slid her a napkin across the table, and Rose accepted it, though she hadn't seen him get up to get it.

"So I tried to save him, I knew CPR, from lifeguarding. Blood was coming out of his mouth, but he was awake, alive, and his sister came running, but he was saying something." Rose's eyes brimmed, and she wiped them with the napkin. She didn't want to tell it, but now she had to. Just one time in her life, it had to come out of inside her. "I bent over, and got a hand under him, but the blood was bubbling, and he said something."

"Rose, it's okay." Leo's voice was back to normal, his eyes filled with concern. He stood up to come around the table to comfort her, but she held up a hand because if he hugged her, she might stop.

"His eyes opened, and they were blue, and he looked right at me, and said, 'Mommy.'" Rose wiped her eyes, the tears coming freely, her nose all clogged. "I was thinking, later, maybe it was because of the Cleopatra makeup, I looked older. In the dark, the way he was, he could have thought I was his mother, or maybe he wished I was. And, I know, it sounds awful, but, I answered him."

Leo blinked. "You did?"

"I still can't believe I did it, I don't even know why. I guess I wanted to comfort him, so he could feel like his mother was with him. It wasn't my place, but I did it."

"What did you say?"

"I answered as if I were his mother. I answered, as her. I said, 'I'm here, and I love you. Your mommy loves you, very, very much.'" Rose burst into tears. "And then, he died. Right there. Right then."

Leo came and put his arms around her, sitting down. "It's okay now, babe. It's all right."

"No, it's not. I killed that child."

"It wasn't your fault." Leo held her tight, his embrace warm and certain. "Accidents happen. Kids run out in front of cars. They do that."

"The mom and dad came running, they were hysterical. His mother screamed for him, 'Thomas!' It was an awful sound. Primal. I'll never forget it. I can hear it now." Rose kept shaking her head. "My mother was sure they'd sue, so she got a lawyer, and he told me never to call them, never to speak to them, so I didn't. I wanted to, I wanted to say I was sorry, as if that would help, but I didn't."

"Babe, relax. Drink something." Leo slid her watery soda to her, but she ignored it. Her tears slowed and she blew her nose, messily.

"I must look awful."

"You don't have to look pretty when you cry. I'm not that guy, so don't be that girl."

Rose nodded, blowing her nose with gusto. She balled up the napkin and set it aside, then drained her soda.

"Want another?"

"No, thanks." Rose heaved a deep sigh, and Leo released her.

"So why did you get arrested? Joan said there was a mug shot on TV."

Rose cringed. "They found vodka bottles in the car, three of them, empty. They were my mother's. I didn't even know they were there. When I braked, they came rolling out from under the front seat, so the cops thought I'd been drinking. They gave me a field sobriety test, and I passed, but they still booked me, on suspicion." Rose stiffened, remembering the fight the next day, with her mother. "And the Pelals never sued us. I kept waiting, expecting it, but they never did. I never heard anything from them, and I didn't contact them, either. I would have, but the lawyers said no, then we moved again. Away, up north."

"So that was that." Leo's mouth made a grim line.

"No, hardly. Sometimes I wished they had sued, and I'd been punished in some way. Then I would have felt like I paid for it, and told what happened, and how sorry I am, every day." Rose felt too upset to articulate her thoughts. "And now this thing, with Amanda, it feels like it's all coming back, full circle."

"It isn't. Don't be silly. It's not karmic."

"How do you know?" Rose looked over, sniffling. "I swear, for a long time, I thought that Melly's birthmark was payback. That my child was being punished for something I did to another woman's child. That Melly was marked, because I was marked. It's the stain of sin, my original sin."

"Stop, no." Leo put a hand up. "That's crazy."

"Not to me. Not in my heart."

"Honey, please." Leo frowned. "You can't carry that kind of crap around, all by yourself. That's what bothers me, that this came out the way it did. Why didn't you just tell me?"

"I didn't want to in the beginning, when we first met, and then we were so happy, right away, I didn't want to ruin it." Rose shook her head. "I never told anybody, if it makes you feel better."

"What about Bernardo?"

"No. No one, not even Annie. It seems wrong now, I know, but I kept it to myself, ever since."

"Not wrong. Distrustful." Leo looked pained, his forehead buckling unhappily under his dark curls. "It's like you don't trust me. You don't trust our relationship."

"Yes, I do."

"No, you don't. You didn't tell me, so you don't. Meanwhile, it's too big a secret to keep to yourself. Did you ever even have therapy about it?"

"A little, but it didn't help." Rose turned to him, finding her emotional footing. "Therapy or no, the fact never changes. I killed that child. I did that. It's a fact. I have to live with that, and I'm the lucky one. Thomas Pelal doesn't get to live, at all." Rose felt terrible, but honest, saying it out loud. "That's why they reported it on the news, and that's why they're right."

"Please." Leo pushed her empty glass aside, maybe just to push something. "They reported it for ratings. Don't buy in."

Suddenly Rose's phone rang, sitting on the table, and the screen lit up, Kurt Rehgard. She was so immersed in the conversation that at first she didn't recognize the name. "I'll get it later."

"Who's that?" Leo asked, glancing at the screen. "A reporter?"

"No, a carpenter, at the school."

"What? What's he want?"

"He said he'd do some asking around for me."

"What do you mean?"

"I was at the school, and I was talking to him about what caused the fire and he said he'd do some looking around and get back to me if he found anything out."

Leo frowned. "Why did you do that? And when?"

"It's nothing, Leo. I had time to kill before I picked Melly up today, so I went over to the cafeteria." Rose blinked. She was thinking about Thomas Pelal. "Look, it doesn't matter."

"It does to me. What's going on? Can you fill me in on my own life, for just a sec?"

Rose set down the soggy napkin. "I didn't even get to tell you about the meeting with Oliver and his partner. They told me that what actually caused the fire was going to be relevant to me, since they want us to sue the school."

"So why are you poking around?"

"Because I want to know."

Leo's lips parted. "Oliver has a firm investigator."

"I know, but I was curious."

"Curious?" Leo opened his hands, his dark eyes flashing. "You shouldn't do that, if you're going to be the subject of a lawsuit, or if we are. You should stay as far away from the scene as you can, and you shouldn't say anything to anybody about the fire or that day."

"All I did was chat with him."

"I know, but whatever you've been saying to this carpenter is discoverable. Admissible in court." Leo got up, shaking his head. "Rose, you're taking on everything, all on your own. You decide to go to that wake, no matter what I think. You chat up carpenters on your own. We're supposed to be partners, you and me. You're acting like a single mom, but you're not, anymore."

"No, I'm not," Rose said, surprised.

"What else don't I know? What else didn't you tell me?" Leo started to pace, then stopped, hands on hips. "I have to hear from my secretary that my own wife has a mug shot? I have to hear from Melly that you're going to the lake house? Now I learn that some carpenter is giving opinions on legal causation in a putative lawsuit against us? Great!"

"It's not like that," Rose said, but it wouldn't help to get into it.

"Can't you talk to me about what you're doing? Can't we make at least *some* of these decisions together? You're not thinking as a family."

"Yes, I am."

"How?"

"Well, for example, going up to the lake house. I thought, with all this terrible stuff coming out, that it would be harder on everyone if we stuck around, especially Melly. You saw that bruise. She got into a fight at school, defending me."

"Okay, that's my point."

"What is?" Rose thought the bruise would prove her point, not his.

"If she got into a fight, then we'll deal with that. We have to. Like you said, we have to make a home here." Leo gestured around the kitchen. "We moved here because you wanted to, and the bullying started all over again. We can't just take off, or you can't. Running away doesn't fix anything."

"Leo, you agreed to the move." Rose raised her voice, then lowered it quickly, glancing at the stairwell. "And I'm not running away, I'm taking a break."

"From me?"

"No, from everything here."

"But *I'm* here."

"No, you're not. You're on trial."

"This again." Leo raked a hand through his hair. "I wish you had told me, is all. I wish I'd known. I'm blindsided." He stopped pacing, with a resigned sigh. "You know what, I take it back. Go to the lake house. Take a few days, take a week. The time apart will do us good."

Rose didn't understand what was happening. It was one thing to go, and another to be sent. The situation was getting away from her. "Leo, it's not about you."

"I know." Leo leaned on the back of the chair and looked at her, dead even. "That's what I'm saying. It's about you and the kids. Your decisions, your reactions, your past, your *guilt,* and I'm on the perimeter. You cut me out, and it has nothing to do with my trial."

"Yes, it does. Everything's been happening so fast, I haven't seen you to catch you up."

"Babe, let me ask you this. If I had no trial, would you have asked me to go to the lake house? Did you even think of me?"

Rose hesitated. She didn't know what to say.

"Be completely honest. Trust me enough to tell the truth, for once."

Ouch. "That's not fair," Rose said, stung.

"Then tell me." Leo folded his arms. "Yes or no?"

"No."

"Thank you," Leo said, with a snort. "Thank you, at least, for that."

Chapter Forty-six

Rose stood in the backyard, letting the dog out before bed. It was dark, and the nighttime breeze felt cool, with a chilly hint of the autumn to come. The sky looked black and starless, but the lights from inside the house cast squares of brightness around the yard. Googie made a white spot near the back fence, her head down, her nose buried in the fallen leaves. Rose had gotten a return call from Oliver, and he'd said there was nothing they could've done to prevent the broadcast, anyway. He'd asked her again about the press release, but she still wanted to talk to Leo about it and told him so.

Rose felt raw and lost, after Leo had gone back to the city. She'd feared that his knowing about Thomas Pelal would end them, and she wondered if this was the beginning of the end. Leo had too good a heart to let Thomas Pelal be the reason for any split; he'd chalk it up later to her distrust, her childhood, their growing apart or whatever; but she wondered if this was the moment when his view of her changed, and years from now, whether she'd think back to tonight and say to herself, this was where our end began.

Rose sighed. The air carried the canned laughter of a sitcom from someone's TV, the mechanical rumble of a garage door rolling down, and an SUV being chirped locked. A couple was arguing somewhere, their shouts echoing, and Princess Google raised her head, sniffing the air, the tips of her ears blown back. Rose's phone started ringing in her pocket, and she pulled it out, hoping it was Leo. The glowing screen read Kurt Rehgard. She'd forgotten that he'd called earlier, after all that had happened. She pressed ANSWER. "Hello, Kurt?"

"Rosie, why didn't you call me back?" Kurt slurred his words slightly. "I gave you good info."

"Are you drunk, Kurt?" Rose asked, annoyed. Maybe she shouldn't have given him her number.

"Nah, come on, tell Matlock you have to get away. You can meet my new buddies."

"Sorry, I have to go." Rose pressed END. The phone rang again almost as soon as she hung up, but she saw it was Kurt and let it go to voicemail. She was about to slip the phone back into her pocket when she remembered he'd said something about good info. She pressed VOICEMAIL for her messages, then listened:

"Rose, I got some inside info on the fire." Kurt's words sounded clear and distinct in the call, earlier. "This will come out, sooner or later, but a buddy of mine heard one of the fire marshals talking, and they think the fire started when the loose wire in the wall sparked with gas and fumes from some polyurethane cans, that some slob left in the teachers' lounge, from shellacking the cabinets. So, if you ask me, it's the general contractor's fault, Campanile. They're ultimately responsible for clean-up. Call me and I'll explain. Take care."

Rose pressed END, slipped the phone back into her pocket, and put the fire out of her mind. The rift with Leo and the news about Thomas Pelal had put everything in perspective. She had to take care of her family, keep praying for Amanda, and let the lawyers and their investigator take care of the litigation and criminal charges. She'd call Oliver in the morning, tell him what Kurt had said, and let it be his problem. She'd use the time at the lake to get herself centered and wrestle with the question of what to tell Melly about Thomas Pelal.

"Googie, come!" Rose called, and the little spaniel looked up, her bugged-out eyes making blood-red spots in the dark. They'd be leaving first thing in the morning, and she wanted to straighten up the kitchen before she went to bed, so she went into bribe mode.

"Googie, treat!" she said, and the dog came trotting. Rose shooed her inside the kitchen and gave her a biscuit, then got to work, straightening the clutter of papers on the counter. She spent a half hour reading the unopened mail, taking the bills out and stacking them for payment, then setting aside the stack of school notices: a flyer for a Pumpkin Carving Contest, a permission slip that had to be returned for a field trip to go apple-picking, and a reminder about the school's Halloween Parade. She flashed on Thomas Pelal in his ghost costume, then skimmed the notice:

Parents, Please remember not to park in the faculty lot the morning of the Halloween Parade! In case of emergency, we need that to keep those extras spaces open . . .

Rose thought of the fire, the ambulance, then Amanda. She gathered up the papers, stacked them, and at the bottom found the school newsletter for September, which they'd given out on opening day. She remembered that day, when Reesburgh Elementary was brand-new and she'd had such great hopes for moving here. She hadn't known Leo felt differently. She looked at the flyer, with its proud banner headline REESBURGH READER. Under **Meet the Office Staff,** the front page showed Mr. Rodriguez, the guidance counselor, and the secretaries standing in front of the counter. She scanned the smiling faces, knowing she could never sue them, ever.

She turned the page, and a subhead read **Meet the Teachers and Staff,** with photos of the gym, music, and art teachers, then the head janitor and his staff, and the two cafeteria ladies, Serena and Ellen. Rose felt a pang, seeing their smiles. It was awful to think they'd been killed because somebody had been careless. She turned to the next page, to **Meet the Library Staff,** and a photo of the librarian and her aide, grinning in the neat stacks. Rose would never forget the kindness of the librarian who had helped her get Melly to the ambulance.

There were two photos under the headline, **Meet the Special Services and Gifted Teachers.** The one on the left showed three special services teachers, who helped kids with ADHD, ADD, and the like, and the photo on the right showed Kristen Canton, who looked pretty and carefree. Rose felt a nub of resentment that Kristen still hadn't called Melly and made a mental note to try tomorrow. Then she looked at the photos again. Both showed the various teachers standing in the teachers' lounge, in front of the counter. The room was small, and the pictures were taken from the door, showing the entire lounge. On the left was a galley kitchen, with a toaster, microwave, and coffeemaker, and next to that was an oven and a tall refrigerator. The room contained six round lunch tables, and there weren't any cans of polyurethane around, or any construction debris. The lounge looked perfectly clean and ready for use, and the cabinets looked shellacked. She turned the newsletter over to double-check the date, and it was dated the first day of school. The picture had to have been taken before school opened, to make it into the newsletter.

Rose thought back to when she had visited the school, the night after the fire. Kurt had taken her around, and it felt like so long ago. She'd been thinking of Amanda then, especially when she'd found the charred videogame. But she'd seen the cafeteria, the kitchen, and clear through to the teachers' lounge. The wall that had blown up had been between the kitchen and the teachers' lounge. That was where the gas leak and faulty wiring must have been. She didn't know what it meant, or if it meant anything, and anyway, it wasn't her problem anymore. She added it to the list of things to tell Oliver, put the newsletter into the pile, and deemed the kitchen cleaned.

"Bedtime, Googie." Rose shooed the dog to the stairwell, then checked the clock on the stove. 10:55, almost time for the eleven o'clock news. She was curious if they'd run the story about Thomas Pelal again, so she went into the family room, picked up the remote, and clicked on the TV, keeping the volume on mute. She didn't need to hear her past played out again, or risk waking the kids up.

Commercials came on for Boniva and Chevy trucks, then the male news anchor popped onto the screen, with a banner behind him that read WAREHOUSE FIRE. If they were going to rerun the feature, it would probably be at the end of the half hour, so Rose sat down on the couch, and the dog jumped up beside her, nudging onto her lap. The next story was of a gas-station shooting, and then an old bridge collapsed outside of Camden; Rose knew because of the banner, and she considered watching the news with the sound off all the time, because none of the stories had any emotional impact. She petted the dog's soft head, which felt like a baseball with fur.

The banner changed again, this time to BREAKING NEWS, and Rose felt impatient, since she had learned long ago that breaking news was neither breaking nor news. She watched as the screen went live to an aerial shot of a highway at night, with the shoulder surrounded by police cruisers, their red lights flashing. There must have been a traffic accident, and she thought instantly of Leo, driving back to the city. She reached for the remote and clicked the sound on.

The anchorman was saying, ". . . called to the scene of a fatal accident on Route 76, heading eastbound."

Rose frowned. Route 76 was the expressway, back to Philly.

"The two passengers in the car were pronounced dead at the scene. They have been identified as Hank Powell, twenty-seven, and Kurt Rehgard, thirty-one, both of Phoenixville."

What? Rose wasn't sure she'd heard correctly. It couldn't be possible. It must have been a different Kurt Rehgard. Her Kurt Rehgard had just called her. She had just listened to his message. She hit PAUSE and ran the TV broadcast back until the highway shots reappeared on the screen, then hit PLAY.

". . . identified as Hank Powell, twenty-seven, and Kurt Rehgard, thirty-one . . ."

Rose watched the rest of the report unfold, stunned. It had to be the same Kurt Rehgard. It was such an uncommon name, and he'd sounded a little buzzed. He'd been out partying with friends.

You can meet my new buddies.

She pulled out her phone, thumbed the rollerball until she got to the phone function, and checked the time of his call. 10:06 P.M. Then she checked the current time. 11:12 P.M. She realized what must have happened. Kurt had left the bar, buzzed, after he'd called her, and driven home with his friend. And now they were dead.

The news went on and on, then the commercials, but Rose didn't hear or see anything on the screen. There had been too much death lately, too much destruction.

It was a long time before she felt strong enough to stand.

Chapter Forty-seven

It was a sunny morning, and Rose hit the BREW button on the Keurig, already on her second cup of coffee. She'd hardly slept last night, thinking of Kurt, Thomas Pelal, and Amanda. Leo hadn't called, and she hadn't called to tell him about Kurt's death because she knew he was busy and it seemed random, after their fight. Melly was asleep upstairs, and John sat contentedly in his high chair, chasing dry Cheerios around his tray with wet fingers.

She went to her laptop and logged onto the newspaper, wondering when she'd gone from being a mom who had an interest in the news, to one who could follow her life in the headlines. She skimmed the home page and breathed a relieved sigh that there was no mention of Amanda, so the child must still be alive.

Thank you, God.

She glanced down the screen, found a link titled *Alcohol a Factor in Expressway Collision,* and clicked, scanning the five lines:

> Two Phoenixville men, identified as Kurt Rehgard, 31, and Hank Powell, 27, both of Bethany Run Construction, were killed in a drunk-driving accident last night. . . .

She read the story but there was no further news, a photo of the men, or listing of survivors, which left her with the same empty feeling she'd had all night. She clicked to the Local News page, where her own photo ran beside one of Thomas Pelal. The sight stunned her: the two of them, side-by-side, joined together forever, villain and victim, life and death, present and past, juxtaposed.

Mommy!

Rose sank into the chair and read the story, REVELATIONS AFTER REESBURGH FIRE. The article said she had "caused the death of a six-year-old boy, when she struck him with her car," ending with a disclaimer that the charges had been withdrawn and she had been "convicted of no wrongdoing." The last paragraph was a quote by Oliver, who had been interviewed on the phone last night:

> "It must be noted that my client, Rose McKenna, was convicted of no wrongdoing in connection with the accident that killed Thomas Pelal. In addition, Ms. McKenna is a hero who was injured trying to save her daughter and three other children, including Amanda Gigot, from the school fire. Rose and her husband are currently contemplating litigation against the state, the school district, the school, and its contractors for negligent fire evacuation procedures and for faulty construction."

What? Rose's mouth dropped open. She'd told Oliver that she wanted to talk to Leo before she'd let him say that she was contemplating suing the school. She couldn't imagine how hurt and betrayed Mr. Rodriguez, Mrs. Nuru, and the rest of the faculty would feel, when they heard. She reached for her phone, pressed in Oliver's number, introduced herself, and asked for him.

The receptionist answered, "Oliver's in court today, Ms. McKenna. Same trial as yesterday."

"How about Tom?"

"Same thing, but they'll both call in."

"Please ask either one of them to call me on my cell as soon as possible."

"Certainly."

"Thanks," Rose said, pressing END. She checked on John, who was gumming a Cheerio. She glanced at the clock; 8:10. Time to call the school and let them know Melly would be absent. Rose pressed in the office number, hoping they hadn't read the papers yet.

"Office," a woman answered, and Rose recognized her voice.

"Jill, how are you? It's Rose McKenna, Melly Cadiz's mother."

"How can I help you?" The voice went stone cold, and Rose's heart sank.

"I just wanted to let you know that Melly won't be in today. I want to take her away—"

"That's fine. Thanks."

"I was hoping it could be counted as excused. Mr. Rodriguez said that if—"

"Not a problem."

"I'm not sure how long I'll be, maybe until the end of the week."

"Fine. If there's nothing else, I have to go." The line went dead, and Rose hung up. The secretaries and the rest of the office had heard she was suing. Her family had gone from outsiders to pariahs. Suddenly the house phone rang, and Rose checked Caller ID. Kristen Canton, it read, and she picked up.

"Kristen, how are you?" Rose asked, grateful that she'd called. "Melly's been asking about you."

"Sorry to call so early, but I didn't want to let another day go by without talking to her. I thought I could reach her before she left for school."

"That's okay, she's not going today." Rose's affection for the teacher returned at the sound of her voice. "We're taking a few days at the lake until things simmer down. How are you doing? Better, I hope."

"Finding my footing. Thanks." Kristen paused. "Sorry I was rude the night I left. I was upset."

"Me, too. I'm sorry I was so tough on you, and that I've been calling your house so much. Were your parents annoyed?"

"No, they're fine with it."

"Are they upset that you quit?"

"No, they get that, too, considering. They're really supportive. I'm gonna take some time for myself, just kick back and let my mom pamper me."

"I'm sure she loves that." Rose smiled. "Let me get Melly. I hear her padding around upstairs. Can you hold on a sec?"

"Sure."

"Great." Rose went to the base of the stairwell. "Melly, it's Ms. Canton on the phone, for you!"

"Yay!" Melly's bare feet pounded on the floor in the upstairs hallway, then she hurried down the stairwell in Leo's T-shirt, sliding her hand down the banister. Princess Google scampered behind her, feathery tail wagging.

"Exciting, huh?"

"Yes!"

Rose went back to the wall phone and hit the SPEAKER button, like they did when Leo called. "I'll put you on speaker, Kristen, and let you two yap away."

"Great. Melly?"

"Ms. Canton!" Melly climbed into her chair, while Rose crossed to the back door, opened it, and let the dog out into the backyard. Then she went to the cabinet, took the box of cereal off the shelf, grabbed a bowl and spoon, and set it all down in front of Melly. She wanted to get an early start on the drive to the lake, which took three hours.

"How are you, Melly?" Kristen asked, her voice sounding warm, despite the mechanical timbre of the speakerphone.

"Good! Is your mom still sick?"

Rose cringed, having forgotten that they'd lied to Melly about why Kristen had left.

Kristen answered, "She's doing better, thanks for asking."

"So are you coming back to school now?"

"No, I have to stay at home. I don't think I'll be back again, Melly. I'm sorry, but I can't help it." Kristen's voice went heavy with regret, and Melly looked disappointed, her lower lip buckling.

"It's okay," she said anyway.

"You know, Melly, I don't have to be your teacher for us to stay in touch. We can email, and I'll call you, and you can call me, too. I'll give my cell phone number and my new email address to your mom before we hang up, okay?"

"Okay. But I don't have email."

"You can use your mom's."

Rose didn't interrupt to say that she didn't have email, either. She went to the refrigerator, picked out the milk, and set it on the table.

"Melly, tell me how you are. How's school?"

"Good."

"Everything going okay?"

"Yep."

Rose noted that Melly didn't mention the fight with Josh.

Kristen said, "I hear you're going up to the lake. It sounds like fun."

"My grandparents live there, not my real ones, you know, and there's raccoons and foxes. I got *The Tales of Beedle the Bard*. I love it!"

"I knew you would. What's your favorite story?"

Rose hadn't realized the recommendation had come from Kristen.

Melly answered, "I like 'The Babbitty Rabbitty and Her Cackling Stump.'"

"That's a good one. My favorite is 'The Warlock's Hairy Heart.'"

"I love that, too!" Melly said, quick to agree. "I like the part where . . ."

Rose zoned out on the Harry Potter details and emptied the dishwasher, cleaned up John's tray, wiped his face and fingers, let the dog in and fed her, turned off the coffeemaker, and nudged Melly to start and finish her cereal during a conversation about wizards, healers, magical fountains, giants, witches, sorcerers, kings, and charlatans, all of which left Rose to conclude that the most magical beings in the universe were teachers.

Kristen was saying, "Melly, I'd better go, and I know you've gotta get to the lake. Rose, are you there? I'll give you my cell and email."

"Right here." Rose picked up her phone, but the battery icon had turned red and it needed charging. "Hold on," she said, moving John to her other hip and finding a scrap of paper and a pen. "Go ahead."

Kristen rattled off her number and email, then said, "Well, goodbye, both of you. I'll talk to you again, and you guys stay in touch."

"We will," Rose said, buoyed. "Thanks again. Stay well."

Kristen added, "Melly, have fun at the lake."

"I will, I'm taking my Hermione wand!"

"Good. See you!"

Rose hung up the phone, then crossed to Melly and gave her a hug. "You know what I was thinking? Maybe for our next family vacation, we can go to the Harry Potter theme park in Florida. Would you like that?"

Melly's eyes lit up. "Is that a real thing? One of my friends in Club Penguin said they have that, but I didn't think it was real."

"Sure it is." Rose gave her an extra squeeze.

"Yay! We can show Johnnie." Melly boosted herself up in her chair and grinned at John, who leaned over and reached for her.

"Then let's go to the lake!" Rose felt her spirits lift, but three hours later, everybody's good mood had evaporated.

Chapter Forty-eight

Rose was in the driver's seat with Melly in the backseat, unhappy. John was gurgling in his car seat, transfixed by his amazing plastic keys, and Princess Google was curled up next to him. They were an hour from the lake house, stuck on the Pennsylvania Turnpike in rush-hour traffic when Melly announced that she wanted to call Kristen back. But Rose had left her cell number on the scrap of paper at home.

"Why didn't you bring it with you?" Melly asked, frowning.

"I forgot, and it's not in my phone because she called us on the house phone. Why do you want to call her back anyway?"

"I want to tell her about the Kristenburgers and a drawing I made for her."

"We can tell her later, or email her."

"Do you have her email?" Melly asked, with hope.

"No. It's on the paper at home, too." Rose couldn't remember the email, which was an incomprehensible combination of letters and numbers, more password than email address. "We can write her when we get back."

"Can't we turn around?"

"No, honey. It's too far." Rose gestured at the traffic, red lights in a line like an airport runway, heat broiling from their hoods in wiggly waves. The clouds had cleared for another unseasonably hot day.

"I really want to talk to her, Mom. She loves Kristenburgers. I told her I would make them."

"We can tell her another time."

"And the picture I made for her, it was of Albus Dumbledore, and she loves him. I never got to give it to her."

"We can send it to her when we go home."

Melly looked out the window, quieting.

Rose felt a pang. She knew it wasn't really about the drawing or the Kristenburgers. Melly was having a hard time saying good-bye to Kristen. "You okay, sweetie?"

"Fine."

"Wait, I have an idea." Rose reached into her purse and extracted her cell phone. "I don't need her cell phone. I have her parents' number and I can call her at the house."

"Good!" Melly looked over, smiling. "But not while we're driving."

"We're stopped now." Rose double-checked. They were not only stopped, they were practically parked. She thumbed to her phone log, got the Cantons' home number, pressed CALL, and let it ring. The call was picked up almost immediately by an older woman, probably Kristen's mother. Rose said, "Hello, Mrs. Canton?"

"No, I'm sorry, who's this?"

"Rose McKenna, the mother of one of Kristen's students. We spoke with her this morning, and I wanted to tell her one more thing. Is she in?"

"Oh, you must be the woman leaving those messages."

"Yes, sorry, that's me. Thanks for giving them to her."

"I didn't. Is she the daughter?"

Rose didn't understand. She felt like they were having a conversation of non sequiturs. "Do you know where Kristen is?"

"No, I never met her or the Cantons. I'm the housesitter. I was sent by the agency. They do the interviewing."

"Is this her parents' home, the Canton residence?" Rose asked, confused. The address she'd written down the other day at school popped into her mind. "Roberts Lane, Boonsboro, Maryland?"

"Yes, this is the Canton residence, but the professor and his wife, Mr. and Mrs. Canton, are on sabbatical in Japan. I don't know the family."

"But isn't Kristen living there?"

"No. Nobody lives here this year, but me and two cats."

Rose felt mystified. Kristen had said she was home with her parents. "Do you have any address or number for Kristen?"

"No. You're the second person who called for her today, though. Now, if you'll excuse me, I'm in the middle of something."

"Sure, thank you." Rose pressed END, and Melly looked over, frowning.

"What's the matter? Did she go out?"

Rose didn't understand, and she didn't want to tell Melly that Kristen had lied. "The woman said she wasn't there."

"Maybe she went to her other house."

"What other house?"

"Her house in Lava Land."

"What's Lava Land?" Rose looked over, confounded. "Is Lava Land a real place? Is this a Harry Potter thing?"

"No, Mom." Melly giggled. "It's real, it's near a beach."

"Ms. Canton has a house at the beach? Where?"

"I don't know."

Rose gave up. It didn't matter where. "How do you know about her beach house?"

"She told me. She loves the beach. We talk about it. I like the lake, and she likes the beach. She says I'm a lake person, and she's a beach person."

The traffic loosened, and Rose fed the car some gas, then braked, checking John in the rearview mirror. His pacifier had dropped out, and he was gnawing on his keys, but he looked happy.

"Ms. Canton said we could come visit her in Lava Land, in the summer."

"Really." Rose kept her foot on the brake. The traffic had stopped again. There must be an accident somewhere; lately, there was always an accident somewhere. Something had gone wrong with the world, and now Kristen was behaving strangely.

"So how can we talk to her?" Melly asked.

"I don't know if we can. Let me think a sec." Rose tried to process what was going on. She hadn't realized how close Melly had gotten to Kristen. "You miss Ms. Canton, don't you?"

Melly turned her head away, to the window. "I'm fine."

"It's okay to miss people."

"You told me that, about Daddy."

"Right." Rose flinched. Melly could be so direct, sometimes it came out of left field. "Someone doesn't have to die for you to miss them. It's a loss for you, just the same. You don't get to see that person, or hear their voice." She was thinking of her father, whom she barely remembered, except for his voice. Low, deep, and gentle. "When you lose someone, it's a sad thing, and it helps to talk about it."

Melly remained silent, and Rose drove forward.

"Mel, what do you like about Ms. Canton? What will you miss?"

"Everything. We like to talk in class, and at lunch."

"Lunch?"

"Yes, like when she saw me in the handicapped bathroom. She would tell me to come eat and talk, with her."

"Over Kristenburgers, like on Fridays?"

"Yes." Melly nodded, still facing away. "She doesn't have anyone to eat with then, and she's left out."

Rose seized the proverbial teaching moment. "You don't have to be a kid to be left out, huh?"

"No." Melly looked over, breaking into a rueful smile.

"You don't have to talk funny or have special needs or wear glasses. Anybody can get left out for any reason, anytime. Or even for no reason."

"Or a *dumb* reason. Like Ryan. Josh won't play with him and calls him Rye Bread because of his name. How dumb is that?"

"Dumb. Ryan can't help his name, and he can't change it."

"I know, right?" Melly rolled her eyes. "He teases you if you have diabetes, like Sarah. She has to wear a pump, she showed us. And he teases Max because he can't eat peanut butter. He has an EpiPen all the time."

"See what I mean? That's just dumb. We can't control what people do or say, even if it's dumb." Rose hit the gas as the traffic started to move. They'd had some of their best talks in cars, and she knew other moms felt the same way. All across the country, kids were captive when that door locked, and cars became family therapy on wheels.

"That's what Ms. Canton says. I made a picture for her. Wanna see? It's in my backpack."

"Sure."

"Wait." Melly got her backpack from the foot well, extracted her binder, and slid out a drawing on a piece of yellow construction paper. "Look. It's me, Albus Dumbledore, and Ms. Canton."

"Wow," Rose said, looking over. Melly had crayoned two smiling girls, one big and one little, and they were holding hands with a figure in a peaked hat. "That's a great drawing."

"Thanks. I made it for Ms. Canton, but I didn't get to give it to her. The fire happened, and I didn't see her."

"Oh, right, you see her in the afternoons, so you didn't see her that day."

"Also she was sick. Mrs. Nuru said she wasn't going to be in, and we'd have a substitute."

"Oh." Rose had known that Kristen was sick the day of the fire, but she hadn't focused on it before. Now she put two and two together. Marylou Battle, the substitute teacher who was killed, must have been called in to substitute for Kristen.

"I'm worried I made Albus's beard too long. It isn't that long in the books."

Rose's mind went elsewhere. "Melly, let me ask you something. When you and Ms. Canton eat the Kristenburgers, is it in the teachers' lounge?"

"Yes."

"It's just you and she, because it's on Friday and she's on a different schedule from the other teachers?"

"Yes."

Rose thought a minute. The substitute teacher had been killed in the teachers' lounge, and the cans of polyurethane had been there, too. If Kristen had been at school that day, she would have been killed in the lounge. And if Melly had been with her, they both would have been killed. Rose's fingers tightened around the steering wheel.

"Do you think his beard is right, Mom?"

"Perfect," Rose answered, but she felt unsettled, uneasy. Kristen had lied about where she was and had left Reesburgh in a hurry, claiming she was upset about the fire and the reporters. But maybe that wasn't the real reason.

"She'll love this picture." Melly placed the drawing back in her binder and slid it into her backpack. "We can mail it to her."

"Sure we can," Rose said, preoccupied. The scenario was fishy, and a series of strange what-ifs popped into her mind. What if Kristen had known the explosion was going to happen? What if she'd made sure she wasn't in school that day? What if she'd been involved somehow, and she'd quit and run away, to avoid being caught?

"Are we almost there?"

"Almost." Rose returned to her thoughts, confused. It made no sense. A devoted teacher wouldn't blow up a school full of children. But then again, Kristen would have known that the kids would be outside the building, at recess, at the time.

"How long will it be?"

"About an hour." Rose would have thought it was crazy, except for the fact that Kristen had lied. Why would Kristen lie about where she was? And if she'd lied about that, what else had she lied about?

Rose had an odd sensation that something was wrong. She couldn't stop the questions from coming, and she couldn't deny that there was one person who would know the answers.

Kristen.

Chapter Forty-nine

Rose pulled into the driveway next to their cabin, a charming, three-bedroom Cape Cod with cedar shakes, which was nestled next to the Vaughns' in the middle of an autumnal woods. Leo had bought the place as a getaway, and when they'd married, he'd called it his dowry. The memory made Rose smile, but she put it out of her mind. She didn't want to think about Leo now.

She cut the engine, parked the car, and waved to Gabriella, who was in front of her house, kneeling as she worked in a garden overflowing with pink asters, poppy-red anemones, and tall black-eyed Susans, their black centers like so many punctuation points. It made a gorgeous sight, but Rose was still preoccupied, her mind on Kristen.

"Hey, Mrs. V!" Melly hollered through the open window, and Gabriella stood up, leaning on a bulb planter with a long handle.

"Melly!" Gabriella smiled, and her hooded eyes followed the car. Her silvery hair was in its chic wedge, and her baggy work shirt and gardener's pants hid a slim body that she kept fit, making her look more forty than sixty-five.

"Girl, you cannot look this good!" Rose called to her, opening the car door. She got out of the seat and stretched, breathing in fresh mountain air. Up here, the sun felt warm and the breeze was balmy, but all she wanted to do was get to her laptop.

"You're wonderful for my ego!" Gabriella came toward the car, tugging off her patterned gloves, black with soil at the fingertips. "What a treat to see you again. I was so glad when you called."

"We're here!" Melly flew out of the car and ran headlong into her arms, followed by Princess Google, caught up in the spirit.

"Melly!" Gabriella gave Melly a big hug and managed to pat the dog, jumping onto her pants in a bid for attention. "How are you, dear?"

"We're on another vacation!" Melly let her go and picked up the bulb planter. "What's this, Mrs. V?"

"A tool for planting bulbs. Give it a whirl, over there." Gabriella pointed to an open patch on their lawn, already raked clean of leaves. "Hold it by the handle, press down, and twist, then drop a tulip bulb inside the hole."

"Like this?" Melly ran over and jumped on the planter, like a pogo stick.

"Perfect." Gabriella beamed.

"Really?" Rose hoisted the sleeping John to her shoulder. "She'll break it that way, won't she?"

"I hope so, I hate that thing." Gabriella chuckled. "Mo got it for me, and I don't have the heart to tell him I'd rather use my hands."

"Ha! So good to see you!" Rose gave Gabriella a hug, breathing in the smells that clung to her work shirt, L'Heure Blue and Merit Lights.

"You, too." Gabriella hugged her back, then stroked John's small back, in his T-shirt. "He's gotten bigger since June."

"I feed and water, as needed."

"Give him to Grandma. I need a fix." Gabriella held out her arms. "I won't wake him."

"An earthquake wouldn't wake him. Please take him, then I can unpack the car. We stopped before we left and got some groceries." Rose handed John over and went around to the back of the car, and Gabriella followed, cuddling him against her cheek.

"I can't say I'm surprised to see you, after what I'm reading about you and this fire at the school." Gabriella eyed her with sympathy. "My heart goes out to you, and thank God Melly's okay."

"No matter what the papers say, I didn't leave that child—"

"Don't even say it." Gabriella raised a hand. "It goes without saying. You'll tell me all when you get a chance, but we know you better than that. We tried to send our love, but we could only leave a message and our email bounced."

"Thanks for trying, but it's a long story." Rose chirped the trunk open and took out three shopping bags, then the tote that held her laptop. "Let's get some lunch and catch up. I have fresh cold cuts."

"Good. Mo can keep Melly occupied. By the way, I'm down to three cigarettes a day. That's why I'm planting bulbs, like mad." Gabriella gestured at a cloth bag of bone meal and a lattice sack. "If this keeps up, we're Holland."

Rose smiled. "Let me get this stuff inside. I'll come out for the rest." She left the trunk open and walked on fallen leaves to the cabin's front door.

"I'll stay out here with Melly. Is Leo coming up?"

"No, he's on trial," Rose answered, and across the driveway, the Vaughns' front door opened and her husband Morris stepped outside, squinting in the sunlight. A former corporate banker in Princeton, he was tall and lean, with the permanent tan of a lifetime sailor and the elegant manners of a Yale grad. His craggy face broke into a broad grin when he spotted Melly.

"Is that Melly The Younger?" he called out, shielding his eyes, and Melly jumped off the bulb planter and went running to him, followed by Princess Google.

"Mr. V!" she squealed, and Rose grinned at him on the way to the front door.

"Hey, Mo!"

"Welcome back!" he called to her, just as Melly caught him in the waist.

Rose unlocked her front door, juggling the keys and bags, then hurried inside, greeted by a cedar smell. The first floor was one great room, which Leo always called the not-so-great room, with an old plaid couch and chairs, a small TV with bookshelves stuffed with old puzzles, board games, and paperbacks on the right, and on the left, a small kitchen with builder's-grade appliances. She hustled to the kitchen area, dumped the bags on the large farm table, and set the tote bag down, then slid out the laptop.

She opened it up, hit POWER, and waited for it to come to life and connect to the Internet. They were in the middle of nowhere, but Leo had made sure his wilderness came equipped with wireless. In minutes, the laptop connected to the web, and she went to MapQuest, clicked to Maps, and plugged in Lava Land, in Pennsylvania, taking a flyer.

We did not find an exact match for your search. Try again.

She knew it couldn't be Lava Land, but it had to be something similar. It sounded like LaLa Land, but nobody around here had a beach house in L.A. Instead she plugged in Lava Land and Maryland, because that was where Kristen's parents had their main house. She hit ENTER, and a box popped up, **We did not find an exact match for your search, but we found a similar location, LaVale, MD.** She clicked on the link, bringing up the region with LaVale starred, but the town was inland, not near a beach.

She typed in Lava Land, PA, and the window came up, **Lavansville, PA,** so she clicked. Lavansville was inland, too. She tried Lava Land, NJ, then clicked the mouse. A window popped up that suggested **Lavallette, NJ.**

"Lavallette," Rose said aloud, and it sounded almost like Lava Land. She clicked the link, and a map filled the screen. Lavallette, NJ, was on a narrow spit of land on the Jersey shore, near Toms River and Seaside Heights. It had to be a beach town. She went to whitepages. com, plugged in Canton and Lavallette, NJ, and in five seconds, she had a street address and an apartment number on Virginia Avenue. There was no phone number, but Rose didn't need one.

She had other plans.

Chapter Fifty

Rose hit the road after lunch with the Vaughns, who were happy to babysit for the day. She was heading east under clear, sunny skies, starting to feel better, stronger. The highway lay open ahead of her, and she hit the gas, whizzing past gorgeous autumn foliage, strip malls, and small towns. It felt good to be moving forward, taking the initiative instead of reacting all the time. She'd been so defensive, ducking for cover since the school fire, and even before, since Thomas Pelal.

Mommy!

Rose heard his voice and honored it, for once, not trying to shake it off. She'd felt horrible and guilty for so long, always dreading that her worst secret would come out, and now that it had, as awful as it was, she could finally exhale. The truth really had set her free, and she was willing to let the chips fall. Now Leo knew everything about her, and while she prayed he still wanted her, she couldn't control him or anybody else.

Her phone rang on the seat beside her, and Rose decreased her speed and picked it up. She recognized Oliver's number on the screen, but she didn't want to have this conversation on the fly. The traffic was light, and she pulled over to the shoulder, spraying gravel, and pressed ANSWER. "Hello, Oliver?"

"Rose, I'm returning your call. I hope you're feeling better since we spoke."

"I am, but not for the reason you think. Oliver, why did you say I was suing the school?"

"I said you were *thinking about* suing the school."

"Oliver, I asked you not to do that. We discussed it, remember?"

"No, you told me you were going to talk with Leo, and I ran into him at the courthouse. I told him about our conversation, and he gave me the go-ahead to say that you two were thinking about suing the school."

"Leo?" Rose asked, surprised. "He said that?"

"I thought you said if it was all right with him, it was all right with you."

"I didn't say that." Rose recovered. "I'm sorry if you misunderstood me. Just because I told you I wanted to talk with him, doesn't mean you can talk to him and get his go-ahead. Leo's not your client, I am."

"He recognizes a good defense strategy when he sees one, and I hope you've come around."

"No, and I won't." Rose didn't get angry. For the first time in a long time, she felt supremely in control. "The very suggestion that I'll sue the school is damaging to my family. The office was stone cold when I called today, and I can't imagine how Melly can attend a school that her parents are suing."

"They have no right to react or retaliate, and I'll send them a cease-and-desist letter, immediately."

"Oliver, they're human, they're people. They have feelings. You can't cease-and-desist feelings." Rose would have laughed, in another mood. "I've tried, and it doesn't work."

"Rose. You're in very serious trouble, have you forgotten? Civil suits and criminal charges may be brought against you, any day now. The smartest thing for you to do is pre-empt them and file first."

"I'm not sacrificing my family for my own hide, and the school didn't do anything wrong."

"Of course they did. The blond teacher at the door let Amanda—"

"Enough." Rose wanted to get real, finally. "It was an emergency, and that teacher did her best in the circumstances, just like I did. Do you think she wanted Amanda to get trapped in the fire? Did anybody really want *this*?"

"They left the doors propped open."

"It was *hot,* Oliver. People make mistakes, and they don't have to get sued for them." Rose was thinking of Thomas Pelal. "Don't you think that teacher feels bad enough? For the rest of her life?"

"Fine," Oliver snapped. "Then we won't sue, but you need good press for the public and the jury pools. We need to spin the story our way."

"No, it's not about the spin, it's about the truth. I'm not suing anybody, or threatening to. That's just being a bully. I hate bullies, and I'll be damned before I'll turn into one." Rose came finally to the point. "Oliver, I'm sorry, but you're fired."

"You can't be serious."

"I am. Bill me for the time we spent, and I'll send you a check."

"Rose, I'm the best criminal lawyer in the state. What are you going to do?"

"I'll figure it out. Good-bye, Oliver." Rose hung up and was about to start the engine when she caught sight of the dashboard clock.

And got a better idea.

Chapter Fifty-one

Rose pressed L for Leo and waited for the call to connect. It was 5:15, and court would be adjourned for the day. She knew the trial schedule because she'd helped him once in court, and he usually got a break before dinner and the night's witness prep began.

"Hey," Leo said coolly, taking the call.

"Hi. Did I catch you at a bad time or a good time?"

"I only have a minute. We're about to go eat."

"I figured, so I'll get to the point." Rose could hear the distance in his tone, but she hadn't expected more. "I just got off the phone with Oliver. He said you told him that it was okay to say we were considering suing. Is that true?"

"Yes."

"Why did you say that? They're angry at me in the office, and I don't blame them."

"I sent you to Oliver because he's one of the smartest lawyers I know, and he came up with a brilliant defense. Let him do his job."

"He won't be doing his job for me anymore, I just fired him. Litigation isn't always the answer, Leo. You're thinking too much like a lawyer."

"Can you blame me?"

Suddenly Rose realized what Leo had meant the other day. "Honey, listen. I'm sorry for not telling you about Thomas Pelal, and for how I've been acting. You were right. I haven't been thinking of us as a family, and now I know how it feels. Lousy. Because you weren't thinking of us as a family, either, by telling Oliver to go ahead."

"I *was* thinking of us. That's why I said that. The best way to protect our family is to sue the school."

"No, it's not. Do you know what they'll do to Melly? Her life will be hell." Rose didn't get it. "If we're really partners, it's fifty-fifty, and nobody has veto power over the other. So I won't do it to you, but you can't do it to me."

"I don't have time to deal with this now." Leo sighed, tense again.

"I'm not expecting you to. Also, I don't want to keep things from you anymore, so I'm telling you that I'm about to visit Kristen and ask her why she left school. I think she might have known about the fire, or maybe have been involved."

"Really?"

"Yes. The kids are with Gabriella and Mo."

"What are you going to do?" Leo asked, his tone changing to concern.

"Talk to her. Find out the truth."

"Is that wise?"

"I think so, and I have to do it."

"That's what law firm investigators do. Whichever lawyer we hire next can deal with it."

"Going to see Kristen is something I have to do, for myself, by myself. You may not understand it or agree, but I'm not asking your permission. I'll let you know what happens. I gotta go."

Leo paused. "Babe, what's come over you?"

"Adulthood," Rose answered, with a smile.

Chapter Fifty-two

It was sundown by the time Rose found Virginia Avenue, parked across the street from Kristen's house, and cut the ignition. Lavallette turned out to be a small, sleepy beach town on an island off the Jersey shore. The street was wide, criss-crossed with sagging telephone wires and lined with two- and three-story homes interspersed with bungalows. The Cantons' address was a newer three-story that looked like it contained several apartments. The apartment was 2-F, and Kristen was probably home, because a light was on in the second floor, front.

Rose grabbed her purse and got out of the car, then walked across the street and up the steps to the house, scanning the names by the buzzers. There were six, and Canton was next to 2-F. She buzzed 1-F, next to William and Mary Friedl. In a minute, an older woman answered. "Yes?"

"Mrs. Friedl, I'm sorry, can you buzz me in? My husband has my key and he's still at the beach."

The door buzzed, and Rose went inside, climbed the stairs, and knocked on 2-F, standing in full view of the peephole. "Kristen, let me in. I have to see you."

"Rose?" Kristen opened the door, her eyes an astonished blue. "What are you doing here?"

"I might ask you the same question." Rose entered the apartment and pushed the door closed behind her. "You told me you were in Maryland."

"You can't stay." Kristen edged backwards, a book in her hand. Her russet hair was in a ponytail, and she had on a gray sweatshirt with black gym shorts. "Please, leave now."

"Why don't you call the police?"

"Why are you here? How did you find me?"

"That's an odd question. Are you alone?" Rose glanced around the small living room, but it seemed empty and still, with a tan couch, matching chairs, and a big TV. Pictures of seashells covered the wall above a white entertainment center. "What are you up to, Kristen? You lied to me this morning about where you were, and I want to know why."

"Go, please." Kristen tried to walk to the door, but Rose stood in the way, sliding her phone from her purse.

"Let's call the police. You can explain to them that you just happened to be out of school the day it exploded, saving your own life but killing three other people, including your sub, Marylou Battle."

Kristen's eyes flared. "What are you saying?"

"I think someone rigged the explosion that caused the fire, either you or someone from the general contractor, Campanile, working with you."

Kristen gasped. "That's crazy! Why would I do that?"

"I don't know, but you're running away from something, and believe me, I know running away when I see it. It's my MO."

"You're wrong." Kristen sank into a wicker chair, placing the book next to the cushion in her seat. "I had nothing to do with the fire. It was an accident."

"Then why were you out that day?"

"I was sick."

"You didn't seem sick when I saw you. You don't seem sick now. And why did you lie to me on the phone today?"

"That's none of your business."

"It is so my business. You used to have lunch with Melly in that lounge. I have a right to know what's going on, because I trusted you with my *child*."

"You're wrong." Kristen flushed behind her pretty freckles. "I'm here because I wanted privacy, like I told you. I'm worried about those crazy parents, and the reporters, too."

"You could have told me or the school where you were."

"I did tell the school."

"That's another lie, Kristen." Rose felt anger flare in her chest. "They're forwarding your mail to your parents' house. That's where you told them you were."

"I don't have to tell everybody everything." Kristen squirmed in her chair, and Rose noticed the book she'd been reading, tucked by her side. Its cover wasn't visible, but she'd know that spine anywhere. Before Kristen could stop her, she reached over and snatched the book from the chair.

"I thought so. I read this book twice. *What to Expect When You're Expecting*."

"This isn't your business," Kristen said, stricken, and Rose dialed back her tone, sitting down opposite her on the couch.

"You're right. But if you ask me, it's time to tell the truth."

"No."

"Try it. It works, and maybe I can help."

"I don't need help."

"Kristen." Rose lowered her voice. "You're pregnant and hiding it from everybody. That sounds like a girl who needs help."

"Okay, so I'm pregnant." Kristen's eyes brimmed, but she blinked her tears back. "My boyfriend Erik's in Reesburgh, in the insurance business. He broke up with me, and I don't know what to do. I don't want to tell my parents, and they're away anyway, so I came here to get back on my feet. That's why I was out of school the day of the fire. I had morning sickness."

"So you didn't know the fire was going to happen?"

"No."

"And you had nothing to do with it?"

"Of course not." Kristen laughed, sadly, and Rose felt relieved and puzzled, both at once.

"So your boyfriend doesn't want the baby?"

"It's not that. He doesn't know I'm pregnant. He broke up with me before I found out, and I'm not about to tell him, now."

"He does have a right to know. I bet he's the one trying to find you. Somebody called your parents' house for you, the housesitter told me."

"It was him. He calls my cell all the time, but he doesn't want me back." Kristen wiped her eyes with the back of her hand. "He wants his stupid truck keys, which I threw in the ocean."

"Aw, I'm sorry."

"Me, too, but not about the truck."

Rose smiled. "Why don't you tell your parents? I'm sure they'll help, and they'd want to know."

"You don't know my dad." Kristen shuddered.

"What are you going to do about the baby, if you don't mind my asking?"

"I think I'm keeping him, or her," Kristen answered, confident. "I think I can do it on my own."

Rose's heart went out to her. "What are you living on?"

"Savings, and I have money I inherited from an aunt. I'm fine, thanks." Kristen's lower lip buckled with regret. "I'm sorry I left Melly in the lurch, I really am. That's why I called you this morning."

"I know." Rose got up, went over, and gave her a hug. "Eat crackers every morning, first thing. Old-school Saltines. You won't feel so sick."

"Thanks."

"I'd better be going. It's a long drive." Rose went to the door, then stopped. "Let me just ask you something. Do you remember seeing cans of polyurethane in the teachers' lounge, recently?"

"Yes. They were varnishing the cabinets. I remember there were WET PAINT signs everywhere, and it reeked."

"When?"

"Thursday, the day before the fire. Why?"

"Somebody told me that the polyurethane is partly the reason for the explosion. It was left there, and it blew up."

"So?"

"So I don't get it." Rose shrugged. "Why does anybody varnish cabinets in October, a month after school opens? Especially if it smells and is going to ruin peoples' lunch. It doesn't make sense."

"I don't know. Maybe a second coat?" Kristen got up, walked to the door, and held it open. "You won't tell anyone I'm here, will you?"

"No, but you should." Rose went into her purse. "Here, take this." She found her wallet, pulled out a hundred bucks, and handed the money to Kristen, who put up her hand like a stop sign.

"No, I couldn't."

"Yes, you have to. Please." Rose put the money in Kristen's hands. "Good luck, sweetie."

"Thanks. This is so nice of you."

"Oh, wait. Take this, too." Rose pulled a folded paper from her purse, opened it, and showed it to Kristen. "This is Melly's drawing of the two of you. That's Albus Dumbledore in the hat."

"I knew that," Kristen said, with a newly teary smile, and Rose gave her a good-bye hug.

"Call me if you need me. And Melly wants you to know we eat Kristenburgers."

"They're yummy, right?"

"Not in bulk."

Kristen laughed. "Can I keep the picture?"

"Sure." Rose went to the door. "I told Melly I mailed it to you, and that's the last lie I'll ever tell my daughter, except for Santa Claus."

It was dark when Rose hit the street, but before she went back to the car, she walked to the beach and took off her shoes, enjoying the sensation of the cool sand as she went down to the shoreline and stood at the edge of the very continent. She still had a blister on her ankle, and the chilly wavelets rolled over her feet, healing and good. The gray foam made pale, shifting lines, one after the other all the way to the black horizon, where sea blended with sky. The stars shone bright white, encrusting heaven, and the full moon was a perfect circle, like a paper hole left by a hole-puncher in school. She breathed in the salty smells and the cool wetness of the air, standing at the intersection of summer and autumn, and at a crossroads in her life, too.

She thought of Leo, hoping she hadn't left him behind, because she wasn't sure where she was going. And she didn't know what to do or think about the school fire, either. She stared into the blackness at the horizon, looking for answers, knowing a line was surely out there, but she couldn't see it. Still, she looked hard and tried to find it, and she found herself thinking of Kurt Rehgard. He was gone, and she didn't know where he was going, either. Or where her mother had gone, or her father.

She thought about death, and life starting anew, in Kristen. And she thought about the place between life and death, where Amanda slept, waiting to wake up, or not. She said a silent prayer for her, and realized that Thomas Pelal had been there, too, in her mind. She had kept him alive, in death, for so long, and it was time to let him go. She realized that letting someone go was setting them free. So she set him free, letting his spirit soar over the great churning sea and up, up, up into the heavens.

The wind blew her hair back from her face, and she breathed in deeply, inhaling one lungful after another, letting it energize and renew her. She kept an eye on the horizon, or where she thought it was, and understood that not everything that existed could be seen. Not every border was clear. She kept thinking of Kurt and the fire, sensing that something still seemed out of whack. She didn't know the answers, and she didn't even know the questions, but they were out there.

As surely as earth met heaven.

Chapter Fifty-three

Back at the cabin, Rose sat over her laptop at the farm table, watching videotapes of the school fire. She'd done it before in her darkest moments, but now she had a new purpose. She was looking for something that could give her a clue about what had happened last Friday at school. She took a sip of fresh coffee, but didn't need the caffeine to keep going, though it was after midnight. Melly and John were sleeping over at the Vaughns', which was their babysitting routine when she and Leo were out past ten o'clock.

She hit PLAY on the most recent link, which was the thirty-fourth new viewer video. She was amazed at how many more there were, from cell phones, flip cams, iPods, and videocameras, made in a world where everybody filmed everything that happened around them, even as it happened, becoming observers in their own lives.

She was having a similar sensation as she watched the video, visualizing herself out of her own body, hunched over the laptop. The only light fixture was the lamp over her head, casting a cone of brightness onto her crown, like Dumbledore's peaked hat. She couldn't help projecting outward into the dim cabin and through its walls to the dark night, its blackness obliterating the outlines of the cabin roofs and the jagged tops of the tall evergreens, cutting into a blanket of dense clouds like so many hunters' knives. The full moon lurked behind, leaving the night opaque and inscrutable.

She hit another video, which showed the same terrified children running from the school, only from a different vantage point. She scanned the video titles backwards in time, reversing the chronology until she was a hero mom. Next to that video was a TV report that she hadn't seen: **More on Moms: Tanya Robertson Speaks with Eileen Gigot.** She clicked the link, and after a web commercial, the anchorwoman came onto the screen:

"I'm Tanya Robertson, and tonight I begin my 'More on Moms' report, which goes behind the scenes in the life of the single mom whose daughter was trapped in the fire at Reesburgh Elementary. Tonight I'd like to answer the question we all have about single moms—how do they do it?"

Rose watched, intrigued.

"By way of background, Eileen Gigot's life changed seven years ago, on August 11, in the world-famous Homestead factory, which started in 1948 with a 6200-foot plant that made only potato chips. Today, Homestead employs almost four thousand people and has grown to a plant totaling fifty-six thousand square feet. It makes potato chips, popcorn, and tons of other snack foods, shipping all over the world from right here in Reesburgh, Pennsylvania."

Rose thought Tanya was angling for a new commercial sponsor until the screen turned to a stop-time photo of the Homestead factory, then morphed into the present-day plant, with her voiceover: "Eileen's husband, William Gigot, loved his job at Homestead, but he was killed in a forklift accident at the plant."

Rose eyed the photo they showed next, of William Gigot and three other men wearing yellow Homestead shirts, with nameplates that read WIJEWSKI, MODJESKA, and FIGGS. Bill Gigot was a tall, handsome man with bright blue eyes that would find their way onto Amanda's pretty face. The screen switched to Tanya, sitting with a teary Eileen, near her breakfront.

Tanya asked, "How did you think you would get along, raising three children on your own?" The camera turned to Eileen, her eyes glistening in a face that looked prematurely lined, and she answered,

"I believe that the Lord gives all of us the burdens we can carry, and no more. Of course, I wish it turned out differently. I miss Bill, every day."

Rose felt a pang, but her thoughts kept coming back to the fire, the polyurethane, and Kurt. She navigated back to the home page, found the story about his crash, and clicked the video. Onto the screen popped the aerial footage, and she watched the coverage again, wondering about what he'd told her.

It's the general contractor's fault, Campanile.

She stopped the video, logged onto Google, plugged in Campanile, and found its website. It had a slick home page with a picture of a huge hotel, and the copy read:

> The Campanile Group is a cutting-edge construction cor-
> poration, a new way of doing things in an age-old business.
> The Campanile family gave us our beginnings over a century
> ago, and though we value our Pennsylvania origins, we have
> expanded and grown nationally. . . .

Rose got the gist. Her gaze fell on the About Us link, and she clicked it. There was a photo of another building, but no listing or bios of corporate officers, only a PR person. She remembered that Kurt had said a "buddy" told him Campanile was at fault, and she wondered if the buddy was somebody working with him at the school. Kurt had worked for Bethany Run Construction, so she plugged their name into Google.

A website popped up, much lower-budget than Campanile. The Bethany Run home page showed three men in brown Carhartt overalls in front of a cinderblock foundation. The caption read, **Vince Palumbo, Frank Reed, and Hank Powell, our famous founders.** The only pages on the sidebar were Current Jobs, Past Jobs, and Contact Us.

Rose clicked on Current Jobs, which turned out to be blank except for a banner that read, **Sorry, Our Current Construction Page Is Under Construction!** Reesburgh Elementary wasn't mentioned, and she clicked to Past Jobs, which showed three small new houses.

There was no About Us. She felt stumped, then thought back to the coverage of Kurt's crash. He'd been killed with a friend, and she had forgotten his name. She clicked back and read the online article until she found the name—Hank Powell. It sounded familiar. She clicked back to the Bethany Run website and double-checked; Hank Powell was one of the "famous founders."

She felt a twinge of sadness, and wondered if Powell was the buddy. A line under the articles had a link for obituaries, and she clicked the one for Kurt. It was brief and ended with **View and Sign the Guest Book.** She clicked, and the screen opened to a webpage designed to look like an open book, with entries for Kurt and Hank Powell:

Uncle Hank, We love you and miss you. We wish we could go to the beach with you again. Your niece and nephew, Mike and Sandy

  Dear Kurt, A light has gone out of our lives. We pray for you, and say hi to Pop when you see him, for us. Love, Carline and Joani

Rose read each one, feeling her heart getting heavy.

Kurt, You were a great friend and a great carpenter. Signed, Vince

Rose remembered the name, Vince. She clicked back to the Bethany Run site, and Vince Palumbo was another of the founders; maybe he was the buddy. She mulled it over. Vince hadn't been out drinking with Kurt that night, and Hank Powell had been the one with Kurt, so Hank seemed more likely to be the buddy. It meant that the two men who knew something about how Campanile was at fault were both dead.

She got up, stretched, and walked around the room, ending at the window, looking out into the blackness. She kept thinking about Kurt, Campanile and the car crash, and she started to wonder if they were related. Another series of what-ifs popped into her mind. What if the crash hadn't been an accident? What if Kurt and Hank had been killed because they knew something about Campanile? What if Kurt was killed because he had been asking about the fire?

Rose didn't know if she was seeing connections that weren't there, or making connections that needed to be made. Kurt had been drinking, but maybe his drinking hadn't been what had caused the accident. He'd said something about new buddies, and she didn't know what he meant. Maybe someone had driven him off the road, or into a tree, or whatever had happened. She looked into the blackness, and all she could see was her own silhouette reflected in the window, an indistinct outline.

She eyed her dark reflection. If Kurt had been killed because he was asking about the fire, she was responsible for his murder. She owed it to him to find out the truth.

She wouldn't settle for anything less.

She couldn't, anymore.

Chapter Fifty-four

"Are you sure you don't mind, baby sitting again, Gabriella?" Rose asked, holding John. He reached up for her nose with splayed fingers, wet from being in his mouth, and she gave his cheek a kiss. "It's one thing to sit for a day, and another to sit for two more, maybe three."

"Not at all." Gabriella dismissed her with a wave. The sun hadn't risen over the trees yet, but the Vaughns' lovely kitchen was already flooded with light. "You know we adore the kids, and Mo loves spending time with Melly."

"Thanks. I hate to go without saying good-bye to her."

"Let her sleep in. We were up late, watching a Harry Potter movie. Call Melly later. She'll be fine."

"And the dog, you can deal?"

"The dog is great, too. I want a Cavalier, I already told Mo. She sleeps on Melly's pillow. It's charming."

"But what if I'm gone until the weekend?"

"Please, take your time."

"I will, thanks." Rose gave John a final kiss and handed him to Gabriella with a wrench in her chest, then walked to the door. "You have my cell number, right?"

"Yes, thanks. And you have mine." Gabriella opened the screen door onto an already warm day, alive with the sound of birds chirping. The Vaughns' front lawn spread out like a dew-laden carpet, and a tall butterfly bush near the door hosted yellow swallowtails and orange monarchs. "What a morning! Why do you have to go back again, anyway?"

"I have a few more appointments, lawyers and such." Rose stepped outside. She hated to lie to them, but they'd worry if they knew the truth. Living without lying was going to be harder than she'd thought, like counting calories.

"Okay, good luck." Gabriella stepped on the front step. "Stay well."

"I will, thanks again." Rose kissed John's warm head one last time, but as she went down the steps, he started to cry, a choked little sob. She turned around at the heartbreaking sound, guilt-stricken when she saw his adorable face pink and contorted. "Aww, see you soon, Johnnie."

"Go on, he'll be fine, I promise." Gabriella waved her on, sympathetic, and Rose turned away with a sigh, vowing to make this trip count.

She hurried to the car, pulling out her phone on the fly, hit the speed-dial for Leo, and listened to the phone ring, then it went to voicemail and she left a message. She put her phone back, got in the car, and started the engine. She took one last look back, and Gabriella was comforting John on the top step.

Rose stifled another sigh, then hit the gas. She felt torn about leaving them again, but she had to figure out what was going on, for herself. She couldn't be right for them if she wasn't right for herself, and she hadn't been right for herself for a long time.

And that time was over, for good.

Chapter Fifty-five

Rose parked on a street south of the school, so the press wouldn't see her car, then got out and chirped it locked. She had on a white man-tailored shirt, jeans, and sneakers, and with sunglasses and her hair under a Phillies cap, no one would recognize her. She walked to the school and made a beeline for the cafeteria, noticing that the plywood wall was being painted by the students. The mural showed a smiling sun overlooking a grassy lawn covered with oversized sunflowers, undersized trees, and polka-dotted butterflies, a kiddie version of paradise that hid an adult version of hell.

Rose walked to the break in the plywood fence, where there was a makeshift entrance that had a clear plastic sheet as a door, then she stopped. It was quiet, for a construction site. No workmen were going in and out, like there had been before. She checked the street, and only one dusty pickup sat parked at the curb, where there had previously been a lineup.

She slid off her sunglasses, turned back to the entrance, and stepped around the plastic sheet. It was dark inside, and the cafeteria was a man-made cave with an eerie azure cast, from the tarp on the roof. It still smelled, though much of the debris had been cleared. Rose felt grit under her sneakers, and realized that she was at the end of the cafeteria, close to the handicapped bathroom. She didn't see anyone around, so she walked ahead, passing a construction lamp with high-intensity bulbs on a metal stalk. Toward the far side of the room, she spotted the broad back of a construction worker, dressed in a white hard hat, dirty white T-shirt, and painter's paints.

"Excuse me," she called out, and the workman turned. He was pushing a wheelbarrow, and his soft belly hung between its handles. Safety goggles dug into his fleshy cheeks, and he was plugged into an iPod.

"Sorry, I didn't see you," he said, with a slight twang. "Do I know you?" He popped out an earbud and squinted through his goggles, then set down the wheelbarrow and walked toward her. "Wait. Yes, I do. You're that chick Kurt liked, aren't you? That mom on TV."

"Uh, yes," Rose said, rethinking her disguise. "I wanted to talk to someone about Kurt."

"Fine." The workman slipped off a worn cotton glove and reached out his hand. "I'm Warren Minuti. I'm with Bethany Run, too. Nice to meet you."

"Rose McKenna." She extended a hand, which was swallowed up by Warren's huge, rough palm.

"My wife and her friends are all talking about you. She's glued to that TV." Warren unstuck his goggles and slipped them onto his hard-hat. "I tell her, you must be a good person because Kurt liked you."

"Thanks. I felt terrible to hear the news that he had been killed. I'm so sorry. He was a sweet guy."

"He was." Warren sighed heavily, his large shoulders sloping down. "We're a small crew at Bethany, only nine of us. We do a job at a time, maybe two, so to lose Kurt and Hank, it's the worst. And Hank, he has a wife and a new baby. *Had* a wife and a new baby." Warren shook his head. "Well, anyway. What is it you want to talk about?"

"Kurt called me Monday night, before the accident, and he mentioned something about a 'buddy of mine,' who told him that some guys from Campanile had left some polyurethane in the teachers' lounge. He said that that helped cause the fire. I was wondering who that buddy might be. Do you know?"

"Well, Kurt's best buddy was Hank."

"Hank Powell, who was killed with him?"

"Yeah. Both wakes are tonight, and the burials are tomorrow."

"Is that where everybody is?"

"Yeah, but I can't go, that's why I'm here. They all just left to go get ready, but I sent my wife. I go to Drexel at night, for law."

"That can't be easy. My husband's a lawyer." Rose paused, thinking. "Kurt said something about new buddies. You know anything about that?"

"No."

"Would Hank have known about Campanile or cans of polyurethane?"

"I don't know."

"Did anybody at Bethany Run used to work for Campanile?"

Warren snorted. "You wouldn't go from Campanile to us, not if you could help it. Campanile, they're a whole 'nother league from us. The bigs."

"Do *you* know anything about Campanile or cans of polyurethane?"

"No."

Rose thought a minute. "Do you think any of the other Bethany Run guys knew somebody at Campanile?"

"Possible, but I don't know. I never met any of the Campanile crew. We only came after the fire."

"What if I wanted to find out who from Campanile worked on the school? Would any of your guys know that?"

"No."

"Then I guess the only way to find out which Campanile guys worked on this job is to ask Campanile."

"Good luck." Warren chuckled. "They're not gonna give out that kind of information, especially if they think a lawsuit's coming down the pike, like they said on the news."

"You're right." Rose took a flyer. "Do you know what happened with Kurt's accident? I mean, how it happened exactly?"

"All I know is Kurt was driving, it was his truck, and it went off the side of the road and hit a tree. There was no shoulder on that stretch of the expressway."

Rose had to tell him what she was worrying about, or she wouldn't get anywhere. "Does it seem strange to you that alcohol was a factor?"

"Yes, I was a little surprised."

"Why?" Rose asked, intrigued.

"I figured that the newspapers played up the alcohol angle, but that wasn't like Kurt. Kurt woulda had a beer or two, at most. He must've been tired, dozed off, and the combination is what did them in."

"What about Hank? Did he drink?"

"Never, not anymore. He was three years sober. Marie woulda drop-kicked his ass."

Rose felt her heartbeat quicken. "When Kurt called me before the crash, he sounded a little drunk, slurring his words, a little."

Warren frowned. "That wouldn't be like him. He was a responsible guy. He took care of his sister and niece."

"I know. I could play you the voice message. I saved it, if you want to hear it." Rose hesitated. "It might be upsetting, now."

"No, play it."

Rose slid her phone from her purse, then thumbed to voicemail and played the message on speaker. Kurt's amplified words echoed eerily through the burned-out cafeteria, then the message clicked off. She eyed Warren for a reaction in the twilight-blue haze.

"Can't say I can explain that," he said, rubbing his chin.

"He sounds kinda drunk, right?"

"Kinda."

"If he was, why would Hank let him drive? Doesn't that seem weird to you? That a guy with a wife and a new baby would let his buzzed friend drive him home?"

"So what are you saying?"

"I'm wondering if someone killed Kurt because he was asking questions about the fire. Or because he knew about the polyurethane."

"*What?*" Warren's small eyes flew open. "You're talking about *murder*."

"I know. I'm just trying to figure it out, and I can't explain why Hank would let Kurt drive drunk. Unless Hank didn't know." Rose thought about it, brainstorming. "Unless Hank saw Kurt have his usual one or two beers, but maybe someone slipped something into his drink. One of these new buddies he mentioned. It's plausible, isn't it? It could have happened."

"Maybe, but murder?"

"I'm just saying it smells, don't you agree? That guy on the tape doesn't sound like Kurt after only two beers, does he?"

"It doesn't but I still don't get why Hank got into the car with him."

"Maybe Hank couldn't tell. What if Kurt wasn't that talkative? What if Hank saw Kurt drink only two beers and figured he was fine to drive, even if he did slur a little?" Rose put her phone away. "Something's wrong with this picture, and two men are dead. And I think it's connected with the fire."

Warren frowned. "We should go to the police."

"With what? What do we say? A buzzed guy got in a truck, drove, and had an accident? That's not suspicious."

"True."

"And they think that the fire was accidental. Besides, I'm the last person who they'd believe, since I'm involved."

"That's true, too." Warren sighed, a huge exhale from his barrel chest. "But if someone murdered Kurt and Hank, I want to be the first to know about it."

"Then maybe you can help," Rose said, with hope.

Chapter Fifty-six

Rose hit the gas, with Warren in the passenger seat. He'd changed into slacks and a fresh polo shirt, which he'd had with him for night school, and he'd shaved in the school's men's room. She could see, in the light, that he was older than she'd thought, maybe thirty-five. Or maybe it was the grim set to his jaw, as if he were gearing up for the task ahead. They were in rush-hour traffic on the bucolic back roads out of Reesburgh, heading to Campanile's headquarters, near West Chester.

"Okay, so what's the plan?" Warren asked, looking over.

"Let's review, okay?" Rose wasn't sure what to do next. "We can't know where we're going if we don't know where we've been."

"That's deep."

"You're telling me. I just learned it." Rose smiled. "Now, Kurt thought that polyurethane left in the teachers' lounge contributed to the explosion, but he was killed before I could ask him how. So far I've heard a few different reasons for the explosion, like faulty wiring, a gas leak, and a snag list not done. What have you heard?"

"The same thing, except for the snag list. Snag lists never get done, and nothing explodes."

"So what caused the explosion?"

Warren shrugged. "The fire marshals' report won't come out for weeks, and that's what the lawsuits will be about, and all that."

"So let's try to figure it out, ourselves. You're an expert, and I'm a . . . mom."

Warren smiled crookedly. "You're kinda nutty, lady."

Rose smiled back. She slowed, passing an Amish man driving a buggy, his head tilted down and only his beard visible under the brim of his straw hat. "We have an advantage. They think it's accidental, and we don't."

"Okay."

"So how exactly do you make an explosion with gas, loose wires, and cans of polyurethane?"

Warren looked over. "Where did you say the poly was?"

"The polyurethane? In the teachers' lounge." Rose thought back to her conversation with Kristen. "Somebody varnished the cabinets on Thursday, the day before the explosion, and left it there. That seems odd to me."

"Why?"

"Varnishing cabinets is the kind of thing they do before you move in, that's what we did at my new house, and it was already done in the lounge, I saw a photo. Why do the cabinets need a second coat, all of a sudden? It was a month after school opened."

Warren nodded slowly. "The teachers eat in there?"

"Some, yes."

Warren wrinkled his nose. "That would stink."

"It did, and that's what I thought." Rose thought again of Kristen. They whizzed by horse pastures with run-in sheds, and hand-painted signs advertising Halloween hay rides and corn mazes. "The lounge reeked of it, and there were WET PAINT signs everywhere."

"That's interesting."

"Why?"

"The poly would have hidden any gas smell."

Rose looked over, her ears pricking up. "So if a bad guy knew he was going to make a gas leak, he might varnish some cabinets to mask the odor."

"Right."

"How do you make a gas leak? Is that hard?"

"No, easy. The gas leaked in the wall between the kitchen and the lounge, and there was a big three-quarter-inch pipe there. I know, I cleaned up the debris. If somebody got into the building on Thursday or Thursday night, they could give the gas valve in the wall a quarter turn."

"Wouldn't that show, a hole in the wall?" Rose asked, as the country scenery gave way to a concrete ramp, heading to Route 202, going north.

"Not if it was behind a cabinet or an appliance. Gas would leak out, but nobody would smell it because of the poly, and they'd also get desensitized to it."

Rose remembered Kurt telling her the same thing, about being desensitized. "So let's say the bad guy varnished the cabinets to hide the gas smell. How does the wall explode?"

"He needs a spark to make an explosion." Warren frowned, in thought.

"Wouldn't the loose wiring provide a spark?"

"It could, but not for sure." Warren shook his head. "It's not necessarily a live spark."

"So what causes a live spark in a wall?"

"The spark didn't have to be in the wall. The poly was in the teachers' lounge, so the spark could have been in the teachers' lounge. An appliance could do it, or the oven."

Rose thought a minute. The Kristenburgers. "How about a microwave?"

"Yes. They could have rigged the micro to spark."

"How?"

Warren looked over. "Ever put tinfoil in a microwave? You get live sparks, blue flashes, the whole nine."

"No, tinfoil wouldn't have worked. The teacher would have seen it."

"Not if it was hidden inside the micro, like in the plastic part on top." Warren's brown eyes came to life. "Here we go, I got it. On Thursday, you varnish the cabinets and leave the poly out. It stinks. Then on Thursday night, when nobody's around, you hide tinfoil in the microwave, turn a valve in the gas pipe, and loosen the wiring in the wall. An electrician could do all those things in fifteen minutes."

"Okay."

"Then, you leave the caps on the poly open a little, so the fumes leak into the micro. Nobody can tell because it stinks anyway, and you put up the signs."

Rose was confused. "But how do fumes leak *into* a microwave?"

"They drift in."

"I thought microwaves were closed, sealed."

"No, they're not. A spark in the micro, with poly fumes inside, would cause an explosion, and if the gas had been leaking in the wall, from a big, three-quarter-inch pipe, it would go *boom!*" Warren made an explosion with his thick fingers.

"What's the loose wiring have to do with it? Isn't that overkill?" Rose thought a minute, answering her own question. "Wait, maybe not."

"Why not?"

"Because that would show up later, when the fire marshals come in. In other words, if you want to make it look like an accident, you need an innocent cause, like faulty wiring." Rose felt astounded. It all made sense. "Like you said, a wire could spark, but you're not sure enough. So it's an explanation, but not a reliable-enough cause."

"True." Warren nodded, shifting forward. "An electrician could do all of this, easy. If he worked the job, he could have a key. Or somebody else would, like one of the higher-ups. Hell, Campanile is the contractor, and they hire the guy who installs the damn locks."

"Right." Rose hadn't thought of that. "So we need to know the electrical subcontractor and the electrical crew that Campanile used on the job, and we take it from there."

"How are you gonna get that?"

"I'm not, you are."

"Me?" Warren looked at her like she was nuts. "How?"

"You're a carpenter, right?"

"All my life. My dad was one."

"Okay, so let's say you could be looking for a job, at Campanile." Rose accelerated. She booked it because it was already 4:15 and they had to get to Campanile before closing time. "You go in, apply for a job, and get the info in an informal way. In conversation."

"How?"

"You can do it." Rose looked over. "You look the part because you *are* the part, and you're not from here, so you can ask a lot of questions without seeming suspicious. Where are you from, with your accent?"

"Arlington, Texas."

"Can you ham it up a little?"

"Sure thang, ma'am," Warren answered, slyly. "What're my lines?"

"Say you're from Texas and you think big. You need a new job and you want to start at the top, with the best. You heard Campanile was the best, stuff like that."

"Kiss some ass."

Rose nodded. "Say you need a new job, you want to move up. You want to work for Campanile and become—what's it called, what you would be?"

"I'd love to be project manager."

"Great. Does Campanile have project managers?"

"Sure. But I bet they promote from within."

"Well, let them say that. Tell them you're new to the area, so you don't know any of the subcontractors, but you can work with anybody."

"Should I mention Reesburgh?"

"No, I'd leave that out. I don't want them connecting you with the fire at all."

"But I have to get them to talk about subcontractors on the Reesburgh job."

"You can't go about it directly." Rose glanced over as the car whizzed along. "Wait. Listen. Subcontractors are important, right?"

"Sure." Warren cocked his head, listening. "The finished job is only as good as the subs."

"Exactly. Say that, and say you're good at managing subs and getting them to do their best work. Tell some dumb story of a sub you managed in Texas."

"I didn't."

"Make it up." Rose didn't know if this plan broke her lie diet, but she wasn't the one lying. "Drop the names of some subs in Arlington, ask if they work with good subs, then bring the conversation around to electrical subs, then maybe you can get a name of an electrician or two on the job. How many could there have been? Not that many. Think you can do it?"

"Yes." Warren straightened up.

"They're big, so they might have a human resources person. If they don't know who the subs are, you might have to get through that interview to somebody who does, like somebody not in administration."

"I thought of that already. I'll say I want to talk to somebody who's been in the field. I'll say I flew up here and don't want to leave until I see somebody tonight."

"Okay, good." Rose felt a wave of worry for him. "If you can't get them to say it, then just leave. Don't do anything to arouse their suspicion. If they came after Kurt, they could come after you."

"Let 'em try." Warren lifted an eyebrow. "I'm from Texas."

Chapter Fifty-seven

Rose slouched down in the driver's seat, pretending to read her BlackBerry, though she could barely see the screen through her sunglasses. Warren had gone into Campanile headquarters at 4:50, and it was 5:45. It meant he had probably gotten to the second interviewer, but she was beginning to worry. She prayed she hadn't gotten him into anything dangerous.

She'd parked the car in the last row of the lot, where it couldn't be seen from the entrance, and kept an eye on the entrance in the rearview mirror, waiting for him to appear. The Campanile offices were in a typical corporate center: low-profile buildings with fieldstone façades and smoked-glass windows. Each company had its own signed parking lot, and there were dried cornstalks tied to the CAMPANILE sign, next to a hay bale and a gigantic pumpkin.

Rose watched as Campanile employees filed in a steady stream from the front doors, wearing white ID tags around their necks, talking, laughing, and lighting up cigarettes. Everybody went to their cars, chirping them unlocked on the way, like so many corporate crickets. It was mostly women in the beginning, then a mixed group later, many of the men in navy-blue Campanile polo shirts, carrying clipboards with navy covers or navy messenger bags that read THE CAMPANILE GROUP.

Rose had the driver's side window open because it was hot and she didn't want to keep the engine running, drawing attention to herself. The breeze carried some of the employees' conversations, and she caught snippets of some: "I told you not to email him, just call, Sue. He owes you an explanation." And, "We need to move the staircase, relocate it on the south side. Problem solved." And, "Run the numbers, Don. Do the math!"

Rose checked the rearview again, and two men in suits came out, one short and bald, and the other with dark hair and a massive build, maybe six-two and two hundred and fifty pounds. The big one struck her as familiar, but she didn't know where she knew him. He walked down the steps, bending to talk with the man, their conversation too low to hear.

She tried to place the big man as he walked toward a car. His suit jacket blew open in the breeze, showing a major paunch and something else. A gun, in a shoulder holster. She blinked, startled. She had seen him before, but she couldn't place him at all. The big man raised his key fob and unlocked a navy-blue SUV that read THE CAMPANILE GROUP on the side door.

Rose stayed low, racking her brain. She hadn't seen the big man at school. She would remember somebody that tall because she was tall. Where had she met him? At a party? She wasn't invited to parties. On the street? She didn't live here. She didn't know anybody at Campanile. She'd never heard of the company until the fire.

Suddenly, the bald man stopped by his car and turned back, calling to the big man. "Hey, Mojo!" he yelled, and the big man turned.

"What?"

"I take it back. Thursday's better!"

The big man waved, acknowledging him, then got into his SUV.

Mojo?

Rose didn't know any Mojo. It was obviously a nickname. She grabbed her phone and thumbed to the photo function as the man reversed in the SUV, then put it in drive and drove past her. As he went by, she snapped his photo, saved it, then hit ZOOM to enlarge it and studied the man's face. He looked so familiar. Long nose, dark hair, huge build.

Rose remembered how she'd recognized him. She'd seen him last night, on one of the videos she'd watched, from Tanya's TV station. She thumbed to the Internet on her phone, plugged in the website for the TV station, and pressed until she got to stories about the fire. She found the link for Tanya's "More on Moms" interview of Eileen Gigot, then pressed PLAY. She sat through the opening about single moms, then the story segued to the boilerplate about the Homestead factory. The photo of some men came onto the screen, and one of them stood much taller than the others.

She pressed STOP. The man in the photo looked like Mojo, but the screen was too small to read his full name. She didn't know if it mattered, but she didn't have time to think about it now.

Warren was walking toward her car.

Chapter Fifty-eight

"You made it, thank God." Rose unlocked the door, and Warren eased his large frame into the passenger seat and sat down.

"Here's the deal. I gotta tell you, I think we were wrong."

"What do you mean?" Rose could hear a change in his tone, and his blue eyes had cooled. She started the engine. "What happened? What'd they do?"

"Nothing. I went in, talked to the HR lady, and filed out an ap. She told me Campanile has no jobs right now. They promote PMs from within."

"PMs? Project managers?" Rose reversed out of the space, then cruised to the exit behind the other cars.

"Yes. I said I wanted to talk to somebody in the field, and they were all hanging out in the hallway, all nice guys, so she pulled one of 'em in. Chip McGlynn. I sat down with him, one-on-one. Take a left up here." Warren pointed. "If you'll drop me off at the train, I can still make my class. They told me the train station is on Lancaster Avenue. They even offered to drop me off."

"Did he tell you who the electrical subcontractor was, on the school?"

"No, he didn't know the job, and I didn't press it."

"He didn't know?" Rose left the parking lot after the other cars. "He's a guy in the field, and he didn't know about a job in the news?"

"To tell the truth, I think he did know, but he didn't want to say. I get that. Lots of big-time construction companies keep quiet about which subs they use. It's like a trade secret."

"You didn't say that before." Rose frowned, driving.

"No, but once I sat down with him, and saw the operation, and how sweet the offices are, and met Chip and the guys, it's ridiculous to think they could murder anybody."

"You can't tell that from—"

"They even told me they'd give me the first job that came up, then move me up to PM if I make the grade. And if they call, I'll take it."

"You'd *work* for them?" Rose asked, surprised. "But they could be—"

"They got this thing they call the Wall of Fame, with tons of awards from every building association you can name, and some from the state, too. They get the big jobs."

"But what about Kurt and Hank? The driving?"

"I can't explain it, but there's a lot of things that people do I can't explain. I can tell you for sure, Chip and those guys didn't kill them, or blow up an elementary school." Warren shrugged his heavy shoulders. "They got photos of their kids everywhere. They sponsor a softball team, and for Make a Wish, they gave a little boy from Allentown a ride on a cherry picker."

"But Kurt said they left the polyurethane."

"Not exactly. He said, *somebody* left poly in the lounge, and I tell you, that's not on purpose. It happens all the time. The average laborer, he's a pig."

Rose flashed on Mojo. "One of their guys carries a gun. I saw it."

"He's probably in security, or carries payroll or petty cash. People have guns, and it doesn't mean they're bad guys. Hell, my dad has two rifles in his truck, and he's honest as they come."

"This guy doesn't look like he carries petty cash. He was an executive, with a tie. His name's Mojo."

"Mojo?" Warren's eyes lit up. "I just met him. He's a *great* guy. He's their security guy. Joe Modjeska."

Rose made a mental note of the name. "What do you mean, security guy?"

"Mojo's the Director of Security. That's why he carries. He shoots a sixty-three."

Rose recoiled. "He shoots who?"

"No, in golf. He shoots a sixty-three. He won the celebrity golf tournament. Cole Hamel was in it, and Werth, too. Mojo told me he'd get me tickets, next year." Warren looked as excited as a little boy. "I love the Phils!"

"Me, too, but Mojo isn't with the Phils." Rose turned onto Lancaster Avenue. "So they won you over."

"No, I got a reality check." Warren's tone stiffened. "You should just forget the whole thing."

"Do you think they manipulated you, intentionally?"

"Why would they? They don't know who I am. I didn't mention Reesburgh."

Rose fell silent, cruising up the street, congested in front of the Dunkin' Donuts, a bank, and a Starbucks. "Why does a construction firm need a Director of Security? Isn't that strange?"

"Not at all. You know how much theft goes on at job sites? People steal everything they can carry. Materials like copper piping, generators, drills, any tools at all. We're not big enough at Bethany Run to have a guy like that, but Campanile is."

Rose tried to imagine it. "So Mojo would travel around and visit the Campanile sites, to check on security?"

"Yes, sure."

"That means he would have access to all the sites, at any time. He'd even have keys."

Warren put up his hands. "Stop, wait, don't get carried away again."

"He could have rigged the microwave or put the poly in the lounge."

"That's crazy." Warren scoffed. "He'd never do that, and he's not an electrician; he's a guy at the top. I loved Kurt and Hank like they were my brothers, but I don't think anybody murdered them."

"I do." Rose felt a shudder run up her spine, saying it out loud.

"Wrong. Kurt made a bad choice, and Hank wasn't thinking, and they're both gone now. Nothing can bring them back, and no sense can be made of their deaths." Warren pointed to the left side of the street. "There's the station."

"Well, thanks for the assist." Rose turned into the parking lot.

"You're welcome." Warren got out of the car, took out his duffel bag, and looked at her. "You're not gonna let it go, are you?"

Rose thought of Leo, saying the same thing. "I can never let it go."

"Suit yourself. Stay well."

"You, too." Rose watched him go, wondering what to do next. She was thinking about Mojo and his gun, and she needed to know more. She slid out her phone, logged onto the Internet, and plugged Joseph Modjeska into Google. There was a page of entries, and she clicked on the first link:

> **Break-In at Corporate Center**
> **" . . . Director of Security Joe Modjeska said that he was pleased that the Campanile's offices weren't burglarized, and all of their laptops were . . ."**

She clicked and read a few more mentions, but they were all press releases, followed by photos of Mojo at the celebrity golf tournament, with Justin Timberlake and Charles Barkley. She scrolled backwards in time and came upon the press release that announced Mojo's hiring:

> **Campanile CEO Ralph Wenziger is pleased to announce the hiring of Joe Modjeska as the company's new Director of Security. Wenziger stated, "Joe comes to us with enormous expertise, having spent the past four years at the Maryland Occupational Safety & Health Administration in Baltimore, Maryland . . ."**

She looked at the date on the press release. It was less than six months ago, which meant that Mojo was new to Campanile. It seemed odd. She hadn't gotten the idea from Warren that Mojo was a new hire. She navigated to whitepages.com, typed in his name, and found his address.

837 Hummingbird Lane Malvern, PA

Rose plugged it into her GPS system and hit START.

Chapter Fifty-nine

Rose parked outside of Mojo's house, surprised. It was a fieldstone mansion, with a grand front door and a huge stone wing on either side. Tall trees surrounded the property in back, forming a screen of autumn color, and the house sat atop a steep hill, so far off the street she didn't have to worry about being spotted. She guessed she was looking at a $1.5 million house and she was practically an expert. She'd done the shopping for the house in Reesburgh and reading the new homes listings was her idea of online porn.

She didn't get it. Mojo had spent the last four years working for the state of Maryland and only six months at Campanile. Even if he was making a fortune now, how could he afford this house? What kind of security director had a multi-million-dollar house? What kind of state employee? Her phone interrupted her reverie, signaling she was getting a text. She picked it up and pressed to the text function. It was Leo:

Sorry, I'm too busy to call back. You okay?

Rose sighed. It wasn't warm and fuzzy, but at least she was still married. She hit REPLY.

Yes. Take care. Love, Me.

She checked the dashboard clock: 7:15 P.M. The sky was darkening, and she could feel the air cooling through the open window. Her thoughts turned to Melly and John, and she called Gabriella, who picked up after one ring.

"Rose, how are you, my dear? Getting things done?"

"Yes, thanks. How are you holding up?"

"We're all wonderful. Melly is out with Mo again, and John is fine, too. He discovered my bracelet, which amused him endlessly. He has expensive tastes."

Rose eyed Mojo's house. "I'm not finished just yet. Can you hang in another day or two, and I'll keep you posted?"

"I hope you let us keep them until the weekend. Melly is making a garden with Mo. Wait'll you see it."

"Thanks so much," Rose said, grateful. "I really appreciate this."

"We know, now let me go. I have a baby to teach to say Grandma. Love you, bye."

"You, too." Rose pressed END, watching darkness fall. She felt at a loss, eyeing the house. She was so used to bouncing ideas off Leo, and it was hard to do all the thinking a cappella. Her gaze fell on the next-to-last text, which she hadn't heard when it came in. It was from Annie.

What's this about Thomas Pelal? Please call. You need me now.

Rose went to her phone log, found Annie's number, and pressed CALL.

Chapter Sixty

Rose sat opposite Annie in a chair, next to a room-service table covered with the remains of roasted chicken. The aroma of rosemary filled the small hotel room, and its window overlooked the lights of Philadelphia and the Delaware River, black and thick as a python. She'd told Annie all about Thomas Pelal, bringing them both to tears, then caught her up on everything else, including Mojo's mansion.

"Well, well, well." Annie scratched her head, her blunt fingernails disappearing in her little corkscrews. "This Mojo guy is wack. He needs a gun, for what? To protect copper piping?"

"I know." Rose hugged her knees to her chest, finally feeling validated. "So I'm not nuts?"

"No, I think he's fishy, too, and it worries me, for your safety." Annie shifted in the patterned chair, tugging the hem of a white sundress over her sleek legs. Her feet were bare, her toenails bright red. "I get that you don't have enough evidence to go to the State Police with, but why don't you hire a private detective? That would be safer."

"I'd have to find one, and right now, I feel like I know what I'm doing and I want to do it myself. I want to get to the bottom of it, and somehow I think I'm the only one who can."

"What if something else is going on, with you?" Annie pursed her lips. "What if you're feeling so guilty about Amanda that you're trying to find some nefarious cause of the fire, so nobody thinks it's your fault?"

"No, I wish the town didn't hate me, but that's not it. It's not about me, Amanda, or even Melly."

"Are you trying to make up for what happened that night, with Thomas Pelal?"

"I don't think so."

"Why didn't you tell me about him, Rose?" Annie cocked her head, her tone gentle. "I wouldn't have judged you. It could have happened to anybody."

"I was ashamed, embarrassed. It's horrifying." Rose ran her fingers through her hair. "But I finally let him go. I'll always mourn him, but that's something different."

"I get that." Annie tilted her heard backwards, appraising Rose with calm, dark eyes. "You know, I see a change in you. You're digging in. Trying to get to what's really going on."

"Instead of running away?"

"Yes." Annie smiled softly. "I'm proud of you."

"Thanks," Rose said, touched.

"The only problem is, I'm also worried." Annie pursed her lips. "These dudes don't play. I don't like you spying on them, and they won't either."

"I know." Rose had been starting to worry, too. She was a mother, and the sight of Mojo's gun stuck in her mind.

Annie brightened. "I have an idea. You're staying the night here, aren't you? I have the extra bed."

"I'd like to, if you don't mind. I don't want to go home to Reesburgh. I'm kind of betwixt and between." Rose knew what the real problem was. "I hate when Leo and I are in a fight."

"I feel you." Annie shook her head, with a smile. "Look at us. Wild girls turned wives."

"I know, right?" Rose thought ahead to seeing Leo, not knowing how that would work, then getting Melly back to school, and not knowing how that would work, either. "All of a sudden, I don't fit into my old life."

"You never did, girl. Now, you finally have a chance. Make a life that fits you. Leo will come around. It's a rough patch, is all. That's marriage."

"We'll see." Rose knew it was more complicated than that. "We have to change a few things, both of us."

"That's just what I was thinking." Annie stood up, newly energized. "I can help you with that."

"How?"

"Get up. You're staying the night, and we need to get started." Annie was already in motion, heading toward her black bags, stacked up like blocks near the luggage carrier.

"What's going on?"

"You'll see."

Chapter Sixty-one

Rose kept her eyes closed, while Annie worked her magic. The built-in vanity was covered with powders, blushes, mascara wands, used Q-tips, and little wedges of white sponges, like tiny pieces of wedding cakes. They'd done the major stuff last night and were putting on the final touches this morning. The hotel room was sunny and bright, and *The Today Show* played in the background, with Meredith Viera interviewing a French chef.

"You almost finished?" Rose sipped her cooling coffee, her eyes shut. They'd had another room-service meal, and she was ready to get going. She had already figured out her next move.

"Now lift your eyebrows, but don't open your eyes. Two minutes until reveal."

Rose felt the pencil filling in her brows. "It doesn't have to be perfect."

"Be still, or I'll make you wear the fake nose."

"I don't need a fake nose."

"So what? I make the best noses in the business. It's a shame you don't need one. It's like ordering the salmon, in a steak house."

"No nose. Hurry."

"Okay, you're a masterpiece. Open your eyes."

"Amazing!" Rose looked at her reflection and almost didn't recognize herself. Her long dark hair was gone, dyed a warm red and cut into feathered layers that skimmed her ears. Annie had reshaped her eyebrows, changing their color to a red-brown, and darkening her skin with foundation. Nobody would recognize her from the TV or newspaper, and that was exactly what she needed for her plans today. She set down her coffee. "Thank you so much!"

"One more thing. Wear these." Annie handed her a pair of large eyeglasses, in pink plastic. "Heinous, right?"

"Yikes." Rose put the glasses on. "Where did you get these?"

"A vintage store in the Village. They're circa 1982. Now you're ready for Main Street, Anywhere, USA. Your distinctive natural beauty is gone, and you're completely forgettable."

"This is great."

"You're welcome." Annie put the eye pencil back. "Are your Band-Aids okay?"

"Yes, thanks." Rose checked her hand and ankle. The burns were healing nicely, and they'd gotten rid of her bandages.

"Now, please be careful and stay in touch. And don't wear your sunglasses anymore. People look longer at people in sunglasses. Love your hair."

"Me, too." Rose shook her head, like Googie drying off. "I feel so free!"

"Every woman does." Annie gathered up her compacts. "Only women equate a haircut with freedom. We're free, ladies. We can vote now."

Rose gave her a good-bye hug. "Mind if I leave you to clean up?"

"No worries. Go get 'em, tiger."

"I'm off." Rose went for her purse, but stopped short when she saw the TV. A local newsbreak had come on, and Tanya Robertson's face filled the screen. On the screen behind Tanya was a school photo of Amanda Gigot. Annie came up from behind, and they both stood watching the news, neither saying anything.

Oh no. Please be alive.

Tanya said, "Young Amanda Gigot remains in a coma, fighting for her life this morning, while the town of Reesburgh reacts this morning to the official report of the county Fire Chief, who has ruled that the school fire was accidental. Students went back for their first full day on Tuesday, and plans are in place to rebuild the cafeteria, as life returns to normal in this lovely community, torn by tragedy and discord."

Rose shook her head. "They're not even looking for anything intentional."

On the TV, Tanya continued, "The District Attorney's Office reports that they are continuing their investigation, and indictments in connection with the school fire and Amanda Gigot's injuries will follow as soon as they are complete."

"That means me," Rose said, newly worried, and Annie clapped her on the back.

"Get going, and prove 'em all wrong."

"On it!" Rose grabbed her bag, rallying, and fifteen minutes later, she was back in the car, driving south on I-95. The sun was rising, the sky clear, and the road lay open ahead of her. Her short hair fluttered in the wind, and her resolve was stronger than ever.

She'd be there in two hours.

Chapter Sixty-two

Rose pushed up her fake glasses and walked up to the counter, holding a steno pad she'd bought at a drugstore down the street. The office of the Maryland Occupational Safety & Health Administration was small and cluttered, with an old-fashioned coat rack, a fake ficus plant, and an umbrella stand. Mismatched government-issue chairs were grouped in the waiting area around a rickety coffee table covered with stacks of Maryland Department of Labor forms, a multi-colored brochure entitled *Workplace Safety and YOU,* and a beat-up copy of *People* magazine.

"May I help you?" asked an older African-American woman behind the counter, smiling in a sweet way.

"Hi, I'm Annie Adler." Rose was sure this was going to be her last lie, but it was hard to quit cold turkey. Maybe if they had a patch, or something. "Joe Modjeska sent me. You know, Mojo? He worked here, until about six months ago."

"Mojo! Of course, how is he? I love that man."

"He's doing great, working for Campanile, just over the border, in Pennsylvania."

"I know. He always said he was meant for better things. A big man with a personality to match."

"Tell me about it. He shoots a sixty-three now, and it's all he talks about."

"Golf, golf, golf! That man *lived* for golf!"

"Don't they all? Me, I live for shoes."

"Ha!" The woman extended a hand over the counter. "I'm Julie Port. How can I help you?"

"I'm a writer for *Hunt Country Life,* a magazine in southern Pennsylvania, where Mojo lives." Rose brandished her steno pad. "We're doing a short profile on him, and I wonder if I can ask you a question or two. He said you might not mind, and the good press would help him out."

"Sure enough." Julie checked the waiting room, which was empty. "We're not busy today, and I can take a couple minutes. If it helps Mojo, I'm in." She moved to the side, opened a swinging door in the counter, and gestured. "Come with me. We'll go in the break room."

"Thanks." Rose followed her past a few workers talking on the phone and typing on computer keyboards, then they went down a hall to a lunchroom with round Formica tables, hard plastic chairs, and a bank of vending machines.

"Please, make yourself comfortable." Julie waved her into a chair, sitting down.

"Thanks." Rose took a seat, put her steno pad on the table, flipped it open to the first page, and slid a pen from her purse. "Now, he began working here about five years ago. He was at Homestead before that, wasn't he? In Reesburgh?"

"Yes, he was. He was their Director of Safety." Julie's face fell into lines, her jowls draping her lipsticked mouth. "He took it very hard."

"What did he take hard?" Rose didn't know what she meant.

"He blamed himself, but it wasn't his fault, any of it." Julie clucked. "Forklift accidents are among the most common, and it wasn't his fault that that man died."

Whoa. Rose realized she meant Bill Gigot. "Mojo has such a big heart."

"He surely does, and he was an excellent safety manager, I'm positive of that. He's very diligent."

"That sounds like him."

"Yes, and from what he told me, the lighting was insufficient in the loading area where the man worked, and he wasn't real experienced with the forklift. In fact, Mojo got him a job in the peanut building."

Rose made rapid notes, for real. "Peanut building?"

"Where they made the peanut butter crackers. They had to use dedicated equipment and such, to protect people with peanut allergies. It's FDA and state regs."

"So you were saying."

"Anyway, to get back to the story, the man didn't have enough experience operating a forklift. Also, they require forklift travel lanes and the like. You can't play fast and loose with a forklift."

"Of course not." Rose kept making notes.

"Mojo didn't like to talk about what happened, but I could tell how sad he was, inside. The man went over the side of the loading dock, killed when his head hit the floor. Mojo found him, on his rounds." Julie clucked. "He made sure the man's widow got herself a nice check without even having to file or sue."

"So that's the kind of man he is, huh?" Rose made another note, and Julie shook her head.

"No good deed goes unpunished, though. Before you know it, Mojo's tossed out."

"Oh no." Rose lowered her voice. "They fired him?"

"I think they asked for his resignation, you know how they do. But he was too proud to let on, with me." Julie frowned. "Don't put that in your story, okay?"

"None of this will be in, I promise." Rose suppressed a guilty pang.

"Thanks." Julie nodded. "Tell you somethin' else about him. He came in as a director after his training, but he never lorded it over anybody."

"What did he do here?"

"Oh, right. You might not know, because the compliance offices in Pennsylvania are run by the feds." Julie cleared her throat. "Well, OSHA, the Occupational Safety and Health Administration, administers workforce safety out of D.C. But some states, like Maryland, have their own compliance agencies, too."

"I see." Rose took notes, and Julie warmed to her topic.

"We cooperate with the feds, and we work hard to ensure that every man and woman in the state has safe and healthful working conditions."

"So Mojo came here after his training. Where did he train?"

"Baltimore, with everybody else."

"Why did he need training, if he'd been a safety manager at Homestead?"

"That's what *he* said!" Julie laughed. "We train anyway, and he didn't know the way we do things down here."

Rose thought a minute. "I didn't ask him, but was he a Maryland resident then?"

"No, he had to move here."

Rose hesitated, and Julie leaned over.

"Next, you're gonna ask me how he got the job, and that I don't know. He moved to Harford County, just over the state line. I knew he wouldn't stay forever. He wanted to go back to Pennsylvania, and they were building the house. You've seen that place of his?"

"Yes, that's where I interviewed him."

"His wife's family, they got money. That, he told me." Julie leaned over again. "How else you think he could afford to build custom, especially from that fancy company? He liked it so much, that's who he went to work for."

"Campanile." Rose made a fake note, and suddenly a fluorescent light began to flicker overhead.

"Uh-oh!" Julie looked up, curled her lip in annoyance. "Here we go again. Building Maintenance's gotta come change that bulb. I don't know how to do fluorescents, you know, those long, skinny ones."

"Me, neither."

"Mojo wouldn't have any of that, of course. If he was here, he'd get on a ladder, grab a screwdriver, take off that panel, and change that bulb himself, no waiting." Julie nodded. "Mojo can fix anything."

"Even lights?"

"Sure enough. That's something else you probably don't know about Mojo. You can put it in your article."

"What?"

"He's a master electrician."

Chapter Sixty-three

Rose hit the road on fire, flying up I-95, heading north. Traffic had picked up, and she kept her foot on the gas, passing slowpokes, full of nervous energy. Mojo was looking more and more like a killer; he had access to the school at any time, so he could have planted the polyurethane in the teachers' lounge, and he knew enough about electrical wiring to rig the microwave, loosen the wiring, and create a gas leak.

Rose sensed that Mojo had done it, but she didn't know why. Campanile had just built the school, so why would he want to blow it up, especially when lawsuits were likely to follow, against his own employer? She raced down the highway, and the questions kept coming. Why would he want to murder children? Even if he had known that they'd be at recess, it would be an awful chance to take, and he'd killed three staff members.

She steered smoothly around a Honda, thinking back. In a matter of days, there had been two deaths that looked like accidents that weren't, and after her trip to Baltimore, she felt even more paranoid. She hadn't realized that Mojo had any connection with Bill Gigot; wherever Mojo went, death seemed to follow, and she was beginning to wonder if Bill Gigot's death had been an accident, too.

Rose sped home, toward Reesburgh, but she wasn't sure of her next move. She still didn't have any evidence that Mojo had committed a murder, much less three of them, so she still couldn't go to the police. She had called Annie and Leo to tell them what was going on, but neither had answered, and this time, she didn't leave a message. She was on her own.

She took the exit ramp, and in time, the terrain grew familiar. White clapboard farms and tall blue silos. Sun-drenched stretches of corn and soybeans, their round, dark-green leaves shuddering in unseen winds. She whizzed past the scenery, thinking about Bill Gigot and Homestead. She had never been inside the plant; she and Melly had missed the school's field trip there, in second grade. Homestead staged the town's Halloween and Christmas parades, and sponsored a team in its softball and basketball leagues. Other than that, Rose knew very little about the company.

Maybe it was time to learn.

After all, she was a reporter.

Chapter Sixty-four

Rose got out of her car in the visitors' lot, breathed in the tantalizing aroma of frying potatoes, and eyed the Homestead factory, which was on the other side of the access road. It wasn't a single building, but a series of five buildings—immense corrugated metal boxes, painted a sparkling white, with a broad yellow stripe. Clouds of steam billowed from metal smokestacks and drifted from square metal vents near the flat rooflines, dissipating into the clear blue sky. Rose had known Homestead was a big company, but she hadn't realized it was this vast.

She turned around, pushed her fake glasses onto her nose, hoisted her purse to her shoulder, and walked to a sidewalk mobbed with kids on field trips, being shepherded by teachers, aides, and moms into lines for factory tours. She waded through the kids to the entrance of the Homestead corporate offices, a large, three-story office building of a sleek modern design, with a façade of dark brick and smoked-glass windows.

HOMESTEAD SNACK FOODS, read a discreet sign in yellow letters, and she reached the office doors, went inside, and found herself in a two-story waiting area dominated by a modern chandelier of frosted glass. A gleaming reception desk was at the back of the room, but the receptionist was talking on the phone, her head down.

Rose looked around. To her left was a waiting area, where two men in suits sat talking in front of a glass coffee table, and on the right was a display case of Homestead products, next to a bigger one of awards, made of engraved glass and Lucite. A set of crystal spikes were annual safety awards, and Rose could guess which year they hadn't won: seven years ago, when Bill Gigot was killed.

"May I help you?" the receptionist called out, and Rose turned, then froze. The receptionist was one of the moms from school, though not in Melly's class. Rose had no choice but to rely on her master disguise.

"Hi." Rose approached the desk. "I'm Annie Adler."

"Hello," the receptionist said, seeming not to recognize her.

"I'm with *Home Baking,* a new magazine. We're doing a story on how home cooks can make their own potato chips, and I was wondering if I could talk to someone about baking in the big leagues, like at Homestead. I'd love to know more about your operation here, including workplace safety practices."

"Of course." The receptionist smiled politely. "Would you like to make an appointment for next week? Our public relations manager, Tricia Hightower, is busy this week. The Harvest Conference, our annual corporate gathering, is held here at headquarters, with all the executives and top sales reps from all our branches."

"Thanks, but I've driven a long way. Does she have an assistant, or someone else I can talk to?"

"No, Trish handles all press relations personally."

Rose tried another tack. "Can I speak with someone in production, perhaps a supervisor on the line? I'd love to speak with someone who'd give me the inside track."

"Sorry, that's not our policy, and it's Group Day today, so there's no admittance to the plant if you're not with a group. Now, would you like to make an appointment for next week? May I take your phone number and she'll get back to you?"

"No thanks, that's past my deadline." Rose wanted to get out while the getting was good. "I'll call again. Thank you for your time."

"Thank you," the receptionist said, and Rose turned and headed for the door. She hit the sidewalk, breathed in the cooked potato aromas, and walked to the car, preoccupied. She wasn't sure what to do next, but she still wanted to know about Mojo and Bill Gigot's accident. The company would probably have had to file all sorts of accident reports, but she didn't know how to get them. Being a fake reporter could only take her so far.

"Line up, Jake!" one of the teachers shouted to the mob of kids. "Guys, come on! Behave, here we go!"

Rose threaded her way through the excited children as the teachers and moms wrangled them like runaway calves. A team of Homestead employees helped corral them for the factory tour.

"Excuse me," one of the employees called to Rose. "Aren't you with Holy Redeemer? You're all signed in and your group is leaving now!"

"Me?" Rose answered, then caught herself. She couldn't get into the factory otherwise, and she wanted to learn more about the loading dock area, where Bill Gigot had been killed. "Hold on, I'm coming!"

Chapter Sixty-five

Rose was herded through a crowded gift shop that contained Homestead snacks, T-shirts, baseball caps, key chains, cookbooks, and stuffed-toy potato chips. The store narrowed like a funnel at the back, into a hallway that reverberated with the noise of excited kids.

"The theater is this way!" called out a ponytailed Homestead employee. "We're gonna see a movie!"

Rose had no choice but to go with the flow, though the last thing she needed was to watch a corporate video with talking potato chips. Luckily, it lasted only twelve minutes, which was the average attention span of a six-year-old and a mom trying to solve a murder.

"Follow me, I'm Linda!" the ponytailed employee called out, and the group was herded down one hallway and another. The kids giggled, pointed, and pushed each other, and Rose decided there was a special place in heaven reserved for teachers and moms who chaperoned on field trips.

"First, the pretzel factory, then the potato chip factory!" Linda called out, taking them into a wide hallway that had floor-to-ceiling plastic windows, providing a complete view onto the factory floor, two stories below. The Holy Redeemer group merged with two other school groups already there, and Rose breathed easier, since all the moms would think she was with one of the other groups.

Linda started her spiel. "So, Homestead Snacks started with the Allen family and today it's a multi-national food producer, which owns seventy-five hundred acres of land in Reesburgh, including the Reesburgh Motor Inn, Reesburgh Visitor Center, the Potato Museum, and other things."

Seventy-five hundred acres? Rose looked over at Linda, amazed. That was practically the whole county.

"Homestead employs almost four thousand people in its Reesburgh headquarters, and many more in its thirty-five branches throughout the Mid-Atlantic states." Linda gestured to the window. "Here you see the first step of our pretzel baking, which is when the dough goes into the kneader, gets mixed up, and is extruded, which means pushed through . . ."

Rose tuned her out, eyeing the factory floor, below. It was a large, well-lit space, filled with huge lines of stainless steel equipment. The walls were white cinderblock, and the floor a dull red industrial tile. Oddly, there were only six employees, performing various tasks in their yellow jumpsuits, earplugs, and hairnets.

Linda asked, "Any questions before we move on?"

Rose caught her eye. "You have so many employees, but there are only six for this whole pretzel operation. Is that typical?"

"Good question!" Linda answered, officially perky. "Most of our employees are route drivers, and we have a fleet of one thousand trucks and vans on the road. And the machinery does all the baking, so our employees don't have to slave away in those hot temperatures. Also, you're seeing only a third of our plant employees at any one time, because we work around the clock, on three shifts; 6–2, 2–10, and the night shift, 10-6."

Rose wondered how many people would have seen what happened the night Bill Gigot was killed. "Do the same number of employees work on each shift?"

"No, many fewer work the night shift. Now, let's go!" Linda shuttled them to another window that showed superwide belts of uncooked pretzels moving slowly into a large oven.

"What are *those* things?" asked a little boy with glasses, pointing to red hoses that came from the production machines.

"Those are wires. Now, before we see the potato chips, we have a few offices to pass and we'll go by them quickly. Here's the office of our Quality Assurance Manager." Linda pointed through the window at an older woman in a hairnet and labcoat. "That lady eats potato chips *five* times a day. Who wants her job?" The kids hollered, and Linda hustled them ahead. "This is the office of our Director of Safety. As you see, all of our employees wear hairnets and earplugs, and there's even hairnets for beards!"

The kids erupted into laughter, but Rose was thinking that it was Mojo's former office, a small box of white cinderblock with a cluttered desk. No one was inside. She asked, "Does the Director of Safety make rounds at night, to check on things?"

"I'm sure he does." Linda smiled in a pat way that let Rose know her welcome was wearing thin. "Now, let's move along to our packing operation and warehouse." She ushered them past the office that read DIRECTOR OF SECURITY and onto a second-floor deck, which overlooked an expanse of floor-to-ceiling Homestead boxes.

"See all these boxes?" Linda took her place at the window. "They go for blocks and blocks! All these boxes will get shipped out tomorrow, not only all over the United States, but to Latin America, Mexico, Jamaica, and the Caribbean, too. You see that number on the side of the box? We know where every ingredient in the pretzels came from, where we bought the yeast, flour, salt, and malt, following strict FDA regulations."

"I have a question." Rose raised a hand. Julie had said that Bill Gigot worked in the peanut building, whatever that meant. "Is there a peanut building here, that's separate? My older son has mild peanut allergies, and I understand you make peanut butter crackers."

Another mother nodded. "My son has a peanut allergy, too. Very severe. We have to watch everything, or he goes into anaphylactic shock. He and another child have to eat alone at school, in the classroom. If they even breathe peanut butter, they could die."

A third mother added, "My daughter has a gluten allergy. It's a lot of trouble, but at least it's not lethal." The rest of the mothers started talking about their kids with soy and other allergies, and Linda raised her hand to get a word in edgewise.

"To answer your question, we do not use any peanuts in the preparation of our products, and they're all peanut-safe. We provide an extensive list of which of our products are allergen-free, soy-free, and gluten-free, and we also make kosher products, which are certified under kosher laws."

The other mom frowned. "But you *do* make peanut butter crackers. I saw them for sale, in the Acme."

"We don't make them, but we sell them under the Homestead name. They're made by another company, out of state."

Rose was thinking about Bill Gigot. "But you used to make peanut butter crackers here, didn't you? I heard there was a peanut building here."

"Yes, and we also made peanut-filled pretzel nuggets, but not in this building." Linda gestured behind her. "We used to make peanut-butter crackers and peanut-filled pretzel nuggets on the other side of the access road, behind the train tracks. That was called the peanut building, but it's been repurposed to make chocolate-filled pretzel nuggets. Now, time for the potato chips!"

"What's *that*?" asked the little boy with glasses, pointing at a long hook on a metal rod, hanging on the factory wall.

"That's what we use if something gets stuck in the machine." Linda led the group down the hall. "It's like a big, long toothpick."

Rose followed the group, lost in thought. It was entirely possible that Mojo had killed Gigot. It had happened on the night shift, in a smaller operation and a separate building. There would have been only one or two other employees there, and as Director of Safety, Mojo would have had free rein. It wasn't impossible to make a forklift injury look accidental. Mojo could have hit Gigot on the head, killing him, then sat him on a forklift and sent it over the side of the loading dock. And Mojo would have known how to disable any surveillance cameras, with his electrical expertise.

The tour ended, and Rose walked to her car, getting out her keys and chirping it unlocked. She couldn't stop wondering about Bill Gigot and if he'd been murdered. She wasn't sure what to do to find out more, and she still didn't know what his death had to do with the school fire, if anything.

She crossed the visitors parking lot, which was less full now, with the kids lining up to board their buses. It had to be after one o'clock, for them to get back to school in time for dismissal. She checked her watch, and it was almost two o'clock. She was about to get into her car but looked across the access road, where employees were leaving their cars in the parking lot and heading inside the factory. The second shift was starting at two, and she eyed the employees, wishing she could get inside the factory, to learn more about how Bill Gigot had been killed and see the loading dock in the peanut building.

Rose stowed her purse in the car, chirped it locked again, and slipped her car keys into her pocket, then walked toward the access road. She didn't know how she'd get inside the peanut building, but she'd play it by ear.

It was a potato chip factory, not the C.I.A.

Chapter Sixty-six

Rose followed the walkway to the other side of the corporate campus, across the access road. The land sloped down, and the walkway forked, with the right leading to the main plant and the left leading to a smaller building, also of corrugated metal, painted white with a yellow stripe. Next to it lay a single train track with round black tank cars, so it had to be the peanut building, where it was almost time for the second shift.

A small parking lot sat to the left of the peanut building, and employees were getting out of their cars, greeting each other, and heading together in a steady stream toward an entrance on its left side. There weren't many of them, maybe twenty or so, which meant she would stand out, unfortunately.

She developed a plan on the fly and took the left fork, noticing yet another building, large and sprawling, with several satellite buildings attached to it by walkways. When she got closer, she was able to read the HOMESTEAD CONFERENCE CENTER sign, decorated with pumpkins and a spooky scarecrow. A parking lot to its right was filling up, and she guessed it was the people arriving for the Harvest Conference.

She reached the steps down to the peanut building, crossed into the employee parking lot and approached the entrance, two yellow doors. Employees swiped in with the laminated ID cards they wore on their yellow lanyards, and Rose fell into step behind two women, one older white woman and one younger black woman, chatting away. The young one swiped her ID card and started through the door, then her friend followed, then Rose.

She found herself standing in a hallway with the two women, who each took a card from a yellow tray on the wall and swiped it into a time clock. Next to that was a sign: NOTICE: HEARING PROTECTION REQUIRED IN ALL PRODUCTION AREAS, and a less official, SAFETY IS EVERYONE'S JOB!

The older woman turned to Rose, smiling politely. She had a halo of curly gray hair and bifocals. "Can I help you?"

"Yes, thanks." Rose pushed up her glasses. "Is this where you make the chocolate-filled pretzel nuggets?"

"Yes, but you can't come in here. It's not open to the public."

"I'm not the public. I'm Annie Hightower. I'm new."

"A new hire?"

"Yes." Rose smiled in a way she hoped was convincing. "I'm supposed to start working here next week, near the loading dock. I'm Tricia Hightower's cousin, in PR. Do you know her?"

"Sure, I've met Trish, but there's no job opening that I know of." The older woman turned to her young friend. "Right, Sue?"

Sue looked nonplussed. She had clear green eyes, dark skin, and a pretty smile. "Not that I know of. We should call Trish."

"We can't." Rose hid her case of nerves. "She's busy with the Harvest Conference. She told me she'd meet me here and show me around, but she must have forgotten. Oh no, maybe I spilled the beans. It's a job that's *going* to be open. I was supposed to come and look around before I start."

"Uh-oh, I understand." Sue grimaced. "Somebody's going to get fired. Who? Do you drive a lift?"

Jeez! "No, wait." Rose wasn't about to fake-drive a forklift. "Did I say *this* shift? Sorry, I meant the *night* shift. That's why I'm here now. Trish wouldn't send me to look at a job that somebody was working, right now. She said I'd be doing the same job, but I'd replace somebody on the night shift."

"Oh, good." Sue grinned with relief. "If you don't drive a lift, I'd bet you'd be a screener. That's right next to the loading dock."

"I knew it!" Her older friend looked over. "Francine's gonna get the boot, and she deserves it, for sure."

"It's about damn time." Sue nodded in agreement, and the older woman turned to Rose, smiling and extending a hand.

"Annie, I'm June Hooster, and welcome to Homestead. You'll love it here, it's a great company. Juanita screens on this shift, and I'll introduce you to her."

"Great, thanks."

"Wonder what Trish was going to do with you? Put you in a uniform?" Sue eyed Rose's loafers. "And you got the wrong shoes on. You need 'shoes for crews,' that's what we call 'em."

"Sorry, she didn't say." Rose stepped aside as another employee walked in the door, punched in, then headed toward a room at the end of the hall. "I hate to go home after I drove all this way. I even got a sitter."

"Now that's a different story." Sue laughed, patting her shoulder. "Don't waste a sitter, I never do. I take the long way home if I have a sitter, just because I can."

June smiled at Rose. "Come with us, and we'll get you a uniform and show you the ropes. We're not allowed to have cell phones or purses on the floor, so you can stow your valuables in a locker."

"Thanks, but I left my purse in the car." Rose followed them down the hall and through the door that read WOMEN'S LOCKER ROOM. She felt bad lying to them, but it was hard to stick to a diet.

Especially in a potato chip factory.

Chapter Sixty-seven

Rose stood on the factory floor next to Juanita, feeling like her twin in an identical yellow jumpsuit, earplugs, and hairnet. Only ten employees worked in the immense room, which contained four huge lines of machinery that almost fully automated the production process, making chocolate-filled crackers and pretzel nuggets, then dropping them counted into bags which were sealed and packed into cardboard boxes. The boxes then traveled via a waist-high track of stainless steel rollers to Juanita and Rose, who X-rayed them.

"This job is easy, and don't let it intimidate you." Juanita kept her eyes trained on the X-ray machine. Its screen glowed an odd green hue, showing twelve ghostly circles. Juanita pointed to the image, her nail polish bright red under her clear plastic gloves. "Look. All you gotta do is make sure there's twelve bags in each box. Like right here, see?"

"Yes." Rose nodded. "Do you count them?"

"Yes, you got to, starting out. When you're experienced, you can eyeball it and tell. But in the beginning, you gotta count 'em."

"Okay."

"Watch." Juanita was already closing the box and sending it along the roller track. "If it's okay, you close the box. If it's not, you take it off the line and put it back here." She gestured to a wheeled table behind them, just as another box rolled in front of her and she had to feed it through the X-ray machine. The green screen came to life. "See, this one's okay, too."

"It's tough to keep up the pace," Rose said, meaning it.

"It is. You gotta be quick. The main thing here is production. We got to keep the lines moving. No stopping."

"It's like *I Love Lucy* and the chocolate factory, huh?"

"Sometimes it is." Juanita smiled.

Rose hadn't realized how stressful a factory job could be. The boxes came at a relentless clip, and the room felt overly warm despite large industrial fans mounted on the ceiling. A low-level hum filled the air, challenging her earplugs, and the floor vibrated from the heavy production machinery.

"The other day, one of the lines broke down, and the engineers fixed it so fast it could make your head spin. Like they say, time is money. If a single line is down a day, it costs us a hundred thousand dollars." Another box appeared, and Juanita fed it into the X-ray machine, checked the green screen, then closed the flaps. "You can't let a box go through with less than twelve bags. Then an account paid for twelve, but only got eleven."

"That's bad."

"Sure is. Bad for me." Juanita pointed to a black number code on the side of the box. "This number tells which lot it was, and they can trace it back to which shift the mistake happened on, and then Scotty comes to me and says, 'Juanita, you're the screener, you screwed up.' You get a few warnings, then you're out, like Francine."

"Who's Scotty?"

"Our boss. Frank Scotty. He's the shift super."

"Is he around?" Rose hadn't counted on a supervisor.

"He stops by usually, but he's crazy with the Harvest Conference. They have their prom with all the muckety-mucks." Juanita rolled her eyes. "You can meet Scotty when he stops by. We've been working together ten years."

"That's a long time." Rose realized that Juanita had been here when Bill Gigot was killed and could still have information about his death, even though they hadn't been on the same shift. "You know,

Trish told me this used to be called the peanut building, back then, right?"

"Yep. We made peanut butter crackers and peanut-filled pretzel nuggets here. Had to keep 'em separate from the other products, because there's no peanuts in the big plant. You know, for the allergies. We're not peanut-free, there's a lot of real complicated rules, so we just go with there's no peanuts, like lots of companies. But that's now." Juanita sent the box on its way, then X-rayed the next one. "Then, we had all sorts of procedures, everything had to be separate. We were so careful, it was a pain. Look." Juniata pointed to the X-ray screen, and in the corner, there was empty space where a bag should have been. "Missing one. No good, right? Deal with it."

Rose grabbed the box and set it on the table behind them.

"Good job." Juanita smiled. "Anyway, back then, the peanut allergy thing was getting bigger. The orders went way down. Schools stopped buying anything with peanuts. Moms didn't want to take a chance and bring in a snack that could get the other kids sick. A kid can die from a peanut allergy, you know." Juanita shuddered. "I'd never want to be responsible for a child's death. I couldn't live with myself."

Rose flashed on Thomas Pelal, but suppressed the thought. She had to bring the conversation around to Bill Gigot.

"The peanut business went bust, especially the peanut-filled pretzel nuggets." Juanita positioned a box in the X-ray machine, then screened it, and sent it on its way. "We had four lines dedicated to peanut products, and we didn't get the orders, and they'd be sitting still for *days*. Meanwhile, the chocolate-filled nuggets were selling like crazy, especially in Latin America and the Caribbean, I think because it's so hot there. With the chocolate inside the pretzel, it doesn't mess up your hand, like M&Ms." Juanita turned with a wink. "We didn't have enough machines in the big plant to fill the orders for the chocolate-filled nuggets, and these machines here, in the peanut building, sat doing nothing, because they could only be used for peanut." Juanita screened another box. "We were losing money, hand over fist."

Rose had to get Juanita off the subject, but she was so chatty. "If you were here ten years ago, did you know—"

"Those were the bad old days. The bosses wanted to switch from peanuts to chocolate, make crackers with chocolate and fill the nuggets with chocolate, but it took time, switching over. We couldn't use the peanut machines right away for the chocolate." Juanita closed another box. "We had to get them completely cleaned, then we had to get them inspected and whatnot. The machines sat still, like they were broken. We had no work, we worked in the big plant. We ran the tours. We filled in. We swept. But the pay wasn't the same, and the managers were going nuts and so were the supers. We were down almost six months, this was seven years ago, I remember because my youngest was three, and he just turned ten."

Rose saw her opening to talk about Bill Gigot. "I heard from Trish that there was even a guy who got killed here, around that time."

"Yep. Bill." Juanita's mouth made a grim line. "He was on the night shift, where you'll be. I remember, because I was worried sick about Christmas. We didn't know what we could afford to get the kids or how long I'd have to take less pay." Juanita eyed the X-ray screen. "Finally, we started back with the chocolate-filled, and even though we don't make the peanut-filled nuggets or crackers anymore, we still don't put peanut-free on the bags. We can't take a chance, on account of the FDA and the lawsuits."

"I heard he had a forklift accident."

"He did." Juanita pointed to the left. "Right over there. You can see the loading dock."

"Creepy." Rose turned around, but she couldn't see around the corner. "Do accidents like that happen a lot, here?"

"A fatality, at Homestead? No way." Juanita eyed the X-ray screen. "Forklifts can be dangerous. Bill came over here from the big plant, wait, lemme think, I don't know exactly when he started"—Juanita positioned the next box—"but I know he was here by July. I remember because of the holiday. We had a company picnic, and he was the new guy, over from the big plant. The peanut people always stuck together. That was our joke." Juanita chuckled. "Bill was a nice guy, and he'd been with the company a long time. Then all of a sudden, I come in, I hear he died."

"I wonder how that happened. I guess he wasn't experienced on the forklift."

"No, he was. Very. Drove a forklift at the big plant, too."

Rose didn't get it. Mojo told Julie that Bill wasn't experienced. "So isn't that strange that he could have an accident, even though he's so experienced?"

"No, accidents happen to experienced people. I think they happen more, because the experienced guys don't watch as much. My neighbor is a roofer thirty years, and last week he fell off a ladder and broke his leg." Juanita shook her head, closing the flaps on the next box. "Still, I was so sad when Bill died."

"I'm sure. Did anybody see what happened, that night?"

"No, there weren't any other employees around. We were down to a skeleton crew at night because of what I told you." Juanita closed another box. "They didn't find him until it was too late. He bled to death."

"Yikes. Who found him?" Rose was verifying her facts.

"The Director of Safety. Joe Modjeska. Mojo." Juanita sent another box on its way. "Great guy."

Right. "Did you have a lot of interaction with him?"

"Mojo was here all the time. He was in our building so much, we called him Mr. Peanut." Juanita smiled, moving the next box along. "He resigned but I heard they asked for it. The captain goes down with the ship."

"Why was Mojo here so much? Did you have more safety problems than the big plant?" Rose didn't want to sound too inquisitive. "I don't want to work in a place with a lot of safety problems."

"Don't worry, the new guy hardly ever comes by." Juanita eyed the screen again. "Mojo just liked us, that's what he said. He thought we were more fun, and we are." Juanita smiled, and Rose joined her, but she was dying to get a look at the loading dock, to check the rest of Mojo's account.

"Can I take a bathroom break, boss?" she asked.

Chapter Sixty-eight

Rose went to the loading dock, slowing her pace as if she were just walking through. Two men in phosphorescent lime green uniforms, maybe for greater visibility, drove scuffed orange forklifts, whipping them around the concrete floor. The loading dock was a long, wide area, with flattened cardboard boxes piled on the floor, next to pallets stacked with boxes, shrink-wrapped with plastic sheets, to make a block. On the left was a line of white garage-type doors, with rectangular windows, and two of the doors were closed. The others opened into the containers of tractor-trailers, and at a glance, it looked as if the containers were a series of long, dark rooms.

Rose remembered Mojo had told Julie it was dark in the loading dock, but it was as light here as the factory floor, with panels of exposed fluorescent fixtures attached to a metal support overhead. She wondered if the lighting had been improved after Bill Gigot's death and made a mental note to ask Juanita. Even if his death was a murder, she was curious if they'd changed the lighting, for show.

Rose stepped aside as one of the men steered a forklift into one of the containers, carrying a pallet of shrink-wrapped boxes. Two large lamps on the cab, like the eyes on a hardshell crab, lit his way, and even if the loading dock had been dark, the lamps would have corrected for that problem. One of the garage doors was wide open, with no truck, and sunlight beamed through it in a slanted shaft. Rose could imagine how a forklift operator could drive too close to the edge of the dock and fall off, but she still didn't think that was what had happened to Bill Gigot.

Rose headed back to the factory floor to ask Juanita about the lighting, but stopped when she noticed a man approaching her at the screening station. It could have been the supervisor, Scotty, and Rose didn't want to take any chances of his calling Trish. She did an about-face, walked back toward the locker room, and hurried out of the building.

Five minutes later, she was in her car and driving away from the plant, in the late-day sun. She whipped off her hairnet, glasses, earplugs, and gloves, but she didn't pull over to take off her uniform. She couldn't risk getting caught, and her brain was buzzing. So Mojo had lied about Bill Gigot's death, trying to make it look more like an accident, which only made it more likely to be murder.

She hit the gas, heading into Reesburgh, where traffic was picking up. She didn't understand why Mojo would have killed Bill Gigot and she wished she could bounce it off of Leo. She glanced at the dashboard clock—5:15. He'd just be getting out of court, so maybe she could reach him. She fished her phone out of her purse, slowed her speed, and when she came to a traffic light, hit L. She waited for it to ring, but the voicemail came on, and she left a message. "Call me when you can. Love you."

She pressed END, then dialed Annie while the traffic light was still red, but there was no answer there, either. The traffic light turned green, and she cruised forward, trying to decide what to do next. She still didn't have any evidence to take to the state police, and she wasn't sure how the murder of Bill Gigot was connected to the school fire, except by Mojo. It was a puzzle with pieces missing, but she felt oddly closer than ever.

She drove ahead, looking through the windshield at the narrow strip of highway, barely seeing the trees with their turning leaves, and her phone rang. She didn't recognize the number on the screen, but didn't want to miss a return call if Leo or Annie were calling from a different phone, so she picked up. "Hello?"

"Rose?" a woman said, between sobs. "It's . . . Kristen."

"Kristen, what's the matter?" Rose asked, alarmed. The teacher sounded like she was crying hard.

"I need . . . help. Please . . . help me."

"My God, is it the baby? Are you okay? Kristen, call 911. I can't get to Lavallette in time."

"No, it's not . . . the baby. I'm so scared. Please, I need to talk to you. There's nobody else."

"What is it? I'm here. I can listen." Rose was already looking for a break in the traffic, to pull over on the shoulder. "What are you afraid of? What's going on?"

"I can't tell you over the phone." Kristen's crying slowed. "Where are you?"

"In Reesburgh. Where are you? Are you in New Jersey?"

"I can't say, but . . . I need to see you. I'll text you when and where to meet me, after we hang up."

"Why? What's going on?"

"Rose, everything I told you was a lie."

Chapter Sixty-nine

"What's going on?" Rose was sitting in her car with Kristen, having convinced the teacher that her appearance was a master disguise. It was after dark, and they were parked at the edge of a cornfield, in the middle of the farm country outside of Reesburgh. The air was cool and fresh, and the only light came from the full moon, her car's high beams, and the dashboard, which shone upward on Kristen's young face, showing the wetness to her eyes. Her gray T-shirt and sweats looked thrown on.

"Rose, I lied to you, about everything. Well, not one thing. I am pregnant."

"Okay." Rose tried to slow her heart, which was hammering. She'd taken off her Homestead uniform, which she'd had on over her clothes.

"But it's not my boyfriend's baby, like I told you."

"Whose is it?"

"Um . . ." Kristen hesitated, sighing. "Let me just say, I wish it was his baby, because he's a great guy. And he didn't break up with me, I broke up with him."

"Who is the baby's father?"

"Paul Martin. Senator Martin."

Rose felt her mouth drop open. "Are you kidding?"

"No. It's true."

"But he's married, older, and a United States Senator."

"I know. I used to think I loved him, but I must've been out of my mind." Kristen shook her head, sadly. "We've been seeing each other on the side since early summer. I met him when I was at school picking up some papers, and he was being shown around the construction site, by people from the school district. One of them introduced us, and I invited him to talk to my class. He called me, and we started up."

Rose remembered that Senator Martin had talked to Melly's class, at Kristen's behest. "Okay, so tell me what's going on."

"That explosion in the school, it was meant for me. I think he tried to kill me."

"*Senator Martin?*" Rose couldn't wrap her mind around it. She had thought that Kristen was involved in the explosion, but it turned out she hadn't been a villain, but a victim. "Senator Martin tried to *kill you?*"

"Well, he didn't do it himself, but I think he ordered it done. If I hadn't been out running this afternoon, they would have killed me."

"How do you know? What the hell's going on?"

"Paul knows my schedule. He knows that every Friday, I eat alone and microwave a veggieburger."

"How does he know that?"

"Because that's when we'd talk. That's the only time we talk during the work day. It's our secret." Kristen bit her lip, her eyes glistening. "You were right. Marylou Battle was where I would have been, at exactly the same time, and I think they did something to make the microwave blow up when I used it. She was killed, instead of me. And Melly could have been there, too. I'm so sorry, really sorry."

Rose didn't want to go there, not now. "Didn't the senator know you'd be out of school that day, sick?"

"No. I got morning sick, that much was true, and decided not to go, at the last minute. I didn't tell him. I figured I'd call him from home, at the same time, the way we always did."

"So why would he kill you? Is it because he doesn't want the baby? The scandal?"

"Of course, he doesn't want the baby. He's worried about the scandal and a divorce, and there's more than that. It's because of what I know, or what he *thinks* I know." Kristen sighed. "It happened this one time, when we were supposed to meet at our country place."

"What country place?"

"A house, about an hour from here, closer to D.C. It belongs to a friend of his, who keeps his mouth shut. We used to meet there when Paul had time. He called it our love shack."

Adorable.

"We were supposed to meet, but Mrs. Nuru wanted to go over a lesson plan. So I called and told him, but then she canceled, and I wanted to see him. I left a message on his cell, telling him I'd meet him there. He didn't call back, but he didn't always, if there were people around. I went, but he wasn't alone."

"Another woman?"

"No. He was with a man."

"He's *gay*?"

"No, it was a man I didn't know, and they were sitting in the living room. I had my key, so I let myself in, and when I came in, I could tell it was tense. You know how you can feel it in the air, when you come into a room after a fight?"

"Yes."

"Paul didn't expect me. Neither did the man."

"Wait. Didn't Paul, uh, the senator, get your voicemail message?"

"He must not have checked it. Or sometimes they get delayed, you know? Does that ever happen to you?"

"Yes." Rose nodded.

"Paul got the man out in a hurry, then we had a huge fight."

"What about?"

"Paul worried I heard what they were talking about, but I only heard one thing, and it made no sense. He was freaked that I saw him with this guy."

"Who was the guy?"

"I didn't know. But then, I saw his picture in the paper, at a celebrity golf tournament."

Rose gasped. "Joe Modjeska."

Kristen blinked. "Yes. Do you know him?"

"No. He works for Campanile, the general contractor at the school." Rose shifted up in the driver's seat. "When did you see them together?"

"The Wednesday before the explosion."

"And the explosion was on Friday." Rose put it together. "Modjeska is the guy who put the polyurethane in the lounge, which was supposed to kill you."

"How do you know all this?" Kristen asked, bewildered.

"Doesn't matter. What did you hear them say, that didn't make sense to you?"

"Something about peanuts and foreign countries."

"What do you mean?" Rose asked, her senses on alert.

"They were saying something about peanuts and Jamaica, Latin America, Chile, like a bunch of foreign countries. I asked him what they were talking about, and he freaked." Kristen threw up her hands, upset. "That's why it's so crazy. I had no idea what they even meant."

"I do. Modjeska killed Bill Gigot."

"Amanda's father?" Kristen's eyes widened. "But I thought he died years ago."

"He did. He worked at Homestead and was killed in a forklift accident, but I think it was murder. Joe Modjeska was Director of Safety at the time. Only one thing, I don't know why. I just can't put my finger on it." Rose looked through the windshield into the darkness. She flashed on the beach, when she'd looked into the darkness for answers, and she'd let her mind run free. Then suddenly, it came. "Oh my God. I think I know."

"What?"

"I found out tonight that during this time, Bill Gigot was transferred to the peanut plant, but the peanut business went bust. They wanted to convert the machinery to chocolate products, but it took time because the machinery had been used for peanuts and—"

"People are allergic to peanuts, like Jason."

Rose blinked. "Jason who?"

"Jason Gigot. Amanda's older brother. He has a severe peanut allergy, and Eileen told me this incredible story about how they found out."

"How?"

"They didn't know he was allergic, but their dad worked at Homestead and they switched him to making peanut-butter crackers or something like that. He came home one night, picked up Jason, and the little boy went into shock."

Rose listened, spellbound. It was the last piece of the puzzle, and she could feel it falling into place.

"Jason's throat swelled up, he couldn't breathe, and they had to rush him to the hospital. He almost died, and they didn't even know he had the allergy. He was, like, six years old. Amanda was a baby at the time."

Rose remembered what Juanita had said, and spun out a scenario. "If a production line isn't working at Homestead, it costs the company a hundred thousand dollars a day. During that time, the peanut machines weren't working for almost six months. That's millions, and Homestead had lots of orders for chocolate-filled nuggets. So they must have used the peanut machines to fill the chocolate orders, at night."

"That's terrible!" Kristen shook her head, incredulous. "Children would die. Would they really do that?"

"For that much money, yes." Rose thought about it, and it made sense. "They ran the machines in secret, making chocolate crackers and chocolate-filled nuggets on the peanut machines. Nobody would know the difference, only the skeleton crew at night and the Director of Safety."

"Modjeska?"

"They called him Mr. Peanut because he was around so often, and now we know why. The night shift knew, but that was only a few people, and they kept the secret. They were probably paid off, too." Rose could visualize how it all went down, having seen the plant and the peanut building herself. "I bet Bill Gigot was with them until his son Jason almost died, then he wanted to put a stop to it."

"What about Eileen? You don't think she knew, do you?"

"I doubt it. She would have known that he'd gotten transferred to the peanut plant, but not that they were running chocolate on the machines. He wouldn't risk telling her that." Rose thought of something else Juanita had said. "Homestead got a lot of orders for the chocolate products from Latin America and the Caribbean, so I'm thinking they filled the orders for export, only. Maybe that's what you heard when you interrupted that meeting."

"I see." Kristen nodded, grimly. "They were talking about countries where they sent the contaminated snacks."

"Right." Rose felt breathless at the depravity of the scheme. "It's sick, but brilliant. If they make the contaminated snacks for export only, there's much less risk. Then the kids who die would be from places that don't have the money to sue Homestead, or the FDA to watch out for them. Modjeska didn't care they were killing kids, as long as it wasn't American kids."

"But Bill Gigot did."

"Bill didn't want them to run the peanut machines anymore, and they killed him for it."

They both fell silent a minute. Rose felt Bill was owed that. A moment of silence for a loving father.

"One thing I don't understand." Kristen cocked her head. "What were Paul and Modjeska fighting about, then? The Gigot murder happened way too long ago."

Rose thought of Modjeska's magnificent house. "I bet Modjeska was blackmailing him, about the Gigot murder."

"But if Modjeska told, they'd both lose."

"The senator had more to lose than Modjeska, and more money to spend. I bet Modjeska's been blackmailing him since the murder. He has too much money to explain, otherwise." Rose thought about Julie. "He tells people it's his wife's money, but I bet that's a lie. The only thing I don't get is why Senator Martin got involved."

"He was at Homestead then."

"Right, he was at Homestead, I forgot!" Rose remembered Senator Martin's speech at the assembly. "He mentioned being at Homestead. When was he there, exactly? What did he do?"

"He was CEO until about seven years ago, when he got elected."

"Bill Gigot was killed seven years ago."

Kristen gasped. "You think that Paul—"

"If he was the CEO, I bet he made the plan."

"No!" Kristen's hand flew to her mouth. "God, this makes me sick. I'm *sick*."

"My God," Rose said, hushed. She felt the realization land like a blow. "He killed people to take care of company profits, and his career. Our U.S. Senator is a murderer."

"You really think?"

"Yes." Rose thought aloud. "When Bill Gigot stopped playing ball, Modjeska killed him, and Senator Martin covered it up. It went down as an accident, and the senator pulled the strings to protect himself and Homestead. I learned on the factory tour that the company owns most of the land in the county. That means it's a powerful contributor to the tax base. Plus I wonder how much it contributed to Martin's campaign. I bet that went up after the Gigot murder, too." Rose thought of something else. "Modjeska went from Homestead to a job in state government in Maryland. I bet the soon-to-be Senator got him the job."

"This is a nightmare." Kristen wiped away a tear. "So what do we do now?"

"We go to the state police, and lay it out. Now, we have proof. You, and your story."

"No, you can't go to them. He knows people there."

"Then we go to the FBI."

Kristen bit her lip. "But they're trying to kill me. Maybe I should get out of the country—"

"Think this through, honey." Rose put a hand on her shoulder. "You can't keep running away. It doesn't work, not for long. Modjeska is dangerous. I think he killed Kurt Rehgard and Hank Powell, carpenters who started asking questions about the fire."

Kristen quieted, her eyes widening with fear.

"That's six people they've killed so far, to protect their secret. They're ruthless, and you're not alone, anymore. You have a child to think of now."

"I know." Kristen's eyes welled up. "What kind of man is he? He'd kill his own child."

"The FBI can protect you, and you can't do it on your own." Rose took her phone from the console and pressed 411 for information. "I'm calling them."

"Think it's open?"

"It has to be. It's the FBI, right? Not a frozen yogurt shop." Rose waited for the mechanical operator to come on and ask for the listing. "In Philadelphia, Pennsylvania, may I have the offices of the Federal Bureau of Investigation? I need to report a crime."

Suddenly, a cell phone started ringing in Kristen's pocket, and she leaned over and retrieved it while Rose waited for her call to connect.

Kristen got the phone, checked the display, and said, "It's Eileen. Should I answer?"

"Eileen Gigot is calling you?" Rose asked, surprised. "Why?" There was a click on her phone line, but no ringing yet.

"I don't know, but she did earlier, when I was driving here. I checked my voicemail, and her message said to call as soon as possible." Kristen's phone kept ringing in her hand, insistent.

Oh no. "It could be about Amanda. Quick, hurry, take it!"

"Yes, hello?" Kristen said into her phone.

"What, hello?" Rose said into her phone. She opened the door and got out of the car, sending up a silent prayer.

Please let her live.

Chapter Seventy

Rose stood talking on her phone at the edge of the cornfield, trying to understand the federal bureaucracy and watching moths fly into her car headlights. There was an analogy there, but she couldn't put her finger on it and she had solved enough mysteries for one night.

"Let me get this straight, sir," she said. "You're with the FBI, aren't you?"

"Yes, I'm a Complaint Agent."

"But you can't take complaints?"

"Not after 4:45 P.M. or on weekends."

"So you're a Complaint Agent who can't take complaints?"

"Not at 8:36 at night, I can't."

Rose had told him that she had information regarding a murder, because six murders would have sounded crazy. For the same reason, she'd left out the Senator Martin part. "But the FBI switchboard operator transferred me to you."

"I know, but we don't take complaints over the phone after business hours."

"Then why did she transfer me?"

"So I could tell you that."

Rose was dumbfounded. "You took the call to tell me you can't take the call?"

The Complaint Agent hesitated. "It's important to the Bureau that the public be able to reach a human being rather than an answering machine, to speak to them as we are, now."

"I don't know if I feel better that I'm talking to a human being, when I tell him that I have information regarding a murder, and he tells me he can't hear it right now. That sounds like a machine, to me." Rose looked over at the car, where Kristen was still on the phone with Eileen, her head down. "Sir, I'm sorry. My friend's life is at stake, and I don't know what to do."

"If your friend is in danger, then he or she should call 911 or the local police."

"But she can't. She's worried they may be in on it, like a conspiracy." Rose heard herself, and even she thought she sounded crazy.

"Then I encourage you and your friend to come down to our offices and make a complaint, or call back tomorrow and we'll take it over the phone."

"Okay, thank you." Rose hung up just as Kristen was getting out of the car and walking toward her, her smooth cheeks stained with new tears. In her outstretched hand was an open cell phone. Rose went weak in the knees, and she flashed on the explosion in the cafeteria. The fireball. Amanda screaming. Blood in her blond hair. The missing sandal.

Kristen held out the phone. "Eileen wants to talk to you."

Rose stared at the phone, but she couldn't take it. She didn't want to know. She couldn't hear it, not now. And not from a grief-stricken mother.

"Take it," Kristen said, softly. "Please."

Rose shook her head, no. The only sound was the crickets chirping and the moths hitting the car headlamps.

"No, it's not that," Kristen said, reading Rose's expression. "Amanda's alive, still in Intensive Care, but I messed up, I'm so sorry. I told Eileen about Bill's being murdered, and she's freaking out. Please, take the phone. Calm her down."

"*What?*" Rose felt stunned. "You *told* her? Why would you do that?"

"It just came out." Kristen covered the phone with her palm,

stricken. "She called to tell me that a man came by the hospital looking for me, saying he was my father. It had to be someone sent by
Modjeska or even Modjeska himself. I said, 'Watch out, he's a murderer,' and she said, 'What are you talking about,' so I told her."

Rose kicked herself. She should have warned Kristen not to blab.

"Rose, talk to her. Explain it to her. She has a right to know, doesn't
she?"

"Of course she does, but not now. Not this way. She's at her daughter's bedside, for God's sake."

"Please talk to her. I told her we're calling the FBI, but she's going
to the plant to confront them."

"To *Homestead*? When?"

"Now. Tonight. She says it's the Harvest Conference, and all the
bosses will be there. She's going to confront them about what really
happened to Bill and the peanut machines and—"

"No, she can't." Rose grabbed the phone. "Eileen, don't go to
Homestead! It's dangerous for you—"

The phone line went dead.

"No!" Rose thumbed to the log, then pressed CALL to call Eileen
back. The phone rang and rang, then went to voicemail, and she left
a message. "Eileen, please stop! Don't go to the plant. They'll kill—"

"End of message," interrupted a mechanical voice.

Chapter Seventy-one

Rose took Kristen by the shoulders and looked her in the eye. "Listen to me. You have to go to the FBI. Right now, by yourself. There's no time to lose."

"I have to go without you?" Kristen's eyes rounded, panicky.

"Yes, I have to stop Eileen. If they think she knows what happened to Bill, they'll kill her before she can breathe a word."

"But what about you? They'll try to kill you—"

"No, they don't know me, and even if they did, I look different than I used to. You hardly knew me, remember? Let's go, hurry." Rose hustled to her car with Kristen behind her, tugging at her elbow.

"But I'm afraid."

"I know, honey." Rose opened the car door. "But there's no other way. You can't go to Reesburgh with me, that's walking into the lion's den."

"Can't I stay here?"

"In a cornfield?" Rose touched her arm. "The sooner you get to the FBI, the safer you are. Isn't there anybody you trust, who could go with you?"

"My boyfriend, I guess. Erik. He's the greatest guy ever, and I dumped him for the senator. He wanted to get married. He'd do anything in the world for me."

"Then call him, right now. Have him come get you. Go to the FBI in Philly, in his car. Do not stop." Rose got into her car, twisted the key in the ignition, and looked out the open window. "Call Eileen back, too. If she doesn't pick up, keep trying. Tell her not to go to Homestead."

"Okay."

"You'll be fine. You can do it. *Alohomora.*"

Kristen smiled, shakily. "That unlocks things."

"Whatever. Be safe."

Kristen straightened up. "Okay. You, too."

Rose hit the gas, steered the car onto the road, and took off. She flew down the country lane, heading for the turnpike toward Reesburgh, keeping an eye out for cops. She passed one car, then another, barreling ahead in the cool, dark night, the gold stripe at the median glowing in her high beams.

Her heart was pounding, her teeth grinding. She hoped she could get to the plant in time. She'd left from farther away, and Eileen would have a forty-minute head start, unless one of her family members at the hospital had talked her out of going or delayed her.

Rose knew she wasn't as safe as she'd let Kristen believe. She'd left a major loose end at the plant today. The supervisor would wonder why the new hire had left and he'd probably call Trish, to check up on her alleged cousin. And when Trish told him she hadn't sent her cousin to the plant, they'd notify security, who'd be on the lookout, especially tonight, with the corporate prom.

Her left hand kept a death grip on the wheel while her right hand fumbled on the seat for her phone. She pressed L, and the phone rang and rang, then went to Leo's voicemail. She didn't want to scare him but she couldn't keep the emotion from her voice. "Babe, call me! I'm on my way to Homestead. Please, hurry—"

BEEP. Suddenly the phone went black. The battery had lost power.

"Damn it!" Rose tossed the phone aside and hit the gas.

Chapter Seventy-two

Rose tore down the turnpike and reached the Reesburgh exit in record time, but she still had the sinking sensation that it wouldn't be good enough. She squinted at the dashboard clock, its red digits aglow. 9:17.

She had failed. She'd be a full fifteen minutes behind Eileen. The realization brought tears to her eyes. There couldn't be one more death, not one. Not while she drew breath.

She blinked the wetness away and kept her foot on the gas, zipping down the fast lane. She flashed her high beams at a white VW to move out of her way, but all the cars were braking, their red taillights on at a curve in the road. She fed more gas, hoping the bottleneck would break up or she could pass on the right.

She zoomed around the curve, but the white VW was slowing even more, below the speed limit. The state cops had pulled somebody over on the right shoulder, and a police cruiser sat idling behind a blue van, its bar lights flashing red, white, and blue. Traffic slowed as it passed the scene, on temporary good behavior or gawking. The VW slowed to a crawl.

"Come on!" Rose slammed her palm on the wheel. She glanced over at the shoulder, then looked again. The driver of the stopped van looked like Eileen.

Rose switched into the slow lane, double-checking. A woman driver. Short blond hair. It *was* Eileen, and she was driving the same car she'd showed up in at the hospital, that awful night.

Well, are you happy now?

Rose passed Eileen and the state police car, her thoughts racing. What if the cop hadn't stopped Eileen for speeding? What if they'd found out that Eileen was on her way to the Harvest Conference? Would they alert someone at the plant? Homestead security? Mojo, too?

Rose's gut churned as the traffic picked up speed. She wasn't following Eileen anymore, she was leading her, and it put her in a better position. She steered off the exit and down the ramp, then took a left onto Allen Road, keeping an eye on the rearview for Eileen's blue van.

She sped up. She had to get to Homestead before Eileen, and now she had a fighting chance. There was no traffic, and Reesburgh was dark and empty, the town gone to sleep. She sped past the CVS, the line of box stores, and finally the elementary school, where it had all begun.

And now, finally, it would end.

Tonight.

Chapter Seventy-three

WELCOME TO HOMESTEAD SNACK FOODS, read the sign, and Rose saw it with new eyes. The campus was quiet without the hubbub of school groups and visitors, but the streetlamps and the windows in the corporate offices blazed with light, like a plastic town in a model train set-up. Bright, false, and lifeless.

She cruised down the access road, passing the exits signed for VISITORS, BUSES, and MAIN PLANT. The main plant had no windows to show the lights inside, but she could hear the faint noise of the production machinery. Clouds of steam spewed from the smokestacks, hissing when they hit the cool night air. The employee parking lot was only partly full, and Rose remembered from the tour that a third of the employees worked the night shift.

She kept an eye out for Eileen's van but it wasn't anywhere in sight. She hadn't seen it in the rearview mirror on the way over, but she hadn't gone slow enough to let Eileen catch up with her. She had a different plan in mind.

She took a left at the Conference Center sign, peeling off onto a long road that wound through the trees and fed into its large parking lot, almost full to capacity. Lamps illuminated the lot at regular intervals, casting cool light on the still cars. She parked at the back near the entrance, as far away from a lamp as possible, then cut the ignition, scanning the scene.

The lot was quiet, because everybody was already at the huge party at the Conference Center. The building had floor-to-ceiling glass windows, and inside, hundreds of dressed-up couples danced on the wooden floor or ate at round banquet tables, lit with candles. A large band played, and the *thumpa-thumpa* of bad seventies rock carried on the night air, then the horn section segued into some sort of fanfare. Men in tuxes ascended a decorated dais, presumably the Homestead CEO and other corporate officers. The last tuxedoed man in line was Senator Martin, who climbed the steps waving his hands, and the crowd broke into applause loud enough to be heard in the parking lot.

Rose checked the building entrance, on the side of the building facing the corporate offices. Smokers stood outside the main doors, the red tips of their cigarettes glowing, and two security guards were talking, visible only because of their bright white shirts and caps. Parked off to the side was a white sedan that read PLANT SECURITY, and she guessed that Senator Martin would have his own security detail inside.

Rose cracked her driver's side door, slipped outside, and stole across the access road to the other side, then ducked behind the shrubs. The ground was cool and the shrubs scratchy, but she stayed low, and waited. It didn't take long.

Eileen's blue van cruised slowly down the access road to the conference center, approaching the parking lot.

Rose got up into a crouching position, but stayed behind the bush.

Eileen glided into the lot and parked in a space far from the entrance to the conference center, near Rose's car. The window on the driver's side was closed, but Rose could see Eileen because of her light hair.

Eileen had faced the van so that she'd be away from the conference center, just as Rose had thought she would.

It was time to go.

Rose counted.

One, two, three.

Chapter Seventy-four

"Eileen, let me in, quick!" Rose whispered, trying the van door, which was locked. She showed her face, plastering her hands to the window. "It's me, Rose!"

Eileen turned in shock, her eyes wild with fear. She scrambled away from the window, toward the passenger seat.

"Let me in! It's okay, it's me, Rose."

Eileen's expression relaxed, then she leaned over and unlocked the door. "What are you doing here? You're a redhead now?"

"Shh, they'll hear us." Rose jumped into the driver's seat and closed the door behind her. "They'll come running. Is that what you want? Shhh."

"What do you want? What's the matter with you?"

"Eileen, we have to get out of here and go to the FBI—"

"Are you crazy?" Eileen's face was an anguished mask in the light from the streetlamps. "Didn't you do enough to my family? You're haunting me?"

"Eileen, it must have been awful to hear, about Bill, but—"

"Don't say his first name, like you know him. You didn't know him. You don't know me. Leave me alone."

"I'm on your side."

"No, you're not. You left Amanda in that fire."

"No, I didn't, but this isn't the time or the place to talk about that. You can hate me all you want, but let's leave now and convict these guys. One is Senator Martin!"

"This is none of your business. This is my business. Why are you in it at all?"

"I was looking into the cause of the fire and it led to Homestead, that's all. I'm sorry if you think I meddled, but this isn't the way to do—"

"Don't tell me what to do," Eileen interrupted, her eyes wild. "This is *my* husband we're talking about. You still have yours!"

"Eileen, listen. They could be watching us right now. I saw you get pulled over on the turnpike. What if they did it to stop you?"

"How do you know I got pulled over? Are you following me? Are you a stalker?"

"They'll kill you, Eileen. They don't want to go to prison and they'll have to, if the truth comes out." Rose gestured at the conference center. "Look at the entrance. They have security guards. What are you going to do? They won't let you in—"

"I know those guys. I've had them over for barbeques. They can't do a thing to me, not in front of the whole company." Eileen turned away, yanked on the door handle, and started to get out of the van, but Rose grabbed her arm.

"Please, don't go—"

"Get off!"

The last thing Rose saw was a manicured fist.

Heading for her face.

Chapter Seventy-five

Rose regained consciousness, groggy. She opened her eyes. She lay slumped in the driver's seat of the van. Her left cheek was killing her. She was alone. She came alive with one thought.

Eileen.

She boosted herself up in the seat and spotted a commotion at the entrance of the conference center. Two Homestead security guards were struggling to put Eileen into the security sedan. One clapped a hand over Eileen's mouth, and the other held her flailing arms, and they succeeded in getting her into the backseat and slamming the door closed.

Oh my God.

Rose looked to the right. Inside the conference center, the party continued as if nothing had happened. Oblivious, the guests filled the banquet tables, all of their attention on the dais, where Senator Martin was talking at the podium in front of the Homestead executives.

Rose looked back, aghast, as one security guard bolted to the driver's seat and the other hustled back to the entrance. The sedan emitted a plume of exhaust and steered smoothly to the left, then turned around and drove toward the access road.

Rose ducked down in the seat as it slid past, her heart hammering. If she got out of the van and screamed, they'd come and take her away, like Eileen. She didn't have a phone to call anybody. Her only advantage was that the security guards didn't know she was here, though they'd come looking for Eileen's van, later. If they killed Eileen, they wouldn't leave her van behind. They wouldn't leave any evidence. They hadn't, before.

Rose checked the ignition, and the keys were still there, hanging. She'd be ready to follow the sedan if it left the campus; but it drove up the access road, took the exit to the main plant, and vanished inside. It was as if the building had swallowed the sedan whole, with Eileen inside.

Rose cracked the door, crept out of the van, left the door open, and walked to the bumper in a crouch. She reached the end of the van and checked the entrance. The security guard remained out front, and a smoker had returned, lighting up. Neither was looking her way.

She took a deep breath and darted across the aisle to the next block of parked cars, still in a crouch. Then waited, catching her breath. The main plant was on the hill, and behind it, on the left side, where the sedan had gone in, was a loading dock, a paved area with huge tractor-trailers parked all around. One of the bays was open, making a rectangle of bright light, but there didn't appear to be any activity there.

She bolted ahead to the next block of cars, and ducked behind them, catching her breath. Her heart started to hammer from exertion and fear. She was a mom, not an action hero. Then she realized something:

Every mom is an action hero.

She ran ahead to the next block, then the next, with only one last set of parked cars between her and edge of the lot. She glanced around the sleek bumper of a Jaguar and checked the entrance. The guard and the smoker were still at the entrance. She ran to the next block of cars, then sized up the hillside ahead. Her knees were killing her, her heart was pumping. She'd be exposed while she ran up the grass to the plant, but she had no choice.

Go, go, go.

She tore up the incline, trying to stay low, but then gave up and ran as hard as she could up the hill. Her breath came in ragged bursts. Her heart thundered in her chest.

She dropped behind the first tractor-trailer she saw, then darted between two other trucks parked together. Bright security lights were mounted along the top of the plant, but there was nobody around outside. Still, she'd have to stay out of sight. She didn't hear any sirens or sounds, and it made her stronger, emboldening her.

She peeked around the front of the truck, trying to figure out her next move. The trucks were parked at the loading docks, cab fronts facing out, and there were four trucks in all; the lighted bay was to the far right, and she had to go left.

She ran from one cab to the next, just as she had with the parked cars, until she raced to the end of the plant, then flattened herself against the building. She could hear the noise of the machinery and feel its vibration against her back. She heard no other sound, so she peeked around the corner.

No one was around. Ahead lay more paved area, and lights mounted on the roofline shone ellipses onto the dry asphalt. It was the back of the plant, and there were no trucks or other vehicles. The building was a stretch of rough, white-painted cinderblock, with no window or door. A third of the way up, there was a break in the wall where she thought the white security sedan had gone.

Go!

She tore along the side of the plant until she got to the break in the wall, then stopped. There was no sound of people talking or cars running, so she peered around the side. The white security sedan sat parked inside a small U-shaped bay lined with blue recycling bins, galvanized cans, and flattened cardboard boxes. No one was inside the car or in sight. The bay had three doors, all painted yellow, none signed. One had to lead to the security office, where Eileen must have been taken, but Rose didn't know which one.

She felt stumped, momentarily. She couldn't remember enough from the factory tour to orient herself. She'd gotten turned around because she'd approached the plant from the back. All she could remember was that the security office was along a hall with the other offices, in the middle of the building.

"You have to be kidding me," said a man, from behind.

Chapter Seventy-six

Rose turned in fear. She was thrown against the building. Her head exploded in pain. A hand clamped over her mouth. She knew who it was before she opened her eyes.

Mojo.

"You're out of your depth, Mom." He snorted, standing so close she could smell the cigar on his breath.

She pushed her terror away. She hadn't come this far to be denied. Mojo thought she was only a mom. He didn't know she was an action hero. She kneed him in the groin with all of her might.

"Ooof!" He staggered backwards, and she took off down the side of the plant, running for her life.

"Help! Help!" Rose veered around the corner toward the lighted bay on the loading dock. It was time for Plan B. There had to be employees driving forklifts there. "Help!"

Suddenly a recorded announcement blared through speakers mounted at the roof of the building: "All Homestead employees, please exit the building immediately, using the main entrance. Please exit the building immediately. This is not a drill."

Oh no. Rose could hear the commotion inside the plant, alarmed voices and chatter, but she kept running.

"I'll kill you!" Mojo panted, almost at her heels. He couldn't use his gun or he would alarm everybody. He was big, but she was faster, scooting ahead.

"Help!" she screamed, but it was drowned out by the recorded announcement, on a continuous loop.

She tore past the tractor-trailers, aiming for the lighted bay. She could barely catch her breath. Terror and adrenaline powered her. Only four trucks to go. Then three, then two, then one. The loading dock was high, up close. Four feet off the ground.

Jump, jump, jump!

She leapt onto the dock, but it caught her in the waist. Pain arced through her stomach. She clawed the concrete for purchase, her legs flailing.

"Goddamn you!" Mojo growled, but Rose scrambled up just ahead of him, got to her feet, and darted through the open bay into the loading area inside the plant.

"Help!" she screamed, but the employees had evacuated. Forklifts stood where they'd been left, their headlights still on. The production machinery chugged away, like a ghost factory.

She raced through the loading area past the X-ray machines, deserted now. Boxes were piling up at the scanner.

She tore past the packing area, her thoughts racing. If she could find the main entrance, she could get help. She couldn't die here. Neither could Eileen.

"You bitch!" Mojo shouted, out of breath, but he kept coming.

Rose blew through two swinging doors, her legs churning. She tore down a long hallway, burst through another set of doors, and found herself surrounded by lines of huge stainless steel machines that read PPM TECHNOLOGIES, with a myriad of red tubes.

She spun around, looking for a place to get out. A line of whirring knives sliced the potatoes. A line of sorters dropped them into a funnel. Conveyor belts fed them into cooking oil in covered tanks. The oil boiled, the air felt hot. She panted, her heart thundered.

There! Go!

She bolted for a set of rubber-tipped metal stairs, praying she could take them easier than the heavyset Mojo. If she ran him hard enough, she could keep the advantage. She bounded up the stairs just ahead of him. At the top was a rickety metal catwalk. She took off, running, setting the catwalk swinging.

"You're dead!" Mojo shouted, charging after her. The catwalk jumped with his extra weight.

The next set of stairs lay ahead, and she ran down them, almost falling, then sprinted along the tile floor. She glanced over her shoulder.

Mojo was right behind her, almost falling, so she sprinted ahead and raced up the next set of stairs up to the catwalk, to tire him out.

"Damn you!" he shouted, but she ran along the catwalk, almost out of breath, clutching the metal rails not to fall.

Mojo ran behind her, keeping pace. She ran above the packing room, where the air got cooler, then got hot again over the next room, where the kettle-cooked chips were made. Stainless steel ovens with red tubes cooked the chips in open trays of boiling oil.

Rose tore down the next set of stairs. The room ended ten feet ahead. She had blown it. She whirled around on her heels, in terror. There was nowhere else to go.

She was trapped.

Chapter Seventy-seven

Mojo jumped from the stairs to the floor, grabbed a long metal hook from the wall, and whipped it at her face.

Rose raised her hands, leaping backwards. The hook sliced her forearm. She screamed in pain. On the downswing, the hook caught one of the red hoses on the machines, severing it. It was a bundle of live wires and it sprang free of the machine as if it were alive, sparking through the air like an electrified anaconda.

"You're dead!" Mojo grimaced. The live wire whipped and crackled in the air. He advanced with grim purpose, his dark eyes glittering.

Rose ran terrified to the back wall. There was nowhere else to go. She was too far from the stair. The only door was on the opposite diagonal.

Mojo stood in her path, swinging the hooked stick with the power of a drive off the fairway. His loafer slipped on the tile floor, and the hook hit the stainless steel oven with so much force that it embedded itself in the side.

Rose fled to the far corner. Above, the live wire lashed through the air, showering sparks.

Mojo yanked the hook from the machine. Boiling oil leaked from the hole onto the tile floor, bubbling hot. He sidestepped it, raising the hook high over his head. He was about to bring it down on Rose, but when he whipped it back, it connected with the live wire.

Mojo spasmed as electricity coursed through his body. His eyes popped. His mouth flew open. His throat emitted an inhuman cry. The skin on his face blistered. A disgusting stench filled the air. He collapsed, electrocuted. The hook fell from his hand, breaking the circuit. The live wire snapped away, showering sparks that ignited the oil, engulfing his body in flames.

Rose flattened herself into the corner, horrified. Oil poured from the hole in the oven, spreading all over the floor. Fire raced along its stream back to the huge oven, which exploded in flames.

Whoomp! went the sound. The fire jumped from one open tray to the next, the oil as flammable as jet fuel. *Whoomp! Whoomp! Whoomp!* In a minute, the ovens were beds of lethal flames.

Alarms blared, deafening. Hoods over the ovens sprayed a chemical mist. Overhead sprinklers showered water. The oil on the floor exploded when the water hit it, raging higher. Any speck of residual oil burst into flame; oil lining the ducts, oil coating the machinery, and oil covering the steps and the catwalk. The room became a blazing inferno.

Rose screamed in terror. A wall of flame stood between her and the exit doors. Sprinklers sprayed water, making the grease fire worse. Smoke billowed everywhere. She couldn't breathe for the heat. She flashed on the school fire. She never thought she'd find herself here again. She couldn't fail this time. She couldn't lose Eileen.

Think, think, think.

Rose knew there had to be fire extinguishers. She ran through the smoke along the wall, where the flames were lowest. She found a round metal fire extinguisher big enough for commercial kitchens, mounted on the wall. It looked like her red one at home, except gigantic. She wrenched the extinguisher off its mount, almost dropping it because it was heavy and hot.

She yanked out its pin, squeezed the handle, and grabbed the nozzle. She sprayed a chemical mist on the fire, smothering a path so she could get through the flames. She reached the doors and banged through them. She dropped the heavy extinguisher, which fell with a *clang* and rolled noisily away.

Thick smoke filled the hallway. Sprinklers drenched her. Fire alarms blared. She heard sirens in the distance, too far away. She coughed and coughed. Her eyes teared. Her lungs burned.

"Eileen!" Rose screamed through the sirens and the water.

Chapter Seventy-eight

Rose looked right, then left. Both hallways were identical cinder-block corridors, filling with smoke. She didn't know which way to go. Her eyes stung. Her lungs burned. She coughed and coughed. She tried to remember the plant layout from the tour. The offices had been in the hallway connecting the pretzel to the potato chip production. She had to find that junction.

She sensed it was to the right. She ran down the hall that way, burst through the double doors, and found herself in another hallway. The window onto the factory floor showed a horrific conflagration that burned cardboard boxes, wooden pallets, cellophane shrink-wrapping, and anything else in its path. Then she realized. If it was boxes, it had to be the warehouse. She flashed on what the tour guide had said:

See all these boxes? They go for blocks and blocks!

Rose remembered that the warehouse was between the chips and pretzel production. She was on the right track. She ran down the hall. Smoke filtered the air but it smelled of something else, too. Pretzels.

Go, go, go.

She flew through another set of double doors, her lungs burning and tears spilling from her eyes. The smell of burned pretzels got stronger and stronger, and each window showed a factory on fire. The hallways twisted left, then right. She pounded through another set of doors, and she was finally there, at the hallway of offices. QUALITY ASSURANCE read the first sign, and she bolted to the next office. DIRECTOR OF SECURITY.

"Eileen!" Rose tried the door. It was locked. She looked through the window beside the door. The anteroom was filling with smoke, slipping underneath the door. No one was inside. The door beyond it was closed. If Eileen was here, she was behind that door. Rose had to get inside.

She looked around for something, anything. On the floor down the hall was a large metal trashcan. She bolted to it, picked it up, and struggled back down the hall with it, trailing garbage. She reached the office and slammed the trashcan at the window.

Bam! The trashcan shattered the window but didn't break it all the way. *Bam!* Rose slammed it again, heaving it as hard as she could, straining with exertion. She couldn't breathe for the smoke. Her eyes teared uncontrollably.

Bam! Bam! She hit it twice more, widening the hole, breathing hard. She couldn't lift the trashcan another minute. She let it fall, and it dropped loudly to the floor.

She broke off pieces of the jagged plastic with her hand, then reached through and twisted the lock on the knob. It turned. She yanked her hand out of the jagged hole, opened the door, and ran inside.

"Eileen!" she screamed. Smoke made it almost impossible to breathe in the small room. She prayed she'd gotten to Eileen in time and that the security guys hadn't taken her away. She went to the door, and it was unlocked.

She twisted the knob and burst through the door.

Chapter Seventy-nine

"Eileen!" Rose cried out in relief. The office was smoky but Eileen was alive, struggling against rope that bound her to a metal chair. Her eyes were wide above duct tape covering her mouth. A bruise on her forehead showed fresh blood. She made guttural noises, trying to talk.

"Don't worry, I got you." Rose rushed to Eileen's side. Duct tape bound her ankles, and her arms were wrenched behind her back.

"Hang on, this'll hurt." Rose yanked the duct tape from her mouth. It came off with a *zzzp,* leaving a wide red welt.

"Oh, God." Eileen took a huge gulp of smoky air and started coughing.

"Wait, we need oxygen." Rose looked around. There was a windowless metal door between metal bookshelves on the back wall, and she hustled to it. "They brought you in through this door, right?"

"Yeah." Eileen coughed, her face turning red.

"Hold on." Rose turned the knob and pushed the door open. The bay was empty. The white security sedan was gone. Sirens sounded louder, closer. Fresh air *whoosh*ed in the office, making a whirlwind of the smoke that set Eileen coughing harder, and Rose went back to her side, kneeling. "You okay?" she asked, touching her back.

"Get your hands off me!" Eileen coughed. "Don't think we're friends now. You should have saved Amanda, instead of me."

Rose didn't have time to discuss it. She grabbed a scissors from the desk and wedged the blade between the rope around Eileen's hands. They had turned bright red, her circulation cut off.

"You left my daughter." Eileen kept coughing. "I'd give my life for hers any day."

Rose sawed through the rope, thinning it. She yanked, and it broke, then she started to cut and unravel the rest.

"Bastards." Eileen squirmed and shimmied, struggling to free herself. "They killed Bill. They were gonna kill me when Mojo got back. I bet he took off."

"No, he didn't." Rose snipped the last rope, flashing on that awful sight. "He's dead."

"How?" Eileen bent over and undid the tape on her left ankle. "In the fire?"

"More or less." Rose bent down and ripped the tape off of her right ankle.

"Sorry I hit you, but you deserved it." Eileen jumped up and shook off the pieces of rope.

"I've had better apologies, but let's get out of here. I'll show you the way, once we get outside."

"Gimme a break. I know this plant like the back of my hand." Eileen scooted out the door, with Rose on her heels.

Chapter Eighty

Rose and Eileen raced around the corner of the plant toward the lights and activity in front. The campus was in a state of emergency, abuzz with motion, shouting, and sirens. The air reeked of burned rubber, plastic, and oil. Black smoke leaked from the exhaust vents and stacks on the plant's roof, sending sparks and cinders into the night sky. Thirty-some firetrucks were already fighting the fire, raging at the opposite side of the plant. Firefighters in heavy coats with reflective stripes ran this way and that, hauling thick hoses that lay on the asphalt like a snakes' nest.

Rose and Eileen ran toward the access road, parked up with state police cruisers, ambulances, black sedans, and boxy white newsvans, forming an improvised cordon between the burning plant and the Homestead corporate offices. A massive crowd filled the corporate parking lot, and Rose and Eileen hurried toward it, out of harm's way.

Tears filled Rose's eyes when she realized that they were finally safe, and all she could think about was Leo and the kids. She felt a surge of deep emotion, a profound and unreasoning yearning to see them all, to be together again, whole and happy. She didn't know if Leo had gotten her message before the battery died, or if he could make it here in time. She looked for him in the crowd, but they were shapeless silhouettes, backlit by the emergency vehicles and illuminated windows of the offices.

Someone started shouting, and Assistant District Attorney Howard Kermisez, his young assistant Rick Artiss, and a cadre of state policemen, FBI agents in navy blue windbreakers, and black-uniformed EMTs came running toward Rose and Eileen.

"Help!" Eileen shouted, with Rose behind, and the first to reach them were the EMTs.

"We need to get you away from this building." An EMT eyed Eileen's forehead on the fly. "Is that bruise impairing your vision? Can you see?"

"I'm fine." Eileen hurried toward Howard, Rick, the state policemen, and the FBI agents, as a second EMT hustled to Rose.

"Let's get you to the hospital," the second EMT said, taking Rose's arm and hustling her forward. "We need to get you treated."

"Thanks." Rose kept looking for Leo, but the crowd was still too far away.

"Thank God you're here!" Eileen met the state police, the Assistant District Attorney, and the FBI on asphalt wet from the firehoses. "I'm Eileen Gigot and I was almost murdered tonight. Three men, security guards at Homestead, tried to kill me. I have their names and descriptions. They killed my husband, seven years ago."

"Mrs. Gigot, come with us," said one of the state policemen, his eyes alarmed under the wide brim of his hat. "You can give us a statement later. Please come away from this area. It's too dangerous."

Howard Kermisez took Eileen's arm, falling into step beside her. "Mrs. Gigot, we're fully briefed at my office—"

"No way, Howard." The FBI agent grabbed Eileen's other arm, flashing a brown billfold with a shiny badge at Eileen. "I'm Special Agent Jacob Morrisette, from the Wilmington office of the FBI. This is a matter of federal jurisdiction, and we'll handle this." He turned to Rose. "I know you're Rose McKenna, and we have Kristen Canton at our office in Philadelphia. Come with us, please."

Howard hurried along. "Jake, this is our case. It's a matter of state law, and the criminal acts took place in Reesburgh County—"

"Not now, gentlemen," the first EMT said firmly, on the fly. "These women need medical attention, first thing."

"No, I said, I'm fine." Eileen waved him away. "We have to catch those men. They left about twenty minutes ago."

"Here's the plan, people." Special Agent Morrisette hustled them along, followed by the authorities and EMTs. "The staties will put out an APB, and we'll get you ladies some medical attention, then we'll sort this all out at our offices. Hurry, come with us."

Rose let herself be hustled toward the crowd, scanning it for Leo. She didn't see him among the state policemen, Homestead employees in yellow jumpsuits, Harvest Conference executives in glittery gowns and tuxes, and Reesburgh residents, of all ages. Everyone's gazes were riveted to the fire, and every face showed shock, pain, and heartbreak. Some Homestead employees cried freely.

Rose thought of Juanita, June, and Sue, who'd been so kind to her, and she wondered if they'd be out of jobs now. She passed the crest-fallen executives and sales reps, thinking of the enormous loss to the employees, the residents, and the town itself. She realized with a shock that somewhere along the line, Reesburgh had become her home.

"Eileen, Rose, over here!" someone shouted. Tanya Robertson and her TV crew hurried toward them, their videocameras whirring and klieglights blinding. Tanya held out her microphone, but the state police rushed to prevent her from crossing the cordon.

"Eileen, why were you in the fire?" Tanya shouted. "What's going on? How did you and Rose get together?"

"Tanya, here's the scoop," Eileen answered, facing the camera. "My husband, Bill, was murdered seven years ago, and tonight they tried to kill me, too."

"*What?*" Tanya said, shocked. "Who?" The crowd burst into ex-cited chatter. People in the back craned their necks, trying to see and hear. The FBI agents tried to pull Eileen away, but she didn't budge, grabbing the microphone.

"We need to find the men who killed my husband. The ones who tried to kill me are Roger Foster, Paul Jensen, and Deke Rainwater. They were in a conspiracy with Joseph Modjeska, who was killed in the fire. I want them arrested for murder and attempted murder."

"Do you have evidence to support these allegations?" Tanya asked, barely containing her excitement.

"I sure do. So does Rose, who saved my life." Eileen jerked a thumb at Rose, and Tanya turned to her, with the microphone.

"Did you really save her life, Ms. McKenna?" Tanya held out the microphone. "Don't you have any comment for me, this time?"

Suddenly, Rose spotted a motorcade of black sedans, behind the crowd. The cars were gliding away from the campus, heading out the access road and toward the highway. It had to be Senator Martin and his entourage.

"Yes, I do have something to say." Rose pointed to the motorcade. "There goes Senator Martin. He's the mastermind behind the conspiracy. He's responsible for the murders of Bill Gigot and also Kurt Rehgard and Hank Powell, of Bethany Run Construction." The crowd gasped, but Rose didn't stop, her voice ringing clear and strong, like truth itself. "He's even behind the fire last week at Reesburgh Elementary School, which killed three people and put my daughter and Amanda Gigot in the hospital. The fire wasn't an accident, it was premeditated murder, by Senator Martin and his coconspirators."

Tanya's mouth dropped open, Eileen cheered, and the crowd erupted into gasps, chatter, and shouting. The FBI agents looked at the state police, the state police looked at the Assistant District Attorneys, and all hell broke loose.

"That's enough of that, ladies," said Special Agent Morrisette, clamping a strong hand on Rose's arm and trying to tug her from the microphone.

"Hey, wait a minute," she said, tugging back, until she saw Leo fighting his way to the front of the roiling crowd, his tie flying.

"Let her speak!" he shouted, struggling past a state policeman, and Special Agent Morrisette turned on him.

"Sir! Get behind that cordon! Who do you think you are?"

"I'm her husband. And if she has something to say, then let her say it. Honey?" Leo turned to Rose, his eyes shining. "Like your new hair, by the way."

"I do have something to say." Rose felt tears come to her eyes and reached for him. "I love you."

Chapter Eighty-one

Rose and Leo left the FBI offices at dawn, holding hands as they walked along Market Street, in Philadelphia. The city was just waking up, and the sun was rising behind the buildings, painting the sky with swaths of yellow, like fresh latex from a roller. Only a few people were on the street, and two uniformed cops stood talking in front of the federal building. A street-cleaning truck with a rotary brush whirred water at the curb, and a SEPTA bus hissed past, half-empty. The only store open was the Dunkin' Donuts across the street.

Rose breathed in fresh air, carrying the scent of glazed doughnuts and the first chill of autumn. "Smells good."

"For a city, yes." Leo looked around. "But I spent all week here. I've had enough."

"Congratulations on your settlement."

"Thanks." Leo looked over with an easy smile. His eyes were tired, and his chin sported stubble, but he looked happy and relaxed, his tie loose and his khaki jacket catching the breeze. "I'd tell you how it went, but it doesn't compare with chasing murderous senators and exposing corporate conspiracies."

Rose smiled. "Not bad for a week's work."

Leo squeezed her hand. "Has it only been a week?"

"Yes." Rose couldn't believe it herself. "It's Friday morning. One week ago today, the cafeteria caught fire."

"Jeez." Leo shook his head, and Rose sent up a silent prayer that Amanda would be okay. Last night, she and Eileen had been questioned by the FBI and the Assistant District Attorneys, but they'd been in two separate interview rooms, and Eileen had left for the hospital before Rose was finished. "Too bad we didn't get to say good-bye to Eileen."

"What?" Leo looked at her like she was nuts. "She punched you in the face, babe."

"I would have done the same thing, if someone left Melly in a fire." Rose was oddly fine with it, maybe because her face didn't hurt that much. She'd iced the bump last night with a gel pack and felt like herself again, having washed off her makeup disguise. Although she was thinking about keeping the red hair, which suited the new her.

"Still, please, don't do anything like this again." Leo shuddered. "You could have been killed."

"It's all over now." Rose squeezed his hand, and she could feel his love in the warmth of his palm. "I'm fine."

"Never again, promise?"

"Promise."

"Nothing can happen to you. I'll never get another wife as good-lookin'."

"Stop."

Leo smiled. "One thing I don't understand. Why would Campanile let Mojo do all the stuff he did?"

"I don't think they knew." Rose had a worry, too. "It really bothers me that they might not be able to prove that Kurt and Hank Powell were murdered. Howard said they don't have the blood to do a toxicology screen, but I bet it would show that his new friends slipped him a drug."

"Maybe they can check out his car, see if it shows evidence that he was hit, like a paint scrape." Leo looked over, brightening. "I have an idea. When this all dies down, why don't we offer to take his niece out, with Melly? Baseball's over but I can get some Eagles tickets."

"That's a nice thought." Rose squeezed his hand. "I wonder when it will die down. I can't wait to see Senator Martin indicted. He played it smart, didn't he? Kept the conspiracy to just a few guys on the night shift and Mojo, who did the dirty work." Rose felt disgusted. "What is it with corporations? Aren't they just made of people? Don't they have kids?"

"They don't think that way when it comes to money. And it's somebody else's kids, not their own." Leo shook his head. "They'll get Martin. He'll be going away for life. Not only for his role in the murders, but for the corruption that was involved in the blackmail. It's just a matter of time."

Rose thought he was right. Late last night, the FBI had arrested the three Homestead security guards, in Virginia. "Maybe one of the security guards will flip."

"Flip?" Leo looked over, eyes narrowing.

"I heard it on *Law & Order.*"

"Don't mess with a lunch mom."

"Exactly." Rose smiled. "I hope they can rebuild the plant. It was awful to see it burn. Would they be insured for that?"

"Sure. The bad guys will go to jail, the board will replace them, and the company will rebuild. It's too successful not to." Leo squeezed her hand again. "And by the way, we're in the clear, eh?"

"Thank God." Rose breathed a relieved sigh. The D.A. wouldn't hold her responsible for Mojo's death or for what had happened to Amanda. "And I really doubt Eileen will sue me now, on her own."

"It better go without saying. You saved her life." Leo smiled. "All's well that ends well."

"Except for one thing." Rose's thoughts kept circling back to the same place. "I hope to God that Amanda comes out of this."

"Me, too." They both lapsed into silence as they reached the corner and turned right toward the parking lot.

The wind disappeared, and they approached the grim gray column of the Federal Detention Center, with its slitted windows. Ahead lay the Police Administration Building and the expressway, where rush hour was starting. Rose felt the pulse of the city beginning to beat, but she didn't miss the excitement. She felt as if her life was starting over, in Reesburgh. She hoped that Melly would have it easier now, but that could be too much to ask.

"Wow." Leo shook his head, musing. "I still don't get how you figured all this out. A school fire that's intentional, set to kill a teacher who's having a senator's baby, and a forklift accident that's no accident, to cover up a scheme that would kill children."

"So many people are gone now." Rose sighed, sadly, thinking of them all. Marylou Battle, Serena Perez, Ellen Conze. Kurt Rehgard, Hank Powell, and Bill Gigot. Even Mojo. All that death, all so tragic and pointless.

"But still, you figured it out. I'm proud of you, and more importantly, I'm sorry." Leo stopped and turned to face her, eyeing her directly. His expression grew serious, and his entire body seemed to still. "I was wrong. I shouldn't have vetoed you with Oliver. We'll get him to make a statement that we won't be suing the school."

"Good."

"And from now on, you and I will talk about everything, until we're sick to death of talking, and we'll make no moves without agreeing. Forgive me, partner?"

"I do."

"You said that already, at the altar. And I do, too." Leo smiled, and Rose smiled back.

"Does this mean we're getting married, all over again?"

"Yes. So now I can kiss the bride, for keeps." Leo leaned over and gave her a soft kiss, then more deeply, and Rose kissed him back fully, feeling them reconnect as a couple, renewing their vows, on the fly.

"I love you," Rose said, when Leo released her.

"I love you, too. And I miss the kids."

"Me, too."

"Let's go get our family." Leo looped an arm around her shoulder, and Rose slid her hand around his waist.

And they walked to the car, together.

Chapter Eighty-two

Rose and Leo pulled into the driveway at the cabin and got out of the car, and Melly came tearing across the Vaughns' lawn toward them, her hair flying. Princess Google scampered behind, her plumed tail wagging furiously.

"Mom, Leo!" Melly called out, and Rose threw open her arms.

"Sweetie!" Rose hugged her close, breathing her in. "I missed you so much!"

"Ready for your surprise?"

"Sure." Rose kissed her and set her down. They'd called on the way, and Melly had told her she'd had a surprise for them. "Let's see."

"It's not here. We have to go somewhere else."

"Okay, you're the boss." Rose smiled, petting Princess Google, who had climbed up on her leg, resting feathery paws on her knee. "Hi, Googie girl!"

"Leo!" Melly ran to Leo, who lifted her up and gave her a bear hug and a little grunt.

"Melly Belly! Where you been all my life?" Leo kissed her on the cheek, and Rose turned to see Mo coming out of the house, in his navy polo and jeans, followed by Gabriella, dressed the same, holding John.

"How's my baby boy?" she said, hurrying toward him, and John burst into a smile, looking so natty in his white T-shirt, Mom jeans, and two whole teeth. "I missed you, buddy boy! I missed my baby!" She scooped him up, hugged him close, and kissed his head, then grinned at Gabriella. "Girl, do we owe you! How can I thank you? Dinner? A night on the town? A car?"

"Nonsense, we loved it." Gabriella beamed. "You're a celebrity. You're all over the news."

"Yes!" Mo came up from behind, grinning. "Why didn't you tell us you were a crimefighter?"

"Ha!" Leo smiled. "She didn't tell me, why would she tell you?"

"Let's go, Mo!" Melly started jumping up and down, and Rose noticed she had on new brown shoes with her jeans and Harry Potter T-shirt.

"Where'd you get those shoes?"

"They're boots! Come on, Mr. V.!" Melly ran to Mo, who checked his watch.

"You're right. Can't be late. Gotta go."

"Where?" Rose smiled, mystified.

"Not far," Gabriella answered. "You all go ahead. I'll stay here with the dog and get lunch ready. Come here, Googie!"

Mo nodded. "Let's hit the road. Rose, why don't you and Leo follow us in your car?"

Melly bounded after Mo. "I'll go with Mr. V."

Rose blinked. She couldn't remember Melly ever choosing not to ride with her. Mischief was afoot. She looked at Leo.

"Don't ask me," he said, with a happy shrug.

Chapter Eighty-three

Rose and Leo stood together in the back pasture of a small horse farm, down the road from the cabin. The trees blazed with orange, red, and gold, and dry, grassy hills rolled on and on. Post-and-rail fences separated the pastures, and in the middle sat a white barn with a tin roof, faded red. Mo and Melly had gone inside, asking Rose and Leo to stay here and wait for the surprise.

"I'm trying not to worry." Rose cuddled John, who hooked his little arm around her neck. "Mo's not putting her on a horse, is he?"

"Relax." Leo smiled easily, slipping an arm around her shoulder. "He wouldn't do anything unsafe with her."

Rose turned, and Melly was sitting atop a furry black horse, grinning as if she'd ridden all her life. She had on a black helmet and buckskin jodhpurs, and even though Mo stood beside her, Rose felt her heart jump into her throat. "Leo, you see this?"

"She'll be fine."

"Bsbsb!" John squealed, pumping his arm when he spotted Melly.

"How do you know she'll be fine?"

"Shh. He's coming over."

"Mo!" Rose managed not to freak as he strode over. "Is this safe? She's not that great in sports. She's double-jointed. She trips a lot."

"Don't worry." Mo put a hand on Rose's shoulder, smiling. "She's in total control."

"Mo, she's *eight*."

"Just the same, and double-jointed is good, for riding. Look at the flex in those ankles. Her heels drop very low. It increases her stability." Mo waved at Melly. "Walk on, Mel!"

Rose held her breath as Melly gave the horse a kick, and it walked quickly around in a circle. "Can't it go slower?"

"Any slower, she'll be in reverse."

Leo smiled, looking away.

Rose asked, "So, Mo, how did this come about?"

"Well, she got tired of mucking, so we went for a hack. She's become quite the barn rat. She has a perfect seat." Mo cupped his hand to his mouth. "Melly, eyes up, heels down! Good girl!"

Melly steered around the circle, and when she came around their side, she waved happily.

Leo waved back. "Lookin' good, cowgirl!"

Rose gasped. "Two hands, honey!"

Mo scoffed. "She can ride with no hands, her balance is that good. Want to see?"

"No," Rose shot back. "I mean, no thanks."

Mo and Leo laughed. Melly walked past them, and the horse swished his thick black tail. Mo cupped his mouth, calling out, "Mel, trot on!"

Melly kicked the horse, and it trotted around the circle, faster. She went up and down in the saddle, keeping the rhythm, even at speed.

Mo nodded. "Churchill said, 'The outside of a horse is good for the inside of a man.'"

"Churchill wasn't a mother." Rose bit her lip. "Why is she going up and down?"

"She's posting. Many people take a few lessons to pick it up, but she got it right away." Mo gestured at Melly. "She's happy as a clam. On a horse, you have to meet the world with your eyes front and your chin up. A girl who directs a thousand-pound animal learns confidence."

Rose watched Melly, who did look happy.

"Horses have a way of going, which means the way they move and relate to the world. People have a way of going, too. Melly's way of going is to keep her head down, to run and hide behind books and computers."

Rose winced. "These aren't the worst things, Mo."

"Don't mistake me. I think she needs all the things already in her life, but she loves horses and she's not afraid of them, even the biggest jumpers here."

"I know she's good with animals. The thing she needs to work on is people. She needs a friend in school, and riding isn't even a school sport."

"Ah, but riding is where it starts." Mo kept an eye on Melly. "She's making a friend, before your eyes."

"She's making friends with a horse."

"Not at all. She's making friends with *herself.*"

Rose hadn't thought of it that way. She watched Melly.

"We all see Melly's problem, but she's got to find confidence in herself. Face the world as she is, on her own, with her eyes front and her chin up. The more she does it here, the more she'll do it at school. Look. She's moving that pony on her own. She's *succeeding.*"

Rose watched Melly riding smoothly in the bright sun, with the lovely pastures and the gorgeous autumn backdrop, and felt her heart fill with emotion. Something had changed, and she was looking at it, and maybe things could turn around for Melly, someday. Maybe someday was starting right now.

"It's worth a try, babe," Leo said softly, his hand on her back.

"It surely is," Mo added. "I can give her a lesson when you come up, and there are plenty of schooling barns in Reesburgh. I looked into it online and found you a list."

Rose felt tears in her eyes, cuddling John close. It was hope, at long last. "Does she want lessons?"

Leo answered, "Ask her."

Chapter Eighty-four

"Hit the sack, kid!" Rose tucked Melly into bed, feeling like herself again, having showered and changed into clean clothes. It was twilight, her favorite time at the cabin, when the day was over and they'd go to bed early, in harmony with the rhythms of nature rather than TV or homework.

"It's cold tonight." Melly tugged up the comforter, next to Princess Google, already asleep. "Isn't Ebony so cute, Mom?"

"Very cute." Rose sat down on the edge of the single bed. The room was bare-bones, containing only a small bookshelf and bureau. A metal reading lamp was clamped to the headboard, and Rose turned it off, leaving them in the dim light from the window.

"Do you really like him?"

"Ebony? Of course. I think he's adorable and furry. You looked great up there."

"Harry rides brooms, and I ride horses." Melly smiled, and Rose gave her a kiss on the cheek.

"Do you like riding horses?"

"I love it. It's so fun, and Ebony is soft, really soft."

"I remember." Rose had petted the horse before they'd left, and he'd looked insanely tall, up close. "You know, I was wondering if you want to take riding lessons. Mo says there's barns around us, at home. Want to give it a try?"

"What do you think?"

Rose fell silent a moment, and through the screen came the scent of horse manure, but that could have been her imagination. She knew if she said the word, it would put a kibosh on this whole crazy venture. Every mother had moments like this, when she could sway things toward what she wanted, and not what her child wanted. Instead, she said, "I think it's a great idea, Mel. You're really good at it, and it's fun and really special."

"But I don't know any kids who ride. Nobody in my class does."

"Kids do it everywhere, like those girls at the barn. You'd have a great time."

"What if the kids make fun of me, at school?"

"If they do, you can deal with it. If they tease you, try not to let it bother you." Rose thought of what Mo had said. "Keep your head up and go forward. Tell yourself, trot on. So what do you say? Wanna give it a try?"

"Think I can do it?"

"I know you can, honey," Rose answered, without hesitation. She heard Leo's footsteps on the staircase, and turned. "Hey, honey. You up here for another good-night kiss?"

"Leo!" Melly called out. "I'm going to take riding lessons!"

"That's great!" Leo entered holding John, then leaned close to Rose's ear. "Phone for you, babe. It's Eileen, about Amanda."

Chapter Eighty-five

Rose walked down the glistening hospital corridor, holding Melly's hand. Amanda had come out of her coma and been moved from Intensive Care, though she'd developed motor problems in her left arm and was recovering her memory only slowly. Eileen had asked them to stop by on Sunday afternoon, and Rose was hoping it was a good idea.

"You okay, Mel?"

"Fine." Melly held their gift under her arm. "Are you giving her the present or am I?"

"You decide. You picked it out, but I'm happy to give it to her and say that."

"I'll give it to her."

"Good." Rose squeezed her hand. "She doesn't remember everything and she might not look very good, but she's going to get better, very slowly. She won't be back at school until the end of the year."

"Does she remember putting the jelly on her cheek?"

Rose flinched. "I don't know."

"Who's going to be there, visiting her? Any kids from my class? Danielle and Emily?"

"I don't think so, but I'm not sure."

Melly fell silent.

"You worried, Mel?"

"I'm trotting on."

Rose burst into laughter, and Melly giggled, releasing the tension. The hallway was empty, and the air smelled vaguely antiseptic. People talked in low tones in one room, and a football game played on a TV in another. They reached Amanda's room, where the door was propped open. Rose knocked on the jamb and peeked inside. "Any Gigots around?"

"Rose!" Eileen got up from her chair by the bed, and Amanda was awake under the covers, her head still bandaged and her face pale. She was hooked up to an IV, and her blue eyes were sleepy.

"Hi, Ms. McKenna." Amanda's voice sounded weak. "Hi, Melly."

"So good to see you both." Eileen came around the foot of the bed, looking relaxed in a sweatshirt and jeans, with light makeup and her hair in fluffy curls.

"I'm so glad Amanda is better."

"Thanks." Eileen nodded, her eyes shining, and she looked down at Melly. "Thanks for coming this afternoon. Amanda really wanted to see you."

"Why?" Melly asked, and Rose tried not to laugh.

"Good question." Eileen turned to Amanda. "Amanda, why don't you tell Melly why you wanted to see her?"

"I'm going home in two or three weeks and we're going to have a big Halloween party. Do you want to come?"

"Okay," Melly answered, her tone wary. She stepped to the bed and held out the present. "We got this for you."

"Thanks." Amanda took the gift with her right hand, though her left arm didn't move, apparently limp. "My arm and hand don't work right anymore. My brain didn't get enough oxygen, and I have to do rehab."

Rose felt a stab of sympathy, and Eileen moved to help her, but Melly beat her to it, and the two girls began to unwrap the package with much fussing, ripping, and eventually, giggling. Behind them, Eileen and Rose exchanged relieved and happy smiles. Never before had such significance been projected onto the unwrapping of a gift, as if it could lead to world peace.

"Cool!" Amanda became animated, holding up the present, an American Girl book. "Look, Mom. It's Lanie, my favorite!" She turned to Melly. "Who's your favorite?"

"Harry Potter."

Rose hid her smile.

Amanda said, "I like Harry Potter movies. Do you?"

"Yes," Melly answered. "If you want, I can bring your homework to the hospital. But I can't do it on Wednesdays because I'm starting my riding lessons."

Amanda's eyes widened. "You ride horses?"

"Yes. I ride Ebony."

"Felicity rides horses. I *love* Felicity. She's my old favorite. Lanie is only my new favorite."

"Who's Felicity?" Melly asked, puzzled.

"She's an American Girl, too. She lives in Virginia. I have the DVD at home. You can come over and watch it when I get home, okay?"

"Okay," Melly answered, cheering. "I never read American Girl but I have one of the books, too. Nicki."

"Nicki is the one who likes dogs."

Behind them, Eileen smiled at Rose. "Amanda knows everything about those American Girl books. She knows all the characters. She's *obsessed*. You can't imagine."

"Uh, yes, I can." Rose laughed, and Eileen motioned to her.

"Let's go outside and let them talk, huh?"

"Good idea." Rose followed her into the hallway, eavesdropping to make sure Melly was okay. The girls began to yammer about Felicity and Hermione, and Rose smiled. "Isn't that great?"

"Great." Eileen's expression grew serious. "But I have to say, in person, I'm really sorry, for everything."

"Forget it." Rose waved her off, but Eileen held up her hand.

"No, listen. I told you on the phone that Amanda's memory is in bad shape. It is. She doesn't remember much, and what she does comes in dribs and drabs."

"Okay."

"So yesterday, we were talking about you and Melly, and, well, she remembered something." Eileen frowned deeply, her regret plain.

"She remembered that when the fire broke out, you took her out to the hallway with Emily. That you told them to go to the playground, but she went back in for Jason's iPod, then got lost in the smoke. It wasn't your fault, at all." Tears brimmed in Eileen's blue eyes. "I'm so sorry, for everything I accused you of."

"Shh, it's okay, don't cry, the kids'll hear." Rose gave her a hug, and Eileen's chest heaved with a sob, then a soft cry escaped her lips.

"I'm so sorry. I thought you abandoned Amanda for Melly, and that you didn't even try."

"Hush a minute. Listen to those kids. They're laughing."

Eileen settled down, her tears subsiding, and the mothers eavesdropped while the daughters yammered about Lanie missing her best friend Dakota, and Harry missing his best friend Ron, then they segued into what costume they would wear for Halloween, which, as any mother knows, is a conversation that lasts several weeks.

And by the end of the visit, the daughters had gotten to know one another better, and so had the mothers.

And as far as Rose was concerned, that was world peace.

Chapter Eighty-six

The morning was clear and cold, finally October in earnest, and Rose walked toward the school, holding Melly's hand. John snoozed happily, cocooned in his Snugli, and Melly was bundled up, her red puffy coat making her backpack fit too tightly.

Rose tugged at her backpack strap, on the fly. "We have to adjust these when you get home."

"It's the coat, Mom. It's too heavy."

"It's cold today."

"Not *that* cold."

Rose smiled, delighted to be talking about normal things again. Meanwhile, mothers were turning their way, smiling and waving as they approached the entrance ramp. The news had been full of stories about her, the Homestead CFO had been indicted, and its board had announced that it was going to rebuild the plant and compensate any victims of its crimes. And the company had already reached a voluntary settlement with Eileen, in connection with Bill's murder.

"Way to go!" one mom called out, and a dad in a suit flashed her a thumbs-up. Another mom shouted, "Hi, Rose. Hi, Melly!"

"Hiya!" Rose called back, and Melly looked up, squinting against the bright sky.

"Who's that, Mom?"

"I have no idea."

Melly giggled, bewildered. "Mom, what's going on?"

"It's what I told you." Rose and Leo had tried to explain what had happened, but it wasn't something any eight-year-old should know in detail. "I helped catch some bad guys, and everybody's happy."

"It's so different." Melly looked around, in wonderment. Heads were turning everywhere, as they approached the ramp. "It's like a birthday party."

Mr. Rodriguez emerged from the front door and headed down the ramp and strode toward them with a big grin, buttoning his jacket. "Rose! Melly!"

"Hi, Mr. Rodriguez." Rose met him on the sidewalk. "Good to see you."

"Rose, I can't thank you enough. We're all so grateful to you. You risked your—" Mr. Rodriguez stopped, catching himself in front of Melly. "Well, we're grateful, leave it at that."

"Thanks, and I have to tell you that Leo and I never had any intention of filing any lawsuit."

"I know. I got a phone call this morning, from Oliver Charriere." Mr. Rodriguez looked down at Melly and touched her shoulder. "And I heard you volunteered to take Amanda her homework."

"Yes." Melly nodded.

"Thanks for helping out. That's the way all of our students should act, at Reesburgh. That's what community is all about." Mr. Rodriguez looked up at Rose. "Would you like to stop by the office? I know the staff wants to thank you in person."

Rose smiled, surprised. "I'd love to, thanks."

"Great. Mind if I escort Melly inside?"

"Not at all."

"Melly, come with me." Mr. Rodriguez smiled, taking Melly's hand. "Let's go to class together. I think there's someone you might want to see."

"Who?" Melly asked, as they went up the walkway.

The front door opened, and standing in the threshold was Kristen Canton, dressed and ready for work.

"Melly!" Kristen called out, and they ran into each other's arms.

Rose hung back, tears filming her eyes, finally letting go.

And setting free.

Chapter Eighty-seven

Halloween at the Gigots' was a houseful of witches, Iron Men, and vampires. Tables were stocked with sandwiches, ginger snaps, and candy bars that kept the boys chasing each other on a sugar high, while the girls bobbed for apples. Rose was dressed as a lawyer in a three-piece suit and a striped tie, Leo was her prisoner in an orange jumpsuit, and John had on a black onesie, as their resident baby judge.

She raised her plastic glass of cider and clicked it to Leo's. "You know what we're toasting, right?"

Leo smiled, his glass raised. "Senator Martin's indictment?"

"No. Guess again."

"That you look so hot as a redhead. Put me in jail and have your way with me. Got handcuffs?"

Rose leaned over. "This is the first Halloween that Melly hasn't worn a mask."

"Whoa, I didn't realize that." Leo looked around for Melly, who had dressed as a horseback rider in fringed chaps, paddock boots, and a sweatshirt that read THE BUCK STOPS HERE. At the moment, however, she was with Amanda, Emily, Danielle, and the other girls, her face stuck in a galvanized washtub of apples. They hadn't become best friends, but the worst of the bullying had stopped, and Amanda had shown a new empathy, after her injury.

"Now drink, felon." Rose raised her glass, Leo clicked it, and they sipped, then kissed over John's head.

"Get a room, you two." Eileen waltzed over, a beaming princess in a rhinestone tiara.

"Hey, girl." Rose smiled. They'd grown closer, with Melly bringing Amanda her homework in the hospital. "Love the costume. Every mom deserves a tiara."

"True, except I'm Paris Hilton." Eileen laughed, then Wanda came over dressed as a witch, followed by some other class parents, Rachel and Jacob Witmer as Barack and Michelle Obama, Susan and Abe Kramer as Bill and Hillary Clinton, and Elida and Ross Kahari as Sarah and Todd Palin. Rose regarded them all as new friends, regardless of political affiliation.

Wanda looked at Rose. "Honey, you know, I have to say it again, I'm so sorry for the way I treated you."

"That's okay," Rose said, meaning it. Lots of people had apologized, and her new email and Facebook page were flooded with virtual love.

"The new CEO at Homestead even mentioned you in his speech. He said the new broom's gonna sweep clean."

Jacob added, "I'm so happy that Martin got his."

"Nobody's happier than I am!" said a voice behind them, and they all turned around.

"Kristen!" Rose gave her a hug, and the young teacher looked pretty, even dressed as Humpty Dumpty.

"Rose, Leo, everybody, let me introduce you." Kristen gestured at the white knight beside her, dressed in tinfoil armor. "This is Erik, my boyfriend. Or should I say, my fiancé."

"Woohoo!" Rose hooted, and all the women clustered around Kristen, who showed off her engagement ring to the sound of much clucking.

"Mom!" a child shouted, and the women looked up, because they all answered to the same name.

"Yes, honey?" Eileen asked. It was Amanda standing there, her face wet from bobbing for apples.

"Can you fix my lightning bolt? It's coming off, from the water." Rose smiled at the sight.

Amanda was dressed as Harry Potter.

Chapter Eighty-eight

Rose parked at the end of the street, twisted off the ignition, and sat in her rental car for a moment. She broke into a light sweat, and her heart pumped a little faster. She checked the dashboard clock—10:49. She was ten minutes early. She inhaled, trying to calm her nerves. She'd felt something come over her the moment she turned onto the street, a shudder that seemed to emanate from her marrow and reverberate out to her skin, like shockwaves from her soul.

She looked around, taking it all in. This end of the street looked different than it had twenty years ago, but she could see the way it had been, the same way she could look into Melly's face and see the baby she'd been. The past lived in the present, and nobody knew it better than a mother.

Mommy!

The houses were still close together, though the paint colors had changed, and the trees grew in the same places, though they were taller and fuller, their roots breaking up the concrete sidewalk, like so many tiny neighborhood earthquakes. Drying leaves littered the sidewalk, and big brown paper bags of them, stamped with the township's name, sat at the curb like a row of tombstones, just like then.

Rose closed her eyes, and it all came back to her. Halloween, and she was eighteen years old. She'd just turned onto the street when she saw the white blur and heard the horrible *thud*. Tears came to her eyes, just as they had then, instantly. That night, her heart knew what had happened before her brain did. It just didn't know how to tell her. Then she'd heard agonized scream of Thomas's mother.

Thomas!

Rose found a Kleenex in her purse and wiped her eyes. She eyed the house, which hadn't changed at all: a three-bedroom colonial, with a front porch, and wooden steps. The Pelals still lived here, and their phone number had been easy to find online. She'd called them yesterday, and they'd recognized her name. She'd asked if she could visit, and they'd suggested the very next day, today, but hadn't asked any questions.

Rose put the Kleenex away and slid the keys from the ignition. She knew that what happened here had set her in a pattern she hadn't recognized, and so couldn't stop. Then, when she was young, she'd been told not to talk to the Pelals, and she didn't want to, anyway. She could only run and hide. But it wasn't about law, any longer. It was about right and wrong, and she had become an adult. Jim and Janine Pelal were parents like her, and she had killed their child. She couldn't let another day pass until she said what needed to be said.

She got out of the car, closed the door, and made her way up the sidewalk to the house. She composed herself, then pressed the doorbell.

Chapter Eighty-nine

"Thanks for seeing me." Rose sat in a wing chair, the nicest seat in the living room, which had a worn brown sofa and a plain wooden coffee table, covered with a folded newspaper and an ashtray with a pipe and a pile of black ash. The air smelled like burned cherry-wood from its smoke.

"Of course." Jim sat down next to Janine, on the sofa. Both of them had short hair, his gray and hers a dark brown, with steel-rimmed bi-focals, plain polo shirts, wide-leg jeans, and newish white sneakers, so they looked paired but not identical, like salt-and-pepper shakers. They had a benevolent way about them, down to their smiles, which were polite, even kind.

"Well," Rose began, her mouth dry. "It was lucky for me that you still live here. It made you easy to find."

"Oh, we'd never move." Jim shook his head, once. "We love it here. It's our hometown, both of us. We're semi-retired, but all our friends are here, and our church. Our daughter lives in Seattle. Her husband's an engineer at Boeing."

Rose flashed on Thomas's sister running from the porch, then put it out of her mind.

"We have two grandchildren now, both boys. We love to visit 'em, but we love to come home, too." Jim chuckled. "I read in the news-paper, online, that you have children."

"Yes, a boy and a girl." Rose felt awkward making small talk, espe-cially since Janine was so quiet, her small hands folded in her lap. Her nails were polished, and she wore a fair amount of makeup, with thick eyeliner. "My call must have come as a surprise."

"We thought we might hear from you someday. You were so young when Thomas died. Just a kid yourself."

"Not that young. I should have come before."

"As I say, we've been reading about you, but that's new. We didn't know where you lived until the fire. Some of our friends up north saw it on TV and called us."

"I hope that didn't cause you further . . . pain." Rose had to grope for the right word.

"Not at all. A TV reporter called us about it, too. Tanya." Jim rubbed his forehead. "What's her name?"

"Robertson?" Rose felt a pang. "She found you?"

"My wife, she didn't want us to talk to her. Seems like you did a bang-up job up there, in Pennsylvania. That crooked senator going to court, and all." Jim glanced at Janine, who remained quiet, so Rose got back on track.

"Thanks, but to come to the reason for my visit, I'm grateful that you agreed to see me. I want to apologize to you both, as inadequate as words may be, and to tell you how sorry I am about Thomas." Her throat caught, but she was determined to keep her emotions in check. "I think of him every day, and I replay that scene. I try to make it end differently. I wish I'd taken another way home, or gone slower, or seen him sooner. I think of how one little thing could have changed every-thing, and he'd be alive now, with you. I mourn him, but he was your son, and I'm so deeply sorry for what I did that night. Please accept my apology, if you can."

Jim met her eye, behind his bifocals. Janine lowered her head, a small gesture that broke Rose's heart.

"Thank you. Thank you for saying that. We do accept, but you don't have to apologize. We know it wasn't your fault. We saw what happened. We weren't that far up the street."

Rose blinked. She hadn't known. The lawyers had assumed that the Pelals hadn't seen it, and even if they had, that they'd sue her anyway.

"Thomas, he ran out in front of the car." Jim's lower lip trembled, then he seemed to recover. "It was horrible, seeing how it happened and knowing we couldn't get there, in time. But Thomas, he liked to run everywhere. He always had ants in his pants. Janine always thought he mighta had, you know, attention deficit. But in those days, well, we didn't get him to a doctor." Jim shook his head. "So he ran into the street. We used to tell him, don't do it, you'll get hurt. It wasn't the first time he did it, it was just the first time you were there, and this time, well, the Lord works in mysterious ways, that much is true."

Rose felt her throat thicken, but didn't cry. And she didn't feel better either. "Regardless, I wish it hadn't happened."

"We have our faith, and we rely on it, always." Jim nodded, his skinny shoulders suddenly slanting down. They both looked so sad for a minute, sagging together in the middle of the sagging couch. Janine said nothing, hanging her silvery head, with a whorl of gray at her crown, like a hurricane.

Jim sighed. "I just wish, well, I guess Janine, she wishes she was there. That she was there with him, for him, at the end. That's what wakes her up at night, almost tortures her, really. Any mother would want that for her child, I suppose."

Rose remembered holding Thomas in the street, then him looking up at her, seeing her in the Cleopatra makeup. Now that she'd gotten a good look at Janine, with her dark hair and eyeliner, Rose understood why he'd mistaken her for his mother, on that dark night.

"You can understand that," Jim continued, more softly. "She wishes that she'd been there, to hold him. Not for her, but for him. That he wouldn't think he was alone in this world. That he knew we loved him, that she loved him, right until the very end. He was our youngest, you know. Our baby. *Her* baby."

Rose swallowed hard. She would never forget what she'd said to Thomas, right before he passed. Maybe there was something she could do for the Pelals, after all. Maybe the words that had been haunting her all these years would be the words that eased Janine's heart.

"You can see that, can't you? Being a mother yourself."

"Yes, I do understand, and I'd feel exactly the same way." Rose took a deep breath. "Janine, I have something I think you should know."

Acknowledgments

I've written seventeen novels in almost as many years, and while I've always had emotionality in my books, more recently I've turned to writing about the most emotional of all relationships, mother and child. There may be some irony to this, now that I'm an empty-nester, but perhaps I finally have the perspective and the distance (and the time!) to examine the relationship and plumb it for my fiction. This is a long way of saying thank you very much to my amazing daughter, Francesca, and to my mother, Mary, both of whom have taught me everything I know about the richness and complexity of the bond between mother and child, not to mention, simply put, about love.

In this regard, thanks, too, to my gal pals, all of whom are terrific mothers: Nan Daley, Jennifer Enderlin, Molly Friedrich, Rachel Kull, Laura Leonard, Paula Menghetti, and Franca Palumbo. They're my kitchen cabinet, and if we're not talking about our daughters, we're talking about our mothers. All of our everyday conversations inform *Save Me*, so thanks, ladies, for being yourselves, and for helping me, every day.

This novel raises a number of legal, ethical, and moral questions, and for those I needed research and help. This is where I get to thank the experts, but also where I have to make clear that any and all mistakes are mine. Thanks to my ace detective, Arthur Mee, criminal lawyer Glenn Gilman, Esq., and special thanks to Nicolas Casenta, of the Chester County District Attorney's Office. I also want to thank Professor Marin Scordato, of the Catholic University of America, Columbus School of Law, for his excellent advice, expertise, and seminal article, *Understanding the Absence of a Duty to Reasonably Rescue in American Tort Law.*

Thanks so much to Principal Christopher Pickell, teacher Ed Jameson, and staff members June Regan, Kathy Kolb, and Brett Willson, and all the rest of the wonderful staff at Charlestown Elementary School. Principal Pickell took his valuable time to answer all of my questions to make *Save Me* as realistic as possible, and we should repeat that Reesburgh Elementary herein is not Charlestown Elementary, but is completely fictional. Still, I could not be more grateful to them all for their time and guidance, and more importantly, for all they do for children. There is no more important job than educating the generations to come. I've always admired teachers, and still do. I wouldn't be a writer but for the great public education I received, and I never realized how exhausting, albeit rewarding, teaching can be until I started teaching a course I developed titled "Justice & Fiction" at the University of Pennsylvania Law School. So thanks so much to all of my teachers, past and present, including my students—who are teachers, too, in their own way.

Thanks so much, too, to the team of genius firefighters who not only keep all of us safe, but even took time out of their day to help me imagine a fictional fire. Thank you so much to Mike Risell, Karen and Duke Griffin, Dave Hicks, and Mark Hughes of Kimberton Fire Company. And thanks for expert EMT advice and counsel to Rebecca Buonavolonta and Sergey Bortsov. And thanks to Robin Lynn Katz.

A special hug of thanks for their time and expertise to everybody at Herr Foods of Nottingham, Pennsylvania. It's important to reiterate here that everything in the book is fictional, but I was helped to create Homestead by the great people at Herr Foods, starting with ace Public Relations Manager Jennifer Arrigo, and most especially the Herr Family: J.M. Herr, Ed Herr, Gene Herr, and Daryl Thomas. A special thanks for the consultation to Fran Dolan, Jim Rock, Bill Beddow, and all the hard-working staff who showed me the ropes.

Thank you to the gang at St. Martin's Press, starting with my great editor and super-supportive coach, Jennifer Enderlin, who inspires me and guided this book, and to John Sargent, Sally Richardson, Matthew Shear, Matt Baldacci, Jeff Capshew, Nancy Trypuc, Monica Katz, John Murphy, John Karle, Sara Goodman, and all the wonderful sales reps. Big thanks to Michael Storrings, for an astounding cover design. Also hugs and kisses to Mary Beth Roche, Laura Wilson, and the great people in audio books. I love and appreciate all of you.

Thanks and big love to my wonderful agent and friend, Molly Friedrich, as well as the Amazing Paul Cirone, and the brilliant Lucy Carson. My dedicated and amazing assistant and best friend is Laura Leonard, and she's invaluable in every way, and has been for twenty years. And she's a great mom! Thanks, too, to Annette Earling, my Web diva, who runs scottoline.com, where I exist only in Photoshopped form.

Thanks to my family and friends, for everything. They know I love them and they usually get the last word, if not the dedication, in my books. But this book is different, because the last word, and the dedication, goes to my dear friend Joseph Drabyak, who recently passed away, much too soon. I dedicated this book to Joe because he was dedicated to books.

I met Joe almost twenty years ago as the bookseller at my local independent bookstore, Chester County Books & Music Company, and I grew to be great friends with him and his wife, Reggie. He was an early champion of my books and advocated for books he loved as well as for independent bookstores, and eventually he became the hardworking president of the New Atlantic Independent Booksellers Association. Joe understood that books bring people together, and that reading empowers, enriches, nurtures, and fuses us, one to the other. Before Joe passed, I sat with him and told him I'd dedicate my next book to him, which made him happy. And though he'd read every one of my books in manuscript form, he didn't get to read this one.

It is, now and forever, my loss.

<u>Ebury Press Fiction Footnotes</u>

Turn the page for more information about *Save Me,*
including a reading guide.

EBURY
PRESS

About the Book

An emotionally powerful novel about a split-second choice, agonising consequences, and the need for justice from a New York Times bestselling author

Rose McKenna volunteers at her daughter Melly's school in order to keep an eye on Amanda, a mean girl who's been bullying her daughter. Her fears come true when the bullying begins, sending Melly to the bathroom in tears. Just as Rose is about to follow after her daughter, a massive explosion goes off in the kitchen, sending the room into chaos. Rose finds herself faced with the horrifying decision of whether or not to run to the bathroom to rescue her daughter or usher Amanda to safety. She believes she has accomplished both, only to discover that Amanda, for an unknown reason, ran back into the school once out of Rose's sight.

In an instance, Rose goes from hero to villain as the small community blames Amanda's injuries on her. In the days that follow, Rose's life starts to fall to pieces, Amanda's mother decides to sue, her marriage is put to the test, and worse, when her daughter returns to school, the bullying only intensifies. Rose must take matters into her own hands and get down to the truth of what really happened that fateful day in order to save herself, her marriage and her family.

About the Author:

Lisa Scottoline graduated magna cum laude from the University of Pennsylvania, in 1976. Lisa then graduated cum laude from the University of Pennsylvania Law School in 1981, where she served as an Associate Editor, *University of Pennsylvania Law Review.* She began her legal career with a clerkship at the Pennsylvania Superior Court. When the clerkship ended, she joined a law firm in Philadelphia as an associate.

In 1986, she left the firm to raise her newborn daughter and began writing legal fiction part-time. In 1994, Scottoline re-entered the legal world as an administrative law clerk to Chief Judge Dolores K. Sloviter of the United States Court of Appeals for the Third Circuit, while beginning a new career as a fiction author, with the publication of her first novel.

Critical Praise for *Save Me*:

'Scottoline knows how to keep readers in her grip...there is one thrill after another, particularly once the narrative moves into the legal and investigative realms where Scottoline excels...'
New York Times

'. . . the Scottoline we love as a virtuoso of suspense, fast action and intricate plot is back in top form in *Save Me,* manipulating pulse rates and heartstrings with all the ruthlessness she showed in *Look Again* . . . Here, as elsewhere in her work, Scottoline is exceptionally good at depicting the feral, pack mentality of public opinion and the impotence of decency and dignity before it.'
Washington Post

'At the start of this gut-wrenching stand-alone from bestseller Scottoline, an explosion rips through the nearly empty cafeteria of Reesburgh Elementary School. Scottoline melds it all into a satisfying nail-biting thriller sure to please her growing audience'
Publishers Weekly

'Scottoline crafts a heartfelt emotional novel with the intensity of a thriller. This stand-alone work will mesmerise readers at the first page and hold them spellbound until the final word. Jodi Picoult fans may crown a new favourite author.'
Library Journal

Other Books by the Author

Fiction
Think Twice
Look Again
Lady Killer
Daddy's Girl
Dirty Blonde
Devil's Corner
Killer Smile
Dead Ringer
Courting Trouble
The Vendetta Defence
Moment of Truth
Mistaken Identity
Rough Justice
Legal Tender
Running from the Law
Final Appeal
Everywhere That Mary Went

Nonfiction
My Nest Isn't Empty, It Just Has More Closet Space
(with Francesca Scottoline Serritella)
Why My Third Husband Will Be a Dog

Suggested Further Reading

19 Minutes Jodi Picoult
This Perfect World Suzanne Bugler
The Woman He Loved Dorothy Koomson
The Year of Fog Michelle Richmond

Additional Online Resources

www.scottoline.com

Questions for Reading Groups:

1. Lisa Scottoline's SAVE ME explores the mother and child relationship. What do you think defines a mother? How is a mother and child relationship different than any other relationship? Look at other forms of culture, like art, for example. How many depictions are there of mother and child? And how many of father and child? Are we discriminating against fathers, or diminishing them, by all this talk of the mother-child bond? And by doing so, do we create a self-fulfilling prophecy?

2. In SAVE ME, Melly is the victim of bullying because of a birthmark on her face. Do you think bullying is different today than years ago? Do you think that the bullying is getting worse, or are we just hearing more about it because of the Internet? What do you think parents and schools should do to help curb bullying? What kind of punishment do you think is appropriate for the child who is doing the bullying? What about those who watch and say nothing? Are they, or aren't they, equally as culpable? Do you think that the school curriculum should include lessons in body-confidence and self-esteem?

3. Rose experienced her own bullying at the hands of the angry parents, which gave her a new perspective on what Melly was going through. Do you have any experience with bullying between adults? In what ways are adults better equipped to deal

with bullying than children? What impact can bullying have on adults, and what can an adult do if they are faced with a bully?

4. Rose steps in to defend Melly against her bully. Do you think it was a good idea? How do you think a parent's involvement hurts or helps the situation? At what point do you think a parent needs to involve themselves in the situation? What steps would you take to help your child if they were being bullied, and how far would you be willing to go?

5. What impact do you think a physical blemish has on a child, and how do you think it effects their identity, their relationship with their family, and their relationship with the outside world? What about other physical differences, like a child in a wheelchair? Or learning challenges, that aren't so visible? Or how about discriminations based on race, religion or sexual orientation? Melly's father reacted very badly to Melly's birthmark. What did his reaction make you feel about him?

6. Many of Lisa's books centre on single mothers or blended families. Do you think the love of one great parent is enough to sustain a child through life? Does it take a father, too?

7. How did you feel about Rose keeping her past secret from Leo? Did you understand her reasoning? Did you agree or disagree with it? What impact do you think Rose's past will have on her marriage as she moves forward? Do you think she will ever really be able to escape what happened? Will he forgive her not telling him? How do secrets impact intimacy in our lives?

8. Rose was called a "helicopter" parent, a term uses sometimes in the media to denote "over-parenting"; a parent who pays extremely close attention to their child's experiences or problems. What separates helicopter parenting from good parenting? What kind of parent do you think Rose was? What mistakes do you think she made? Do you think she was a good mother? Do you think she favours Melly, or the baby? Or treats them equally?

9. How did you feel about Amanda in the beginning of the book? How, if at all, did your opinion of her change by the end of the book? What do you think causes children to be bullies? Under

what circumstances would you ever feel bad for the bully? In punishing a bully, do you think their personal circumstances should be taken into account?

10. What did you think of Rose's lawyers' strategy? Did you agree or disagree with it? Do you think they were just passing the blame, or do you think the school had a responsibility in what happened?

An interview with Lisa Scottoline

Where did the inspiration for SAVE ME come from?
The story idea actually grew out of a conversation I was having with my friend. She had been asked to take another child home with her from the baseball field. When she went to leave, she realised she only had one car seat. She was faced with a decision of who should get the car seat, her child or her friend's child. I instantly thought that this was a book idea and SAVE ME is that book. In it, an explosion rocks a school cafeteria and a lunch mom must make a split-second decision to save her daughter who is a distance away, or her daughter's bully, who is right next to her.

Have you ever had any experience of bullying either as a child or a parent?
Yes, when I was younger there were not many Italian Americans in my neighbourhood and my nickname was 'Rat' because the joke was that Italians lived in sewers. When you are little you think you are on the outside. When you get older you realise that even the people on the inside feel like outsiders.

'Every mom is an action hero' – do you think this is true? Which action hero would you be if you could choose one?
The whole point is that she doesn't think she is an action hero, but comes to realise that she is one. I want people to rethink what

defines an action hero. Moms are the unsung and often under-appreciated superheroes, and I want to change that thinking in society. Moms are superheroes and I think my mom is a superhero.

Dream casting time – who ideally would play Rose in a movie of SAVE ME?

It is always exciting to have your book optioned for TV or the movies, but my first love is books. I like the characters to exist in the readers' imagination and my own. For that reason, I wouldn't want to put a face to a character that has a face in the readers' minds. That is the magic of books.

Your books often seem to feature strong resilient female characters. To what extent do they mirror aspects of your own life and personality?

My favourite quote is one by Eleanor Roosevelt. "Women are like tea bags, you don't know how strong they are until they are in hot water." I like to think that is true of all women and it is what I try to portray in my characters; ordinary women who are faced with extraordinary challenges and must find their own inner strength to save others and themselves. Often women, as well as my characters, don't realise how strong they are until they are in trouble, and from that they come to learn about themselves, just like a lot of people in real life.

What are your favourite and least favourite things about being a writer?

My favourite thing about being a writer is that I love books and I feel lucky to be able to create them and honour women by portraying them as the stars. The least favourite thing is that it is a little of a solitary life and I am a people person. Luckily, I like my own company and it is a small price to pay for having the freedom to do such an enriching job.

What do you do in your spare time, when you aren't writing?

I love to walk my dogs, ride my pony and do anything outdoors. I love to read, and if I can read outdoors, all the better.

Where do you research information for your books?
I do tons of research for my books because I think the details matter and there is no substitute for research. I always go directly to source, so if I need to figure out what the police would do, I go to the police, for emergency room doctors, I go to the hospital, and potato chip factories, I go there. For SAVE ME, I spent several days in an elementary school and a day in a firehouse to come up with a realistic conflagration. I've always admired teachers and the work they do, and for SAVE ME, I also spent time observing teachers in order to accurately depict some of the rewards and the trials of being a teacher.

SAVE ME is a wonderful blend of emotional pageturner and thriller, brilliantly suspenseful with lots of unexpected twists. Did you know how it would all end when you started out? Are you a planner when it comes to your writing?
Each story starts with one idea and grows from there. I don't write with an outline and I never know how the book will end. In fact, I never even know how it will middle. Impressed? I like the book to unfold naturally, so as I go, I think what would happen next, and that is what I write next. I think it allows the book to develop along the way and provides a flexibility that encourages creativity. That is what works for me, but many people feel very different and work better with an outline and knowing the entire book before they write. I believe that everyone should write the way that works best for them.

Which classic novel have you always meant to read and never got round to it?
I was an English major in college and did get around to almost all of the novels that could be considered a classic. The truth is that I tend not to categorise novels that way. Contemporary fiction can be just as worthy as period fiction, and can ultimately turn out to be the classics of the future.

What are your top five books of all time?
Here is what I think is interesting: I read all the time and am constantly impressed with the depth of fiction and non-fiction. My

favourites changes over time, just like when I was twenty my favourite food is pizza and now it is kale.

What book are you currently reading?
Life by Keith Richards, and I love it.

Do you have a favourite time of day to write? A favourite place?
I always work in my house and write all day and many evenings. I tend to write emotional scenes in the evening because I'm more relaxed and the emotions flow more easily.

Which fictional character would you most like to meet?
Again, there are too many to name.

Who, in your opinion, is the greatest writer of all time?
I value the diversity of speech, thought, and voice, and for that reason, to me, there is no single greatest writer.

Other than writing and the law, what other jobs or professions have you undertaken or considered?
I teach a course I created called "Justice and Fiction" at the University of Pennsylvania Law School, and I've had a host of different jobs when I was younger. Overall, my most important and rewarding job is being a mother.